Bello:

hidden talent rediscovered

Bello is a digital only imprint of Pan Macmillan,
established to breathe new life into previously published,
classic books.

At Bello we believe in the timeless power of the imagination,
of good story, narrative and entertainment and we want to use
digital technology to ensure that many more readers
can enjoy these books into the future.

We publish in ebook and Print on Demand formats
to bring these wonderful books to new audiences.

www.panmacmillan.co.uk/bello

D0921350

Jill McGown

Jill McGown, who died in 2007, lived in Northamptonshire and was best known for her mystery series featuring Chief Inspector Lloyd and Sergeant Judy Hill. The first novel, *A Perfect Match*, was published in 1983 and *A Shred of Evidence* was made into a television drama starring Philip Glenister and Michelle Collins.

Jill McGown

DEATH OF
A DANCER

B E L L

First published in 1989 by Macmillan

This edition published 2014 by Bello
an imprint of Pan Macmillan, a division of Macmillan Publishers Limited
Pan Macmillan, 20 New Wharf Road, London N1 9RR
Basingstoke and Oxford
Associated companies throughout the world

www.panmacmillan.co.uk/bello

ISBN 978-1-4472-6853-6 EPUB
ISBN 978-1-4472-7952-2 HB
ISBN 978-1-4472-6850-5 PB

Copyright © Jill McGown, 1989

The right of Jill McGown to be identified as the
author of this work has been asserted in accordance
with the Copyright, Designs and Patents Act 1988.

A CIP catalogue record for this book is available from the British Library.

Visit **www.panmacmillan.com** to read more about all our books
and to buy them. You will also find features, author interviews and
news of any author events, and you can sign up for e-newsletters
so that you're always first to hear about our new releases.

Chapter One

NO ROAD TRAFFIC BEYOND THIS POINT –
ALL VEHICLES TO CAR PARK

Philip Newby turned in the direction of the arrow, along a road which ran between two buildings. Behind the larger of the two, he could see the car park, and pulled in, thankful to find a space close to the road. He emerged from the car with difficulty, shivering as he stepped out into the bitter January wind. This winter was never going to end. There were always going to be heaps of snow along the pavements, making them narrower than they were to start with. The frost that lay along every branch of every tree, every television aerial, every telegraph wire, was there for ever, frozen and permanent.

Reaching back into the car, he took out the walking-stick, and made his way back along the side road. It seemed like a long way to the school itself, which was on the other side of the grounds, its roof visible above the other buildings. Between him and the grey, dignified building was a curving tarmac roadway slippery with slush; it might just as well have been a minefield. But the school had been there for a hundred and fifty years, and he didn't suppose it was going to come to him. He clamped his teeth together as he walked up the slight incline that he once wouldn't have recognised as one.

He walked quickly; too quickly, the doctor had said. Certainly too quickly for the conditions. But he *walked*, and there had been a long time when it was thought that he might not, because of the back injury. It had healed more quickly than his leg, as it had turned out. It ached, from time to time. He couldn't turn quickly. But he did exercises, and through the pain he could feel it strengthening. With the leg exercises, all he could feel was the pain. His long stint in a wheelchair had, however, made his arms stronger than they'd ever been; an ironic twist.

He made the final assault with a burst of speed that took him up the stone steps at the front of the building in seconds; the best way to deal with steps, he'd found. He winced each time his weight came on to his right foot, as it had to, but the pain afforded him some pleasure; it was proof that his leg was still there, and still functioning.

Heat wrapped round him like a blanket as he went into the building, and he stood for a moment, savouring it. In the large entrance-hall, an old-fashioned finger-post pointed the way to the office, where he joined a queue, a mixture of boys and staff, who looked at him curiously or incuriously, depending on their nature. Staff didn't get preferential treatment, he noticed. First come, first served. He approved of that.

Another finger-post greeted him: CLASSROOMS 1–14, STAFF ROOM, LADIES' REST ROOM, STOREROOM, BOILER ROOM. It pointed in all directions, including up. CLASSROOMS 15–21, that one read. HEADMASTER'S STUDY, PHYSICS LAB, LAVATORIES. He looked at the wide, curved staircase, counting the steps he could see, in case LAVATORIES indicated the only facilities available. Like an old man. An old man with a stick, afraid of a flight of stairs. He'd bought the stick specially; the hospital had said that theirs was very carefully designed to give the best support, and hadn't been too keen on the idea, but if he had to walk with a stick it would be a stick to be proud of. It was a silver-topped walking-stick, slim and elegant. All right, the surgeon had said grudgingly. But keep the other one in case that one snaps. The balance was all wrong, with that heavy knob; these sticks weren't for *walking* with, they were for show. So Philip was showing it. The other one was with his luggage, in the car.

First day of term; that was the reason for the queue. There were questions to be answered, children to be checked and registered and comforted, staff to be given timetables and instructions and notes about epileptics and Muslims. He joined the end, and shuffled up with the others. He'd been told not to, in a letter. The headmaster would meet him, show him round, it said. But none of the people he had seen had been the headmaster. His memory was a bit faulty, but not that bad. Treadwell had come to see him just before Christmas, to check that everything was all right, and that he could start in the new year.

He had seemed very solicitous. Too solicitous. Philip must tell him, he had said, if there were any obstacles that could perhaps be overcome or made less troublesome. There would be no obstacles, Philip thought darkly. He was thirty-seven, God damn it. He was in the prime of a life that he enjoyed, an uncomplicated life, doing more or less what he pleased. He was ... he was just temporarily inconvenienced. He wasn't disabled, and he never would be. He just used a walking-stick, that was all.

An all-male queue; but in the office two women came into view as Philip at last achieved the window position, with only a man and a small boy ahead of him. The blonde receptionist was dealing with the queries; she caught his eye, as she would, for Philip was taller than the rest of the queue, and she smiled. Philip smiled back automatically, but he was looking past her to where another woman sat perched on the desk, talking on the phone. She was a little younger than he was, at a guess. Dark eyes, clear skin, dark hair drawn away from her face. Delicately coloured eyelids, and lips that matched the pale, polished nails. A wedding ring encircled one slim finger. No other jewellery. He felt as though he knew her, but he didn't.

'Are you sure you don't mind?' she was saying. 'It's just that it's only on that one night. But I did say I'd—?' She paused. 'Thank you,' she said. 'I'm really grateful, Diana.' She twisted the telephone cord lightly in her fingers as she spoke.

Lifting her hand to his mouth, kissing the long, slim fingers ....

'You'll have to hire one,' the receptionist was saying to the man. He was about fifty, stockily built, slightly overweight, wearing jeans and a sweatshirt.

'Hire one?' the man repeated, in a London accent which, if it ever had been polished up, had returned to its native roughness. 'Do you know how much the bloody things *cost* to hire?'

His lips touching her eyes, her cheekbones . . . .

'Fucking dinner-jacket,' the man said, walking down the corridor.

There were embarrassed giggles from the boys, but neither of the ladies seemed shocked, or even surprised.

'You'll have to excuse Sam,' the dark one said, her hand over the mouthpiece as she addressed him over the head of the small boy in front. 'He's a law unto himself.' She turned back to the phone. 'Just apologising for Sam,' she explained to the caller. 'He's trying to shock people, as usual.'

'They'll all be taller than me,' the boy now at the head of the queue complained, and Philip could see that this would indeed be the case, whatever the child was talking about.

Like the previous customer, the child left disgruntled, but refrained from swearing, at least in anyone's hearing.

His mouth seeking hers . . . .

'Can I help you?'

Unwillingly, Philip's eyes turned to the young receptionist. 'Newby,' he said. 'I believe you're expecting me.'

'Mrs Knight,' the girl said, over her shoulder, 'Mr Newby's here, but Mr Treadwell isn't in his office.'

She was Andrew Knight's widow.

'Oh – thank you, Kitty,' she said, and hurriedly finished her call. She stood up and went out of sight for a moment, then came out of a corridor door. She was taller than he'd thought. Longer legs.

'I'm Caroline,' she said. 'Mr Treadwell must have got held up – you know how it is on the first day. Everything that can go wrong does.' She smiled.

'Philip.' He shook the hand she extended, and frowned slightly. Her greeting had reminded him of something. It was always happening – things people said, did – sometimes just the tone of voice or a gesture, and he would be groping around in the void of his memory-gap. Bits were coming back, slowly. Nothing came back this time.

She smiled. 'I heard a lot about you from Andrew,' she said.

4

He had probably heard a lot about her. But he couldn't remember anything about that day. Or the days that followed it.

'I expect you'd like to go straight to the flat,' she said.

The staff block turned out to be the smaller of the two buildings by the car park. That side of the grounds could be reached through a sort of alleyway that he hadn't noticed. It made the walk shorter, but he embarked with dread on the cobblestoned surface, and tried to look as though he was strolling, rather than picking his way. It was a difficult effect to achieve in the biting wind that whistled through the alley.

'Is your stuff in your car?' she asked, with a glance down the side road towards the car park. 'We'll collar a child to bring it in.'

They were at what had once upon a time been a single house, which had been split into two flats. Caroline opened the door, and let him in to the ground-floor rooms; large, cold, sparsely furnished, but adequate.

'You'll be sharing,' she warned him. 'Did someone tell you?'

He nodded.

'Well,' she said. 'At least you're here at last.'

Philip should have started at the school almost eighteen months before. He had come for the interview, had been offered and had accepted the job. He was to have started that September. Andrew Knight had been running him back to London when the accident had happened. He had known Andrew since their school days; they would surely have done a lot of catching-up, but he couldn't remember. He couldn't even remember whether or not he had met Caroline; from what she had said, he assumed that he hadn't.

Smiling, mouths meeting, the tip of his tongue moving over perfect teeth ....

She shivered. 'Sam should have put the fire on,' she said, going over to the gas fire, and kneeling in front of it. She looked up. 'That's who you're sharing with,' she said, her voice slightly apologetic. 'Do you have matches?'

The driver of an oncoming car had seen fit to overtake the vehicle in front, on a road too narrow for such a manoeuvre, and hadn't survived the experience; neither had Andrew Knight. Philip had, but he had no recollection of it.

Trying not to lean too heavily on the stick, he knelt beside her. Kneeling was one of the few physical feats he could achieve without too much difficulty. He produced matches, and the jets lit with a quiet little explosion.

'This is terrible,' she said, holding her hands out to the warmth. 'We can't even offer you hot food today, I'm afraid – some crisis in the kitchen. But there's a pub just down the road that does lunches.'

'It's better than last time,' he said.

'Tt must have been dreadful for you,' she said. 'All that time in hospital.'

'I survived.' There *was* something familiar about her, he thought, and he coloured slightly, not wanting to admit any non-visible defects. 'This is the first time we've met, isn't it?' he asked.

'Not quite,' she said. 'I came to see you in hospital.'

'Things from before and after the accident are sometimes a bit hazy,' he said.

'It doesn't matter,' she said. 'I didn't expect you to remember me. You were in a bad way.'

Her lips parting to admit his questing tongue . . ..

He must have seen the car coming, he supposed; he must have closed his eyes and waited for the impact, but he could remember nothing. He couldn't even remember arriving at the school, or anything about the interview, except tiny, fragmentary, frustrating snatches. The last thing he really remembered was getting on the train to come here.

'It seems amnesia's not uncommon,' he said. 'Something to do with the pain. Your memory blanks it out.'

'I wish mine could,' she said.

'It was good of the school to keep the job open all this time,' he said.

Unbuttoning her top button, slipping a hand inside her blouse . . ..

'The least they could do,' she said.

6

'It wasn't the school's fault.'

Cupping her warm, silk-encased breast in the palm of his hand . . ..

'Perhaps not,' she said, handing him back the matches, and standing up. 'Well – I expect you'd like to rest before you start looking round.' And she left, closing the door behind her.

Philip closed his eyes, hearing the quiet roar of the gas fire. He leaned on the stick, and slowly, painfully, got to his feet, standing motionless for a moment. Then his hand gripped the wooden shaft of his stick, and he raised it above his head, bringing it down on the table with all the strength he possessed. Pain shot through his body as the stick shuddered in his hand, and he let it go, watching it roll along the floor.

Now he would have to pick the damn thing up again.

Barry Treadwell watched Diana Hamlyn from the window as she crossed the courtyard, towards the playing-field, on her way to the junior dormitory. He sighed, sliding open his desk drawer, and feeling at the back for the bottle. He drank from it twice before replacing the cork, and putting it back. The phone rang as he did so; he answered it to Kitty, the receptionist.

'Mr Treadwell – Mrs Knight said to tell you that she's looking after Mr Newby.'

Damn. He'd forgotten all about him. 'Good,' he said. 'Thank you, Kitty.'

'And . . . .'

He knew he didn't want her to go on.

'. . . there's been another theft,' she said. 'A ring.'

Treadwell took the receiver from his ear, and sat with it in his hand for a moment; when he put it back, she was still on the other end of the line. 'Where from?' he asked wearily.

'The ladies' loo,' said Kitty. 'Miss Castle says she took it off to wash her hands, and remembered about it as soon as she got back to the staff room. She went back, but it had gone.'

'Is she sure?' he implored. Treadwell was fifty-six, but on the first day of term he always felt twenty years older. Now this.

'She's quite sure. She's here. Do you want her to come up?'

No, he didn't want her to come up. A boys' school shouldn't *have* ladies' loos, was his first reactionary thought. Then it wouldn't have ladies taking their rings off in them. So no one could steal them. He had been at the school for two and a half years. The previous head had agreed with the governors' odd notions when it came to staff; employing women was just one of them. If he had had anything to do with it, he would have fought the idea, just as he was fighting the suggestion that they admit girls. But he had already lost that, and the first of the female pupils would be starting next year whether he liked it or not.

The first woman had been Caroline Knight, who had come four years ago as some sort of package deal with her husband, Andrew. Two vacancies had been advertised, the newly married Knights had applied, and the idea had appealed apparently. It would not have appealed to Treadwell, but it had been an established fact when he arrived, and it seemed to have worked, for as long as it had lasted.

His heart felt heavy as he thought of Andrew Knight; deputy head, a good teacher, a good man. For poor Andrew had been wiped out in a car crash less than a year after Treadwell started, and Treadwell didn't want to think about that.

Anyway, Caroline had been the first, and save for the months immediately following Andrew's death she was level-headed and logical and even quite good company. But she had opened the door for the others, and now one of the damn women was saying her ring had been stolen.

'Send her up,' he said.

He listened to her story, and had to admit that unless (as he tended to suspect) the woman had no brain at all, then she had taken her ring off in the ladies', walked along ten feet of corridor into the staff room, remembered, walked backhand it had gone. Yes, she said coyly when he asked her, there had been someone else in there, but she didn't want to accuse anyone.

But Treadwell knew, without her assistance, who it must have been. Perhaps if he called in the police it might bring her to her senses; he needn't voice his suspicions.

'We'll have to get the police this time,' he said to her and, sighing, he picked up the phone.

'Oh,' she said. 'It wasn't my engagement ring.' She waved her left hand at him to indicate its continuing presence on her finger. 'I mean, it isn't valuable or anything.'

No, he hadn't supposed it would be. The things that went missing never were.

He asked for the chief superintendent, and saw Miss Castle raise her eyebrows just a little. Why shouldn't he? The man was a friend of his. He wanted to be sure it was all handled properly, he thought, running a hand through springy grey hair. Nothing irritated the middle classes so much as having their sons suspected of theft.

He just wished it was one of their sons he suspected.

The canteen was virtually empty, much to Sam's delight. There were many things about teaching art in a small, fifth-rate private school that he didn't like; eating with blazered youths was just one of them.

'Salads?' he said incredulously. 'What do you mean, there's only salads?'

'The electricity went off to the cookers,' the girl explained patiently. 'It's only just been fixed, because we couldn't get an electrician any sooner.'

'You can't call salad *food*, woman! How do you expect me to exist on—?'

'Hello, Sam. Still complaining?'

Sam turned to see one of the few things he did like about the place.

She rubbed her cold hands together. 'Oh, it's cold out there,' she said, shivering.

'Good afternoon, Caroline,' he said. 'Don't expect any rib-sticking stew to take the cold out of your bones, whatever you do. We're being fed like sodding rabbits today.'

'I know,' she said. 'So would you if you ever read any notices.'

'This place has got more signs and notices than a bloody—' He broke off, being unable to think than what. 'Besides, I'm an artist – I don't have to be able to read.'

They picked up their salads, and went to a table beside one of the old-fashioned radiators. Sam sat down and looked reflectively at Caroline. 'I take it that was Philip Newby at the office this morning?' he asked.

'Yes,' she said.

'Are you all right?'

She frowned. 'Why shouldn't I be?' she asked.

'Well – it's a reminder, and all that.'

Her eyes grew hard. 'I hadn't forgotten,' she said.

'No, well,' said Sam, 'you know what I mean. Anyway – what's he like?'

'He's all right, I suppose.'

'Oh, come on! I've got to live with the guy – I want to know what he's like. For all I know he's queer.

'I don't think you need worry on that score.'

'Oh – what's up? Did he make a pass at you?'

'Of course not!'

'Well – what didn't you like about him?'

'Nothing,' she said, decidedly on the defensive. 'He's all right, that's all. He didn't say much.'

'There's something about him you didn't like,' Sam persisted.

'Oh, for God's sake! I exchanged about three sentences with the man. He'd had a long drive, his leg was probably hurting him, you were the first member of staff that he clapped eyes on, and then he found out he was sharing a flat with you! No wonder he seemed a bit odd.'

'He has to be odd,' Sam said, 'or he wouldn't be eligible to work here.' He looked up as some more members of staff wandered in. 'Look at them,' he said. 'Flotsam and jetsam – we take what other schools throw out. How this place has staggered on for a hundred and fifty years is beyond me.'

She looked up. 'I wasn't thrown out by another school,' she said.

No. But she had come as one of an inseparable pair; Sam knew for a fact that they had tried several schools before this one. Positively unnatural, in Sam's view, being so wrapped up in one another. Especially at their age. And she was an odd one herself. Blew hot and cold.

Maybe she fancied this Newby; he'd heard it took some people like that. Though it was hard to imagine Caroline fancying anyone. He'd taken her out once or twice since she had begun to get over Andrew's death, and the relationship had moved from entirely platonic through sub-teenage to long discussions about how she didn't feel ready. Sam didn't really mind. He liked her company, and if it developed beyond that – fine. But in between the outings and the discussions he seemed to be the last person on earth that she wanted to spend time with. Perhaps he embarrassed her. He hoped he did. At any rate, she had never given the least hint that she was remotely interested in him other than as an occasionally necessary social accessory.

'How long was he in hospital?' he asked.

A little frown creased her forehead. 'Who?' she asked.

'Newby.' She knew damn well who.

'He was in and out for about a year, I believe. He's had dozens of operations.' She gave a short sigh. 'He's been at some sort of recuperation place for six months.'

'It was hard luck,' Sam said.

'Hard luck? Is that all you think it was?'

Sam shrugged. 'What else? Some nutter comes out of a line of cars, Andrew gets killed, Newby gets crippled – bad luck. Fate, if you'd rather.'

She just looked at him, not speaking, not arguing.

'Well,' he said, 'what would you call it? '

She sighed. 'Forget it,' she said.

'What's he doing for lunch?' Sam asked.

'I don't know. I told him he could get something hot at the pub.'

Sam frowned. 'Does he know where it is?' he asked.

'I don't know!'

'You mean you just left him to fend for himself?'

'Can we drop the subject of Philip Newby?' Oh, well. Presumably his presence had upset her. But someone had better see that the man got fed.

'Are you going to this party tonight?' Caroline asked.

'If you are,' he said. 'Does cocktails with the Hamlyns turn you on?'

'Not really,' she said. 'But I suppose it would be a bit off not to celebrate his promotion.'

'Robert Hamlyn – deputy head,' said Sam, in tones of wonderment. 'Who would credit it?'

'Robert's all right,' said Caroline, determined to disagree with him about everything, obviously.

'*He's* all right,' Sam agreed. 'But I don't think the deputy headmaster's wife should be the good time that was had by all, do you?'

She shook her head. 'Probably not,' she said.

'No other school would employ him, never mind make him the deputy head.'

The deputy between Andrew and Robert Hamlyn had abandoned ship during the summer break, having realised all too quickly what he had got himself into. Sam had his own ideas as to why Hamlyn had been thus exalted.

'What's wrong?' asked Caroline. 'Do you think it should have been you?'

'Oh, very funny. No, but there are one or two people I think it could have been. You, for instance.'

She looked at him strangely, again, then smiled, shaking her head.

'The boys would have been queuing up to have you discipline them,' he said, pushing away his barely touched salad, and standing up. 'I think I'll see if Newby wants to come to the pub,' he said.

Caroline was no fun when she was in one of her moods, and it was with something like relief that Sam stepped out into the sleet which was now slicing its way through the air, and walked down to the staff block, letting himself in to find Newby sitting by the fire.

'Waters,' he said. 'Sam. I teach art because no one buys my paintings.' He held out his hand.

Newby looked a little startled, then smiled. 'Newby,' he said. 'Philip. I teach English because I like it.'

'They're feeding us on grass at the canteen,' said Sam. 'I wondered if you fancied something at the pub.'

'I've heard of you,' Newby said slowly. 'You had an exhibition at the Tate – it was quite successful, wasn't it?'

'It was five years ago,' Sam said, surprised as he always was when anyone had heard of him. 'Are you interested in art?'

'Yes,' said Newby. 'I went to the Tate a lot when I was in London – I like the things the tabloids make fun of.'

'So do I,' said Sam thoughtfully. 'Yes – the exhibition was quite successful. But you have to die in my business before you earn enough to live on.'

Newby smiled. 'I don't suppose you're too pleased about having a room-mate,' he said.

'Oh, I don't know,' said Sam truthfully. 'I'll be glad of the company.'

'I'll be looking for somewhere of my own,' Newby said.

'Good luck. The nearest town is Stansfield, and that's twenty miles away,' said Sam. 'And if you get anywhere in one of the villages you'll have even less privacy than you get here.'

There was a knock at the door, and Sam watched as Newby went to answer it, moving in the oddly quick way he had, almost as though the stick wasn't there at all. He could have gone, but he had a feeling in his bones that that wouldn't have been a wise move.

'Philip,' Barry Treadwell's voice boomed. 'So sorry I couldn't meet you myself this morning, but there were a million things to do.' He walked in, nodded to Sam, then turned back to Newby. 'Still,' he said, 'I'm sure you'd rather have Caroline showing you round than me!'

Newby didn't react with the expected polite smile. If Sam were to be asked, he would say that he saw a faint flush on Newby's face.

'Now – are you settling in all right? Got someone lined up to bring in your stuff?'

'Not yet,' said Newby.

'Soon remedy that.' He went back to the door, and bellowed at the youth who was passing to get someone else and start unpacking Newby's car. 'Keys?' he said, turning back.

'It's open,' said the still bemused Newby. 'The back door doesn't lock.'

Treadwell relayed this information to the young man who had answered his summons; Matthew Cawston, head boy and smooth bastard. Sam didn't care for him.

'Good,' Treadwell said. 'That's got that organised. You didn't see much of the place when you came for the interview, did you? And it was a long time ago, now. So have a good look round, and anything you think you need – come to me. Anything we can do to make things easier . . . just pop into my office – any time. Sorry I can't stay and chat.'

Sam looked at Philip Newby when Barry had gone. 'So,' he said. 'You've met the lovely Caroline?'

Newby nodded.

'Forget it,' Sam said. 'I've got my name down.'

'I'm sorry?' Newby said.

There was another knock on the door, which opened to reveal Cawston and a bearer. The smaller boy staggered in, loaded down with suitcases.

'Where would you like your things, sir?' asked Cawston.

'Oh – just dump them in my room,' said Newby, going to open the door for the panting child. 'Anywhere,' he said.

Sam watched as Cawston supervised. 'Cawston,' he said. 'Try going back to the car and picking up a few things yourself. You never know, it might just work.'

Cawston's back stiffened for a moment. 'Yes, sir,' he said.

'And don't call me fucking sir!' roared Sam, as Cawston left. 'Lazy young sod,' he said to Newby, as the other one emerged from the bedroom and scampered out before he got sworn at, too.

Newby was trying not to look startled, and manfully got back to the matter in hand. 'Er ... you and ... Mrs Knight,' he said. 'Are you ...?' He finished with a movement of his head.

'Well,' said Sam. 'Let's put it this way. There are four hundred males and twenty-three females in this place.'

Cawston and his labourer returned with various items of Newby's luggage.

'Eight of them are under ten – I don't know if you're into paedophilia, but I'm not,' Sam continued, enjoying Newby's consternation at his discussing such things within the boys' earshot. 'Twelve of them are married, and one, as we all know only too well, is engaged to be married. If they stray, they don't do it here.'

'Is there more in the boot, sir?' asked Cawston.

'Except for one, of course,' said Sam. 'But she's a nympho.'

'No,' Newby said, with a quick, disapproving glance at Sam. 'It was frozen up this morning – I couldn't use it.' He dug in his pocket for change.

'And you can get too much of a good thing,' Sam went on, ignoring Newby's embarrassment.

Newby hurriedly tipped the boys, thanking them, shepherding them to the door.

'One is Matron,' continued Sam, 'who is twice my size and coming up for sixty-five. And the other one is Caroline.'

Newby closed the door with a sigh of relief, and took cigarettes from his jacket pocket. He lit one as he considered Sam's words. 'Which one's the nympho?' he asked.

Sam had been expecting a reproof. He grinned. 'You'll find out,' he said. 'Are you coming to the pub?'

'Mrs Knight! Mrs Knight!'

Caroline turned in the direction of the peremptory treble.

'Mrs Knight – Mrs Hamlyn says could you possibly pop up to see her if you have a moment?'

The faithful reproduction of Diana Hamlyn's request made Caroline smile, and she followed the child back to the junior dormitory, and popped up to see Diana, who sat amid trunks and suitcases and sundry grey-blazered small boys, a blonde, vivacious splash of colour.

'. . . and this has no name-tag.' She looked at the child over her reading-glasses, which were perched on the end of her nose. 'You can write your name, can you, young man?'

The child smiled shyly at her mock sternness, and Diana went on. 'Two white shirts, two—' She looked up and smiled. 'Oh, super, Caroline. Are you on your way back to the staff block by any chance? The thing is that I only found out about this new chap this morning – I mean, he hasn't had an invitation for drinks. I'm stuck here with these horrors, and I'm hours behind – could you be an angel and pop in to tell him he's more than welcome?'

I'll bet he is, thought Caroline, as she tried to think of a way of refusing. Diana always welcomed a new man. She was an odd mixture of sense and sensibility.

'Can you?' Diana asked. 'Or are you fearfully busy?'

No, Caroline wasn't fearfully busy. But she hadn't been able to get away from Philip Newby fast enough, and she had no desire to go back. She still tried to think of a plausible excuse, but none presented itself. She supposed she was being silly; it wasn't as if he *had* actually made a pass at her or anything. And, if the worst came to the worst, she could certainly run faster than him.

Diana smiled her thanks. 'Two vests,' she said, carrying on with her inventory. 'I'm assuming you have one on.'

He smiled again, pinkly confirming her supposition. Diana was in her element with the little ones, thought Caroline, and not for the first time wondered why she had none of her own.

And she delivered Philip's message from Diana. At first he was diffident, almost shy; she wondered if she had imagined the whole thing until after a few moments she became aware of his intense interest once more.

It surprised her a little that she thought of him as Philip. Not as Philip Newby, or Mr Newby, or just Newby, as Sam called him. There was something about Philip that she recognised, and understood. The shared experience of the accident, perhaps; she didn't know.

'Is it the sort of thing I ought to go to?' he asked her calves.

'Well, he's just been appointed deputy head,' she said. 'That's what they're celebrating. I don't know how strong you are on keeping in with the bosses. But it's a good way to meet the rest of the staff.'

His eyes travelled up, lingering now and then, before meeting hers. 'I suppose I should go,' he said.

She resisted the temptation to pull the collar of her blouse together as his eyes rested on the little line of cleavage of which she was now as intensely aware as he was. She stood up. 'They live at the top of the junior dormitory,' she said. 'That's the building just across the side-road.'

'The one that backs on to the car park?'

'That's right,' she said, going to the door, wondering if he was actually listening to anything she said.

'What about the Grand Tour?' he asked, getting to his feet.

Damn. She'd forgotten about that. He did listen, apparently. 'Of course,' she said, her heart sinking at the thought.

He wanted to see everything, but she could see that trying to keep his feet on the slippery cobbles of the little lane through the buildings was painfully difficult. She was uncharitably grateful to the road surface for taking his mind off her anatomy.

Over the years, buildings had been added to the grounds until it looked like a small village; a tour merely confused new people. But, she assured Philip as they went into the main building, he would find his way about eventually.

She showed him the staff room, and one of the classrooms, then popped her head round Barry Treadwell's door.

'Oh, I beg your pardon,' she said, when she saw that he had someone with him. 'I was just showing Philip round.'

'Come in, come in,' Treadwell said. 'Philip may as well find out that it's not all roses.' He gestured towards the dark-haired woman with him. 'This is Detective Sergeant Hill,' he said.

Sergeant Hill was about her own age, well dressed, and attractive. Caroline nodded to her, puzzled by her presence, and delighted that she was female, which would not please Barry at all.

'Something's gone missing,' Barry said by way of explanation. 'Already.'

'We've got a thief,' she said to Philip. 'Watch your valuables.' She turned back to Treadwell. 'I'll leave you to it,' she said.

They left the headmaster's study, and went back downstairs, where she ticked off doors as they passed. 'Storeroom, boiler room – and this', she said, opening the insignificant door at the end of the corridor, 'will surprise you.'

She liked introducing people to the Great Hall by its internal door, watching their faces as they found themselves in its baronial splendour.

Philip looked up at the exposed beams arching across the high ceiling, and walked slowly towards one of the carved pillars, his face breaking into a slow smile at the sheer chaotic bad taste of it all.

'It's called the Great Hall,' she said, as they crossed over, towards the double doors by which people more usually entered. 'The original school had it built on, for reasons best-known to the founder. It's used for assembly, prize-giving, lectures – that sort of thing. This is where we'll be holding the Sesquicentennial Ball.'

'Lovely word,' he said. 'You'd have to celebrate it just so you could use it. It's next month, isn't it?' he asked.

'Yes. Friday the fourteenth. St Valentine's Day.'

His face broke into a sudden and engaging smile. '*That's* what Sam needs the adjectival dinner-jacket for!' he said.

'Correct,' she said, laughing, as she pushed open the double doors to the entrance-hall.

'Loos, cloakroom, telephone,' she said, tackling the huge, arched outside door which weighed about a ton, and stepped out into the courtyard.

Philip followed her, his step becoming unsure once more as he made his way across the cobbles.

'What are all these buildings?' he asked, stopping by one, trying not to look as though he was recovering from his short journey across the courtyard.

Caroline pointed to the one behind the Hall. 'That's the Dining

Hall,' she said. 'Most people just call it the canteen. And the new one behind that is the gymnasium.'

Philip nodded. 'What's in here?' he asked, trying the handle of the door he was pretending not to lean on. 'Oh,' he said, as visitors always did, when he found himself looking directly at the snow-covered playing-field through the open wall at the other side.

'The Barn,' said Caroline. 'At least that's what it used to be. It's even got a hay-loft.' She led the way in.

'So it has,' said Philip. 'Do you have some use for hay?'

Caroline stiffened slightly. 'Not to feed animals,' she said. Diana sometimes had a use for hay, she thought, but she didn't burden Philip with explanations. He looked a little puzzled at her cryptic answer, and she smiled briefly. 'Anyway – that lot's well past its sell-by date,' she said. 'We tend to use this place like other people use attics.'

'So I see,' said Philip.

Boxes, old books, builders' left-overs lined the floor along the walls. But you could still have held a dance in what was left. They almost had, but the effort of getting it cleared out had proved too much for Barry.

'Couldn't it be put to some better use?' asked Philip. 'All this space?'

'Ah – you and Sam had better get together,' Caroline said. 'He wants it to be turned into a new art room. The big doors face north, apparently. He wants glass put in their place, and all sorts of things.' She smiled. 'But that costs money, and this school doesn't have a lot of that.'

They wandered out, and Caroline slid the barn doors shut. 'They're supposed to be kept closed,' she said. 'But the kids play in here.' She turned. 'That's the junior dormitory,' she said, pointing across the playing-field. 'The Hamlyns' flat is at the top.' She smiled at his confused expression. 'You'll get your bearings,' she said.

'Don't you have a garden, or something?' Philip asked.

'No,' she said. 'There's no room. We've got buildings everywhere there was once a space.'

He frowned a little. 'I thought I remembered a garden,' he said.

As they moved off again, his stick skidded on the frozen cobbles, shooting out of his hand; Caroline retrieved it, examining it for damage.

'There's a little crack just about halfway down,' she said concernedly.

He almost snatched it from her. 'I know,' he said.

They carried on, more slowly now that he was taking care with the stick, and on their way back to the staff block Caroline explained the buildings that huddled round the lane. There had been a time when the enrolment had increased rather than decreased every year, and the result was a wonderful mixture of periods and mock-periods. The whole place was an architect's nightmare, and Caroline liked it.

Philip suddenly stopped, as they emerged from the lane. 'There's no need to see me home,' he snapped.

Caroline raised an eyebrow. 'I live here, too,' she pointed out.

His unexpected smile appeared again. 'Sorry,' he said.

Caroline smiled back. When he wasn't ogling her, or biting her head off, he wasn't all that bad. In fact, he reminded her of Andrew; she wasn't surprised that they had been friends.

Outside the light faded, and Judy Hill tried to sound interested in Mr Treadwell's problems.

'And it began about eighteen months ago?' she asked, taking out her notebook.

'Yes, just about. A year ago last September – at the beginning of the autumn term. At first, we didn't even realise we had a thief – the odd thing went missing now and then, but it wasn't constant. There would be months when nothing went missing. But eventually we knew it couldn't be coincidence.'

'Do you have a list of the stolen items?'

'Not as such,' he said. 'I've noted them down here and there, but I haven't done an actual list. I can let you have one, if you like.'

'Yes, please,' she said, trying not to yawn. 'Have you done anything yourself about the thefts?'

'I made an announcement at assembly. Told everyone to keep a careful eye on anything that might be stolen, and to report anything that was. I advised the thief to stop, because if he was caught he would be expelled.'

Dynamic leadership, Judy thought, and her brown eyes widened a little as she wrote. 'You're certain it is one of the boys?' she asked.

'Well,' he said, 'yes. Yes, I imagine it is.' He got up and looked out at the darkening sky. 'I think we must be seen to be doing something about it.'

'What's gone missing today?'

'A ring – not worth much but, then, none of it is. It belongs to one of the teachers. She'd left it on the .... '

Judy wrote down what he was saying. There wasn't much you could do about this sort of stealing, with upwards of four hundred suspects. On the first day of term, everyone was all over the place. There were no classes; there was nothing to pin anyone down to a particular place at a particular time. Whoever it was, he bided his time, and took great care not to get caught. It was obviously purely to irritate.

Trust Lloyd to land her with this on her first day back. 'As a favour to Chief Superintendent Allison,' he had said, blue eyes shining with suspect honesty. 'The headmaster doesn't want uniforms all over the show.'

'What's wrong with Sandwell?' she had asked.

'Mr Allison thinks a woman would be less threatening to the lads.' He had grinned mischievously. 'And I thought it would be a nice way to ease you back into harness.'

This, of course, was Lloyd's way of getting at her, Judy thought darkly, as she glanced at her notes, at the list she had made of where the thefts had occurred.

'Would I be right in thinking that these are mainly staff areas?' She glanced down the list. 'Staff room, sports pavilion, secretary's office, kitchen, storeroom ...' she read.

'Yes,' he said testily, then apologised. 'It is popularly believed to be a member of staff,' he admitted. 'But that's out of the question.'

'Well,' said Judy, 'I'd better start with the boys, if you think it's one of them.'

'How?' asked Treadwell, alarmed.

'Do you have a head boy?' Judy asked.

'Oh, yes.'

'Perhaps if I speak to him. If it is one of the boys, he quite probably has an idea who.'

'He'd never tell you if he did. That would be sneaking.'

'I know. But he might warn off whoever it is. Or just knowing that the police have been called in might put the thief off. And, if it is a member of staff, they might get an attack of conscience if the boys seem to be being suspected.'

That was what Treadwell was hoping.

She closed her notebook. 'It isn't very satisfactory, but . . . .

'Yes, yes.' Treadwell stood up. 'I'll send Matthew in,' he said. 'In the meantime, I'm sure you could do with a cup of tea.'

Judy smiled, and Treadwell left. Again, she found her thoughts turning to Lloyd, and was irritated with herself for being unable to divorce her personal life from her professional life. She had always been able to before.

The tea came, brought in by a youth who looked to Judy far older than most of the constables with whom she worked. She stood up and relieved him of the cup and saucer. He was slightly taller than she was, and somehow contrived to make his uniform look like what the fashionable man-about-town was wearing, with exactly the correct amount of cuff showing, and an air of elegance that Lloyd would have envied. Lloyd somehow never looked like that. Someone she knew did, though; he reminded her of someone. Not his features. His manner, his personality.

'Matthew Cawston,' he said smoothly. 'Mr Treadwell said that you wanted to speak to me.'

Judy turned her mind once more to work, until at last she was leaving the school, and on her way home.

Two weeks since her promise. Two weeks of steeling herself, lecturing herself, loathing herself for being such a coward, had crystallised into two words. Tell him. Tell him at breakfast, before he goes to work. Tell him when he comes home from work. Tell him in the evening, when he's settling down to watch television. Tell him before you go to bed, tell him at breakfast. It wasn't as if it would come as all that much of a surprise to him; Michael had probably already guessed about her and Lloyd. But somehow none of that made it any easier. And it had only been a fortnight ago that she had made her mind up to leave him; she had to pick the right moment.

She drove home with the words beating in her mind like a pulse. It was a half-hour drive from the school, which contrived almost literally to be in the middle of nowhere, but which somehow came under the purview of Stansfield Constabulary. At last she saw the orange lights flanking the snow-lined dual carriageway into the new town, and now-familiar landmarks came into view. The industrial estate with its neat factory units looking like terraced houses, and the superstore looking like an enormous Swiss chalet, with its seemingly permanent covering of snow. The DIY store with swings and see-saws and slides; the adventure playground, with tyres and planks.

A left turn, and she would be in the village that had been there since Elizabethan times. The old Stansfield, where Lloyd lived.

Tell Lloyd that you still haven't told Michael. I dare you.

She took the right turn.

Michael smiled when she came in. Don't *smile*, why would you smile? Criticise me for something, God knows that's what you usually do. Say that it's high time we moved out of this town. Go on about how much we'd get for the house if we put it on the market. Tell me that you've got filing clerks earning more than I do, so it's not as though my job's that important, and you could get a job anywhere. Prove you don't understand, don't want to understand – *don't smile.*

'How did it go?' he asked.

'What?'

'Your first day back.'

'Oh. Fine.'

'Are they going to give you a medal or something?'

'Good God, I hope not.' She took off her coat and went out into the hallway to hang it up.

'Why not?' he called through. 'You were hurt in the line of duty – you could have got killed.'

She went back. 'Well, I wasn't,' she said.

'No, thank God.'

Tell him. 'Michael, I want to tell you—'

'Shall I tell you something funny?' he said, interrupting her.

She sat down with a sigh.

'When I came home, and the house was in darkness – I forgot you were back at work. I was expecting you to be here.'

Oh, here we go, she thought. How nice it was to have her at home. So why didn't she just give up her job and go with him to a nice middle-class town and have a baby before it was too late?

'And for a moment . . . .' He laughed a little shyly. 'For a moment, I thought you'd left me.'

She looked up at him. 'Left you?' she repeated dully.

'It wasn't such a strange thing to think,' he said. 'Was it? I mean – we're not even. . . . Well, I just thought you had. And then I realised you were just at work,' he said. 'But I thought . . . other men don't think their wives have left them just because the light's out. And I know things haven't been too good since I got the promotion – but that's just because we're not used to being together all the time. We've drifted apart, that's all.'

Judy couldn't speak.

'But we've stayed together ten years, and I don't want to lose you, Judy.' His eyes dropped away from hers. 'I really thought you'd gone,' he said. 'And I felt exactly like I did when I was three years old and lost my mother in Woolworth's. Total panic.'

Judy listened to the little speech with a dismay which she felt must show on her face, but he didn't seem to notice.

He metaphorically picked himself up and dusted himself off. 'Well, now I've said it. What were you going to tell me?'

'Oh,' she said, looking away from him as she told a rare lie. 'Nothing. I don't remember.'

'Can't have been anything important, then,' he said, with a smile. 'Would you like a drink?'

Matthew Cawston looked up at the windows of Palmerston House, checking that all the lights were out. His fellow-prefects would go from room to room, opening the doors; Matthew thought that a waste of energy. Tonight, something was going on in the junior dorm which interested him. And they hadn't all arrived yet.

He stepped out of the shadow of the building, and walked to the end of the lane, where he lit an illicit cigarette. He shook the match out and buttoned his jacket against the chill. He was glad to be back at school, and away from all the rowing at home. He had caused it, of course, by refusing to be put into some sort of pigeon-hole by his father. His mother had taken his side, as she always did, so before long it was his mother and father who were shouting at one another.

School was infinitely preferable to that. Here, they only wanted him to shine for them, and he could do that without trying. He drew deeply on the cigarette, watching stars begin to appear as the clouds drifted off, and the temperature fell once more.

'What are you intending doing with your life?' his father had demanded to know during one of the interminable sessions.

Matthew didn't know, but he couldn't explain that to his father. He was sixteen. Why should he start mapping his life out? He didn't know if what interested him now would still interest him at twenty-six, or forty-six. He wasn't sure what did interest him now, anyway. He was good at most things; studying came easily to him, and passing exams was taken for granted. His father expected him to go on and get a double first at Oxford, but that didn't interest Matthew. There was no challenge in that.

The only subject in which he had any real interest was English. English wasn't like other subjects, where everything was cut and dried, right or wrong. He enjoyed the books that the others moaned about having to read; he liked discussing thhem, dissecting them, criticising them. He'd seen the new English teacher limping about with Mrs Knight, and wondered what he'd be like. He must be good, for them to have kept his job open for such a long time.

The tip of the cigarette glowed red in the darkness, and Matthew moved back into the lane, in case some over-zealous fellow-prefect spotted it. The housemaster was at the Hamlyns' do, so no fear of his creeping up behind him. All in all, it wasn't a bad school. It had rules and regulations, like all schools, and Matthew enjoyed that; it gave him the chance to break them without getting caught. His expertise was evidenced by the fact of his having been made head boy, an honour which Treadwell had solemnly conferred upon him while Matthew kept a straight face.

Footsteps came along the road from the staff block; Matthew dropped the cigarette and stood on it, strolling out into the light again.

'Good evening, Mrs Knight,' he said.

'Hello, Matthew. Is there something wrong?'

'No, not at all. I just felt like a breath of air.'

'How did you get on with the policewoman?' she asked.

'Very well, thank you. She said that it was really crime prevention at this stage – a case of advising everyone to lock desks and rooms, and so on. She said we should report to Mr Treadwell if we saw anyone hanging round the lockers or anything like that.'

She nodded. 'I don't suppose there's much the police can do about it, really,' she said.

'No.' Matthew let her get a couple of steps away. 'Oh – Mrs Knight. I was pleased to hear about Mr Hamlyn.'

'I'll tell him,' she said, smiling.

Matthew watched her go. He *had* been pleased to hear about Hamlyn's promotion; he liked him, liked his absent-minded professor air, which was entirely genuine. Hamlyn knew what he wanted to do with his life, and he was doing it, to the exclusion of all else. He wanted to immerse himself in maths and logic and solve complicated puzzles. It wouldn't do for Matthew, but he admired Hamlyn's single-mindedness, his courage. Because it took courage to do what you wanted to do, and to hell with what people thought. And that even included his choice of wife. Matthew smiled as he thought of Mrs Hamlyn, as unlike her husband as it was possible to get, and still be of the same species.

He gave Mrs Knight time to get upstairs to the Hamlyns' living-quarters, then walked quickly across the road, down the side-road to the car park, and along to the junior dorm's fire-escape. The light went on in the Hamlyns' bedroom as it had with each new arrival, and went off again after a moment.

Mrs Knight's late arrival had made it more of a challenge than it might have been; people might even be thinking of leaving soon. But, then, again, people were innately polite, and wouldn't go as soon as someone had arrived. He would give himself three minutes, he thought, glancing at his watch in the dim, almost nonexistent car park lighting.

A glance over his shoulder, before he ascended the metal steps; there was no one else about on this cold night.

On the balcony, it was simplicity itself. Interior décor was not something for which the school was renowned, and the curtains, made for a quite different window, left a gap down the side through which he could see the darkened room. It was easy to step from the balcony to the window-ledge, after he had knocked away the frozen snow. The window didn't close properly; Matthew had already established that. It pivoted open, and he put his arm through, pushing down the handle of the balcony door.

Slowly, carefully, he opened it; to his surprise and horror, it made a deafening squeak, but it couldn't have been that loud inside the house. He waited a second or two before going in, and noiselessly crossed to the light-switch. He smiled at the heap of coats on the bed, and began going through the pockets. He didn't care what he found; if he found nothing, he would take the travelling alarm-clock that sat on the bedside table. But he would prefer it to be something out of a coat, or a jacket.

It had been accidental, to start with. The very first thing he had taken had made them all decide it had to have been Mrs Knight; now, he shadowed her, taking things when the opportunity presented itself. It was fun. And this morning he had struck gold in the ladies' loo, waiting until she had left it empty, then slipping in unseen. He could hardly believe his luck when he saw the ring.

He moved to the side of the bed, standing still as the door blew shut again, with another loud squeak. Then he picked up the sheepskin jacket affected by Newby, the English teacher, and his hand closed over a packet of cigarettes, followed by a box of matches. They went into his pocket, joining his own; a further search of the coats produced a lady's comb and a pound coin.

At first, he didn't recognise the sound; by the time he realised that it was the tap of Newby's stick on the corridor, it was too late. He thought he would have time to make it back out before Newby got to the room, but Newby moved faster than he'd suspected; desperate, Matthew slipped behind the curtains, drawing his feet up on to the window-sill as the door opened. He couldn't get out without pushing open the balcony door, and he couldn't do that without attracting attention. So he just had to stay there.

Through the gap in the curtains, Matthew watched as Newby pulled coats aside to reach his jacket. He was feeling in the pockets, frowning, when Mrs Hamlyn appeared, standing in the doorway.

'Not leaving us, are you, Philip?'

'Just came to get my cigarettes,' Newby said. 'But I must have left them at the flat.'

'Is that why you left?' she asked. 'Or is it because Caroline's arrived?'

Newby looked down at his feet for a moment. 'I don't know what you mean,' he said.

'Yes, you do. But she's much too complicated for you, Philip. Take my advice – don't get involved.'

'I don't even know her, Mrs Hamlyn. I only met her this morning.'

'I'm very uncomplicated,' she went on. 'You'd be much better off with me.'

Matthew held his breath.

'Mrs Hamlyn, I—'

'She's never got over Andrew,' Mrs Hamlyn went on.

'That's hardly any of my business,' said Newby.

'It's everyone's business,' said Mrs Hamlyn. 'She's making it everyone's business – if your cigarettes have gone, that's probably because Caroline's just been up here.'

'What?' said Newby.

Mrs Hamlyn gave a slight shrug.

'You're not suggesting that Caroline—?'

Matthew so far forgot his unenviable position to permit himself a smile.

'She can't help it,' said Mrs Hamlyn. 'I'm just warning you.'

'I've probably left my cigarettes in the flat,' Newby said again, his tone growing angry. 'And I hardly think they merit warnings being issued.'

Mrs Hamlyn smiled. 'I'm not warning you to keep an eye on your cigarettes,' she said. 'I'm warning you not to get involved with Caroline. She's supposed to be seeing a psychiatrist or something, but she doesn't.'

'I can't imagine what you mean, "get involved".'

'Oh, come on, Philip. I saw the way you looked at her.'

There was an uncomfortable silence, during which Matthew didn't dare breathe, and Newby grew red and sullen, like one of the first-years caught reading a girlie magazine.

Mrs Hamlyn glanced down at Newby's leg. 'Does it give you much trouble?' she asked, nodding at it as she spoke.

'Not really,' said Newby, recovering some composure now that the subject had been changed.

'I mean – it would be a frightful bore if it interfered with your normal activities.' She lifted her eyes to his again. 'I do hope it doesn't,' she said.

It sounded like an innocent remark, but its implication was not lost on Matthew, or Newby.

'Hardly at all,' he said. 'I'd better be getting back.' Newby went towards the door in the sudden way he had of moving. He didn't look awkward with the stick; it was as if it was just a part of him. 'If you'll excuse me, Mrs Hamlyn,' he said.

She didn't move.

'Could you excuse me?' he asked again.

'I'm sure you could squeeze past,' she said, not moving.

Matthew's eyes widened. He'd heard the stories about Diana Hamlyn, but he had always assumed they were exaggerated.

'Mrs Hamlyn, I—'

'How formal. Do call me Diana.'

'Mrs Hamlyn,' he said firmly. 'I think I should get back.'

She smiled. 'I'd be more fun than a cigarette,' she said. 'And much better for you.'

Newby gave a brief smile. 'If you could just move, please,' he said.

She came in, then, closing the door, and leaning on it. 'I've moved,' she said.

A mixture of fear and fascination warred within Matthew as, open-mouthed, he watched her turn the key and remove it from the lock. Fascination won; he forgot his own predicament as he watched Newby deal with his.

'I presume this is your idea of a joke,' Newby said.

'It is quite amusing.' She came up close to Newby, and smiled.

'We met exactly an hour ago, Mrs Hamlyn,' said Newby. 'I hardly know you.'

'We could remedy that,' she said, lightly touching his chest.

Newby moved away from her, and sat down, his hands crossed over the top of his walking-stick. 'If the positions were reversed,' he said, 'you could slap my face – even shout for help. As it is, I'll just have to wait for you to get bored.'

'You were a friend of Andrew Knight's, weren't you?' she asked.

'Yes.' Newby sounded guarded.

'Oh, don't worry,' she said. 'I wasn't. Not like that, anyway. He had no time for me – he was too much in love with Caroline.' She sighed. 'I've a dreadful suspicion that so are you,' she said, and smiled, throwing him the key.

He didn't try to catch it; it clattered to the ground, perilously close to the window, and Matthew closed his eyes. He opened them as Newby addressed himself to the problem; he saw the pain on his face as he leaned as much of his weight as he could on the stick, and scooped up the key. For a moment, as Newby straightened up, it was as if he were looking directly at Matthew, but he wasn't.

He was waiting for the pain to go before he turned to face Mrs Hamlyn.

'Thank you,' he said, going to the door, unlocking it.

'Making sheep's eyes at Caroline won't get you anywhere,' Mrs Hamlyn said. 'Sam's been trying for months.'

Newby coloured a little. His stick tapped quickly down the corridor, and Mrs Hamlyn smiled to herself, putting out the light as she left.

Matthew let out a long sigh of relief, and waited until it was safe before pushing open the treacherous balcony-door and making his exit. Outside, he repeated the exercise in reverse; his arm through the window, he pulled the door shut. He closed the window as much as it ever closed, checked that he still had everything he had taken, and almost strolled back down the fire-escape steps, back to Palmerston House.

Detective Chief Inspector Lloyd poured himself a beer, picked up his plate of sandwiches, and went through to the living-room, kicking the door shut behind him.

He put the sandwiches on the table, the beer on the floor, and eased off his shoes, sitting down in the reclining chair that had been his first major purchase after his divorce. He picked up the television remote control, and the television flashed into silent life as he muted the sound. He'd waited years for this film to be shown again. He'd had hair the last time it had been on. Well, rather more than he'd got now, anyway.

There was something to be said for living alone, he thought, as he reached for the video remote. You could watch films that went on until one fifteen in the morning, *and* record them, without being nagged to death.

Judy would think he was quite mad, of course.

'Why watch it in the middle of the night when you're recording it anyway? Why record it when you've seen it three times already? Why even watch it twice?'

'Oh, for God's sake, I just want to watch the film. Go to bed if you don't like it.'

'I'll hear it through the wall – how can I sleep?'

'Then, watch it with me.'

'I don't want to watch it.'

He smiled. It would be better, he conceded, if she was actually there, saying all that, instead of just in his head. As it was, she had never stayed all night with him, and all their rows were about their situation, not about normal domestic differences.

'*As for people fantasising rows ...*'

Judy would have him certified if she knew everything that went on in his head.

He wondered what she was doing now, then wished he hadn't. Her assurances that the marriage was all over bar the shouting didn't help, though he knew it was the truth. She still spent her nights with Michael instead of with him, and what was or wasn't happening was of secondary importance.

She had promised to tell Michael, and she would. But she hadn't promised when, and Judy had a positive phobia about commitment.

But perhaps, he thought, with a total lack of conviction, perhaps she was telling him even now. Perhaps she would turn up at his door in half an hour, saying that she had finally left him. He smiled to himself. If she did, she would spoil the film, and wouldn't that be just like her?

The credits rolled on the news programme, to which he had not been listening, and he turned up the sound. He checked the video. Right channel. As a slide of tomorrow's early programmes went up, he started the tape, and paused it, ready to roll on cue.

'*And now*,' said the announcer smoothly, '*in a change to our advertised programme ...*'

Lloyd stared at the screen, at the 'tribute' to the actor whose death had presumably been reported in the previous programme. One of his old films. How dragging a few reels of film out could possibly be regarded as a tribute was beyond him. Anyone who wanted to see the damn thing wouldn't know it was on.

He was still watching, still recording, as though it would somehow transform itself into *his* old film, but it wouldn't. With a deep sigh, he switched off the television, and stopped the tape.

He bit disconsolately into a sandwich. No chance of her turning up now.

Chapter Two

The Sesquicentennial Ball had finally arrived; Caroline had other plans, which included Sam. 'Are we still on for tonight?' he asked, sitting opposite her.

She barely looked up from her newspaper. 'Yes,' she said.

It was hardly enthusiastic, but it was in the affirmative. Sam picked up his knife and fork, as she turned her attention once more to what seemed to be the racing pages. He prodded the potatoes. 'What did you have?' he asked.

'The quiche.'

'I think so should I have done.' But despite his misgivings he began to eat; he was ravenous. He glanced up now and then at Caroline's absorbed face. 'Are you fond of a flutter?' he asked.

'No.'

God. Was she going to be like this tonight? Sam didn't care for hard work, and that's just what Caroline was. He was beginning to see Matron's attractions. She presumably had the appropriate anatomy, which was the only qualification required.

But Caroline had got hold of tickets for a midnight showing of some foreign film of which he'd never heard, but which, it appeared, anyone worth his artistic salt would kill to see. And since it was at midnight she obviously didn't want to go alone. So, call for Sam, who she knew would welcome any excuse to leave the festivities. He was under no illusion about why he had been thus honoured, but he had no pride.

He was to leave the ball at eleven, and pick Caroline up from the junior dorm. The film, he understood, concerned itself high-mindedly with erotica; perhaps she had picked him because she imagined that artists, like doctors, viewed these things with a detached professionalism.

They didn't. At any rate, *he* didn't. He couldn't wait any longer for Caroline.

'I trust Diana's suitably grateful for your offer to babysit,' he said. 'Imagine – the Great Hall full of men, and she might have been stuck with a load of eleven-year-olds.'

'Diana isn't obliged to look after them,' she said, not lifting her head from the paper.

'Then, I trust the school is suitably grateful,' he persisted. At least he'd got a whole sentence out of her.

'Look – I didn't mind organising it, but I certainly didn't want to go to this thing. Both Robert and Diana have to be there at least until the speeches are over. Someone has to supervise the kids, so I volunteered – is that all right with you?'

Sam decided that saying nothing was the wisest course.

'And she is leaving early so that you and I can go to this film,' Caroline added.

'She's probably, got some man lined up,' said Sam.

'My God – they say women are bitchy.'

'You're a woman,' said Sam. 'You don't know what she's like. Ask Newby, if you don't believe me. She's been trying to seduce him for weeks.' He sat back a little. 'But he's only got eyes for you,' he said.

'Have you got your dinner-jacket?' she asked, transparently changing the subject.

'Not yet.'

'Oh, Sam!' She got up.

Sam shrugged. 'I'm picking it up this afternoon,' he said. 'Don't you worry.'

'I'm not worried,' she said. 'But you can only get away with being just so eccentric, you know. Even famous artists have to conform sometimes – or they might lose their cushy jobs.'

She walked off, and Sam watched her go out of the corner of his eye. Cushy job, he thought sourly, returning to his stew and potatoes. Trying to teach the rudiments of art to a lot of talentless youths who wouldn't know a Picasso from a pikestaff. That wasn't cushy; it was soul-destroying.

And now they wanted him to sing for his supper; stand up and make speeches to blue-rinsed women and paunchy men about how they should keep the school going for another hundred and fifty years by sponsoring scholarships which would be named after them; sales-talking local yuppies into sending their sons there. And, come to that, their daughters – next year, they were accepting girls – how positively modern could you get? And who better than 'one of our foremost modern artists' to give them the sales pitch?

He supposed, to be fair, that anyone would be better than Barry Treadwell, who thought women were of no practical use whatsoever – and who could blame him, with Marcia for a wife? And who was to say that he was wrong, come to that?

He couldn't think why he was so hungry; he persuaded the girl to give him a second helping, and sat down. He hadn't felt as hungry as this since he was doing stuff for the exhibition. In the golden days, when inspiration never seemed to dry up; when the desire to work was so strong that it sharpened his senses and his appetites, and he would eat and drink and . . .

It had been so long that he had failed to recognise the symptoms. He looked round. Yes. Yes, there were things here, even here, that could inspire. Look at *that*, he thought, as the girl splashed tea into a mug from a push-button urn. Machines. He loved machines. He didn't know what he would paint yet. That still had to come. But he would paint something, soon. And in the meantime the hunger would burn, and would have to be staved off in other ways. Food. Women. Only when he started painting, could it truly be satisfied. It was difficult, this period of increased awareness; difficult to live through, difficult to control. But it meant that he was working again. He might look as though he was sitting here eating stew, but he was working. And this school could stuff its contract. And its dinner dance. He smiled. But no, it would be a shame to waste the opportunity.

He pushed his plate away. He'd go, complete with dinner-jacket. And he'd make them sit up.

As the speeches droned on, Matthew glanced round the Hall at the talent, as his father called females. Earlier in the day, they had been the subject of brisk trade-offs.

'*And* your pen-knife.'

'It's a Swiss army knife! She's not worth that.'

'Then, you can't have her.'

'You hang on to your knife, Simmons – women aren't worth it.'

'You'd know, and I don't think.'

The reason for the black-marketeering was the First Dance, which was how it had been described in the handout from the office, and the only way in which Matthew could think of it, with capital letters.

The senior boys had each been allocated a partner for the First Dance; they were to politely request (sic) the First Dance, dance with the lady, and return her to her table. This was in honour of St Valentine, apparently, in view of the 'happy coincidence' of the dates.

The ladies were a mixture of staff, governors, various wives, and sundry local schoolgirls, and it was this last which had brought out the entrepreneurial skills of those who had drawn them.

After the First Dance, the boys could dance or not, as they wished. The desirability of getting the right partner first time round was obvious. They were in school uniform, which hadn't pleased anyone, and therefore the chance to impress was more necessary than ever. Not necessary enough, however, to part with a Swiss army knife. In the end, the lady went, for a give-away solar-powered calculator, to another bidder altogether.

Matthew had drawn the headmaster's wife, but he hadn't joined in the bidding for a more suitable partner, because she would give him access to the top table, and that had given Matthew an idea.

He was working on something very special for tonight, and Marcia Treadwell was going to help him, albeit unwittingly, to achieve it. Trust Treadwell, he thought, to have married someone like that. A woman for whom the word vacant might have been coined; a downtrodden doormat of a woman who was about as exciting as a piece of boiled cod, and who went pink if she thought she had done or said anything of which others might disapprove.

Matthew's eyes were fixed firmly on the top table, as he waited for his moment to arrive. Anything would do; he didn't mind what it was, just as long as it was on the top table.

Sam Waters finished his speech; what little Matthew had noticed of it had seemed very ordinary. People were clapping with some enthusiasm, which was a disappointment. Matthew had rather hoped that Sam at least could be relied upon to say something deeply offensive. He had imagined that their illustrious and foul-mouthed art teacher might sit down to boos, but no such luck. His jacket took a bit of getting used to, though, he had to give him that.

The applause had barely died away when Waters just walked out. Matthew smiled, as Treadwell, already on his feet, watched him leave. Good old Sam, he thought, frowning a little as he tried to make out the object on the table where Sam had been sitting.

When he realised what it was, he smiled broadly, and clapped vigorously as Treadwell cleared his throat to indicate the start of his speech.

It was his chance.

The knock at the door made Caroline jump; she wasn't expecting anyone. Please God, don't let it be one of the boys, she thought. No temperatures, no spots, no sore throats, not tonight. She opened the door to Sam, and stared at him without speaking, not sure whether it was his presence or his attire that had actually struck her dumb.

'What on earth are you doing here?' she said at last.

'The speeches are over.' He smiled. 'Mine is, at any rate, and who wants to hear any other bugger's? I thought I'd come and keep you company.' He looked at her expectantly. 'Well,' he said. 'Do I get to come in?'

'Did you really wear that to the dinner?' she asked, as he walked in past her.

'I did. And very splendid everyone agreed it was.'

'Where in God's name did you get it?'

He grinned. 'Theatrical costumier,' he said. 'A friend of mine. I asked him for something which would be worn by an MC at a strip show, and this is what he came up with.' He strolled up and down, modelling it. 'Good, isn't it?'

Caroline didn't smile. 'You enjoyed showing Barry up, did you?'

'Yes,' he said. 'Yes, I think I did.'

'We can't go yet,' she said. 'Diana isn't due for at least an hour.'

'I know,' he replied conspiratorially. 'How about a cup of coffee, then?'

And she found herself in the kitchen, making coffee, wishing Sam was anywhere but there, wishing that the Hamlyns had a more plebeian taste in coffee. It seemed to be taking for ever.

'What kind of music do the Hamlyns run to?' Sam called through.

'I don't know. Don't put it on too loud.'

'Boys that age can sleep through anything,' Sam said. 'Besides, they're downstairs. Oh – *Hits of the Fifties* – that sounds like my scene. Who'd have thought Hamlyn was a rock fan? You're a bit young, I suppose. Still – we'll give your ears a treat, shall we?'

When she took the coffee through, the record was being played at what even she had to agree was a modest level. He had removed the jacket to reveal an even more hideous shirt; he sat in one armchair, and the jacket lay over the other. She handed him his coffee, and sat on the sofa.

'I'm not going anywhere with you dressed like that,' she said.

'I thought it was a dressing-up do,' he said.

'It is. It isn't a fancy-dress do.'

He grinned. 'Don't worry. I'll change into a respectable suit before we go.' He got up, and joined her on the sofa. 'But I had to let you see it, didn't I?'

His arm was round her shoulders, and his lips planted a chaste kiss on her cheek. 'Fifties music, fifties ploy,' he said.

'What?'

'Sit in one chair, throw jacket over the other. The girl feels obliged to sit on the sofa, where, in due course, you join her.'

His lips were on hers, and she turned her head away. 'Don't, Sam, please.'

He sat back with a sigh. 'Christ, you're hard work,' he said. 'It's St Valentine's night – relax, for God's sake.'

'Don't be silly, Sam,' she said, pushing him off. 'I think you should go and get changed.'

'I'm willing to get out of these clothes any time you say.' His lips were at her temple.

'Stop it, Sam,' she said. 'Please. We've been through all this.'

'Don't I know it? You're not ready. Great. Well, I am, and we're not kids any more.'

Go away, she thought. Just go away.

'We've been going out for months – it's time to get grown-up, Caroline. We're much too old for goodnight kisses on the doorstep.'

'We haven't been anywhere,' she reminded him.

'I could have waited until I brought you home,' he said, the wheedling tone back since masterful dominance wasn't working. 'But you'd have thought it was the film that had given me ideas.'

'So what has given you ideas?'

'You,' he said. 'I don't need erotic movies. I find you sexy even when I've been listening to Robert Hamlyn make a speech.'

She laughed at the little joke, and instantly his mouth was on hers in a prolonged, passionless, tongue-thrusting kiss. Her lack of response didn't put him off; it was probable, indeed, that he hadn't even noticed.

He began to unbutton her shirt, his hands everywhere; grappling with her bra, groping her with bruising thoroughness. She passively endured the invasion, because maybe he was right; maybe it was all she needed to put her grief behind her.

Forcing her bra up, out of his way, he grasped her exposed breast, squeezing it hard, muttering some form of encouragement before his mouth turned its attention to it, and his hands were free to continue undressing her. And still she didn't stop him, because he might be right.

He was already fumbling under the navy satin cummerbund for his zip, and she didn't even like him. It wasn't necessary to like him, she told herself. Sex never used to be that important to her, in her single days. It had always just been a bit of fun, no big deal, before she met Andrew. Perhaps it should be again. Sam might be right. It might be all she needed.

It might be. But it wasn't going to be here, and it wasn't going to be now, and it wasn't going to be Sam.

The speeches were no more or less boring than speeches usually were; Robert's, indeed, had really been quite amusing, which had surprised Philip. Sam Waters's had been entirely conventional, unlike his dinner-jacket. Philip smiled again as he thought of it.

It was a quite wonderful dinner-jacket; midnight-blue velvet with pale-blue shot-silk lapels and pocket flaps, it set off the ice-blue dress-shirt with navy ruffle and solitaire-studded bow-tie to perfection.

Sam had left as soon as he'd finished speaking, and just as Treadwell had stood up to speak, in what seemed to have been a calculated insult. He'd get away with it, of course, thought Philip. He always did.

Philip's eyes had searched the Hall in vain for Caroline, and it was with a mixture of relief and disappointment that he had learned of her babysitting activities. He had tried to talk to her, even rehearsed asking her out for a drink, but he couldn't. All he could do was so pathetically sick that it destroyed him, but he couldn't stop it. St Valentine's Day, he thought sourly. Once, it would have been easy.

Barry was using index cards for his speech; it was impossible to tell whether he was in the middle of it or nearly at the end; one could only hope it was the latter, as he had been speaking for over twenty minutes. He got a murmured laugh, and seemed to be winding up; Philip shifted slightly in his seat as his leg began to complain, and joined in the applause.

Philip drank to the next hundred and fifty years, feeling a bit as though he had been there for the first hundred and fifty. He had drunk to everything; indeed, the speeches had been made easier on the ear by virtue of finishing off each glass of wine while the next one droned on. The young woman who kept refilling his glass was by now wearing a permanently worried expression. Philip smiled at her.

The music struck up; a plague of grey blazers suddenly rose from the tables, and descended on the ladies, who tried to look surprised as they took to the floor.

Philip watched as they danced; people who could move, some more elegantly than others, exactly as they chose, and he hated them all. He sighed, wishing Caroline was there, and turned to the other two men who remained at the table as they included him in the inconsequential conversation, but he was having some difficulty following what they were saying.

The dance was over; the boys began to see their ladies back. Returned to the top table, Diana Hamlyn didn't even sit down, but instead came back across the room towards him, almost, it seemed, pushing people out of her way in order to get there. The music began again, and his companions rose to dance with their returned ladies.

He was alone at the table when Diana arrived.

'Is this a frightful bore for you, Philip?' She leaned over as she spoke, her face close to his.

He didn't answer.

'How's the leg holding up?' she asked, as her hand rested lightly on his good leg.

The girl he had been seeing before the accident had come to the hospital when he lay paralysed, with no one able to say if the immobility was permanent or not. It had been the most casual of relationships; she had not unnaturally taken fright at the possibility of being cast in the rôle of paraplegic's loyal girlfriend, and he hadn't seen her again.

But he hadn't had fantasies about her, to whom he really had made love. And he didn't have fantasies about Diana Hamlyn, whose hand really was pressing his thigh.

She straightened up, slowly slipping her hand away. 'Sorry I can't stay,' she said. 'Duty calls.'

And she made her way to the exit, just as Sam had done; Philip watched her go, swearing under his breath. Damn the woman.

Damn her. She'd been using him as some sort of decoy. But he couldn't even ask her to dance, never mind anything else, so what good would he be to her? He didn't want her anyway.

He wanted Caroline.

'Isn't Mr Waters coming back?' asked the wife of the chairman of governors, whose name Treadwell was constitutionally incapable of remembering.

'Er . . . no,' he said, his eyes still on Diana as she left the Hall. 'He did say that he wouldn't be able to stay long,' he said. 'He had a previous appointment.'

'What a pity,' she said. 'I had hoped to get the chance to talk to him.'

Thank God you didn't, Treadwell thought. He had scarcely been able to conceal his relief when Waters told him he wouldn't be staying. When he had seen the jacket, the relief had been doubled; if that was the Statement, then the speech would probably be free of four-letter words and innuendo, which had proved to be the case.

'But he and Caroline aren't leaving until eleven,' said Marcia, with the wide-eyed innocence that Treadwell, despite having been married to her for over thirty years, still wondered about. 'Are they?'

'Eleven?' repeated Hamlyn, in a startled voice. 'Then, why did he leave at half past nine?'

'Just a misunderstanding, I expect,' Treadwell said. He glared at his wife, who looked flustered.

'Diana seems to have misunderstood, too,' said Hamlyn. 'She also left as soon as she had discharged her duties.'

Treadwell smiled weakly. 'I'm sure there's an explanation,' he said.

'I think we all know the explanation,' said Hamlyn.

Treadwell wanted to die; he signalled frantically to the girl to bring more wine. Hemlock, for preference.

'It's an odd time to have an appointment,' laughed the bloody woman who wouldn't let the subject of Sam Waters go. 'Whenever it's for. Still, artists are supposed to be unconventional.'

'Mr Waters is certainly that,' said Hamlyn. 'Wouldn't you say, Barry?'

The new bottle arrived. 'More wine?' Treadwell asked, his voice a shade desperate. But any hopes he had of the subject having been dropped were dashed.

'You'd think the man would have more of an idea of dress sense, if he's meant to be an artist,' said the bloody woman's husband.

'I think', said Robert Hamlyn quietly, 'that that was Sam's idea of a joke, rather than his idea of dress sense.'

'A joke?'

Treadwell smiled broadly. 'As your wife says,' he laughed, 'artists are supposed to be unconventional.' He poured more wine for himself.

'I don't really see the point, if it was a joke.'

'We're the point,' said Hamlyn.

'Sorry?'

'We never see ourselves, do we?' He smiled. 'As others see us,' he added.

Treadwell watched with dismay as his guests' faces grew slightly pink.

'Here we are,' Hamlyn went on, in the quiet voice that carried as far as it had to, after years of lectures and talks. 'Here we are, sitting up straight in our best bibs and tuckers, and there's Sam, doing exactly what he pleases.' He paused, and looked straight at Treadwell. 'With my wife,' he added.

Treadwell's glass froze at his lips. He had expected trouble from Waters; he had anticipated it, told him in no uncertain manner that his fixed-term contract had not been agreed by him, and did not have to be renewed. It would never have occurred to him that Hamlyn, who lived for the most part in a world composed entirely of logic and mathematics, would be the nigger in the woodpile. Almost automatically, he told himself that he mustn't use that expression any more. The fly in the ointment, then. Presumably there were no pressure groups for fly rights yet. Why now, for God's sake? Why now? Why here?

'You're worrying these good people,' he said, trying to laugh, sounding hysterical, he knew he sounded hysterical. 'They'll think you mean it.'

'You mean I'm worrying you,' said Hamlyn, still smiling.

Treadwell shot a look at Marcia, who looked like she always did. Polite, a little apprehensive, not understanding what was going on, and quite unaware that she had caused it all.

It was just then that he saw Philip Newby get up and move quickly through the dancers to the doors.

'Do you want coffee?' Lloyd asked, his voice as surly as he could make it, given the deliberately non-contentious nature of the question.

They were in Lloyd's flat, surfacing from yet another row; Judy shook her head, not turning to look at him, and opened the window a little to watch the rain pouring down, leaving a slippery film on everything, as it battered away at the piles of snow. It had come suddenly, unpredicted by the weathermen. Hopefully, it was at least signalling the end of winter.

She had looked at her watch, apparently. Not, she would have thought, the most inflammatory of gestures, but it had sparked off the quick temper to which she doubted if she would ever become accustomed. Michael was at a colleague's stag party, and wasn't going to be home until the early hours. But it was well after midnight, and, bearing in mind her Cinderella status, she had looked at her watch.

And she was getting no better at holding her own during such hostilities; the cutting remarks and wild accusations perhaps stung a little less than they used to, but not much.

The question had broken the ten minutes of silence which had followed the angry words; it was, Judy knew from experience, the prelude to a more reasoned statement of grievances, to which she was supposed to reply in equally reasonable tones, until Lloyd made some feeble joke that they would both pretend was funny.

She let the cold air cool the cheeks that had grown hot with indignation as the hurtful words had been hurled at her; she had no weapon to match Lloyd's tongue, and he knew it. Afterwards – after the silence and the peaceful negotiations, which Judy hated even more than the row, after the pipe of peace had been smoked – he would blame his Welshness, and try to make her laugh at the English reserve which stopped her giving as good as she got.

She closed the window and braced herself for the unnecessary but obligatory discussion of their situation; when Lloyd didn't speak, she turned to look at him. He stood up, and held out his arms.

'This is crazy,' he said, hugging her. 'I want you to live with me, and all I can do is fight with you.'

It was far from all he could do. The rows blew over, and he had every right to feel frustrated and angry as the weeks went by. But she couldn't explain to Lloyd why she hadn't made the break. Michael's dependence on her, unsuspected and unsought, was a factor that Lloyd didn't know came into it, and to tell him would seem more like a betrayal of Michael than her infidelity ever had.

'Are you having second thoughts about leaving him?' he asked.

'No!' She pulled back to look at him. 'He just won't accept that it's all over. We've got separate rooms, Lloyd, I told you.'

It was an unnecessary denial of one of his angry suggestions, and he pulled her close to him again. 'I didn't mean any of that,' he said. 'But you can't leave him in stages, Judy.' His lips touched her cheek. 'Hoping he won't notice.'

She closed her eyes. 'Do you ever take time off?' she asked.

He gave a little laugh. 'Sixteen years ago it was Barbara you didn't want to hurt,' he said. 'But someone is going to get hurt.'

She had known Lloyd since she was twenty years old; she had loved him since she was twenty years old. But he had been married to Barbara then, with two young children. So – as a direct result – she had married Michael, with whom she had had an easy relationship for years. Marriage had put an end to that. Her path had crossed Lloyd's again two years ago, when she and Michael had come to live in Stansfield.

46

Thus began what was supposed to have been a no-strings-attached relationship with Lloyd, except that there were strings attached, and always had been. They had just pretended that they couldn't see them, until they pulled so tightly that it hurt, and even she had to admit to their presence.

With that admission, and the spoken acknowledgement of it, had come a flood of relief, and love, and guilt, laced with a generous measure of panic. But the panic was over; now she truly didn't want to hurt Michael. So she was hurting Lloyd instead.

'You,' she said miserably. 'I know I'm hurting you. Because you'll put up with it.'

He smiled. 'You'd better go,' he said, kissing her gently.

Judy looked at her watch again, but this time she took it from her wrist, and slipped it into Lloyd's pocket.

'Sure?' he asked. 'It's even later now.'

'I'm not going anywhere,' she said, as the phone rang.

Lloyd picked it up with a shrug of apology to her, then listened, his face growing grave. He sighed. 'Yes,' he said. 'I'm on my way.'

She was going somewhere now, she thought, as they went out to their cars. Hers coughed and spluttered like a sixty-a-day smoker, and she had to abandon it and go in Lloyd's. They were going, as fast as they could in the non-stop rain, to what Lloyd had described as 'that school of yours'. He seemed to hold her personally responsible for the rape and murder which had apparently taken place there.

They arrived to find what seemed like half of the county constabulary there already; squad cars, doors open, radios crackling messages, were parked in the wonderfully eccentric fashion known only to squad-car drivers. Lloyd pulled up beside the pitch-dark playing-field, where the knot of onlookers suggested that they would find the body.

'Get rid of them,' Lloyd muttered, as he got out of the car.

Judy sometimes wished he wouldn't make allowances, but on the whole she was glad that he did. It helped a little if she could get into her stride before she had to look at the victim.

She got out, and prepared to go into the routine of telling them that there was nothing to see; this time it was entirely true. Portable lighting equipment was on its way, but for the moment there was only the light from the building, and it lit the onlookers, not the scene of the incident. But the crowd, mostly boys, wasn't sightseeing. It was quiet, and still, shocked by the news. The boys spoke to her of someone they had liked, someone who had meant a great deal to each of them. She caught a glimpse of the one she had spoken to about the thefts, but she couldn't remember his name. Coatless, he stood shivering in the rain, and in the aftermath of tragedy he looked like the schoolboy he was. Not the elegant man-about-town; an awkward schoolboy, all wrists and ankles. Another blinked furiously as he told her that he would have run away when he was eleven if it hadn't been for her. None of them could help with what had happened; they only knew what they had been told, and what they had overheard. She moved them away, and watched them go, moving off slowly, looking back over their shoulders at the dismal, rainsoaked scene. They were still boys, still children. They were sad, not angry.

She was angry.

Her husband had found her, almost falling over her in the darkness as he had crossed the playing-field from the Great Hall to the junior dormitory. The ambulancemen who had been called had treated him for shock; there was nothing they or anyone else could do for his wife.

The ambulance had had to leave almost as soon as it had arrived, to pick up the injured from a crash on the treacherous road. It had happened close enough to the school for the mournful sound of a jammed car horn to reach them, and Lloyd had sent someone to investigate. Now half the men were out at the accident, coping with something which had taken and continued to take more lives than all the murderers there had ever been.

But deliberate destruction was still much harder to take. Lloyd watched as at last they set up the lights, which had taken an hour to arrive because of the road diversion, and another hour to fix up. By torchlight, they had cordoned off the playing-field. Now, in the steady rain, they ran ribbon along either side of the tarmac path, and round the area where the attack had taken place. No murder weapon was immediately to hand; they would have to start searching at first light. So much time was wasted in winter, waiting for the sun to come up. The cold, relentless rain was washing away evidence, and the killer was getting further and further from their reach.

The lights went on, illuminating the little patch of playing-field like day; Freddie looked round the small lit area for anything that might give them a clue to her attacker, but there was nothing. He shook his head, and crouched down beside the young woman's body, under the canvas that sheltered it from the rain; it seemed an uncomfortable position for his tall frame, but he wouldn't move until he'd finished, for fear of disturbing some minute piece of evidence. He had done what he could when he arrived, two hours ago. Now he could really begin his work. His thin face looked pinched and cold as he drew a quick sketch of the area, and dictated initial thoughts and findings to his assistant, a slight frown furrowing his brow. The girl wrote with blue hands, stopping now and then to rub them together.

Even with the lights, they could see nothing in the immediate area that could have inflicted the injuries. Slowly, Lloyd moved back towards the body, under the makeshift shelter. It had been bad enough by torchlight.

'Several blows to the head,' Freddie was saying, as the girl wrote. 'Non-manual. Our old friend the blunt instrument.' He peered closely at the body. 'An attempt, possibly successful, at strangulation,' he said. 'Bare legs and feet, no shoes. No underpants. No coat. One, two – two buttons missing from dress at front. Brassiere torn. Injuries to—'

'Sex murders,' Lloyd said bitterly, like the obscenity they were.

'Don't knock them, Lloyd,' said Freddie cheerfully. 'Chances are I can learn a lot more from a sex murder than from any other kind.'

'Well, that's all right, then,' said Lloyd. 'I'm sure Mrs Hamlyn was pleased about that, if nothing else.'

Freddie looked the part, all right. All tall thin seriousness, until you became aware that his looks disguised a genuine, even engaging enjoyment of his work. But Lloyd couldn't share his appreciation of rape as an aid to detection.

The photographer arrived, and began setting up, as Lloyd heard another car arrive; its headlamps lit up the gentle slope from the gates as it joined the other cars. He looked out from the bright light into the wet, cold darkness, taking a moment to make out the chief superintendent's figure.

'Morning, Lloyd.'

'Sir.'

Chief Superintendent Allison was twelve years younger than Lloyd, which had illogically irked Lloyd when he first arrived. His grudging admission that at least Allison was better than his predecessor had given way in the end to a slightly less grudging respect for the man's ability. And he wasn't all that much taller than Lloyd, which gave him several merit points.

Together, they sorted out what was being done, what could and would be done. There was someone on the gates, checking cars in and out; that would continue until the living-in member of staff who was missing had either come back, been accounted for or placed firmly on the suspect-list. Judy had spoken to the gathering in the Great Hall, and was currently taking statements from anyone with anything to say.

Allison would be addressing the school at assembly next day. There were other women at the school, small children and young boys; neither the police nor the school could take chances with their safety. The evening assemblies would be suspended until further notice to avoid the necessity of the younger boys walking round after dark.

Theoretically, anyone could have come into the school grounds and attacked Mrs Hamlyn as she walked across to the junior dormitory. Realistically, it was unlikely that a total stranger would chance on a night when everyone was safely in one place, rather than coming or going. Everyone except the victim, that was. She was using the short cut from the Hall to the dormitory, alone and in the darkness. Anyone in the school, however, could have known that; it had hardly been a secret. Any of the guests could have followed her.

And statistically it was more likely to be someone she knew. Lloyd sighed. It was the same problem as Judy had with the thefts. Too many suspects.

Allison glanced round the dark playing-field. 'How wide a search are you doing?' he asked.

'Ten feet either side of the footpath,' Lloyd said. 'To start with.' Daylight was still hours away. He sighed again.

'Do you want any more photographs?' asked the thin man with the beard. 'The doctor's got all he wants for tonight. I'll be back in daylight.'

'Fine.' Allison sighed, too.

It was the universal reaction to something that could never be righted. Insurance replaced burgled goods; shop windows could be renewed; supermarkets could mark up their prices to take account of shoplifting. But, no matter what anyone did, the young woman on the ground was no more. Lloyd's anger might help him get to the bottom of it, but it wouldn't bring her back.

'Bob Sandwell's been talking to the catering staff, I understand,' the chief superintendent said, as the photographer thankfully packed away his camera.

Detective Constable Sandwell seemed to discover things by osmosis. Already, he was the one everyone asked if they wanted to know which building was which; he doubtless knew all the catering staff by their first names. Lloyd waited to hear what he had discovered from the ladies.

'And it seems that Mrs Hamlyn had something of a reputation,' said Allison. 'To put it mildly.'

'Does that matter?' said Judy's voice, from behind them, startling them. 'Sir,' she added, with a delayed, acid politeness that bordered on insubordination.

'All right, Sergeant,' he said good-humouredly. 'I'm not suggesting it was her own fault.' He looked down at Diana Hamlyn's corpse.

Carefully, Freddie turned the body, and continued his patient eyes-only examination before taking samples. He finished with a minute description of the still-frozen ground below the body, and a final taking of the temperature.

'We'll be in a better position once we've had the postmortem results,' said Allison, for want of something to say, in Lloyd's opinion.

'. . . as at two fifty-five hours,' Freddie said, dictating the body temperature to his assistant, whose own didn't look much higher. He gave her the ground temperature, and looked up at them.

'That's about it until I can examine her properly,' he said, packing away swabs and tapes. 'She can go to the mortuary now.' He stood up, flexing his back. 'Is there somewhere Kathy can go and thaw out?' he asked, taking the notebook from her.

'Yes,' said Sandwell eagerly, appearing from nowhere. 'I'll show you,' he said to Kathy, who gratefully followed his tall figure out of the light, towards warmth.

'How long?' asked Judy.

'I'd say between two and five hours,' Freddie said with suspicious promptness. He was normally very loath to give estimates at any time, and never liked to be asked before the post-mortem.

Lloyd looked at his watch. Between ten and one. But they already knew that, of course. She'd been seen in the Hall at ten, and the treble nine call had been made at ten past one. 'Thank you,' he said to the smiling Freddie.

'What do you expect? There's dozens of factors to be taken into consideration.' He stepped carefully back, out of the shelter.

'Is there a chance of narrowing it down?' Lloyd asked into the darkness.

'For once there might be,' Freddie's disembodied voice said. 'She'd just had dinner for a start.' He came back into the light. 'And the temperature readings are interesting – I think I'll be able to narrow it down a little. She was nice and fresh.'

He couldn't disguise his enthusiasm, and never tried to. Freddie liked dead bodies.

'Sir?' A young uniformed constable looked uncertainly from the chief superintendent to Lloyd. 'Mr Waters has just come in. He's the art teacher – the one that was missing. We've asked him to wait in the Hall.'

'All yours,' said Allison. 'I'll have another word with the head.' He turned back. 'He seems to have been a bit liberal with the medicinal brandy,' he said. 'I don't think you'll get much out of him until the morning. Shall I tell him to expect you then?'

Allison left as Sandwell delivered Freddie's assistant back to him, and they roared off in Freddie's powerful car, with little regard for the younger residents, who until then had slept on, unaware of the drama going on.

Lloyd and Judy walked into the building, through a cloakroom in which only Mrs Hamlyn's coat remained.

'She didn't mean to be out in the rain for long,' Judy said.

The catering staff moved round the Great Hall in a silent pall of disbelief, having been told that they could at last clear away. The party's abrupt and shocking end was evidenced by the balloons still trapped in the netting slung from the rafters.

They found Mr Waters sitting at a cluttered table, wearing jeans, a thick sweater, and a surly expression.

Lloyd introduced himself and Judy, and asked Mr Waters where he had been, immediately eliciting hostility.

'Why should that concern you? What's going on?'

'A crime's been committed here,' Lloyd said.

Waters raised his eyebrows. 'So? I wasn't here, was I?'

'What time did you leave here, Mr Waters?' Judy asked, her notebook at the ready.

'How the hell should I know?'

'Were you at the dinner here tonight?'

'Yes. I left early.'

'Would you mind telling us why?'

'Yes.'

Lloyd sat down beside Judy, opposite Waters. 'Someone was murdered here tonight,' he said, his voice almost conversational. 'Would you know anything about that?'

Waters's eyes widened. 'Murdered?' he repeated. 'Who?'

'A Mrs Diana Hamlyn,' said Lloyd, watching carefully for Waters's reaction. It wasn't any of the things he had expected.

'Diana?' he said. 'Murdered?' He looked almost amused. 'Are you telling me that Hamlyn finally cracked?'

Lloyd sat back in his chair and regarded Waters for some moments; until Waters began to look uncomfortable. 'Do you have some reason to think that Mr Hamlyn murdered his wife?' he asked at last.

'I'd have murdered her,' he replied.

Lloyd smiled coldly. 'But you didn't,' he said.

Waters shook his head. 'She wasn't my wife,' he said.

'And had she been your wife? What would have been your motive for murder?' asked Lloyd.

'Only that she was screwing half the men in this school,' Waters replied.

'Does that include you?' Judy asked, with polite interest, not looking up from her notebook.

Judy waited for a reply, as Lloyd watched Waters argue with himself.

She looked up. 'Does that include you?' she asked again, as though he might not have heard.

'Yes, all right. It did, at one time.'

'Mrs Hamlyn was raped,' said Lloyd.

A broad smile spread over Waters's features. 'Raped?' he repeated incredulously. 'Diana Hamlyn, *raped*? You have to be joking.'

'I wish I were. But it would be a joke in very bad taste.'

'Who the hell would need to rape Diana?' he said.

'Why did you leave the dinner?' Judy asked.

Waters didn't reply.

'Where did you go?'

Waters just looked at her without speaking.

'What were you doing?' she tried.

'Minding my own fucking business,' said Waters.

'That'll do, Mr Waters,' said Lloyd.

Waters clapped his hand to his mouth. 'Oh, am I offending the lady?' he asked.

'I wouldn't know,' said Lloyd. 'You're offending me.' He got up, and walked round the table to Waters, bending down to talk to him. 'The English language is a very flexible instrument, Mr Waters. The use of entirely inapposite adjectives offends me very deeply.'

It was a lie, of course. Lloyd could throw in as many inapposite adjectives as the next man. But Judy would never forgive him if he admitted that it was using them in her presence that he found offensive. He stood up, and looked again at Sam Waters. 'I take it you didn't attend the dinner dressed like that?' he asked.

Waters raised his eyebrows. 'No,' he said. 'Is my dress something else that offends you?'

'Not in the least,' said Lloyd smoothly. 'But you've changed your clothes, Mr Waters. And I'd rather like to see the ones you were wearing earlier.'

'What?' Waters stared at him. 'You think I did it?'

'You won't tell us what you *were* doing,' said Lloyd.

'It's none of your bloody business, if you'll forgive another inapposite adjective.'

'Oh, but this time the adjective is right, and you're wrong. It is a bloody business – but it *is* mine. And I'd like to see the clothes you were wearing this evening.'

'Don't you need some sort of warrant?' Waters said, and got up. 'Oh, what the f—' He put a finger to his lips. 'Oops,' he said. 'Hell. Is that all right?'

Lloyd ignored him.

'They're in my flat. And since I've had a bloody awful evening which culminated in being sent five miles out of my way by a road diversion, only to be accused of murder when I finally get here, that is where I'm going.'

Lloyd smiled again, with no more warmth than before. 'Then, we had better come with you,' he said.

'Suit yourself,' he said, striding away.

Lloyd had rarely disliked anyone as much in so short a time. But, he reminded himself as he and Judy followed Waters out of the Hall, that didn't make him a murderer.

It just made him an inapposite adjective good candidate.

Chapter Three

Philip Newby lay awake in the darkness. It was cold in the little unheated bedroom, but there were beads of perspiration on his temple as he lay still clothed on top of the bed, afraid to move. He would have to move, sooner or later. It would be daylight in a few hours, and he could hardly walk around like this. Thank God it was Saturday.

He swallowed, his mouth dry, and forced himself to sit up, closing his eyes as the pain gripped his lower back. Perhaps he wouldn't be walking around at all by the morning. But he *could* sit up; he could ease himself off the bed. He stood one-legged, and moved round the room, supporting his weight on the chair-back, the dressing-table, the end of the bed, until he reached the light-switch.

He could see himself in the dressing-table mirror. Bent over like an old man, his blood-stained shirt hanging out, his jacket and trousers smeared with mud. He had to straighten up. He had to. The image went as he screwed his eyes up against the pain, and lifted his head, wanting to howl like the wounded animal he was. Little dots of light swam in front of his eyes when he opened them, but when they cleared he could see himself again. Erect. And that was a joke, he thought.

Now, no joke – he had to get the clothes off. It was difficult enough at the best of times. He weighed up the pros and cons, and decided to start with the trousers. It was a slow, agonising operation.

He had got the trousers and the jacket off, and was standing in his shirt and underpants when he heard Sam's key turn in the door. One hand on the desk, he allowed as little of his weight as possible to fall on his bad leg as his good one kicked the clothes out of sight under the bed. Just in case he was too stiff to get rid of them in the morning.

He could hear voices; a woman's, and at least one other man's. He could hear the rise and fall of a voice that wasn't Sam's.

The wardrobe was just within his reach, and he pulled open the door, fumbling amongst the clothes for the stick. It was the middle of the night, and the voices sounded urgent, official. He had no desire to be discovered in this condition.

His hand grasped the metal, and he pulled the stick out. At last he could move more freely. He got into his dressing-gown, pulling the belt tight, covering his shirt. Perhaps the pain was lessening, he told himself, as he opened the door.

'What's going on?' he asked, his voice failing as the agony seized him again.

He could hardly think, as the man introduced himself. Chief Inspector Lloyd, he heard, and those three words were all that went through his head, like a mantra, as he tried to cope with the pain. Other words fought their way through. This is Sergeant Hill. Sorry to have disturbed you at this time of night. Serious incident.

'Would you be better sitting down, Mr Newby?'

He didn't know if he could sit down. Or get up again if he did. He shook his head.

'Are you all right?' Sam asked, the first time he had spoken.

Philip nodded, teeth clenched together.

'What happened to you?' the sergeant asked.

'Car crash,' he said.

'When did it happen?'

'Eighteen months ago. It's not usually as bad as this.'

'Well, Mr Waters?' asked Chief Inspector Lloyd.

'It's over there,' Sam said, jerking his head towards a large box in the corner of the room. 'Help yourself.'

The chief inspector went over, and took out the suit, his eyes widening when he saw it. Philip frowned as he watched him examine it.

'It's damp,' said the chief inspector.

Sam shrugged.

'Is it hired?'

'Borrowed,' said Sam. 'Do you want to take it away? Examine it for blonde hairs?'

'Yes, thank you. Since you have been kind enough to offer. Do you want to tell us where you were tonight between ten and midnight, Mr Waters? It would save a great deal of time.'

Sam told the chief inspector that he had no intention of divulging this information, but he took only two words to do it.

Philip stared at him, at the chief inspector, at the sergeant.

'Very well, Mr Waters,' said Lloyd. 'We'll be back, I've no doubt.'

Philip marshalled his wits, and looked again at Sam. 'What's this *about*?' he asked.

Sam smiled. 'Someone raped Diana,' he said.

'*Raped* her?' said Philip. 'What do you mean, raped her?'

Matthew had hidden the evidence somewhere which was itself a challenge; he'd have to get rid of it all now, but for the moment he was safe. He had got back to the Hall, and had asked Mrs Treadwell to dance; as far as he could tell, he hadn't even been missed, but it didn't really matter if he had.

The ball had been almost over when Hamlyn had come stumbling in like a drunk; Matthew had been contemplating whether it would be going over the top to invite Mrs Treadwell up for the last waltz. It was, after all, conceivable that Mr Treadwell would feel obliged to take his wife on to the floor, but he hadn't danced with her all night, and Matthew had thought she might appreciate the gesture. But the moment never came; Hamlyn had run blindly up to the top table, Treadwell had stared at him for a moment, then had moved uncertainly towards the dais, and the music had petered out. Then he had said that there had been a serious incident, and that the police would have to be called, and asked everyone to stay until they got there.

Matthew was awake, working out what to do next, how much – if anything – he should tell the police. The others hadn't talked much about what had happened; they had silently got into bed, and eventually had gone to sleep.

But Matthew watched. From the window, he could see the line of police cars at the far side of the playing-fields. He was stiff and cold, after hours of watching. Two of the cars still sat there, but the one the sergeant had come in had moved, and just five minutes ago he had watched it sweep round the road to where it now stood outside the junior dormitory. Sergeant Hill and the man had got out of it, and had gone into the building, presumably up to the Hamlyns' flat, where the fight had burned all night.

Matthew didn't like it when he didn't know exactly what was happening. He even contemplated the fire-escape again, to eavesdrop, if he could. He abandoned that idea, but he was going to carry on watching.

All night, if he had to.

'Raped?' Caroline Knight stared at Chief Inspector Lloyd.

'Yes, Mrs Knight,' he said, with just a trace of a Welsh accent. 'I'm afraid so.'

She had been told, when someone had finally got round to telling her, that Diana was dead. That her body had been found on the playing-field. No more.

'Does that surprise you, Mrs Knight?' The cool question came from the sergeant. Caroline remembered her from last month, when she had come about the thefts.

'Well . . . .' Caroline felt a little uncomfortable under the sergeant's steady brown gaze. 'No one's really told me what's going on. I knew someone had . . . .' She broke off, not wanting to say the word. 'But I had no idea that she had been raped.' She sat down. 'That's dreadful,' she said.

Sergeant Hill wrote something in her notebook, and Chief Inspector Lloyd took over.

'Forgive me, Mrs Knight,' he said. 'But you did seem a little more surprised than shocked.'

'Yes,' she admitted. 'It was silly of me.'

Robert Hamlyn was being attended to by Matron, and Caroline

had found herself in sole charge of the junior dormitory by default. The police had asked if they could speak to her, but had said that it could wait until the next day. Caroline had said they could come in; she couldn't sleep anyway. But she hadn't been prepared for the almost hostile sergeant.

'Shall I tell you some of the other reactions we've had?' Sergeant Hill was saying, as she made a business of turning back the pages of her notebook. 'We've had "Who the hell would need to rape Diana Hamlyn?", and "What do you mean, raped?" Now you say you're surprised. Why?'

Caroline Knight looked at her thoughtfully. 'If you've been asking questions, then I expect you already know the answer,' she said. 'Diana had . . . well, a problem.'

'A problem?' queried Lloyd.

'With men. I mean – I'm no psychiatrist, but she seemed to me to be a . . . .' She paused, not wishing to sound melodramatic. But it was the truth, after all. 'A nymphomaniac, I suppose,' she said. 'She was promiscuous, at any rate.'

'Oh?' said Sergeant Hill. 'Does that mean she can't have been raped?'

'No, of course not.' Caroline didn't want to think about it; she really ought to tell them, but perhaps she'd imagined it. She wasn't sure. And, if she said anything, the crazy thought that went through her head at the time might get spoken, and she really couldn't do that to Sam. She'd been jumpy, that was all. Better not to say anything at all, unless she had to.

'Well,' said Chief Inspector Lloyd, 'let's get away from that. I understand, Mrs Knight, that you intended supervising the children until about eleven, when Mrs Hamlyn was due to relieve you. Is that right?'

'Quite right.' She pushed her long hair away from her face. 'I rang the Hall at about quarter to, and was told that she had left about half an hour before that.'

'Were you worried?'

'I thought it was odd, but I wasn't exactly worried.'

'You must forgive me again,' Lloyd said. 'But I'm not all that sure how the school runs. Am I right in thinking that Mrs Hamlyn was not actually employed by the school in any capacity?'

She nodded. 'But housemasters' wives do find themselves in this position,' she said. 'And she had said she'd be pleased to let me go at eleven – I was going out, you see.' She glanced down at herself, all dressed up. 'So it did seem odd that she hadn't turned up, but – well, I never dreamed anything had *happened* to her. Not until Mr Dearden came and—' She broke off.

Lloyd nodded. 'And Mr Hamlyn?' he asked. 'Was he worried? I take it that's who you spoke to at the Hall?'

'No,' she said slowly. 'Robert didn't come to the phone. Barry did. He said he'd have a look round for her, but he didn't ring back or anything. So I just stayed. I ... we ... well, Barry and I both thought she might have gone off with someone.'

'You didn't ring Mr Treadwell back?' asked Lloyd.

'No – because my plans had fallen through anyway. The next thing I heard was when Mr Dearden came and told me she was dead. That someone had killed her. I couldn't believe it.'

'Did he leave you here on your own?' asked the sergeant.

'Well – you ... the police were all over the place. I told him I'd be all right.'

'Now,' said Chief Inspector Lloyd, 'you didn't hear from Mrs Hamlyn at all?'

Caroline shook her head.

'The path across the playing-field,' he said. 'It's a short cut, I take it. How many people would be likely to be using it?'

'No one,' said Caroline. Sam. Sam must have used it.

'No one?' Lloyd frowned a little. 'Why is there a path, then?'

'The younger boys have always used the playing-field to get from the school and the Hall to here. For years. Eventually, they wore a path, so in the end they tarmacked it. Mr and Mrs Hamlyn use it, of course. But everyone else uses the lane.'

'What lane?' Sergeant Hill and the chief inspector chorused.

'There's an old lane from the main buildings,' Caroline explained. 'The senior boys are in houses – the lane runs past them.'

'How come we didn't see that?' asked Lloyd.

'It goes through the buildings,' she explained. 'You wouldn't know it was there unless you were looking for it. That's why we can't allow cars to come right in – it would be too dangerous, with boys shooting out of there.'

'And everyone else uses that rather than the footpath?'

'Well – anyone going to the boys' houses, of course, or any of me other buildings off the lane. Or anyone going to the staff block or the headmaster's house. The field's only a short cut to this building. The lane's the quickest route to everywhere else.'

'Thank you, Mrs Knight,' Lloyd said, standing up. 'I suggest you try to get some sleep now. There will be officers patrolling, so you don't have to worry.'

'I still don't think I'll sleep,' she said.

Lloyd and Judy left the junior dormitory and crossed over to the other side of the road. The lane snaked and zig-zagged along, shadowed by the darkened buildings that flanked it; the boys' houses, the sick-bay, and others that only Bob Sandwell could have sorted out.

Lloyd glanced at Judy. 'I want this place searched,' he said. It seemed to him a much more likely trysting-place than the middle of the playing-field. It was dark, private. Perhaps she had come along here with someone, on their way to the staff block; he tried not to see it as Sam Waters, but without success. Perhaps she had been killed here, and dumped on the playing-field. Freddie might be able to tell them that. It looked like a good place to hide the weapon. Plenty of nooks and crannies.

The doctor who had been called to Mr Hamlyn had said that he mustn't be disturbed until the next day, so there was no more to be done until then. The living-in staff were all accounted for now; a couple of other members of staff and the odd guest had gone AWOL from the ball, and that all still had to be sorted out. Lloyd wrapped it up for the night, and four-thirty found them on their way back to Stansfield.

'Do you want to try your car again?' he asked.

'No,' she said. 'There's no point until it dries out a bit.'

Lloyd smiled. 'That might not be until August.' He took her watch from his jacket pocket and handed it to her with a shrug. 'I'll take you home,' he said.

The road had been cleared, but they could see the debris of the accident.

Lloyd shivered a little. 'Any thoughts?' he asked her.

'Well,' she said, 'I think it's a bit of a coincidence that both Sam Waters and Caroline Knight seem to have had appointments that late at night. If they were going somewhere with each other – I think I'd like to know why the plans fell through.'

'And why Waters was so reluctant to tell us what his plans had been,' said Lloyd. He sighed as he thought of Waters.

'Aren't you always trying to convince me that artists are sensitive?' said Judy, her voice mischievous.

Lloyd spent a great deal of time trying to educate Judy in the fine arts; it was probably a lost cause, but he tried anyway. 'Sometimes,' he said, 'I feel I should apologise for the male of the species. This is one of the times.'

And Waters may have thought he had got off lightly, but he hadn't. He had left the Hall about three-quarters of an hour before Mrs Hamlyn, which hardly suggested a tryst, but he wasn't prepared to tell them what he had been doing. He would get another visit from Lloyd before he was much older.

'None of them seemed to care all that much,' he said. 'At least Waters was truthful about it, I suppose.'

'Caroline Knight was upset about the rape,' Judy said encouragingly.

'Yes,' Lloyd said. 'Though I would have thought that being dead was the more pressing of Mrs Hamlyn's problems.' He yawned wearily.

'Do you want me to talk to Treadwell tomorrow?' she asked, after a moment. 'I have met him before,' she added.

He grinned. She was never going to forgive him for that. 'Yes,' he said. 'My first appointment's going to be with the chief super,' he said. 'I'll meet you at the school after I've been to the post-mortem. I don't suppose you want to join me?'

He didn't want her to join him. Freddie's black humour usually went down better with Judy than it did with him, but he had a feeling that he might find himself being the referee if she went this time. It wasn't difficult to dissuade Judy from attending a post-mortem, and she didn't even bother to confirm his supposition.

The rain stopped suddenly as they came into Stansfield. You could almost hear the sigh of relief.

'It could just have been someone who got in, and was wandering about the grounds,' Judy said. 'Is Allison setting up an incident room?'

'They're sorting out an office for us,' said Lloyd. He glanced at her. 'But you know as well as I do that it was probably someone she knew.'

'Why does that sound as though it was all her own fault?' Judy asked, as the car made its way through Stansfield.

Lloyd didn't answer as his tyres threw up spray from the side of the road where the rain had at least made some impression on the heaps of snow. He moved out a little. The car's tyres hissed through slushy puddles which reflected the orange street-lamps, and Lloyd knew how people felt when Judy was questioning them. She was waiting for him to answer, and the question would hang in the air until he did.

'Because women *do* sometimes play with fire,' he said carefully. 'Sex *is* an aggressive act. From the male point of view.'

She snorted.

'All right, assertive, then. If the assertiveness wasn't there, it couldn't happen at all. And it doesn't take much to turn it to aggression – there is sometimes a very thin line between sex and violence. It's not always nonsense when the man says he was led on.'

'And being led on gives him the right to rape her?'

'No,' he said vehemently, shaking his head. 'It doesn't excuse it. But it gives him a reason.'

'Oh,' she said. 'So it's *reasonable* for him to rape her?'

Lloyd sighed. 'Yes, in a manner of speaking,' he said. 'It implies that he had not lost his reason. That he knew what he was doing.'

'Is that better or worse than if he *had* lost his reason?' she asked.

Lloyd shook his head. 'I don't know,' he said tiredly. 'But it's more likely to be someone she was with – someone she felt safe with. Safe enough to cross a pitch-dark field with.'

'You ended at least two sentences with prepositions there,' she said wickedly, as she got out of the car. 'I'll report you.' She leaned back in. 'I'm telling Michael today,' she said, kissing him on the cheek. 'I'll have left by tonight, I promise.' She smiled, and closed the door.

He was startled, as she had intended; he smiled broadly as she walked up her front path, her shoulders set in the way he recognised when nothing and no one was going to stop her doing what she intended to do. He had almost given up hope of seeing that resolve being used out of working hours. But this time she meant it, and he watched until she went into the house. She waved, and he drove off.

He knew that the suggestion that the victim might have played a part upset Judy, but it was something which had to be considered. Because if it wasn't someone Diana Hamlyn was with, then they could soon be playing a repeat performance of tonight, and that sort of show could run and run.

That was why the victim's own contribution was important; if she had made one, it made investigation easier, and a solution more likely. It reduced the likelihood of further crimes, and the proportions of the one being investigated to ones that he could understand. That a lot of men could understand, including judges. And that was what angered a lot of women, including Judy.

Back in his flat, he poured himself a large whisky, and put on an episode of an old, entirely escapist, quite ridiculous television series, the entire rerun of which he had taped. He went to bed at half-past six, allowing himself two hours' sleep.

Judy would think he was quite, quite mad.

Judy's alarm brought her to consciousness, and she opened her eyes to Saturday morning proper with some reluctance. The injury received in the line of duty had caused her to see what a mess she was making of everyone's life; she had made her original promise to Lloyd, and had used the excuse of a painful leg to move into the spare room. She had never moved out again. She pulled on her dressing-gown, and went downstairs, to find Michael in uncharacteristic pose, at the cooker.

'Good morning,' she said.

'Morning. I didn't think you'd be getting up yet,' he said, serving himself his large English breakfast as he spoke. 'I heard about the murder on Radio Barton.'

Judy raised her eyebrows. 'Do you actually *listen* to local radio?' she asked. 'I mean, when there are no extremes of weather?'

'No,' he said. 'I do when my wife's out all night, and I want to know why. You didn't leave a note.'

'Sorry,' she said. 'I didn't know it would take so long. There was a bad accident as well – it held everything up for hours.'

'Where's your car?' he asked, as he picked up his knife and fork.

'It wouldn't start,' she said. 'I had to leave it.' It was so easy, telling selective truths. So easy and, now, completely automatic. But it had to stop.

'Oh, of course,' he said, and carried on eating, unfolding the morning paper. 'The rain.'

'Michael,' she said.

There was a silence after she had spoken his name, during which he pretended to read. Then he shut his eyes briefly, and looked up at her.

'The car's at Lloyd's,' she said. 'I was with him when we got called out. That's why I didn't leave a note. Because I wasn't here.'

'I see,' he said, arranging a look of slight puzzlement on his face, then turned back to the paper.

'Don't pretend you don't know what I mean!'

His eyes didn't leave the newspaper. 'You were in bed with Lloyd,' he said. 'Is that what you mean?'

'No, as it happens,' said Judy. 'But I have been, and I would have been if we hadn't got called out. And I'd have stayed the night, and I would have told you when you asked where I'd been.'

He nodded slowly at the newspaper. 'And despite fate's intervention you're telling me anyway?' he said.

'I've been trying to tell you for weeks.'

'I know. I didn't want you to tell me.' He looked up, and it was her turn to look away.

'I'm sorry,' she said.

'Are you?'

'I'm sorry about the whole thing! I should have told you a long time ago. I shouldn't have married you, come to that.' She met his eyes.

'Was it going on when we got married?' he asked.

Judy had met Lloyd in London, when she was a WPC and he was a detective sergeant. Almost sixteen years ago. What a waste of time. 'Yes,' she said. 'I wasn't sleeping with him, but ... yes.'

'Why *did* you marry me?' He sat down, and looked at her, his thin face showing no emotion as he asked the question.

She took out cigarettes and lit one before answering. 'Because I liked you,' she said. 'Because we got on well together, and because you were going back to live in Nottingham, which was a long way away from Lloyd and Barbara and the children.'

'How very strong-minded of you.'

'I didn't see myself as a home-wrecker,' she said wearily.

'But you don't mind wrecking this one?'

'This isn't a home! We share a house – it's all we've ever done. And it's my fault, I'm not pretending it isn't.'

'How long has it been going on?' he asked. 'If you'll forgive the cliché – one can hardly avoid them.'

'Does it matter?'

'Yes.' He picked up his plate and tipped its contents into the swing-bin. 'Did you know he was in Stansfield? When I applied for this job?'

She nodded. 'And I knew he'd been divorced,' she said. Lloyd's marriage had ended the year before Judy arrived in Stansfield.

'You kept in touch with him? All that time?'

She nodded again.

'So when did it start? As soon as you got here?'

She shook her head. 'It wasn't quite the way it sounds,' she said, and gave a short sigh. 'It was about six months after we came here.'

'And I didn't know,' said Michael. 'Not for certain. I've no doubt everyone else did – all your friends at the police station, for instance – but I didn't.' He smiled coldly. 'Until you moved out of my bed, I was sharing you with Mr Lloyd. And I didn't know.'

Lloyd had envied Michael that; he had hated knowing. And poor Michael was under a handicap just discussing it. Lloyd's first name was so awful that even she didn't know it, and he was universally referred to by his surname. Michael had to put in the 'Mr' to indicate his hostility.

'You've had other women,' she said. 'Don't pretend you haven't.'

'I'm not. But a one-night stand in Brussels isn't quite the same thing, is it? I think I could have lived with it if you'd been filling in time between planes, as it were. But that's not how it is.'

'No, it isn't,' she agreed hotly.

'For God's sake, Judy, you knew about all that! They didn't mean anything – they were casual girlfriends, that's all!'

'A girl in every port?' said Judy. 'I know, Michael. I was one of them. And it should have stayed like that. But you decided it was time you were married. Now you've decided it's time you had a family. But the fact is that it's time we were divorced.'

He shook his head.

'I don't care, Michael,' Judy said. 'Don't you see? I don't care, I've never cared about other women. This has never been a marriage – we've never been a unit. You should have someone else,' she said. 'Someone who loves you. Someone who wants children – someone *you* love. You don't love me.'

'Don't I?'

'Do you?' she asked, getting up.

'It rather depends on what we mean by it. If it means not being able to live without you, then – no, I don't love you. I don't claim the grand passion that you and Mr Lloyd have apparently found.' He looked away. 'I don't know, Judy,' he said. 'I know how I felt when you got hurt. You can't live with someone for ten years and feel nothing for them!' He looked up at her. 'Or can you?'

'No,' she said, sinking tiredly down again. 'But it's over, Michael. Whatever it was, whatever it is. It's over, and I'm leaving.'

'And moving in with Mr Lloyd?'

'Eventually,' she said. 'When I get my transfer.'

'Because the powers that be wouldn't like it while you're both still at Stansfield?'

'Quite.'

'So where will you go in the meantime?'

'I'll get somewhere,' she said. 'I can share with someone. It's only until June.'

'Stay here,' he said.

Judy's eyes widened. 'What?' she asked disbelievingly.

'Stay here. Why not? We've got separate rooms – if you're going to share with someone, share with me.'

'I can't do that!' she said.

He nodded. 'Of course. Mr Lloyd wouldn't like it. Well,' he said, with a grim little smile, 'I know where I come in the pecking order, don't? I come a poor third to your bosses and your boyfriend.'

Judy shook her head. 'Why on earth do you *want* me to stay?' she asked.

He dropped his eyes away from hers. 'I can't cope with this,' he said. 'I can't cope on my own.'

'Michael, you're a grown man!'

He put his head in his hands. 'Maybe that's just what I'm not,' he said.

A little boy in Woolworth's. Judy got up, and put her arm round his shoulders. 'You can't hold on to this,' she said. 'Not just because of—'

'I know,' he said, interrupting her. He took his hands away, and looked up. 'Just stay,' he said. 'Until your transfer. Give me time to get used to the idea. Don't walk out on me now. Please. Give me time to find somewhere. I can't rattle about this place on my own.'

Judy frowned slightly as she looked at him. 'I never knew you felt like that,' she said.

'Well, I never knew about Lloyd. That makes us quits,' he said.

Her arm was still round his shoulders. She gave him a squeeze. 'No,' she said. 'It doesn't.' She straightened up. She would have to break her promise. 'I'll stay until the transfer,' she said. Her heart sank at the thought of telling Lloyd, but she managed a smile. 'And this does make us quits,' she said. 'OK?'

He smiled. 'OK,' he said.

The rain had offered false hope; it was falling again, but this time as sleet, as snow, adding to the problem that they already had. It was difficult just to keep upright on the slippery pavement. Judy took a taxi to Lloyd's flat. The obliging driver took her into the garage area, and waited until her own car was coaxed into starting, driving off with two cheerful blasts of the horn when the exhaust fumes belched out, indicating success.

She was looking forward to living here, in an apprehensive sort of way. In the relentlessly modern Stansfield, the old village was reassuring, with listed buildings and family shops and people who had lived there all their lives. But it was enough like part of a much larger town to be reasonably anonymous. Her comings and goings from Lloyd's flat doubtless amused his neighbours, but it remained none of their business. And Lloyd's flat itself was a kind of haven; a little bit of the initial magic was always there.

Judy got ready to go and interview Treadwell, trying to bring her mind back to work, and away from how she was going to tell Lloyd what she had agreed with Michael.

Sam prepared a canvas; he would be painting soon. The image danced just beyond his vision, but it was there. Outside, teams of police combed the playing-field, and nosed up and down the lane; they didn't know what they were looking for, either.

He looked up as the knock came to the door, and Caroline walked in.

'Philip said I'd find you here,' she said, wrinkling her nose a little at the smell.

'Philip was right.' He went back to his canvas. Fifties song, fifties ploy, fifties frustration. He hadn't ached like that since he was fifteen. The brief moments of gratification that he had finally achieved hadn't been worth it. Women never were.

'I owe you an apology,' she said.

'Yes,' he said, still not looking at her.

'I'm just not ready,' she said.

'You seemed ready enough to me.' He looked up. 'Are you ready to come to the pictures?'

'What?'

'Well, we missed out last night,' he said, wiping his hands on a rag. 'So let's go this afternoon. To a real cinema. Saturday afternoon flicks. It won't be very artistic, but what the hell? I don't know what's on, but that doesn't matter.'

She looked shocked. 'We can't do that,' she said.

'Why not? It's Saturday, isn't it?'

'That's got nothing to do with it!'

'Oh,' Sam said. 'Because Diana Hamlyn's dead? Not coming to the pictures with me isn't going to change that.'

'I can't! What would people think?'

'I don't give a f—' He gave a mock bow. 'A fig what people think. And Diana Hamlyn's demise is another thing I don't give a fig about.' He gave a broad smile. 'It looks like she had one fig too many,' he said. 'Doesn't it?'

Caroline just looked at him.

'So,' he said. 'The afternoon showing's at about three, I think. I'll pick you up in the car park at quarter past two – all right?'

'I'm not coming to the pictures with you,' she said carefully, as though he were a bit slow. 'Do you understand?'

'Of course you will. You want to.' Why was he being so persistent, for God's sake? They were all the same in the dark. But he wanted *her*, for the same reasons, he supposed, that a fisherman might struggle for hours to land an inedible fish.

'Is Philip all right?' she asked, ignoring him.

'I think so,' said Sam. He didn't, but he wasn't about to discuss Newby with Caroline.

'He seemed to be in a lot of pain when I saw him,' she said.

Sam grinned again. 'He always looks like that when you're around,' he said. 'Hadn't you noticed? Everyone else has.'

This time he achieved a real blush. You would think it would make her angry, the way Newby looked at her sometimes. But it didn't. At least it embarrassed her.

She turned away and walked to the door.

'Two-fifteen,' he said. 'I'll be waiting with bated breath for your arrival.'

He went to the window then, as there was a flurry of activity in the lane outside. They seemed to have found something.

'I wouldn't, if I were you,' she said. 'Because I won't come.'

Sam grinned. 'I wouldn't really expect you to,' he said. 'Not in the back row of the cinema.'

'Is that it?' asked Treadwell, pointing to the ring.

'Yes,' said Miss Castle, and reached out a hand to take it.

'I'm sorry,' said Sergeant Hill. 'But we'll have to hang on to it for the moment.'

'Oh, of course,' she said.

Treadwell indicated that she could leave, and Miss Castle reluctantly took the hint.

'Where did you say they were found?' he asked.

'In the loft above one of the houses,' she said, tagging the ring.

'Which one?'

'The one at the far end of the lane,' she said, consulting her notebook. 'Palmerston.'

'Worrying about theft seems a bit ridiculous after what's happened,' he said gloomily, then brightened. 'Still, it does seem to have been one of the boys after all,' he said.

There was a little group of items which remained untagged; they were all things that people might never even have missed. Loose change, cigarettes, a pocket handkerchief. Except that there was a pen there – it looked expensive.

'It's odd that the pen wasn't reported,' he said, picking up the plastic bag. It was old; well used. The pattern along the side had almost worn away.

'Yes,' agreed the sergeant. 'I'll see if anyone recognises it. But to get back to why I'm really here,' she said briskly. 'Was there much coming and going from the Hall last night?'

Treadwell thought for a moment. 'No, I don't think so. Waters left at about half past nine, and Mrs Hamlyn went just after quarter past ten. And Newby went early . . . . I left briefly, when I went to look for Mrs Hamlyn. And Robert went back to the flat at about one o'clock – that's when he found her, of course.'

'Mr Newby left early?'

'Yes. He said his leg was bothering him, I'm told.'

She jotted something down. 'He seemed to be in quite a lot of pain when we saw him,' she said, responding to the note of disbelief.

Treadwell shrugged. 'He moved fast enough when he left,' he said.

'When was that?'

'Just minutes after Mrs Hamlyn left. Five at the most.'

He sat down, motioning to the sergeant to do the same. His office felt cold this morning.

'Did Mr Waters mention to you where he was going last night?'

'Is he being difficult?' he asked, but she didn't answer.

'He was supposed to be going out with Caroline Knight,' he said.

'Mrs Knight didn't attend the dinner,' said the sergeant. 'Why was that?'

'She didn't want to, and I didn't press her. She was in a very bad way after Andrew's death.' He sighed. 'I asked her to organise the dinner. I thought having something specific to do might help. And it did seem to – she's quite like her old self. But she wouldn't attend. Not without Andrew, she said – so . . .'He shrugged. 'Perhaps I'm not such a good doctor,' he said, with a smile.

'But she was going out with Mr Waters?'

'Well,' said Treadwell. 'She said she was. Some film, I believe.'

She frowned. 'At that time of night?'

'It was a special showing for St Valentine's Day. Midnight.' He smiled again. 'It doesn't sound like Waters's cup of tea to me. I think it was an excuse they cooked up to get him out of having to stay at the ball.'

She wrote what seemed to be all of that down. 'Is that obligatory?' he asked, pointing to the thick pad.

She smiled. 'It is if you've got a memory like mine,' she said. 'Do you mean you don't think that he was really going out with her? You don't believe the film existed?'

He held up his hands. 'Who knows? Sam – well, you've met him. Enough said, I imagine. But Caroline is quite friendly with him, for some reason. She might have let herself be used as an excuse.'

'Mrs Knight telephoned to speak to Mrs Hamlyn at ...' She consulted her notebook. 'Ten forty-five. Why was it you rather than Mr Hamlyn who spoke to her?'

Treadwell wasn't sure how to handle this. The woman must have heard about Diana by this time, but ... well, she *was* a woman. It was all a little indelicate. 'Hamlyn thought she'd gone somewhere with Sam Waters,' he said. 'He refused to take the call.'

She gave a little nod. 'You were gone from the table for about quarter of an hour?'

'Yes,' he said. 'Yes, I must have been.'

A little frown appeared between the sergeant's eyebrows. 'I got the impression from Mrs Knight that the call was quite brief,' she said.

'It was. But she wanted to speak to Diana, and I said I'd look for her.'

'Where did you look?'

'Does it really matter?' Treadwell snapped. He hadn't expected a *woman*. Simon Allison had said the chief inspector would see him. Not a woman.

'Well, one of the people at your table told me that when you returned you were ... .' Again, she leafed through the notebook. '... "soaked to the skin",' she said. She looked up at him. 'Were you?' she asked.

'Hardly,' said Treadwell. 'But I did get wet. It was raining very hard.'

'Where did you look?' she asked again.

Treadwell could feel perspiration on the back of his neck. He wished the woman would just go away, but she was waiting patiently for an answer.

'Various places. Places she might have gone with ... with ... well, you know.'

'Mr Treadwell – do I understand that as soon as you were told that Mrs Hamlyn wasn't where she was expected you assumed that she was with a man somewhere?'

'Yes, I'm afraid so.'

'Wasn't she a bit of a liability?'

'In some respects.' He resisted the temptation to run his finger round his shirt collar. 'But she was a very good housemother. She understood children – the youngsters are devastated.'

'Did you ever try to do anything about her behaviour?'

'Like what? It's Hamlyn that we employ, not his wife. What she did was her business.'

'And yet you went looking for her?'

'Mrs Knight wanted to speak to her.'

'Where did you look?' she asked.

Treadwell thought he'd got her off that. 'I went across to the Barn,' he said. 'I just thought she might be there.'

'The Barn?'

'The building behind this one.' He waved a hand behind his shoulder, indicating the Barn through the window.

She got up to look out. 'Why?' she asked.

He closed his eyes briefly. 'I once had occasion to go into the Barn for something,' he said, his voice flat. 'She was in there with someone.'

'Who?'

'Does it matter? He's no longer employed by the school.'

'Yes, it matters,' she said, in a voice as crisp as the white blouse she wore.

Treadwell sighed. 'It was a young man who was employed as a sort of handyman,' he said. 'I dismissed him on the spot.'

'So he might well feel very resentful towards Mrs Hamlyn?'

'I don't see why. Anyway, it was eighteen months ago – it was a year ago last July.'

'She got him into trouble – she lost him his job.'

'Hardly,' said Treadwell. 'It is the man who takes the lead in these matters.'

He could only be thankful that Marcia had never looked at anyone like Sergeant Hill was looking at him.

Chapter Four

'. . . internal bruising, together with injuries—' Freddie broke off as he realised that Lloyd had come in. He smiled. 'Good morning, Chief Inspector,' he said. 'You almost missed it all.' He smiled broadly.

'Pity I didn't,' Lloyd said sourly, as Freddie finished off the note he'd been making.

'– to neck, breasts, and thighs, consistent with sexual assault.' He looked up. 'Swabs are positive,' said Freddie. 'If it was someone at the school, we might clear this up quite quickly. But it's an interesting one, Lloyd.'

Lloyd groaned. Freddie's 'interesting' was everyone else's headache. He looked at Kathy, which was a more pleasant activity than looking at what Freddie was doing. She smiled at him, as she wrote down Freddie's findings. How could a nice girl like her possibly want to do this for a living? Sandwell was smitten; Lloyd didn't blame him. But he wasn't sure that he could fall for a pathologist's assistant.

'She died of asphyxiation,' Freddie said, peering at something.

Lloyd frowned. 'What about the head injuries?' he asked.

'They didn't kill her,' he said. 'They would have done. He hit her often enough to drop an ox.'

Lloyd nodded, and was left in limbo while Freddie worked, whistling quietly to himself, stopping to get Kathy to make notes, then picking up the tune where he left off. At last, he looked up.

'But all her attacker knew was that she wasn't dead. He thought he wasn't making much of a job of it like that, so he restricted her air supply instead.'

'What with?'

'Ah – well, that's one of the more interesting aspects,' Freddie said eagerly. 'Something rigid – quite thin, probably quite long. Made of wood. And it broke, eventually. We're working on the splinters – should know the sort of wood quite soon, I imagine.'

'Can you give me some sort of description?'

Freddie nodded. 'The blows were made with something blunt, about five, six inches long, with rounded edges. Probably metal, but not particularly heavy – that's why it didn't do the job very efficiently. Unless he went with a positive armoury of weapons, I'd say he adapted whatever he'd been using; just pressed it down on her throat instead of hitting her with it.'

'Can you hazard a guess as to what he used?'

'Taken in conjunction with the neck injury, I'd say you were looking for something with a long, stiff wooden shaft, and a protuberance at one end. Like a golf-club,' he said, and smiled. 'Can't get much closer,' he said. 'I'm not sure what I'd take – a sand iron, do you think?'

'I wish you sometimes had a hangover,' Lloyd said. 'Maybe you wouldn't be so cheerful.'

'Anyway,' Freddie said, 'he underclubbed, whatever he took.'

'Is the golfing analogy going to be a feature of this investigation?' Lloyd asked.

'Just trying to bring a little sunshine into your life,' Freddie said. 'Speaking of which – why do you keep Sergeant Hill away from me?'

'Freddie, believe me. In this case, I'm doing you a favour. She wouldn't take too kindly to your remarks – it's quite difficult to say anything, never mind make jokes.'

'Why?'

'Sex murders don't exactly give her a warm, secure feeling.'

'No, I don't suppose they do. This is a funny one, though.'

'Freddie,' Lloyd sighed. 'Don't make difficulties.'

'I'm not,' said Freddie, sounding a little hurt. 'But it's possible that we're not dealing with rape and murder.'

'Freddie,' said Lloyd, with exaggerated patience. 'She was found in the middle of a field, in the middle of February, in the middle of a downpour, in the middle of the night. Her clothes were torn. She wasn't wearing any underwear. She had been beaten and strangled.'

'I know it wasn't her *day*,' said Freddie. 'I'm just saying she might not have been raped.'

'Oh, come off it!' said Lloyd.

'She was very sexually experienced,' Freddie persisted.

Lloyd raised his eyebrows. 'There would be a lot more blood and guts in here if Judy heard you say that,' he said. 'What's her sexual history got to do with it?'

'It makes rape easier to achieve, and harder to detect, for one thing,' said Freddie. 'And with rape and murder you usually find—'

'Usually!' snorted Lloyd. 'Rape murders aren't usual.'

'They're getting that way,' said Kathy.

They both turned, to look at her, rather as if the corpse had spoken, and Kathy looked faintly guilty for having an opinion at all, but she carried on, glaring at Lloyd.

'It used to be something people did if they went crazy,' she said. 'Now it's something they do if there's nothing good on the telly.'

'– that the rape itself is extremely violent,' Freddie said, determinedly finishing his sentence.

'It sounded violent enough to me,' Lloyd said, waving a hand at Kathy's notes.

'And me,' said Kathy, obviously emboldened by the discovery that she did not get struck by lightning for speaking her mind.

'There was a not inconsiderable degree of sexual violence,' agreed Freddie. 'It was crude, and very forceful. But, if that had been that, it's quite probable that she wouldn't even have sought medical assistance. Her injuries would have mended themselves. And they were occasioned before the head injuries,' he added. 'But she didn't fight back.' He indicated her fingernails. 'These could do a lot of damage,' he said. 'She didn't use them.'

'Perhaps she couldn't get her hands free,' said Lloyd.

Freddie admitted the possibility with a slight nod of his head. 'Perhaps,' he said. 'If the attack had taken place in a confined area, where she couldn't move freely. But, as you so Welshly point out, it took place in the middle of a field, et cetera. And there is no indication that she was restrained in any way.' He smiled suddenly. 'In any sense of the word,' he added.

Lloyd glanced at Kathy, but she was letting that pass. Judy wouldn't have.

'The ground was rock hard, and uneven,' Freddie went on. 'She wasn't forcibly pinned to it, or there would be indications.' He paused. 'The sexual violence was' – Freddie thought for a moment – 'cynical, if you like. The sexual equivalent of a professional foul. He wasn't out of control. He knew what he was doing.'

Lloyd listened thoughtfully as Freddie almost echoed his words to Judy.

'I don't think you're looking for someone who frenziedly raped and murdered her as she was crossing the field,' said Freddie.

'What *are* we looking for?' Lloyd asked.

'Whoever killed her was certainly very frightened – or very angry. The murder *was* particularly violent. And in that context the sex wasn't. She could have put that down to experience. Quite probably a not entirely new experience – possibly not even an unwelcome experience.'

Lloyd's eyes narrowed a little as he tried to work out what Freddie really thought. Freddie's opinions were rarely offered; it didn't do to dismiss them. Or very angry, he had said. 'Do you think she was killed because she had been discovered with someone?' he asked.

Freddie raised reproving eyebrows. 'That's a theory, Lloyd,' he said. 'I don't have theories. Facts, the odd opinion if I feel strongly enough . . . .'

'The very odd opinion,' grumbled Lloyd. 'Are you seriously saying that she *consented* to sex in the middle of a field, et cetera? I don't care how many men she had before breakfast – she wasn't about to do that.'

'No,' conceded Freddie. 'But she could have been chased on to the field from somewhere else. We've found nothing yet to confirm that anything other than the murder took place on the field – we're still looking, of course, but the intercourse could well have happened somewhere else.'

'Why do you have to take a perfectly obvious rape murder and complicate it?'

But he was giving Freddie's opinion his consideration all the same. Hamlyn? Did he find her with someone, and kill her in a terrible rage? That seemed to be what Freddie was unofficially suggesting. Freddie who never had theories, because they always came to grief.

'Where would he get hold of a golf-club?' Lloyd asked. 'If it was some sort of row that blew up after the sex?'

Freddie smiled. 'Not my job,' he said. 'The facts are that it certainly looks like rape, and that the rape' – he glanced at Kathy, and smiled seriously – 'though fairly violent, wasn't as violent as the murder. We won't have the results of the tests for a while – before that, anything is guesswork. So, as far as my preliminary report is concerned, Mrs Hamlyn was raped and murdered.'

'Good,' said Lloyd.

'She died between ten-fifteen and eleven-fifteen,' Freddie said. 'I could stretch that to eleven-thirty, but no more. She had been dead at least two hours when I first saw her, and she was last seen alive at ten-fifteen.'

Lloyd nodded. At last, something was going his way. Most murders weren't discovered soon enough to have that good an estimate of the time. But it meant that his theory about Hamlyn had come to grief already.

Waters had a little bit of talking to do, though, and he wasn't going to find Lloyd such an uncritical listener this time.

'Did you think Mrs Hamlyn was with Sam Waters?'

Treadwell rubbed his hands over his face. He had a hangover, and this woman was going to be here for the rest of his life, asking him questions, the same questions, over and over again. 'She did have a bit of a . . . a thing with him, once. But that was well over a year ago. It wasn't still going on.'

'But her husband thought she was with him?'

'Well, as I said, she left forty-five minutes after he did,' said Treadwell. 'That doesn't sound like even circumstantial evidence to me. But Robert made a bit of an exhibition of himself about it.'

'Are you surprised?' she asked.

'Well, I don't think—' He stopped. He'd already been made to discuss things that he would never normally discuss with a woman. Not even Marcia. He had never spoken to her about Mrs Hamlyn's behaviour with that young man in the Barn; he had not wanted to speak to Sergeant Hill about it.

'You didn't think she was with Mr Waters,' she said, her pen moving over the pages.

Perhaps he could try to make it clear without having to go into any sort of detail. 'The boys danced the first dance with the ladies – just a silly sort of token thing for Valentine's Day,' he said. 'As soon as Diana had finished dancing, she made a bee-line for Philip Newby. I'm not exaggerating – she practically fell over young Matthew Cawston in her hurry to get to him. She talked to him for a few moments, and then she left.'

She waited patiently while he worked out how to phrase the next part.

'He watched her leave,' he said. 'And I understand that he said his leg was bad. But he moved out of there fast enough, believe me.'

She wrote it all down, but her question wasn't about Newby, and she couldn't have made it much plainer.

'Do you know if Mr Waters did go straight to see Mrs Knight?' she asked.

'How would I know?' he said, almost shouting at the stupid woman who couldn't see what was staring her in the face.

'Was he with her when she was told about Mrs Hamlyn?'

'No,' said Treadwell. This seemed to have nothing to do with anything, but at least he could talk about it. 'Dearden said she was on her own – he was a bit worried, because he already thought she seemed jumpy, even before he told her about Diana. But that was half past two in the morning, so I'd hardly expect Sam to have been with her.'

'Everyone left her on her own?' Sergeant Hill asked. 'After what had happened to Mrs Hamlyn?'

Oh, God. 'Yes,' said Treadwell. 'I know it must seem a bit—'

'No one even went to check up on her until half past two?' she asked incredulously.

'No.'

'You didn't ring Mrs Knight back,' the sergeant carried on remorselessly.

'Sorry?' said Treadwell, desperately hanging on to the ropes.

'When you failed to find Mrs Hamlyn – you didn't ring Mrs Knight. Why was that?'

'I had left my guests for rather too long as it was,' said Treadwell. 'Caroline would have gathered that I hadn't found her.'

She didn't believe him, but if she had been going to question him further, he was saved by the door opening, and two of the boys tumbling in excitedly, without even knocking.

'Sir! We've found these!'

'I'm glad I caught you,' Sergeant Hill said. 'I'd like to have another word with you, if it's convenient.'

Caroline invited her in. 'Take a seat,' she said.

Sergeant Hill sat down, and took her notebook from her handbag.

Caroline sat down, too, a little warily. 'I don't think I can tell you any more than I did last night,' she said.

The sergeant smiled. 'I think perhaps you can,' she said pleasantly. 'There are a few things – things that might not have seemed relevant last night.'

Caroline sat back a little, trying to look relaxed, like she did at the dentist. But the efficient, smartly dressed, quick-witted Sergeant Hill made her feel even more uncomfortable than the dentist's chair ever had.

'Did Mr Waters stand you up last night?' she asked suddenly.

Caroline was taken by surprise, as she was meant to be, and she had no time to think. 'No,' she said. 'No, he didn't.' What if he had? Caroline didn't know why she was being asked.

'But your plans – to go to the cinema, was it? – fell through.'

Caroline shrugged slightly. 'It's a film club,' she said. 'Not really a cinema. Of course they fell through. Diana didn't turn up,' she said sarcastically.

A tiny frown appeared on Sergeant Hill's brow. 'I don't think', she said, consulting her notebook, 'that that was what you said yesterday, was it?'

Caroline didn't know what she'd said yesterday. She wasn't sure what she was saying now.

'Here it is,' said Sergeant Hill. 'My *plans had fallen through anyway*.' She looked up. '*Anyway*,' she repeated. 'Whether or not Mr Treadwell had been able to locate Mrs Hamlyn?'

Caroline felt cornered. 'Yes,' she said. 'It was going to be too late for us to go by then.'

'At quarter to eleven? Surely it didn't start until midnight?'

Caroline assumed the question was rhetorical. 'Was Mr Waters with you when you rang the Hall?'

'No,' said Caroline.

Sergeant Hill looked puzzled. 'But he had been with you?'

'Yes.'

'So when did he leave?'

Caroline didn't answer, as she tried to gather her thoughts. She didn't know why they were so interested in Sam. But all his remarks and comments about Diana were echoing in her head, and if he'd said that sort of thing to the police . . . .

'About what time did Mr Waters arrive?'

'Half past nine or so.'

'And leave?'

'He left at about ten past ten, I think,' Caroline said, still not sure what relevance Sam's movements had.

'Oh? Did you have some sort of argument?'

'He went to change his clothes,' said Caroline, feigning puzzlement. 'He was wearing a ridiculous dinner-jacket – I wasn't going out with him in that.'

'But when Mr Waters did go out he wore jeans and a sweater. You were all dressed up, Mrs Knight.'

'I don't understand!' Caroline shouted. 'Why are you asking me all these questions?'

'On television they ask if the deceased had any enemies,' said Sergeant Hill. 'I'm afraid we're more likely to ask if she had any friends.'

'But why pick on Sam?'

'We're not picking on him,' the sergeant said calmly. 'But Mr Waters has refused to tell us anything, including where he was. So I have to find out from other people. It's my job, Mrs Knight.'

'To suspect everyone who isn't prepared to tell you all his private business?'

'I'm afraid privacy is at something of a premium in the wake of a murder,' she said.

Caroline made an exasperated noise. 'Sam's just being pig-headed!'

'Perhaps he is,' she said. 'Had you had an argument? Or were you never really going out with him at all? Was that an excuse so that Mr Waters could leave the ball early?'

Caroline frowned. What was that supposed to mean? It was none of her business anyway.

'If he was here, he left early. Did you have a row?'

Oh, God. Caroline could see his baffled face again, and her own face grew hot. 'What makes you think that?' she asked, trying to give herself time to think.

'I think perhaps you rang to tell Mrs Hamlyn that she needn't come at all.'

'So?'

'You were meant to be going out together, but Mr Waters left after half an hour.' She raised her eyebrows. 'In my experience, that equals a row.'

'Yes, all right! We had a . . . disagreement – what of it?' Caroline didn't know how to cope with this. Everything she said seemed to get her in deeper.

'What was it about?'

'It's got nothing to do with you!'

'Someone raped and killed Mrs Hamlyn,' she said, her voice still maddeningly calm, like someone manning a Samaritan line. 'That's got something to do with me.'

My God, she thought it was Sam.

'Sam didn't rape her!' she shouted, more to convince herself than Sergeant Hill. 'I know what he's like – I know the sort of things he says and does. But he wouldn't *rape* someone! My God, if he'd been going to rape anyone, it would have been me!' She could hear her own voice echoing in the air for what seemed like hours after she had spoken.

'It would have been you?' repeated Sergeant Hill quietly.

Now what had she done? Caroline couldn't believe she'd said it. How had she made her say it? She dropped her head in her hands.

'Mrs Knight,' she heard the sergeant say. 'You are going to have to explain that.'

Caroline wouldn't look at her. Her hands still covered her face.

'Mrs Knight?' she said again, after a moment. Still calm, still patient.

Caroline looked at her.

'Are you saying that Mr Waters tried to assault you?'

'No!' said Caroline, horrified. She took a moment, then tried to explain. 'I know Sam swears and says outrageous things,' she said. 'He tries to shock people all the time. I don't even like him all that much. And last night was a mistake – things just got out of hand. It wasn't his fault,' she said quickly. She pushed back a straying strand of hair. 'I didn't mean to, but ... I – I suppose I gave him the wrong idea.' Her nerve deserted her a little under the sergeant's unwavering gaze, and she stopped speaking.

'Go on,' said Sergeant Hill.

'I stopped him,' she said. 'He wasn't very happy about it – that's why he left. He didn't do anything.'

Sergeant Hill showed no reaction.

'I don't know why he didn't just say he was with me, except that it did end like that, and – well, that might just be Sam's version of chivalry.'

The truth. It was a relief, in a way. But now what would she think about Sam? And what if he *had* . . . .

'I was going to tell Diana not to bother coming back early,' she said, in a low voice. 'But when I couldn't speak to her I decided to go anyway. By myself.' She sighed. 'I don't suppose I would have had the nerve.'

She was going, thank God. But she stopped at the door. 'Did Mr Waters frighten you?' she asked.

Caroline shook her head.

'Did something frighten you? Mr Dearden seemed to think you were already a little nervous before you knew about Mrs Hamlyn.'

Caroline sighed. 'I think there was some sort of prowler here last night,' she said.

'Oh?' She came back in, and sat down again.

'I . . . I think someone was watching me,' she said. 'When I was changing.'

'Where did you change?' she asked.

'In the Hamlyns' bedroom. I felt as if someone was watching – but I ignored it. And then – well, the curtains don't close properly, and . . . .' She shivered again, as she thought of it. 'I'm sure I saw someone,' she said.

'Did you look out?'

'No!' No, she had run into the living-room, too scared to look.

'When was this?'

'Just after eleven,' she said.

'Were you going to keep that to yourself?' Sergeant Hill asked, her tone still polite, interested, like a television interviewer.

'I – I thought perhaps it was . . . 'No. No, she couldn't say she thought it was Sam, trying to upset her. 'My imagination,' she finished.

The sergeant wrote that down. 'Thank you,' she said, standing up again.

Caroline showed her downstairs, and out of the building, more to assure herself that the woman had actually gone than out of courtesy. She began to climb the stairs again, then stopped, and looked reflectively at the door of the downstairs flat. Then she turned, came back down, and knocked.

After a moment, Philip opened it, and smiled, but she could see the pain he was in.

'Wasn't he in the art room?' he asked. 'He's not back yet, I'm afraid.'

'Oh – yes, he was,' she said. 'I just came to see if you were all right.'

'Of course I am,' he said, affecting surprise.

She shook her head. 'You can hardly walk,' she said.

'I was in a road accident,' he said, his voice bitter. 'Didn't I tell you?'

'You know what I mean! You can't even stand up straight. Should you see your doctor?'

'No!' he said firmly. But he stood aside. 'Are you coming in?' he asked.

She hesitated, then went in. 'Does it often get as bad as this?' she asked, sitting down.

He moved slowly to the sofa, and lowered himself down, leaning on his stick. There was something different about him, apart from the obvious difficulty he was having in moving. Caroline couldn't quite work out what it was.

'Now and then,' he said. 'It's probably the weather.'

She nodded. 'Have the police been to see you?' she asked.

'Why should they see me?'

'No reason. They seem to have spoken to everyone else, that's all.'

He shook his head. 'I saw them,' he said. 'In the middle of the night – but it was Sam they were interested in. They didn't ask me anything.'

In the middle of the night? What on earth had Sam done that had got them so suspicious?

'Why were they interested in Sam?' she asked.

'I think it was just because he wasn't around when they arrived,' he said. 'And he'd changed.'

Caroline swallowed. 'He wasn't here? Do you know where he was?'

'He wouldn't tell me.' He shrugged. 'And of course he wouldn't tell them.' He smiled again. 'Can't you get done for using abusive language to a police officer?'

Caroline began to understand that the police weren't really picking on Sam. He was picking on them, enjoying being under suspicion, wanting to make them look foolish, if he could.

Philip was looking at her again, his eyes hungry. She tried to ignore it; it wasn't easy, but she was used to it by now.

'Is Sam working on a painting?' she asked, breaking the silence.

'No idea.'

'Do you get on all right with him?'

'Yes,' he said. 'He's not too bad.'

Caroline wasn't at all sure she agreed, but she smiled. 'What did you think of his dinner-jacket?' she asked.

Philip's face broke into his sudden smile, despite the pain, despite whatever his imagination was up to. 'It was fantastic, wasn't it?' he said, turning back into the person she liked. 'Can I get you a cup of coffee or something?'

'I'll get it,' she said.

'No.' He got to his feet, his face growing pale with the effort.

'Philip – are you sure you shouldn't go to the doctor?'

'I'm all right!' He limped over to the kettle, and shook it before plugging it in. 'When did you see his jacket?' he asked.

'He came to see me at the Hamlyns',' she said.

Philip smiled a little shyly. 'Are you and Sam ... well, a couple?'

'No!' she said vehemently. 'We've been out a few times. That's all.'

'Oh – none of my business. I just .... '

'What's he been saying?'

'Nothing,' Philip said, spooning coffee into two mugs. 'Well – you know Sam.'

Yes, she knew Sam.

Philip poured the water on to the coffee, then picked up one mug, and reached over to her, the knuckles of his other hand white as they gripped the stick.

The stick. That was what it was. He was using an NHS one.

'Where's your proper stick?' she asked.

'This one's better when it's bad,' he said.

Caroline drank her coffee, but he was at it again before she'd finished; she hurried it, and left.

Matthew watched with dismay the comings and goings of the police, of lab technicians, photographers. They were everywhere. They'd found his hiding-place.

Could they prove anything? If they could, it would be better if he told them himself. Admitted the thefts, saved them the time and trouble of finding him. Let them get on with the serious business. Almost heroic, he told himself.

No – not heroic. Frightened. That would be better. He'd get sympathy then. He could tell them he had been too scared to come forward. Too scared, by what he knew. The sergeant would go for that, he decided, as he watched her talking to one of the teachers. She had a kind face. He would make a full confession. But not now. Not here. After a struggle with his conscience; after he had convinced himself that the police wouldn't let any harm come to him.

Yes, he thought, as he left the house and walked along the lane to the school, that would be best.

He was going to offer Mrs Knight some help in setting up some project that she was doing for Monday. He'd heard her mention it to Treadwell; she had said she would need the key for the storeroom. Before, that would have presented a glorious opportunity to take something, and make it look like she had done it. He walked quickly through the drizzle to the main building, and along past the office to the storeroom, where the door was open, and he could see Mrs Knight reaching up to the top shelf for some old books.

'I'll do that,' he said.

She turned quickly, her hand at her mouth, her eyes wide with alarm. 'Oh, Matthew,' she said, breathless. 'I thought there was no one else in the building. You gave me a fright.'

'I'm sorry,' he said. 'I didn't think.'

'Not your fault,' she said. 'Are you taller than me?'

He came in and stood beside her, but there was no difference in their heights. 'I'm afraid not,' he said, looking round.

There was a pile of out-of-date encyclopaedias, and he began piling up the enormous old books.

'No,' she said. 'What if you fell?'

'I won't fall.' He really did seem to have frightened her; he supposed, now he came to think of it, that it wasn't surprising. He constructed a platform of books, and tested it with one foot. It seemed quite stable.

'Well,' she said. 'All right. You hand them down to me.'

They got them all down, and began transporting them to the classroom. He met her on the stair as he went back down after dumping his first load; she seemed calmer. But she had been nervy since her husband's accident; Mrs Hamlyn's being murdered wouldn't have done her much good.

'In the Barn,' said Judy. 'Some of the boys found them. Shoes, bag, tights, the lot. One of the shoes was squashed. And the underwear and tights were in the bag.'

'Why didn't anyone check the Barn last night?' Lloyd demanded.

They had obediently parked in the car park, and were walking through the lane, making for the main building. Lloyd held the door open for her with a flourish. 'Ladies first,' he said, with a grin.

'Because no one knew the Barn had anything to do with it,' said Judy. Including Lloyd, but she thought it wiser not to point that out.

It was like any other school building on a Saturday; somewhere, they could hear the caretaker, raking out the boiler, doing whatever uncanny things caretakers did to heating systems to ensure that they belted out heat all weekend and broke down at precisely six o'clock on Monday morning. Judy was instantly transported to her grandmother's warm kitchen; would that she could be, she thought, as her heels rang out on the uncarpeted corridor, making the place seem chillier than ever.

'I suppose every kid in the school got his fingerprints all over them,' said Lloyd gloomily, as he pushed open the office door.

They had temporarily taken over Treadwell's office; Judy once again looked out at the Barn, and was furious with herself for not having got it checked as soon as Treadwell mentioned it. 'Of course they did,' she said, turning from the window. 'I suppose everyone makes mistakes,' she added, almost to herself.

Lloyd laughed. 'Yes,' he said. 'Even me.'

'But Treadwell said he'd looked there,' she said, turning back.

'I don't know who you're arguing with. No one's blaming you. As you said – no one knew it had anything to do with it.' He joined her at the window as one of the scene-of-crime officers emerged from the Barn and lit a cigarette.

'So what do you make of it?' he asked.

'She was raped in the Barn, ran away, and he caught up with her on the playing-field,' she said.

'You know Freddie's theory.'

Judy knew Freddie's theory, and she didn't think much of it. And the Barn seemed no more likely a place for consenting sex than the field, not in the middle of winter.

'Her pants and tights were in her bag,' Lloyd said, correctly interpreting her silence. 'Isn't that more likely to be something she would do?'

'You're asking that as though I were some sort of expert on the protocol,' she said.

'Oh, come on!' he laughed. 'It's not always been in bed, has it?'

She didn't reply.

'It has,' he said gleefully. 'We'll have to remedy that.'

'Don't you have some sort of rule about not mixing our private lives and our professional lives?' she reminded him sharply.

'I didn't mean right *now*,' he said.

He was in one of his skittish moods, when she would wonder what she ever saw in him in the first place. Sometimes if she so much as said his name in the wrong tone of voice he'd be reminding her about his rule.

'Let's hope Freddie can tell us a bit more tonight,' he said.

'Tonight?' Judy repeated.

'We're all going for a drink,' he said.

'You and me and Freddie?' she said. 'Tonight?'

'You and I and Freddie,' he corrected.

'Why?'

'We've got something to celebrate,' he said.

Her heart plunged, but she didn't let it sway her from her investigation. 'You invited Freddie for a drink because we've got something to celebrate?' she asked.

'Well, no. Freddie invited me. Yesterday. But since we've got something to celebrate, I'm inviting you.'

'Oh.'

'It'll just be for an hour or so,' he said. 'Before he goes home to the long-suffering Mrs Freddie. But he might be able to tell us something in advance of the report. You don't mind, do you?'

She shook her head, smiling. She liked Freddie. And she liked the fact that he constantly chatted her up, and that this irritated Lloyd, which served him right for being at times so excessively irritating himself.

She gave him the gist of her interview with Caroline Knight.

'Do you think Sam's our man?' he asked.

Judy shrugged. 'We only know as much as she's prepared to say. Women do sometimes protect men in these circumstances.'

'You concede that, do you?' said Lloyd.

'And she was careful to say that she wasn't all that keen on him,' Judy said, ignoring him.

'We'll talk to Waters. Tell him we know what sort of mood he was in when he left Mrs Knight. That might rattle him a bit.'

'Any chance of eating first?' Judy asked, alarmed that he might abandon lunch in favour of talking to Waters. She had to get the chance to tell him, or she would have to go round with this lead weight inside her all day, and she didn't think she could stand that.

'You bet,' he said. 'I'm told there's a pub round here does a very good lunch. We'll tackle Mr Waters after some food.'

She wished he wasn't in such a good mood, as they went back along the lane to the car park through a cold snow-filled rain that saturated everything.

'It's all right,' he said, as they drove out of the gates. 'We won't get lost – I got directions from Bob Sandwell.'

They didn't get lost, and already she could see the pub sign. Lloyd would soon be off-duty and available to be Spoken To. He pulled into the car park, which was up a three-in-one gradient, and parked the car in an impossible space, with an ease that Judy always envied.

Judy's stomach churned. Music played at a pleasant level, and they were in a private, intimate booth for two in the dining-room. The place was full; people must come for miles, Judy thought, so the food must be good. She wouldn't know, as she pushed it about her plate, but he was enjoying it, and she had no desire to ruin his lunch into the bargain. She would have to wait until he had finished.

As the coffee arrived, Lloyd beamed at her. 'I was talking to the chief super this morning,' he said.

Please, please, don't let it be a long story, she thought. He was deliberately not asking her about Michael. Saving it up, in the same way as he opened all his bills and junk mail before he opened real letters.

'Lloyd, I —'

'And he said to me, "Lloyd," he said, "is Sergeant Hill really a left-wing feminist lesbian from Islington, or is someone having me on?" And I said, "Someone is having you on, sir. She's a left-wing feminist lesbian from Southwark." '

Judy managed a smile. She wasn't going to be able to stop him, so she might as well let him tell his story. 'I take it that the bit about talking to the chief super is true,' she said. 'Let's go from there.'

'He asked if last night was just a gut reaction on your part, or were you a bit political about it.'

'He actually said "gut reaction"?' she asked.

Lloyd smiled. 'He did. Don't blame me. So I said that you held very firm views on the treatment of rape. And he said that he might give you an argument on some of the finer points, but that he just wanted to be sure it wasn't a feminist stand.'

Judy frowned a little.

'And then he said that they were thinking of transferring you to Malworth, instead of to Barton.'

Her face fell. 'Barton would be more exciting,' she said. 'I thought they needed a DI.'

'They do. But they can have any old DI. At Malworth, you would be heading up a small CID section, and second-in-command of the station. Congratulations.' He smiled. 'He said some stuff about ability and leadership and courage – but you don't want to hear all that.'

'Well,' she said.

'That's it? Well?' He called the waiter, and gave him his credit card. 'They're trying you out, Judy. Seeing how you handle command. Before I know where I am you'll be back here as my superintendent.'

'That'll be the day,' she said, and took a breath. 'Well, maybe I should give you my news now.' And she told him, watching him go from delighted to disbelieving.

'Judy – leaving him means that you move *out*!'

The waiter came back, and Lloyd signed the chit angrily. She had known it would be like this. She waited for the waiter to go away again. 'Lloyd, Michael and I, have been married for over ten years, and this is the first favour he's asked.'

'So of course you have to grant it.'

'Yes!' she said hotly.

'Why, for God's sake? He's going to try to hang on to you! You know that as well as I do! What sort of basis will it be on? A sort of *ménage à* trots? "I'm off now, dear, just popping over to Lloyd's. I'll be back in time to make your hot chocolate." I know you! You'll still be looking at your bloody watch!'

His voice was growing louder; Judy could see people look round the corners of the other booths.

'He's given you a safety-net. You're not going to leave him.'

'Of course I am,' she said.

'He knows you'll never go if he can stop you now.'

'It's not like that,' she protested in an agonised whisper. She should have known not to embark on this in a public place. 'It's – it's difficult,' she said. 'I can't just walk out like I was going to.' And now she would have to betray Michael, too. She had to explain. 'I didn't realise how much he needs me.'

'And I don't?'

'You've got me.'

Lloyd got up and left.

Judy looked under her eyelashes at the people who tried not to look as though they were looking at her. The waiter brought back the credit card, and left it on the table.

With slow determination, Judy finished her coffee, picked up his credit card, left a tip, thanked the staff, and walked out into the car park. He was still there.

Judy got in, and neither of them spoke until she finally broke the deadlock.

'I owe him this much,' she said stubbornly. 'It's only until June.'

He didn't even look at her, as he started the car, and lunchtime was over.

They drove in silence back to the school; this time, Lloyd swept angrily past the NO ROAD TRAFFIC BEYOND THIS POINT notice, and parked right in front of the building.

Back up in Treadwell's office, Lloyd made phone calls while Judy went over her notes. That pen was odd, she thought. Why wasn't it reported? Maybe she should show it to a few people. She took it out again, and looked at it more closely.

'Waters,' Lloyd said, as he hung up the phone. 'Let's talk to him.'

'Just what I was going to say,' she said, and followed Lloyd out into the corridor.

They frowned at one another as the noises reached them from one of the classrooms, the door of which stood ajar; a strange scraping sound, and a woman's voice uttering mild, slightly breathless oaths. Lloyd went first, pushing open the door, and they watched

Caroline Knight continue her argument with the easel she was setting up until it was finally upright; she straightened up, and saw them.

'You win on points,' said Lloyd.

'Were you looking for someone?' she asked, smiling.

'No,' said Lloyd. 'We've commandeered the headmaster's office.'

'That's the lot, Mrs Knight.'

Judy turned to see the head boy again. She still couldn't remember his name.

'Hello, Sergeant Hill,' he said politely.

'Hello,' she said. 'It's . . .'

'Matthew,' he said, with a smile.

'Of course. I'm sorry.'

He put down the briefcase he carried, and shrugged on the expensively casual leather jacket that lay over one of the chairs, his elegance fully restored. He still reminded her of someone.

'Matthew's helping me set up a project,' said Mrs Knight.

'He might have done better helping you set up the easel,' said Lloyd.

She laughed.

'I locked the door,' said Matthew, handing her a key. 'Thank you,' she said. 'You've been a great help, Matthew.'

It was as he turned to leave that Judy finally nailed it. Michael. He reminded her of Michael. Articulate, easy with people, self-confident. And vulnerable. She remembered the bewildered, angular boy who had stared at the police activity, and thought of Michael, a little boy who had lost his mother in Woolworth's. Matthew and Michael, she thought. Hebrew names. Like Sam's, like her own. She knew a lot about names since trying to discover Lloyd's dark secret. She glanced at him, struck by a new thought. Was it *biblical*, this frightful name?

'We'll let you get on,' Lloyd said to Mrs Knight. He turned to go, then turned back. 'You wouldn't know where we'd be likely to find Sam Waters at this time of day, would you?'

She looked at her watch. 'Well,' she said, with a look that suggested a private joke, 'it's just possible that you'll find him in the car park.'

Half past two. Sam came to the conclusion that Caroline was not going to meet him.

He got out of the car just as another car pulled in, containing the chief inspector and his sidekick. Good legs, he noticed, as Sergeant Hill emerged from the car into the fine snow that had again begun to fall. In fact, she was all right, was Detective Sergeant Hill.

'Mr Waters,' said Lloyd. 'Just the man we want to see.' He walked up to him. 'Perhaps we could go inside?'

'Perhaps you couldn't,' said Sam. 'What do you want this time? Found tell-tale strands of navy blue velvet on the corpse?'

Lloyd blinked a little against the rain. 'Does Mrs Hamlyn's death touch you at all?' he asked.

Sam shook his head, then nodded to indicate a concession. 'As a facility, she will be sorely missed,' he said. 'By some.'

The sergeant held up a plastic bag. 'Have you ever seen this?' she asked.

He walked slowly up to her, and looked at the pen enclosed in the bag, his eyes widening in mock excitement. 'Is it a *clue*?' he asked breathlessly. 'Don't tell me – it's the murder weapon, isn't it?'

Lloyd came up to him again, his hands deep in the pockets of his coat. 'What do you suppose the murder weapon was, Mr Waters?' he asked.

'I know this bit,' said Sam. 'I say I didn't kill her by stabbing her with a poisoned fountain pen, and you say how do I know she was poisoned. Right?'

'No,' said the sergeant. 'I say how do you know it's a fountain pen?'

Sam's eyebrows rose, then he laughed. 'All right,' he said. 'For that, you can come in out of the cold.'

Sam let them into the flat, where the gas fire was belting out heat. He snapped it off and invited them to sit down, pleased that

Sergeant Hill was there. He was going to have a little fun with the chief inspector's sense of fitness. And she was nice to look at. He wondered if Newby had even noticed her last night. She was his type: dark and slim, like Caroline. But Newby had been in a bad way, and none too comfortable, with the police there. Sam would be willing to bet that Newby couldn't even say what Sergeant Hill looked like.

'It's my pen,' he said. 'It went missing – but I don't suppose you're going to believe that.'

'When did it go missing?' the sergeant asked.

'Last night,' said Sam. 'I know I had it at dinner. I had to put some finishing touches to my speech. I thought I'd left it on the table.'

'Who was at your table?'

Sam grinned. 'Mr and Mrs Treadwell, Mr and Mrs Hamlyn, myself, some boring old fart of a governor and his good lady wife – I don't know their names, but I've no doubt Barry Treadwell does. Failing that, try Caroline Knight – she invited them.'

'When did you notice it had gone?'

'When I put my jacket on to leave the Hamlyns' flat,' he said. 'I had been visiting Caroline,' he added, by way of explanation. 'It wasn't there, so I looked outside for it, but it was too dark.'

'Where did you look for it?'

'I took a walk back across the playing-field,' said Sam.

'Are you sure you were still in the Hamlyns' flat when you noticed it had gone?' asked Lloyd.

'Yes,' said Sam.

'What made you notice?'

'I had had it in the inside pocket,' Sam explained, with great patience. 'The jacket was over a chair, with the inside pocket visible, and the pen wasn't there. Why in God's name do you want to know that?'

'It seems to me that it could have been when you were changing your clothes that you noticed the pen was gone,' said Lloyd. 'You know, transferring things from one set of clothes to the other.'

Sam frowned. 'Well, it wasn't,' he said. 'And so what, if it had been?'

'Then we could be examining the wrong clothes,' said Lloyd.

Christ. Sam went into the bedroom, picked up the jeans and sweater that still lay on the floor where he'd left them, and threw them down on to the sofa. 'I was wearing the dinner-jacket when I looked for the pen,' he said. 'It started to pour down while I was out – that's why it was still damp. I thought you were supposed to be a detective? But you're welcome to waste your time on these if you like.'

Lloyd was looking out of the window, his back to him. 'Thank you, Mr Waters,' he said. 'Of course, you are under no obligation. I appreciate your co-operation.'

Sam offered a suggestion as to what Lloyd could do with the clothes. 'Or get the sergeant here to do it for you,' he added. 'I'm sure she knows her way around.'

Lloyd turned from the window, his face dark and angry, as Sam stared at him defiantly. Sergeant Hill had taken it in her stride. Pity. He'd much rather ruffle her feathers – Lloyd was too easy.

'Well, Sergeant,' said Lloyd. 'The thefts are your province, I believe. Perhaps you could deal with that now?'

Sam felt the chill as she looked at Lloyd, and stood up. 'Yes, sir,' she said. 'If you'll excuse me, Mr Waters.'

'That's it,' said Sam. 'Put 'em in their place.'

She didn't exactly slam the door. She shut it very firmly. Sam grinned.

'Why didn't you tell us before that you went to see Caroline Knight?' Lloyd asked, in a sudden and disorientating change of subject.

Sam sighed. 'Where were *you* between ten and midnight last night?' he asked.

'Just answer the question,' Lloyd said wearily. 'You left the Hall at nine-thirty. What did you do then?'

'Before or after I raped and murdered Diana Hamlyn?' Sam asked earnestly.

'She was very probably raped and quite definitely murdered,' said Lloyd. 'It may be a joke to you, Mr Waters, but no one else finds it very funny.'

Sam smiled. 'I see it's turned into very probable rape,' he said. 'Very improbable would be a more suitable description – I'm aware of your interest in such things.'

'Mrs Knight has told us what happened between you and her last night, so you had better stop trying to be clever,' said Lloyd.

Sam felt as if he had been punched. 'The bitch,' he said, almost to himself, then looked at the chief inspector, waiting for him to say something. 'Nothing happened!' he shouted, when Lloyd remained silent. 'I misread the signals, that's all. I was more bothered about the bloody pen than I was about Mrs Knight, I can tell you that.'

'All right. You failed to find the pen. Then what did you do?'

'Came back here, changed my clothes, and went out.'

'Where did you go?'

'I went to a club in Stansfield.'

'What time did you leave here?' asked Lloyd.

'I don't know!'

'Just tell me,' Lloyd said wearily. 'A straight answer wouldn't go wrong, Mr Waters.'

'After eleven. Ten, quarter past. I don't know. I wasn't checking my watch.'

'Did anyone see you leave?'

Sam shrugged.

'Mrs Knight thinks someone was watching her last night. From the fire-escape – around eleven.'

'Oh – I'm a Peeping Tom now? The woman's paranoid, that's her trouble.'

'Did you see anyone hanging around?' Lloyd asked, raising his voice slightly.

'No.'

'I don't suppose this club has a name?'

Sam told him, and Lloyd wrote it down. He gathered up the clothes. 'You left Mrs Knight at ten past ten or so. Where exactly were you between then and eleven-fifteen?'

'Here, mostly.'

'Alone?' He walked over to the window, his back to Sam.

'Alone.'

'But you looked for the pen before you came back here.'

'Correct.'

'Did you see Mrs Hamlyn while you were out?'

'I didn't have to step over her corpse,' Sam said. 'If that's any help.'

'Did you see Mrs Hamlyn?' Lloyd repeated, getting angry.

'Yes, I saw her.'

'Why didn't you tell us that?'

Sam smiled. 'You didn't ask until now,' he said.

'When you saw Mrs Hamlyn,' Lloyd said, turning slowly to face him, 'did you speak to her?'

'No,' said Sam. 'She wasn't alone.'

'You saw her *with* someone, and didn't bother mentioning that to us?' he asked, his voice low. 'Who was she with?'

'I've no idea,' said Sam. 'I just saw his back view for a few seconds. They were going into the Barn. I can tell you what he was wearing,' he said. 'But it won't narrow the field much.'

Lloyd nodded. 'Dinner-jackets,' he said. 'Unfortunately, they weren't all as distinctive as yours.'

Sam looked at him for a moment. 'I didn't see a dinner-jacket,' he said.

Lloyd looked up sharply. 'What the hell did you see, then?' he shouted.

Sam smiled. 'I saw a school blazer,' he said.

They were in a burger bar in the Square – the centre of Stansfield's main shopping area. Outside, the afternoon light faded, and people walked, heads down against the incessant hard sleet which was turning inexorably back into snow; inside, they talked and laughed, and ate and drank, complained about the weather and their children's inability to keep still, or their unwillingness to eat what they had ordered.

'Would you like me to take that back?' Caroline asked, nodding at the box on the seat beside Philip.

'Sorry?' he said.

Pushing up the folds of her skirt . . . .

He replayed her question with difficulty. 'Oh, no,' he said. 'Thank you.' He glanced at the box. He didn't know what to do about it, really. Did they just accept that things might happen to hired clothes?

His fingers moving over nylon, finding bare skin . . . .

She had seen him just as he was getting into the car to come here. He mustn't drive, she'd said. She would take him to the town. She was going anyway.

The muscles of her thigh growing taut to his touch; the brush of silk on his hand . . . .

'It's just that it is a bit slippery out there,' she said. 'I could take it and meet you back here – unless you've something else to do.'

Touching her through the thin material . . . .

'No,' he said. 'But it's all right – I'll take it myself.'

Pressing his hand between her thighs; her breath catching in her throat . . . .

'If you're sure,' she said. 'We'll meet back at the car, shall we? In what – ten, fifteen minutes?'

'Better make it fifteen,' he said, reaching for his stick.

She buttoned up her coat as she got to the door, shivering as she stepped out, and they went their separate ways.

They just took the box; didn't even open it. Philip escaped from the men's outfitters, and walked cautiously over paving that seemed designed to catch him out. His back ached, his leg felt numb.

She had locked the car; sensible precaution. Things happened when you didn't. He stood for some time in the wind-driven snow that drenched the top deck of the car park.

'Philip; I'm sorry!' She came hurrying over to him. 'Did I lock you out?'

'It's all right,' he said. 'I've just arrived.'

It was getting worse; he could barely bend to get into the car.

'Philip – have you got a doctor in Stansfield?' she asked.

'Not yet,' he answered, as the pain made him close his eyes until it subsided.

'You should see someone,' she said, as he finally sat beside her.

'I'm fine.'

And he was; he had no stiffness, no aches, no gripping pain as he began all over again, starting with her coat. He never needed to undress; magically, his clothes disappeared. No slow, painful process of removing them. But he removed hers, item by item.

Slipping the blouse off; putting a hand to her hair, releasing it, letting it fall over her bared shoulders. Unfastening her brassiere; drawing it away. Touching the small round breasts, his fingers moving delicately over the silk-soft skin; removing her skirt, her slip, revealing French knickers . . . .

Not Marks & Spencer briefs.

'Would you like to come up for a drink?' she asked, as she pulled into the school car park.

Drawing her close, feeling firm buttocks under the soft, soft silk . . ..

'That would be nice,' he said, wondering if he would manage the stairs.

She stopped the car, and he had to work out how to get out of it again. As he planted his stick on the ground, and heaved himself up from the seat, his eye met a faintly familiar figure. He looked up to see the police officers who had arrived with Sam the night before.

'Mr Newby?' the man said.

Chief Inspector Lloyd. Chief Inspector Lloyd. His mantra.

'Could we have a word, do you think?'

Philip turned to Caroline. 'Sorry,' he said.

'That's all right.' She smiled. 'Perhaps later?'

Later, he would be even more stiff. Later, he would be frightened of the stairs, and of her. 'Perhaps,' he said.

She ran up to her flat. If he could run; if he could run after her, chasing her, catching her. They would laugh, and hug . . . .

He opened the door, and the flat was empty. Sam had turned the fire off. Damn the man – didn't he ever feel the cold? Of course he did. But it was macho not to care. Philip picked up the big box of matches he had purchased as a hint, and addressed himself to the task of getting down far enough to light the jets.

'I'll do it,' the girl said, smiling.

'I can do it!'

She looked a little startled. 'Sorry,' she said.

'No. I'm . . . You're right.' Philip handed her the box of matches. 'I can't do anything much,' he muttered through his teeth.

The fire's glow lit the darkening room. 'What do you want?' Philip asked.

'You were at the ball last night, Mr Newby.'

Philip nodded. Chief Inspector Lloyd, Chief Inspector Lloyd, he thought, as the pain gripped his back.

'Why did you leave?'

Chief Inspector Lloyd, Chief . . . 'Sorry?' he said, too busy fighting the pain to hear what he had said. 'What did you ask me?'

'Can you tell us why you left early last night?'

'I was sick,' Philip said. 'I have to take pills. The doctor told me not to drink too much, but I did, and now I know why I shouldn't.'

The chief inspector nodded. The woman was taking out a notebook.

'What time did you leave the Hall?' she asked.

'I don't know. I was just about to throw up.'

'We've been told twenty past ten,' said Lloyd. 'Would you agree?'

Philip nodded.

'Mrs Hamlyn left at quarter past. Did you see her at all?'

'No,' said Philip, as his fists clenched. Carefully, deliberately, he relaxed his hands. 'Not in the gents'.'

'How long were you in there?'

'About half an hour,' Philip said, blinking with pain. He shifted his feet slightly, in the hope that that would ease the ache, but it didn't. 'It was busy, with the speeches having finished. I waited until everyone was gone before I came out. And I know what time that was. It was ten to eleven.'

'What did you do then?'

'I came here.'

Sam came in then, and acknowledged Lloyd and Sergeant Hill. 'Are you going to take a look at his dinner-jacket, or is that reserved for me?' he asked.

'I've taken it back to the shop.' Philip twisted round to look at Sam; it was a mistake. He held his breath for a moment, as his back seized.

'Highly suspicious, wouldn't you say, Mr Lloyd?'

'You left the Hall at ten to eleven, and came directly here?' Lloyd repeated, ignoring Sam.

'Yes,' said Philip. He felt the pain subside; he turned slowly to face them.

Sam walked into his line of vision, tutting, shaking his head, as though Philip had played a bad shot. He sat on the sofa, smiling slightly. Philip stared at him.

'Mr Waters says he was here alone until after eleven,' said the chief inspector.

Philip's head began to clear a little, and his heartbeat slowly returned to normal. Maybe he could sit down. He moved towards the sofa, and leaned heavily on the unfamiliar stick, lowering himself carefully down.

'I didn't come in,' he said. 'I didn't want company.'

'Where did you go?'

Philip thought for an instant before he answered. 'To the car park,' he said. 'I sat in the car.'

Sam tutted again.

Lloyd turned to him. 'You have something to say, Mr Waters?'

'His car was in the car park,' said Sam. 'He wasn't in it.'

'Mr Newby?'

'Sam must have just missed me,' said Philip, feeling flustered. 'I didn't stay in the car. I took a walk.'

'Weak,' said Sam. 'They don't like people who don't behave the way they think they should. They always do very definite things at very definite times and make a note of the witnesses present.'

'Wasn't it raining?' asked the sergeant.

'That's why you're so stiff,' said Sam archly. 'Walking about in the pouring rain like that.'

'Mr Newby,' said Lloyd. 'Did you see anyone in the car park?'

'Sam. I saw him leave. And – and maybe someone else.'

'Maybe?'

Philip couldn't be sure. He could have sworn, at the time, but, then, he had had a lot to drink. 'I was in the car with the window down,' he said. 'And I thought I heard someone on the fire-escape.' He looked up. 'There seemed to be a figure, but it might have been a shadow, or something. That's why I got out. That's why I was walking about in the rain,' he added, addressing himself to the sergeant. He found himself speaking almost at dictation pace as she noted everything down.

The chief inspector was interested. 'What did this person look like?' he asked.

'Oh – I don't know. It was too dark. It was just a movement – a figure. Maybe nothing at all.'

'Could it have been, say, Mr Waters?' the sergeant asked. 'Or me? Or the chief inspector?'

Philip frowned, then realised what she was doing. If he had seen someone at all, he must have got an impression, however fleeting a glimpse. But he couldn't be sure he'd really seen something. Maybe he was just giving himself an excuse. He looked at the assembled company. They were all different shapes and sizes. It couldn't have been Sam. Or the chief inspector.

'It could have been you,' he said to the sergeant. 'I thought it was one of the boys, larking about.'

'What did you do?'

'Nothing,' he said quickly. 'There was no one there when I got to the fire-escape. I thought I must have imagined it.'

They didn't comment; they thanked him for his time, and left.

Sam stood up when they had gone. 'Maybe we should do a runner before they stitch us both up,' he said.

Philip thought it was the mode of speech that probably irritated him most of all. Waters had been educated at a hideously expensive public school before getting a good degree at Oxford; he assumed a pseudo-cockney accent, unless he was rattled, when it would return to the received pronunciation which he more naturally employed.

'Maybe you should go and see your girlfriend,' Sam said, opening a can. 'If you can get up the stairs.'

Philip frowned slightly. 'Why?' he asked.

'She seemed a bit upset when I left.' Sam smiled. 'Must have been something I said.'

Slowly, Philip pulled himself up from the sofa. 'Like what?' he asked.

The smile remained. 'I may have forgotten my manners,' he said. 'What are you going to do, Newby? Hit me?'

Philip didn't speak.

'Now's your chance, son. She needs a shoulder to cry on. Nothing wrong with your shoulders, is there?'

Chapter Five

Caroline couldn't stop the tears. They'd started while Sam was still there, and that had made him worse.

She stared at the door when she heard the knock. Had he remembered some obscenities that he hadn't used? 'Who is it?' she asked, her voice betraying the tears.

'It's Philip.'

Philip. Come for his drink. Come to stare at her with his hungry eyes while he pretended to carry on a conversation. She didn't know why she had asked him up for a drink in the first place. She opened the door.

'What's he been doing?' Philip asked, limping badly as he came in.

She wiped away the tears, but they still kept coming. 'Didn't he tell you?' she asked, closing the door.

'He said he'd upset you,' said Philip. 'Why? What did he say to you?'

Caroline smiled, despite the tears. 'I really wouldn't like to repeat any of it,' she said.

Philip looked baffled. 'What's it all about?' he asked.

Caroline shook her head, and wiped the tears again. This time they stayed away.

'Tell me,' he said. 'You can delete the expletives.'

'That would leave a few pronouns and the odd conjunction,' she said.

There was, of course, a word for people like her. There were, as it turned out, several words. And they might not have shocked her, hurt her so much if he had been railing at her, shouting his graphic abuse; but he hadn't raised his voice once.

The gist was that she had caused the police to suspect him owing to an overestimation of her desirability, that she had nothing that other women didn't have, and that what she did have was less than tantalising. He had not been reduced to a frenzy of sexual frustration because she had denied him her body, and she was deluding herself if she thought that she was capable of inspiring such a thing in anyone other than the sexual inadequate whose sick fantasies' – given vivid expression – fed her own.

'Let's forget it,' she said, as Philip, after much mental preparation for the effort, sat down at last. 'I promised you a drink.'

She poured two glasses from the bottle of wine she had bought in the town to give herself both a reason for being there and a drink to offer him.

'Won't you even tell me what it was about?' he asked, as she handed him his glass.

She sat beside him. 'Maybe he was just telling me some home truths,' she said.

Perhaps Sam wouldn't have upset her so much if she didn't feel so frightened, all the time. Someone had been watching her, perhaps whoever raped Diana. It hadn't been her imagination. And she had thought at the time that it was Sam. She shivered.

Concerned eyes looked into hers, and then he gave a little smile. 'Sam', he said, clinking his glass with hers, 'is a fake from head to toe. He wouldn't know a home truth from a home perm. If he happened to hit on one or two, then it was because he used machine-gun tactics, and he had to hit something.'

That was when she knew why what he had said about Philip had been the most hurtful part; that was what had made her cry. Because every now and then she could see the man that Philip was, behind the constant pain and the frustration about which Sam had been so crudely eloquent.

The Philip that Andrew had told her about; the Philip who lived his life and let other people live theirs, the Philip to whom people turned if they had a problem. Who always had some girl in love with him, who was always going to write a novel, and who had once described himself as living life in the bus lane. She smiled at the memory; Philip asked why she was smiling, and she told him.

He laughed. 'I've never understood yuppies,' he said. 'Screaming down a car phone in your Porsche and giving yourself ulcers doesn't sound like fun to me.'

'Why are you teaching at a school full of embryonic yuppies?' she asked. The wine was beginning to make her feel better. Philip was, too; for the first time, they were just talking.

'I liked the idea of being in the countryside,' he said. 'And of working with Andrew—' He broke off, his face slightly pink. 'Sorry,' he said.

'It's all right,' she said. 'I like talking about him.'

He nodded. 'And maybe I hoped I could get one or two of the boys to smell the roses.'

'Are you succeeding?'

'I have quite high hopes of Matthew Cawston,' said Philip. 'He likes reading – it's a start.'

'Andrew liked Matthew,' said Caroline. 'I'm never very sure that I do.'

'What's wrong with him?' Philip asked.

'I always feel as though he follows me about,' she said, and then wondered what Sam would have to say about that. 'He *does* follow me about,' she said defiantly, as though Sam were there.

'I don't blame him,' was all Philip said.

'And he's a bit too smooth,' she said. 'Too charming.'

Philip grinned. 'Well, there you are,' he said. 'That's one complaint you can't have about Sam.'

'There must be a happy medium,' she laughed.

'There is,' he said. 'Me.' He smiled at her for a moment without speaking. Then his face grew serious. 'Do the police really suspect Sam?' he asked.

'He's done his best to make himself seem suspicious,' Caroline said. 'It was only because they were asking about him that I ever told them about—' She broke off.

'About what?' he asked gently.

'Oh – I just . . . .' She could feel herself begin to blush. At the memory, at Sam's subsequent thoughts on the matter. 'Sam made a pass at me last night,' she said. 'I encouraged him, I suppose. Well – not really. But I didn't discourage him. And then I . . . .' She smiled, gave a little shrug. 'I would have said that I let him down, but he says it was no let-down at all, so I'm overestimating myself, as he pointed out.'

And it was true, she conceded, that the discovery that his pen was missing had made Sam even angrier than she had; she had put it down to sheer frustration, but Sam had assured her during his visit that it was because the pen meant more to him than anything she had to offer. Or a colourful phrase to that effect.

Philip put down his glass. 'This morning you said that you and he weren't involved.'

'We're not,' Caroline said quickly. 'I don't even *like* him!'

So why had she encouraged him at all? She waited, but Philip didn't ask the question.

'I know it makes no sense,' she said. 'But it's the truth.'

'I'd better be going,' Philip said suddenly, arranging the stick to take his weight.

'Philip – it's the truth. There's nothing between me and Sam.'

'None of my business if there is,' he said, grunting with the strain as he heaved himself to his feet.

'I want you to understand,' she said.

'Why?' But he sat down again, with a little grunt of pain. Caroline wished he would see a doctor; and maybe Sam was right, she thought. Maybe she was attracted to Philip because they were two of a kind.

They had both been damaged in an accident that was none of their making.

'I still haven't told you about my further enquiries into the thefts,' Judy said.

They had met up at Lloyd's car, the atmosphere between them frostier than the weather.

Lloyd grunted, uninterested, as they drove through the

interminable snow to the main building. That was the second rime she'd tried to give him chapter and verse on the thefts. All right, so she was going to make a federal case out of it. Let her. He hadn't wanted her to stay there, with Waters making remarks. It wasn't that he had one rule for Judy and another for other officers, he told himself. Her presence was hampering the interview, that was all. But he had wanted to annoy her. It was childish, but there it was.

'We've got a murder inquiry,' he said. 'I'm not interested in petty theft right now.' He pushed open the door at the top of the steps, standing to one side to let Judy through. Their footsteps on the wooden flooring echoed round the emptiness of the school building. But it wasn't like any other school Lloyd had ever come across.

'Is the entire teaching profession comprised of weirdos, or do they just come here to die?' he asked, as they climbed the stairs to Treadwell's office.

'Ssh,' said Judy. 'Someone might be in.'

'Would they care? Most of them seem quite proud of it.'

'Well,' said Judy, 'I did some checking when I had to come about the thefts in the first place.' The sentence was accompanied by a glare in his direction. 'And it costs less to send your child here, and it pays less to teach here, than at any other school of comparable size. So . . . .' She shrugged. 'You get what you pay for, I suppose. Though it has as good if not better an academic record as the others.'

Lloyd toyed with the grammar lesson, but decided that it was too advanced, and too likely to get him a smack in the mouth. He wished he hadn't snapped at her. He wished he hadn't done a lot of things.

'So weirdos make good teachers?' he said.

'Looks like it,' she said. 'But, to be fair, Sam Waters is the only out-and-out weirdo, isn't he?'

'Is he?' said Lloyd, pushing Treadwell's open door. 'What about Hamlyn?'

A man rose as they came in. Not tall; thin, bespectacled, well into his fifties, possibly sixties. 'Mr Lloyd?' he said.

Lloyd, startled, nodded. 'I don't believe we've—'

'No,' he said, a little shyly. 'Robert Hamlyn.' He extended a hand.

Oh, God. Well, nothing to do about it now. Lloyd grasped the outstretched hand more warmly than he might otherwise have done. He had expected a much younger man. 'Mr Hamlyn,' he said, 'I am very sorry about your wife. We're doing all we can.'

He nodded, and looked down at the floor.

'This is Sergeant Hill,' said Lloyd. 'We didn't want to bother you with questions until you felt up to it.'

'I realise', he said, lifting his eyes with difficulty, 'that you will have a great many questions. But – I would like to say something to you first, if I may.'

'Of course,' Lloyd said, sitting behind the desk. 'Would you have any objection to my sergeant taking notes?'

'None,' said Hamlyn, but he still stood.

Lloyd watched Judy become aware that Hamlyn wasn't going to sit down until she did. She took a chair from the wall, and she and Hamlyn sat down in unison.

'People here', said Hamlyn, in his quiet, clear voice, 'find – found – my relationship with my wife difficult to understand.' He smiled a little. 'Perhaps I should say *even* people here,' he said. 'I couldn't help overhearing your conversation.'

Judy shifted a little in her chair. Lloyd nodded slightly. 'I'm sorry,' he said, there not being much more he could say.

'No need for apology,' said Hamlyn. 'Sam Waters calls us flotsam and jetsam – you call us weirdos. People have a need to label others.'

Lloyd took a breath, intending to defend himself, until he realised he really didn't have a defence.

Hamlyn continued. 'And it's true,' he said. 'In a way. The school has a – well, policy would be too definite a word – a tendency, let's say, to recruit from the ranks of non-career teachers, to put it politely. It's a matter of economy as far as the school is concerned, but it does have an odd side-effect. You see, sometimes those who aim for the top forget what they originally set out to do. By employing those who would be rejected by a more rigid system, the school gets – as your sergeant said – as good a result as schools charging several times the fee.'

Judy wasn't taking notes, but surely she should be, Lloyd thought. Wasn't this a lecture? Lloyd hoped that Hamlyn would get to the point in the end.

'And I am one such,' he said. 'I love what I teach. And I love being able to teach my way. Not teaching by numbers.'

There was a pause, but Lloyd knew that it was still not his turn to speak.

'I didn't become a teacher until I was almost forty. I was a bachelor, I was in industry, and one day I realised how much I hated it. They needed teachers, in those days, and I went back to college. I started out teaching in a private day-school, twenty years ago.'

The man spoke like a book. In neat paragraphs, with a space left between them. It was like listening to the radio.

'Diana was fourteen years old when I met her.'

Lloyd's eyes widened slightly, and he refrained from catching Judy's.

Hamlyn's hands were clasped in front of him. They twisted constantly and nervously, belying the calm delivery. 'It was wrong, obviously. I didn't even want it to be like that, but Diana . . . .' He hunched his shoulders slightly.

'Well, it was what she wanted, and I didn't want to lose her.'

Humbert Humbert lives, thought Lloyd. Lolita, on the other hand . . . .

'We married when she was eighteen,' he said. 'We ran away; at the age of forty-three, I eloped with an eighteen-year-old girl, Mr Lloyd. It doesn't do a lot for your career chances.'

Lloyd could see that it wouldn't.

'I think it had probably started by then. Her . . . infidelity.' He looked up. 'I am assuming that someone – if not everyone – has told you about Diana,' he said. 'I was the first. But I was very far from being the last.'

'Someone did mention that she might have had a bit of a problem,' said Judy carefully, rescuing Lloyd.

Hamlyn nodded. 'I shudder to think how she would have lived if she hadn't married me,' he said, then looked away again. 'But, then, she might not have died.' He gave a long sigh. 'She couldn't help herself,' he said. 'She was perfectly ordinary in other respects.' He smiled sadly. 'She was sensible about everything,' he said. 'Except men.'

This time Lloyd couldn't resist sneaking a look at Judy. Baffled brown eyes looked back for an instant, before returning to her notebook.

'When I could no longer pretend that it wasn't happening, we had rows. We separated, even. But we weren't happy apart. You see' – the hands clasped and unclasped, the fingers twisting round one another – 'we were very fond of each other,' he said. 'But I was never very keen on . . . the physical . . .' His hands came together in a helpless little mime. 'In a way, I think that that's what Diana liked about me.'

Lloyd became aware that his mouth was slightly open.

'And I realised that I simply wasn't being logical. I was acting the aggrieved husband. I was doing what I thought other people would do. What other people expected me to do. But she needed me, and I needed her. So, we settled for a platonic relationship, which we both enjoyed very much. What Diana did was no concern of mine.'

Lloyd nodded, trying to look as if he came across this every day.

'It had begun to concern me – that is – I was concerned about Diana, with all the talk of disease, and so on. But other than that . . . .' He shook his head.

'Mr Hamlyn—' Lloyd began, but Hamlyn moved his hand just enough to indicate that he had not finished. Lloyd glanced at Judy again, but she was steadfastly writing in her notebook.

'I understand', he said, 'that you have been questioning Sam Waters about my wife's death.'

Lloyd was taken by surprise at the sudden return to the matter in hand.

'I – we – are talking to everyone, Mr Hamlyn.'

'But you are paying very close attention to Sam.'

'I'm sorry – I can't . . . .'

'No,' said Hamlyn. 'Of course not. But I feel that I may inadvertently have caused you to suspect Sam rather more definitely than you should.' He paused. 'Last night, at dinner, I deliberately indicated that I believed Sam was with Diana.'

Lloyd scratched his forehead. 'But you didn't believe that?' he asked, tentative for the first time that he could remember since childhood.

'I had no reason at all to think that he was with Diana. She was involved with him – but that was all over eighteen months ago. Sam ended it.'

Lloyd saw the little frown that came and went on Judy's brow.

'You *know* it was Sam who ended it?' he said.

'Yes.'

'Did – er – did Mrs Hamlyn talk to you about her relationships with – er – other . . .?' He tailed off, out of his depth.

'No,' Hamlyn said. 'But I'm afraid everyone knew about her new man, once they had been discovered together – and it isn't hard to tell when Sam is offended. Besides which, Diana simply wouldn't have ended it.'

'Mr Hamlyn,' Judy said, just as tentative as Lloyd had been. 'Forgive me. Would that have been the incident with the handyman?'

He nodded. 'All a bit Lady Chatterley, I'm afraid,' he said.

'Doesn't anyone do any work here?' Lloyd asked, unable to keep quiet any longer.

'The school wasn't open,' said Hamlyn, obviously feeling he had to defend what was left of the school's honour. 'It was during the summer break. And he wasn't a handyman, not really. He mended the odd broken window, but we have a caretaker for that. Treadwell got a two-year driving ban, and he needed a driver.' He gave a wry smile. 'I don't think he is ever entirely sober,' he said. 'That's *his* little drawback. We've all got one.'

Lloyd wasn't sure if he meant that it was a qualification for working at the school, or if he was being philosophical.

'Anyway, he called him a handyman on the books. The young man had a lot of time on his hands, and so did Diana.'

Lloyd lapsed into silence again.

'Treadwell discovered them – he was shocked, not unnaturally. Sacked the young man instantly. It was all round the school in no time, and Sam was far from pleased. I came in for some barely veiled comments about her availability, and just who was taking advantage of it – he presumably thought I didn't know what she was like. The truth was that Sam didn't know what she was like, and once he did it was all over, as far as he was concerned.'

Lloyd groped around for the question that would, he supposed, have a logical answer. But it was Alice-in-Wonderland logic. 'Then – Mr Hamlyn – why did you say that you thought she was with Sam?'

'I had my reasons. Childish revenge, I suppose. And I don't like Sam Waters. He was trying to make a fool of everyone, as usual, and I had no qualms about dropping him in it, as the boys would say. But I can't let you suspect him of murder because of what I said. I've no idea who she was with; I have no doubt that she was with someone. I suggest – purely from experience – that you look at the new man.'

'Mr Newby?' said Lloyd.

He nodded. 'That was the pattern,' he said. 'The handyman was new. Newby is the new man now, and Diana would doubtless be interested in him. He, of course, may not have reciprocated; it didn't follow that the new men were necessarily interested in her. But that was the sequence.'

Which number comes last in this sequence? Logic, thought Lloyd. It was all very logical. Judy would like it.

'Do you have any more questions you'd like to ask me?' Hamlyn said.

Yes, thought Lloyd. Why is a raven like a writing-desk, Mr Hamlyn?

'No,' was what he actually said. 'Thank you for being so frank with us.'

Hamlyn removed his glasses, putting them away in a pouch. 'I want you to find out who did that to Diana,' he said, standing up.

'We will,' said Lloyd quietly.

Hamlyn nodded, his eyes sad and trusting, like a basset hound's. 'I believe', he said to Judy, 'that some men buy their wives flowers when they have erred in some way. That's how I felt. As though I had been bought flowers.'

Lloyd waited until the door had closed before he looked at Judy. He sighed. 'Well?' he said.

'Wel.' She closed the notebook, her hand resting on it. 'And you think *our* relationship's irregular,' she said.

Lloyd put his hand on hers. 'Just not quite regular enough,' he said, and smiled. He didn't want to fight with her.

'He thinks we should lay off Sam,' Judy said, with her disconcerting ability to switch instantly back to work. Lloyd had made the rule; only Judy ever kept it.

'Mm,' he said, reluctantly following suit. He told Judy Sam's latest revelation. 'But he says he saw her with one of the boys,' he concluded.

'One of the *boys*?' repeated Judy.

'I don't know why that should surprise you, in this place,' said Lloyd.

'Which one?'

Lloyd shrugged. He wasn't at all sure that he believed Waters anyway. He told Judy what Sam said he had seen, and she looked thoughtful.

'What?' he asked. He knew that look. 'What is it?'

'The boys were allocated ladies to dance with,' she said. 'Who did Diana Hamlyn get?'

For once, he had got there before her. 'I've checked that out,' he said. 'The boy has a dozen witnesses to prove that he went back to his table, and stayed there all evening. Good thought, though,' he said, smiling.

Treadwell walked into the office, preventing Judy from giving vent to her obvious irritation at his patronising approbation.

'Did Robert Hamlyn see you?' he asked. 'I told him he should wait in here.'

'Yes, thank you,' said Lloyd.

'How well did you know Mrs Hamlyn?' Judy asked, as Treadwell looked through papers in a drawer.

'Not particularly well,' he said. 'We didn't have a lot in common.' He found what he was looking for and straightened up.

'It's been suggested that she might have been seeing one of the boys,' said Judy.

Treadwell stared at her for a long moment before speaking. 'By whom?' he demanded, when he did speak. 'Who made the suggestion?' He made an impatient noise. 'As if I need to ask! There's only one person in this school whose mind works like that.'

'Then you don't think that there's any truth in it?' said Lloyd.

'Of course there's no truth in it! She would never have *dreamed* of having a relationship with one of the boys. It's just the sort of foul suggestion I'd expect from Waters!'

'But you've just said you didn't know her very well,' Judy pointed out, her voice quiet and reasonable.

'I didn't,' Treadwell repeated. 'But I did tell you this morning, Sergeant. Mrs Hamlyn was good with the boys.' He shot a look at Lloyd. 'And I don't want any ribald comments,' he said.

Lloyd's eyes widened. 'You weren't going to get any, Mr Treadwell,' he said angrily.

'No,' he said, slightly flustered. 'I do beg your pardon – I'm obviously too used to dealing with Mr Waters. Mrs Hamlyn understood the boys. Youngsters have problems with everything from acne to arson – she could deal with them, better than anyone else here. The deputy head has responsibility for pastoral care, and I had no doubt that it would be Mrs Hamlyn who provided it. Robert's too logical to understand what adolescents are going through, and Mrs Hamlyn would have been an asset. The suggestion is monstrous.' He closed the drawer. 'If you could let me know when you've finished with my office,' he said, by way of a full stop.

'Won't be long now,' said Lloyd.

Treadwell left, and Lloyd looked out of the window at the starlit night, and the frost which was already forming. So much for spring. A silence fell; idly he flicked through the little brochure which advised new parents of their responsibilities. His eyebrows rose as he read; according to Judy, it was cheaper to send your offspring here than to anywhere else, and he would need a loan just to get the clothes required. A policeman's lot.

'About the thefts,' Judy said.

God. He'd thought they'd reached a truce. 'We've got a *murder* inquiry, Judy,' he said. But really, he should have known her better than that. He knew it as soon as he had spoken.

'You never know, sir,' she said. 'It might help with your murder inquiry, sir. If it's all right for me to get involved in important things, sir.'

'How could it help?' he asked, trying to ignore her.

'I follow orders,' she said. 'I was told to work on the thefts, so that's what I did.'

Lloyd knew he was walking into something, and he didn't know what.

'I finally got Treadwell to do me a list. And one item hasn't been recovered. Something he described as ... .' She turned back the pages of her notebook. 'Here it is – a "niblick" – wasn't accounted for. I didn't know what that was, so I asked him.'

Lloyd closed his eyes. 'I know what it is,' he groaned.

'It's an old golf-club,' she went on. 'It was in the Barn one minute, and gone the next, apparently. It was stolen just before Christmas.'

'Why didn't you tell me?' he demanded.

'I tried to. Twice. You said you weren't interested.'

'What have you done about it?'

'I've got people looking for it – what do you think I've done about it? I'm checking who was here and who wasn't. I've given the lab details of the sort of club it was. I've—'

Lloyd held up a hand. She had, of course, done everything that he would have done. He looked at her, feeling ashamed of the streak of pettiness that had made him pull rank in front of Waters, of all people. 'Sorry,' he said. 'I expect I deserved that.'

'Yes,' she said firmly. 'You did.'

Sam opened the door, and smiled. 'Well, well,' he said. 'It's the fuzz.'

Chief Inspector Lloyd eyed him with distaste but, then, almost everyone did.

'What now?' Sam asked. 'Come to arrest me, have you?'

They walked in without being asked, and Sam stood extravagantly to one side, his arm extending an invitation to the empty doorway.

'Mr Newby,' said Lloyd unexpectedly. 'Is he in?'

'No,' said Sam, closing the door. 'He's upstairs, visiting. And that required considerable fortitude, let me tell you, because going anywhere at all is excruciatingly difficult for our Mr Newby at the moment, never mind tackling a flight of stairs.' He sat down. 'But, then, he lusts after our Mrs Knight.'

'Do you have another topic of conversation?' enquired the chief inspector.

Sam grinned. 'Now and then,' he said. 'But a sex murder on the premises does make you think a bit about the power of our sexual urges, doesn't it? I mean,' he went on, picking up a can of beer, 'it's an urge that gets Newby up a flight of stairs when he can hardly walk – even though he'd be too knackered when he got to the top to do anything anyway. If he *can* do anything, which I doubt.'

'Oh?' said Lloyd.

Another knock at the door; Sam raised his eyebrows. 'Popular chap I am, all of a sudden,' he said, opening the door to someone's chest. He looked up into the face of a young man who could have been nothing else on this earth but a policeman.

'Sir?' the young man said to Lloyd, failing even to acknowledge Sam, but at least refraining from entering without permission.

Lloyd went out, closing the door. Sam looked across at Sergeant Hill. 'Finally got around to wondering about our Mr Newby, have you? Caroline didn't tell you about him, did she? Oh, no. She enjoys it. As soon as someone takes a healthy interest in her, that's when she blows the whistle.'

'And Mr Newby's interest is unhealthy?'

'It all goes on in his head,' said Sam, tapping his own head as he spoke. 'And that's where she wants it to stay. Give her a touch of the real thing, and she has the vapours.'

'You mean because she rejected you she must be frigid?' enquired the sergeant.

'She's got the same problem as you, sweetheart,' he said. 'Nothing that a good seeing-to wouldn't cure.' She didn't react at all, not like the more volatile chief inspector.

'Sorted out your thefts, have you?' he asked, opening the beer.

'The inquiry is proceeding,' she said.

'When do I get my pen back?' he asked, twisting off the ring-pull. She smiled. 'Your pen will be returned in due course.'

'When?' he said. 'I want it back.'

'We wouldn't dream of depriving you of it,' she said. 'But the culprit hasn't been discovered yet.'

'You can't hang on to it! I don't give a shit who stole it.'

'I do. Your pen went missing on the night of the murder – it could be evidence.'

'Evidence my arse! You're doing this on purpose, you bitch. That pen's important to me, and I want it back.'

The door opened. 'Trouble, Sergeant?' asked Lloyd, coming in without even knocking this time.

'Nothing I can't handle,' said the sergeant.

'You should be a traffic warden, you know that?' said Sam. 'Hard-faced—'

'Mr Waters,' Lloyd said, timing the interruption to cut him off. 'Don't say it.' He sat down. 'Suppose you tell me again what you were doing on Friday night.'

'I was getting pills and potions, and goodness knows what all,' said Caroline. 'We hadn't been married long – I suppose that's why it hit me so hard.'

His mouth caressing her breasts, tongue tracing erect nipples . . ..

'It must have been terrible,' he said. 'How long were you married?' He should know. Andrew must have told him.

Releasing the fastenings at the top of her stockings, sliding sheer nylon down long, long legs . . . .

'Almost three years,' she said. 'It would have been our third anniversary that month.'

'Andrew and I had lost touch,' he said. 'I didn't even know he was married.'

His mouth claiming hers; their bodies coming together, only silk between them . . . her gasps at the thrusting pressure against the soft barrier . . . .

'He'd lost your address,' she said. 'He was so pleased when you applied for this job.'

Hooking his fingers over the waistband, drawing the silk down; lips travelling back up the smooth legs, gently, expertly, stimulating her . . . her back arching, twisting her against him . . . her groan of pleasure as he entered her, repeated over and over with the rhythmic movements . . . her body writhing, shuddering under his; slowly bringing her to a climax, the soft moans under her quickened breath growing louder, louder, turning to cries of ecstasy—

'Why don't you let me join in?' she asked.

The rush of blood burned his face while everything else in the universe froze into solid ice. He could hear; he could hear the radio playing downstairs. He could hear the water gurgling through the old-fashioned radiator. He could hear the ever-present police call to one another. He could see; he could see the faded, threadbare rug beneath his feet. He could see scuff marks on his shoes. He could see the empty wine-glass on the floor. He could have seen Caroline, if he had looked up, but he couldn't look at her. Not ever again.

'I'm sure it would be better fun if I was doing it, too,' she said.

Say something, you fool. Say *something*. 'I was staring, wasn't I?' he muttered. 'I'm sorry – I . . .'

'You were doing a bit more than staring,' she said. 'You've been doing it ever since you arrived.'

'I . . . .' He couldn't look at her at all. He tried to get up. 'I'm sorry, I'm sorry. I don't mean to do it. I don't know I'm doing it

– I . . . well, I do, but . . . .' He grasped the arm of the sofa, trying desperately to get to his feet. 'I'm sorry.'

'You don't have to go,' she said.

'Why don't you tell me to sod off?' It wasn't a question; it was a plea, mumbled, his eyes firmly fixed on his shoes. Why wasn't she angry? He could take anger.

'If you were anyone else, I would. But you're not. You're Andrew's friend, and I know you. Feel as if I know you.'

Oh, God, if only he could move. Then he could run away from this.

'Why, Philip?' she asked.

His skin was on fire again. 'I don't know,' he said. 'I don't know. I can't . . . can't . . . .' His courage failed him.

'Can't what?' she said.

His shoes looked back at him, no help. 'I can't do anything else,' he said.

'Have you tried?'

He shook his head.

'Then how do you know you can't?'

'I know,' he muttered. Oh, God, let him get out of here.

She was pouring him another drink, handing it to him. He took it, looking at the glass, not at her.

'What does the doctor say?' she asked.

'He just keeps saying that it isn't physical.' That wasn't true; it was not all the doctor said. He said a lot of things that didn't help.

'That much was fairly obvious,' she said.

Oh, God. The humiliation burned on his face. Was that supposed to be some sort of comfort to him? It had all been in his mind; he hadn't had to wrestle with his clothes, to heave his body into doing what was required of it Because it couldn't, he knew it couldn't. It could only make him want to die of embarrassment.

'Sorry,' she said. He could hear the smile in her voice, and he wanted to *die*. Please, please let me leave, he begged God, Caroline, anyone with the power to grant his wish. Please don't make me talk about it. Please let me die.

'Philip,' she said.

He stared at the rug. He wanted to crawl into its faded pattern, and fade with it. Disappear. Die.

'What sort of doctor?' she asked.

'Psychiatrist,' he muttered.

'Are you straight with him? Do you tell him everything?'

He had to look at her. She wasn't going to let him go.

She sat beside him, fully clothed. For the first time, he tried deliberately to have his fantasy, but he couldn't. He couldn't even have that, not now that she had faced him with it.

'I told him,' he said miserably. 'When it started. Total strangers – women in bus queues, girls behind the counter at the bank. I told him. I was frightened I'd molest someone. But he – he just says it's because I'm depressed.'

'He's probably right.'

Philip shook his head. 'That's *why* I'm depressed,' he said. 'Why can't the fool see that? I don't want pills and pep-talks. I'm frightened.'

'You're not going to molest anyone,' she said, smiling again.

'That's what he says.'

'What else does he say?'

'He says I'm avoiding physical contact, not looking for it. He says that's why I pick women I can't have.'

'What makes you think you can't have me?' she asked.

'You were Andrew's wife!'

'You were Andrew's best friend,' she said. 'I'm not going to let you turn into a dirty old man.' And she smiled again.

The knock at the door made him jump, jarring his back. It was impossible. Whatever she said, whatever the doctor said.

'Don't go away,' she said, going to the door.

'I believe Mr Newby's with you?'

It was, of course, Chief Inspector Lloyd. He always seemed to appear just when his discomfort was at its height. Philip reached for his stick, and even that was agony. He wanted his fantasy back, because there could be nothing else.

'I'm glad you're together,' said Lloyd breezily. 'Because you both reported seeing someone on the fire-escape outside the Hamlyns' bedroom window. I'd like to talk to you about that, if I may.'

Caroline was open-mouthed. 'You saw him?' she said. 'You saw him, too?'

Philip nodded, intensely grateful to Lloyd for the change of subject, even if it was to this one. 'Yes,' he said. 'Well – thought I did. Just a glimpse.'

'I didn't imagine it.' She shivered. 'I thought maybe it was just my reflection or something.'

Philip wanted to reassure her, but how could he?

'Well – perhaps we can get a reasonably precise time,' said Lloyd. 'Mr Newby – about when did you see this person?'

'I don't know for certain. It was just after I'd arrived in the car park. About five to eleven, or so.'

'I thought it was a few minutes after eleven,' said Caroline. 'I told your sergeant.'

'Still – we're agreed that it was about eleven o'clock,' Lloyd said. He looked at Philip. 'You didn't see whoever it was come down again?'

'No. It was just a figure – it was there, and it was gone. I thought I'd imagined it, too.'

'Did you put the bedroom light out when you left, Mrs Knight?'

'I don't honestly know,' she said.

'But you might have, automatically. In which case . . .'. He turned back to Philip. 'He could have come down again without your seeing him. It's very dark out there.'

'Yes,' said Philip, his voice flat. 'But the light didn't go out,' he said.

'So where did he go?'

Philip shook his head. 'I don't know,' he said.

'No,' said Lloyd. 'Well – thank you both. I apologise for the intrusion.'

Lloyd went, and Philip got to his feet. He had the stick now, and he could leave at last. 'I'm sorry,' he said. 'I'm terribly sorry I upset you.'

'Don't go,' she said.

'I must.' He opened the door.

'Don't think you won't be welcome here,' she said. 'Please, Philip. Come back tomorrow. When you've had a chance to think.'

Matthew had watched as the daylight faded, and the playing-field emptied. They seemed to be checking every blade of grass. There had been a whole team of people in the Barn, looking for something. He had spoken to the pathologist; he had been pleased to be asked, and explained that the tiniest of objects could yield clues. Murderers rarely left anything obvious behind, not if they were intent on getting away with it. Most of them weren't, oddly enough, he told Matthew. Some of them gave themselves up, some even killed themselves. But most just waited for the reckoning, and didn't bother to deny it.

The interesting ones were the ones who thought they could beat the investigation teams. But if they only knew, he said, what they could discover from mud, from blood – from anything that was found in the area. It wasn't just in Sherlock Holmes that footprints – he called them footmarks – and cigarette ends gave the murderer away. They really did.

He had shown Matthew how they took casts of footmarks, explained how even the way the soles were worn down was sometimes how they proved someone's presence at the scene. But the ground in this case had still been frozen, despite the rain, and hadn't proved much help. But there were other things, he said. He had explained how the injuries themselves could point to someone in particular – someone left-handed, for instance. And how they could work out how many blows had been struck – that, he said, gave you an idea of the state of mind of the attacker.

Matthew had been fascinated.

'Do you think forensics might interest you?' he had asked.

'I'm sure it would,' Matthew had replied.

The pathologist had beamed; a sudden, wide smile that changed his whole face. 'Then, you should talk to your careers master,' he had said. 'Do you have one?'

Matthew had nodded.

'If he needs to know anything – tell him to contact me.' He had given Matthew a card. 'I'll show you round,' he said. 'When we're not so busy.'

Matthew had watched him drive away, and had raised his hand in salute, still holding the card. It was the first profession that had ever really caught his attention, the first time he had ever known what he wanted to do. His father had suggested the law, which had had some appeal. But this was much better. Piecing evidence together, like a jigsaw. Proving what must have happened, perhaps even proving who must have done it, from tiny fragments of information. A piece here, a piece there, the pathologist had said. He did his job, the police did theirs and, if they were lucky, it all came together to prove or disprove someone's story.

Of course, he had said, they didn't always win. But there was always excitement, always urgency, always something interesting to work on.

It was what he wanted to do, he realised, as he saw the chief inspector and the sergeant leave the staff block, and walk towards the car park. He had been waiting for them when he met the pathologist, but he couldn't tell them anything. Not now.

'Right,' Lloyd said to Judy, as they sat in his car in the school car park.

Everyone else had gone with the daylight; they would be back at dawn, looking for the murder weapon.

'What have we got?' he asked.

Judy smiled. 'Do you really want to know?' she asked, reaching into her bag for her notebook, turning on the interior light.

'No, but I expect we'd better make some sense of it all, if we can.'

'We've got Newby. Whose explanation about what he was doing between ten twenty-five and ten fifty-five is uncorroborated.'

'Except Sam reckons he's impotent,' said Lloyd.

'Sam reckons he's an expert on everyone's sexuality,' said Judy. She smiled. 'Including mine. But would Newby have had the strength to kill her? He can hardly move, and you can *see* he's in real pain. All the time.'

'But only since last night,' said Lloyd. 'If we are to believe Sam. Again. And if that's true – what happened to him? Would throwing up be enough exertion to do that to him?'

Judy shrugged. 'He could certainly walk better than that when I saw him last month,' she said. Something still bothered her about that. She would have to think about it.

'And both Caroline Knight and Philip Newby say that someone was hanging round the junior dormitory,' said Lloyd. 'What do you make of that?'

Judy looked up at the bedroom window, and the easy access it gave to the fire-escape door on the balcony. The window should have a lock, she thought, with her crime prevention officer's hat on. 'It's quite possible,' she said. 'The lab might come up with something.'

Lloyd sighed. 'All right,' he said. 'So what was he doing? Trying to get in? Was Mrs Knight going to be his victim if Newby hadn't turned up?' He thought for a moment. 'Unless he thought the flat would be empty,' he said. 'He might have been trying to get into the building to hide somewhere, *after* he'd killed Mrs Hamlyn.'

'I've got them looking for this handyman person,' Judy said. 'His name is James Lacey. But the golf-club doesn't make sense. He was long gone when it went missing.'

Lloyd grunted. 'It's not just the golf-club that doesn't make sense,' he said. 'It could just be a coincidence, I suppose. But I doubt it. That's what Freddie thought it was straight away.' He sighed, a deep sigh of frustration. 'I don't *know* these people,' he said. 'And Sam Waters is right about one thing.'

'Really?' said Judy, unwilling to concede that the odious Mr Waters was right about anything.

'Flotsam and jetsam,' Lloyd said. 'They all work here and live here, but that's it. They're all loners, they're all failures. Putting Diana Hamlyn in amongst them was bound to end in disaster.'

Judy nodded a little sadly.

'They don't like one another,' Lloyd went on. 'They don't trust one another. They accuse one another – but I'd swear not one of them has told us the truth. Sam Waters did go to a club, like he said. Sandwell checked up – that's what he came to tell me. They know him in there – he was there from about half past midnight until about two, according to the owner. But he says he left here at about ten past eleven. It only takes half an hour to get into Stansfield.'

'But Newby confirms that he saw him leave,' said Judy. 'And Freddie says she was dead by then anyway. Does it matter?'

'But where did he go?' asked Lloyd. 'To dump the murder weapon? But I'll let Mr Waters stew for the moment. He's coming to the station to make a statement about what he saw. I'll have a few more questions for him when he does.'

'He could be making it up about seeing a boy with her,' Judy said. 'Treadwell certainly thinks he was.'

Lloyd sighed. 'He could,' he said. 'And we ought to check up on that film he was supposed to be taking Caroline Knight to – it could be some sort of alibi. You said Treadwell isn't convinced that there was a film. We should pay the club secretary a visit.'

'I rang,' said Judy. 'You had to book – and Mrs Knight booked two tickets in January.'

Lloyd looked a little disappointed.

'You just want to see if the club secretary can get a pirate video of that film that was supposed to be on,' Judy said.

'How do you know about that?' he asked.

'Because I tried to watch it.'

'Why? I thought it wasn't your kind of thing.'

She gave a little sigh. 'Because I knew you'd be watching it,' she said. 'We might as well go straight to the pub,' she added quickly, before he could say anything. 'We don't want to keep Freddie waiting.'

Lloyd smiled. 'All right,' he said, and waited until she had got the car started before leading the way out of the school, and into Stansfield, and the car park of the Derbyshire Hotel.

'Anyway, Sherlock,' he said, as they sat down with their drinks.

'You scored a bull's-eye with the pen. How did you know it was his?'

Judy smiled. 'You know the pattern down the side?'

'Yes,' said Lloyd warily.

'When I looked at it more closely, I realised it was "SW" linked over and over again.' She smiled. 'And I enjoyed taking the wind out of his sails for a moment,' she said.

Freddie was good company when it was possible to steer him away from pathology humour. He had come with bits and pieces of information; the bag and shoes were covered with too many prints to be of any use. But the squashed shoe had been run over by a car wheel.

Judy frowned. 'Are you sure?' she asked.

Freddie didn't deign to reply. 'So there must have been a car involved,' he said.

Which sounded as though it hardly needed to be said, except that Judy knew what he meant. A car furthered his theory, which he didn't have, because he didn't have theories. The back seat of a car seemed a quite likely place for consenting sex, even to Judy.

'But cars aren't allowed up at that end of the school,' Judy said.

Freddie spread out his hands. 'Allowed or not, there was a car in the Barn,' he said. 'And we haven't found her buttons in the Barn or the field,' he said. 'I presume Mrs Hamlyn wouldn't go to a dinner dance with buttons missing from the front of her dress, so it's a reasonable assumption that they came off in the car.'

'Oh, good,' said Lloyd, his voice heavily sarcastic. 'All we have to do is find out which car it was. There were only about two hundred people there. Have you any idea?'

'We're checking,' said Freddie. 'It all takes time, Lloyd.'

A niblick fitted the bill, he said, and pointed out to Lloyd that he hadn't been so far off when he suggested a sand iron. Sam Waters's suit had yielded nothing of interest. He was delighted because he had apparently made a convert while he was at the school.

Judy excused herself to make a phone call, and ordered another slimline tonic when Freddie got another round.

'Did you have to?' Lloyd muttered, as Freddie went to the bar. 'I just want to get out of this place.'

'You're the one who made the arrangement for you and Freddie and I to have a drink,' she said. 'So we're having a drink. All right?'

'You and Freddie and me,' he said, and smiled.

Freddie came back with the drinks. 'We've found a couple of strands of grey wool on Mrs Hamlyn's clothes,' he said, also, it would appear, a saver of the best till last.

'Grey wool?' said Lloyd. 'Like a school blazer?'

'Could be,' said Freddie. 'Get me one of the blazers, and I'll tell you.'

When they left the pub, and got into their separate cars, she didn't go home, but followed Lloyd to the flat. She pulled in beside him, and got out of the car.

It was dark in the garage area. She couldn't see his face.

'Judy,' he said, his voice tired. 'I'm getting too old for this. Setting alarms, looking at watches. It's not for me.'

'No alarms,' she said, and it seemed that her voice echoed quietly through the buildings.

There was a little silence. 'Does this mean you're not going to stay with him after all?'

'No,' she said. 'But it means I can spend the night with you.'

'And then go home to your husband?'

She was cold, shivering inside her coat, and it wasn't just the weather. 'No,' she said. 'And then go home. Michael just lives there, too, that's all.'

She still couldn't see his face. Just his shape, as he stood irresolutely beside his car.

'I can't stay here anyway,' she said. 'It would be silly moving to a flat, just to have to move again in a few months.'

'That's Michael talking. I can hear him.'

Having a relationship with a mind-reader wasn't easy. 'It's true, all the same,' she said.

He came up to her then, and she could just see his face in the strand of light from the street-lamp. He was angry. 'Was it Michael you phoned from the hotel?' he asked.

'Yes.'

He looked at her for a moment. 'Do you mean we have Michael's *permission*?'

'No, of course not! I just told him I wouldn't be home tonight.'

'Well, you were wrong. Unless you've somewhere else to go.'

Judy's heart was beating painfully hard. 'What?' she said. 'You don't mean that.' She was shivering.

'You have no intention of leaving him.'

'I *have*,' she said helplessly. 'But not until the transfer. I made him a promise.'

'You made me a promise.'

'I kept it! I told him – and I *am* leaving. I just didn't know it would hurt him like this!'

'It was going to hurt someone,' said Lloyd. 'Just as long as it wasn't you.'

'That isn't fair!'

'Fair?' he said. 'What's fair? Is what you're doing fair? Go back to Michael, Judy. I don't want this any more. Do you understand? No more. I don't care what you do – leave him, stay with him, do what the hell you like. But don't come back here. I've had enough.'

He turned, and walked away, into the flats.

Judy waited motionless by the car, until she could no longer hear his footsteps on the stairs. Numbly, she drove away, her hands and feet automatically manipulating the controls, her mind blankly refusing to face the situation. The road seemed to steer; she made signals and turned comers, but there was no will, no decision. The car stopped outside the house, and the path took her to the front door. They key opened it, her feet took her into the sitting-room.

'Change of plan?' asked Michael.

'I don't want to talk just now,' she heard her voice saying, as she turned back into the hallway to go upstairs. She stopped, frowning, at the suitcases.

'I do,' Michael said. 'I'll be making an early start. Since you're here, we might as well get things sorted out.'

Still frowning with the effort of regaining her thinking processes, she went back into the room. 'Have you got a business trip?' she asked.

'No,' he said. 'I'm moving into the penthouse.'

The penthouse was the flattering name given to the flat at the top of the office block where Michael worked.

'Ronnie and Lisa moved into their cottage today,' he went on. 'Shirley and I are moving into the penthouse tomorrow. I've got the removal people coming on Monday – it's furnished, so we won't need much. But I want the stuff from my study, and the hi-fi and records, and so on. Just my own things.'

Carefully, Judy searched for her wits, and gathered them gingerly together. 'You and Shirley?' she repeated, her voice small.

'Oh, you don't know her. She came to work for us about six months ago.'

Judy stared at him, sudden tears pricking the backs of her eyes. 'Then ... what was all that stuff about Woolworth's?' she said.

'Well – you'd just gone back to work. Seen Mr Lloyd again. I had to do something.'

'Why?' Her voice was a whisper.

'I couldn't have you leaving first,' he said. 'It would have spoiled the surprise.'

She blinked painfully as he smiled at her.

'What was all that about, this morning?' she asked, bewildered.

'I wasn't going to let you upstage me,' he said. 'Why should I make it easy for you?'

She gave an uncomprehending shake of her head.

'If you'd ever bothered getting to know me, you would have known it was rubbish,' he said, and shook his head as he looked at her. 'You were good enough to tell me this morning why you married me. Do you want to know why I married you? A reason that won't have occurred to you.'

She could feel the tears hot on her face.

'I loved you,' he said. 'But I don't any more. And I sincerely hope that your unexpected return means that I have screwed things up between you and Mr Lloyd.'

She turned and ran blindly upstairs. She was opening drawers, delving in the wardrobe, taking out underwear and clothes and shoving them into a laundry-bag. She couldn't see what she was doing because of the tears; she had no idea what she was taking.

Her toothbrush. She ought to have her toothbrush. She went into the bathroom, elbowing Michael aside as he arrived on the landing.

Toothbrush, comb, make-up. She swept them all up, taking a sponge-bag from the back of the door. Some of the things fell as she tried to undo the drawstring, and she knelt down, picking them up, trying to wipe away the tears. She got everything into the bag, and pulled the string tight. A nightdress. She would need a nightdress.

She turned to the door, and stopped. My God, Lloyd had never seen her in a nightdress, she realised, as she went back into the bedroom, with Michael still on the landing.

She was trying to open the drawer that always jammed, tugging at it uselessly as Michael came into the bedroom. The surge of anger served to open the drawer. She looked at him through a mist. 'Loved me?' she said, and it hurt to speak. She consigned the nightdress to the bag, and picked it up.

'We should talk,' he said. 'About the house, and so on.'

She ignored him.

'Where are you going?' he asked.

'Lloyd's.'

'Are you so sure you'll be welcome?'

'No,' she said.

She threw the bag into the back of the car, and sat in it until the tears subsided. She drove off, back to Lloyd. No, she wasn't sure she would be welcome.

But he would let her in. And that, she told the absent Michael, *that* was love.

Treadwell read for a while after going to bed, but he couldn't get interested. He leaned over Marcia to turn off the light.

'No, Barry,' she said.

Nothing had been further from his thoughts; her response was automatic, produced at the first sign of anything that might be construed as an overture. It had made him smile once, long ago; it was a hangover from their chaste courting days, he had thought, given that in those early months of marriage it had not apparently been a serious rejection. As time wore on, however, the cajoling and persuasion had become wearisome, the objective hardly worth the time and trouble expended on its achievement.

Without discussion, an understanding had evolved that his requests – it would be overstating the urgency to call them demands – would be met, despite the token protest, at infrequent intervals. This was one such, and he availed himself of the opportunity on the grounds that it might be a while before the next time, and it might serve to make him feel better. Marcia took little notice of the proceedings; he expected no more than her occasional compliance.

He supposed he must have slept, or he couldn't, presumably, have woken up. He had no idea what time it was; it felt like morning, despite the darkness. He looked across at the smudged blur of light on the bedside table. Six forty-five; it was morning, despite the blackness beyond the window, despite the lack of noise. Schools were unbelievably noisy places, with hundreds of feet scurrying along uncarpeted floors, hundreds of voices raised at once in separate, animated conversations. The walls echoed with sound from dawn till dusk; only now was the place still and silent. But this morning the silence had a different quality.

Treadwell got out of bed, shivering a little in the chill air of the room. He reached for his dressing-gown, and was still struggling with it in the darkness as he crossed over to the window. Outside, the dim lighting revealed the outlines of the buildings. Beyond them, though he couldn't see it, lay the playing-field. The rain that had drenched that dreadful night had gone as though it had never been; even the sleety snow had gone, and the ground was dry and cold once more.

Perhaps it had all been a bad dream. Perhaps the rain hadn't happened. Perhaps – Treadwell sighed – perhaps none of it had happened. Perhaps Diana was still vibrantly alive. And it seemed almost possible that none of it had happened. He had had dreams that had remained real for minutes after waking. How did he know? He couldn't tell what was real and what wasn't, standing here in the dark with the school lying as frostily still below him as Marcia had. It didn't look like a place where a murder had happened.

Treadwell left the bedroom, went downstairs, and out into the cold, dark morning. Past the staff block, across to the junior dormitory, going to where he could see the playing-field, its frost-covered surface gleaming as dawn broke.

He had had to see for himself the proof that it had all happened. He hadn't really believed that it had just been a dream, but some sort of desperate hope had made him go and check. And there they were, two lines of ribbon across the field, as if it had been marked out for a cross-country run. Tomorrow, once again, police would inch their way across the grass, looking for something, anything, to lead them to Diana's killer.

Treadwell turned away, and became consciously aware of the muffled sound. He had been aware of it all along, he supposed. The peculiar quality of this morning's silence was that it *wasn't* silent; sounds of the rude world were intruding. A sound. An engine, running.

Puzzled, a little tentative, he walked round the side of the junior dormitory. The sound was marginally louder, but not loud enough to be coming from one of the dark shapes in the car park. He walked slowly, disbelievingly, towards the sound, towards the private garage that came with the junior dormitory. His hand reached out of its own accord, and he tried to push the door open. Something was jamming it; cloth, paper, something.

He pushed harder, almost falling as the door swung up, releasing the dense, choking fumes into the morning air.

Chapter Six

Wearing Lloyd's spare dressing-gown, Judy pulled the cord on the blind, which ran up the kitchen window with a loud snap as it reached the top. Daylight slanted into the kitchen as the sun reflected on the hard frost.

The flat was a kind of antidote to Lloyd himself; it was even more tranquil in the early morning. Hardy British birds called to one another through the cold air, and below the window the village street still slept. So did Lloyd; it remained to be seen what he was like first thing.

She surveyed the fridge. Bacon, eggs. Good. Frying-pan – where did he keep his frying-pan? On the rare occasions that she had eaten in the flat, Lloyd had done the cooking. It was ridiculous that she didn't know where he kept the frying-pan. Ah – up there. She took it down, glancing out of the window at the sleeping street.

Bread. She opened the bread-bin, but only a few crumbs remained. He had used the last of the bread to make sandwiches last night.

During the drive to the flat, the shock had turned to anger; she had announced as Lloyd opened the door that since everyone was agreed that she was a selfish pig who never thought of anyone but herself, perhaps they could take that as read and skip the part where she got told it all again. Then, tight-lipped, she had told Lloyd what a fool Michael had made of her, just so that he could watch her jump through hoops. Lloyd had listened, and then had asked what she had had to eat.

She had realised that she had eaten virtually nothing all day, and he had made sandwiches. You should not, he had said, make commitments on an empty stomach. It gave you cramp.

Now she was hungry again.

It was a gas cooker, and she wasn't used to one. It was Lloyd's opinion that she shouldn't be allowed near any sort of cooker, but she could at least make breakfast, if she knew how to make the thing work. It was supposed to be automatic, but the clicking noises that it made when she turned the tap seemed to have no intention of fighting the gas.

She had just given up when she heard the kitchen door open, felt Lloyd's arms come round her waist.

She twisted round to look at him. 'Oh, it's you,' she said, smiling at him.

'I was supposed to get up first,' he said. 'And bring you breakfast in bed.'

She kissed him. 'I don't like breakfast in bed,' she said.

'You amaze me,' he smiled. 'Oh, well, the rose on the breakfast-tray is out, I suppose.'

'I'll bring you breakfast in bed, if you like,' she said. 'If you tell me how to light the damn cooker.'

'I never eat breakfast.'

Judy couldn't conceive of anyone not eating breakfast as a deliberate policy. Especially on a Sunday.

She kissed him again, hugging him close to her.

'What was that for?' he asked.

'For being such a nice man,' she said.

'Wait a minute,' he said suspiciously. 'What have you done with Judy Hill? I know all about body-snatchers – I'm a film buff, you know.'

'Shut up.' She hit him.

'What have I done that's so nice?' he asked. 'I thought I was horrible to you.'

Judy took the bacon out of the fridge, and set about finding scissors for the rind.

'How come you're up so early?' he asked.

'A thought occurred to me.'

He smiled. 'I know I'm going to regret this,' he said. 'A thought about what?'

'Diana Hamlyn.'

Lloyd nodded slowly. 'The earth moved for me, too,' he said.

'Doesn't it always?' said Judy, and smiled. 'I did put her out of my mind for a while.'

'So what brought her back?'

'In a way,' said Judy slowly, 'that *was* what brought her back. She never had that.'

Lloyd raised his eyebrows. 'I rather thought the whole point was that she got too much of that,' he said.

'No, she didn't,' Judy argued. 'Hamlyn says he loved her, but he didn't want her. And the men who did want her didn't give a damn.' She shook her head. 'It was so joyless,' she said.

Lloyd frowned, puzzled. 'That's what kept you off your sleep?' he said, his voice disbelieving. 'You're not developing a soul at this late stage, are you? I don't know if I could cope with that.'

'Don't worry,' said Judy, shaking her head. 'It was just a passing thought. But it made me think about Sam Waters.'

'How very distressing,' said Lloyd.

'He said he saw her with a boy.' Judy cut off the rind, and nicked the bacon as she spoke. 'How do you light this thing?' she asked.

'Ah,' said Lloyd.

'Ah?'

'I had a thought, too,' he said. 'I don't think the grey thread means much. All the boys danced with the ladies – I expect we could have found grey threads on any of their clothes.'

'But he says he saw her with a boy, nevertheless,' said Judy.

'You don't think that's just Waters stirring it?'

'Not necessarily. Do you have any tomato, or anything?'

'Mushrooms?' he suggested. 'Salad drawer. I tend to agree with the headmaster,' he said. 'She doesn't sound as if she would be interested in one of the boys. She wasn't interested in them when she was an adolescent herself. It was Hamlyn she went after, remember.'

'I don't think she was interested in a boy,' said Judy. 'Not for that reason, at any rate. But Waters's pen went missing during the dinner. From the top table. Suppose Mrs Hamlyn saw who took the pen, and *that's* why Waters saw her with one of the boys?'

'She takes him outside rather than make a fuss with all these people there?' Lloyd said, nodding slowly. 'Could be. Do you have anyone in mind?' he asked.

'How do you light this cooker?' she demanded.

'You have to use matches,' Lloyd said, frowning distractedly as he spoke. 'The automatic thing doesn't work.' He took matches from the cupboard. 'I'm the one who is supposed to come up with theories,' he complained. 'Not you.'

She applied the match to the grill, half of which remained unlit then exploded into life. 'That's dangerous,' she said, as she left it to heat up.

'So are theories, as Freddie never tires of reminding me,' said Lloyd. '*Do* you have anyone in mind?'

'Well – it depends. The other ladies at the top table were the wife of the chairman of governors and Mrs Treadwell. First, I want to find out which boys danced with them. Because they'd have access to the pen.'

'And?' said Lloyd.

'And if one of them was Matthew Cawston, then I've got someone in mind,' she said. 'Treadwell said that Mrs Hamlyn almost knocked Cawston over on her way to talk to Newby. And, apart from Newby himself, she only had contact with the boy she danced with and Cawston. So, if she was with a boy at all, he seems the most likely. And he's in Palmerston House, which is where the stuff was found.'

Lloyd was still frowning slightly as he went to answer the phone, which was ringing unaccountably early for a Sunday. 'And to think', he said, 'I just fell asleep while all that was going on.'

She smiled. 'You obviously inspired me,' she called after him.

'Huh,' he called back, as he picked up the phone.

Two minutes later, Judy was reluctantly turning off the gas, putting the bacon back in the fridge, and getting ready to head out to the school again.

They arrived to yet another tangle of emergency vehicles, and drove into the car park, almost mowing down the headmaster.

'I don't believe it,' Treadwell kept saying, over and over again, as they got out of the car. 'I don't believe it.'

Freddie was already there; he called them over to the garage. As they walked across the quiet car park, a banshee's wail made Judy freeze. She looked up to see nothing more alarming than WPC Alexander at the balcony door, which would have benefited from some oil on its hinges.

'Sergeant Hill,' she said. 'There's a note up here, addressed to the chief inspector.'

They went round to the front of the building, and up to the Hamlyns' living-quarters. Lloyd read the note, then stood aside to let Judy see it.

'*Dear Mr Lloyd*,' it read, '*I am writing this to you in order to make it clear that I died by my own hand. I can see that my death in the middle of your inquiry into my wife's murder could seem suspicious.*

'*I wasn't happy until I met Diana. I was unhappy during our brief separation. I don't believe I can possibly be happy without her, and I cannot live with the belief that I caused her death. Forgive me for causing you more work, as I know I will*,' It was signed, and dated.

'I'll get the handwriting checked out,' said Freddie. 'And check it for prints. Just in case.'

Judy looked out of the open door at the scene below. Poor Mr Hamlyn, she thought. Calmly, logically, arriving at the conclusion that life wouldn't be worth living. Her eye caught the fire-escape on which the scene-of-crime people had been working. They had found some threads of material, and what might be blood-stains at the foot of the steps; they were working on the evidence as fast as they could, but it all took time, and Hamlyn couldn't face having any more time.

They went back down. Lloyd went into the garage with Freddie, and Judy went in search of Treadwell. At least he was alive.

As she arrived at the house, a motorbike drew up beside her.

'Excuse me.'

She turned to see a dark young man, who was removing his helmet the better to converse with her.

'I'm looking for a Detective Sergeant Hill,' he said. 'Is he here, do you know?'

'You've found him,' Judy said, smiling.

'Oh – sorry. The message just said . . . so I assumed . . . sorry.'

'That's all right,' she said. 'Did you want me?'

'You want me,' he said. 'Jim Lacey. I kept being told a Sergeant Hill was looking for me, but no one said what about, or where you were.'

'I think we kept just missing you,' she said.

'I'm on the move all day,' he said. 'Anyway, I heard about . . . well – what happened, and put two and two together.' He shook his head, and blinked a little. 'I still can't believe it,' he said. 'What sort of a nutter does something like that?'

'I'll find somewhere we can talk,' she said. She rather liked Mr Lacey, and at least he seemed more forthcoming than anyone else she had spoken to.

'I don't think you'll have to,' he said. He unzipped a pocket in his leather jacket. 'That's where I was on Friday night,' he said. He handed her a hospital appointment card. 'I was in a bit of a punch-up,' he said. 'I had to go to casualty. You can check up,' he said.

'Thank you,' she said, smiling. Mr Lacey was probably no stranger to the police, and he was anxious to prove that he had had nothing to do with events at the school. She made a note of his address.

'Since you're here,' she said, 'can you tell me anything about Diana Hamlyn?'

'She was all right!' he said, almost angrily. 'I know what everyone thinks, but – well, she was all right.'

Matthew Cawston was standing a little way off, watching what was going on, looking rather like a model for the sharp clothes he was wearing. She wondered if she was right about him. She had better go entirely by the book in case she wasn't – Matthew would know all about his rights, she was sure.

'We have got the right story about you and her, have we?' Judy asked Lacey, but she had lost her audience, as an older man came past them, and caught his attention.

'Des – how are you doing?' Lacey raised his voice to speak to the other man.

Des put down his tool-kit. 'How do you think I'm doing?' he demanded loudly enough to make people turn their heads. 'Have you heard what's been going on here?'

'Yes,' said Lacey. 'That's why I'm here.'

'Well, if you've come to pay your respects to her husband, don't bother. He's gone, too. This place has gone mad. It was never normal, but this is ridiculous. And you didn't help.'

'What do you mean, he's gone, too?'

'He did himself in. This morning.'

Lacey looked at Judy. 'Hamlyn?' he said.

She nodded.

'Poor old sod,' he said.

'Who's this, then?' asked Des. 'Another of your conquests?'

Lacey smiled. 'No. This is Sergeant Hill, Des. I'm a suspect.'

'What?' He cupped his hand to his ear.

'A suspect! They think I might have done it.'

He was smiling as he spoke, but it seemed to Judy that the heartiness was just a little overdone; he didn't want Des to think that Mrs Hamlyn's death had touched him.

'Get on! You couldn't knock the skin off a rice pudding, for all your leather gear and your motorbike.' He wagged a finger at Lacey. 'Didn't I tell you not to get involved with her?'

'Yes, Des.'

'Well. Won't be told, will you? You and your good for a laugh. She isn't good for a laugh now, is she?'

Judy turned as she heard the sound of Philip Newby's stick on the pavement. He acknowledged her, and went into the flat.

'What happened to him?' asked Lacey.

Judy turned back. 'Do you know him?' she asked.

'Well – met him. He was here for an interview. I'm not likely to forget – it was the day I was sacked.'

'What's that?' said Des.

'I'm saying that bloke was here for an interview the day me and Mrs H got caught,' shouted Lacey. 'What happened to him?'

Des leaned forward, eyebrows knotted together, to indicate that he hadn't quite heard the question, despite its having been bellowed.

'He was in a car crash,' said Judy.

Lacey shook his head.

'What was that?' said Des.

'Will he always have to use a stick?' Lacey asked.

'I don't know,' said Judy.

'What?' said Des. 'Why do all you people *mumble*?' With that, he picked up his tool-bag, and went towards the junior dormitory.

'OK if I go now?' asked Lacey, swinging his leg over the bike and kicking it into life.

'Yes,' said Judy. 'Thank you for coming.'

She watched as he roared off down the drive. She had rather enjoyed meeting Jim Lacey. He was the first person she had met who actually seemed to care that Mrs Hamlyn was dead. She hoped she wouldn't have to talk to him again, and grabbed Sandwell as he passed, handing him the hospital card. 'Check that out, will you?' she said sweetly. Barton General was not noted for its swift response to enquiries.

She had to pass Matthew on her way into the Treadwells' house. He smiled politely, and gravely.

Treadwell came to his front door, a large whisky in his hand. 'A bit early,' he said, ushering her in. 'But I needed it.'

Judy asked him which of the boys had danced with the other ladies at the top table, and he shrugged. 'God knows,' he said. 'And Marcia, I expect.' He tilted his head back slightly. 'Marcia!' he shouted.

Marcia appeared. She didn't speak.

'Who danced with you and what's-her-name on Friday night?'

'Lots of people danced with *her*,' she said.

'No – the boys.'

'Oh, that.' She went slightly pink. 'Sorry,' she said. 'I thought you meant—'

'Just tell her who danced with you,' he said impatiently.

Judy looked apologetically at Marcia Treadwell, though why she felt she should apologise for the woman's own husband she wasn't sure.

'I can't remember who the other boy was,' she said, a little fearfully. 'But Matthew Cawston danced with me. Twice – the first dance, and then one later on.'

'Thank you, Mrs Treadwell.'

Marcia Treadwell took herself back to wherever she had come from.

'Mr Treadwell,' said Judy, 'the chief inspector and I would like to talk to Matthew. You should be present.'

'Why do you want to talk to Matthew?' he asked.

'It's about the thefts,' she said.

'Does it really matter about the thefts? Don't you think you've got more important things to do than that?'

'We'd like to speak to Matthew,' she repeated firmly, and went to the door. 'I'll find Chief Inspector Lloyd,' she said.

Outside, Sandwell was waiting with confirmation that an ambulance had picked up James Lacey outside a pub at 9.30 on Friday night, and that he had been attended to just after midnight.

'How did you get that so quickly?' she asked, in awe of anyone who could get an answer of any sort from medical sources.

Sandwell grinned. 'My sister was on night duty in casualty on Friday night,' he said. 'It's not what you know, Sergeant . . . .'

'Why the hell would he kill himself?' said Sam.

Philip looked across at him. 'Maybe he loved her,' he said.

Sam gave his opinion in two words, which was how he often communicated quite complex thoughts. Philip mused a little on the versatility of one small word, as he shifted slightly in his chair. He could move more easily again. He had spent a sleepless night, thinking about Caroline, but not the way he'd thought of her before. It wasn't a terrible, secret vice any more. It never had been. She'd known, all along.

And what had horrified him at the time seemed somehow to

comfort him during the night. Despite the lack of sleep, he had been relaxed, for once, and the pain had relaxed with him.

'I take it you don't think he loved her,' said Philip, realising just how much he disliked Sam Waters.

'Who could love someone that everyone in the school was knocking off?' asked Sam, then grinned unpleasantly. 'Present company excepted, of course.'

'But she was loved,' said Philip. 'She was like a second mother to the juniors – you only have to look at them since it happened. You can't get a word out of the first-years. They loved her – why shouldn't Hamlyn have felt the same?'

'They haven't all topped themselves, have they? They've got more bloody sense.'

'Have you ever loved *anyone*, Sam?' Philip asked.

'Not a woman,' he said. 'Don't get me wrong, I'm not queer. Gay. Whatever they want to call it now. You just can't make a friend of a woman.'

'I'm not surprised, if you think of them the way you do.'

'That's rich, if I may say so. Can't go to jail for what you're thinking, eh, Newby?'

Philip felt himself grow pink. Did everyone know? Had it been that obvious? It seemed it had, as Sam went on.

'At least I can do something about it,' he said. 'And it's all they're good for.'

Philip sighed. 'Am I supposed to go digging round in your psyche to find out that someone let you down in your impressionable youth or something?'

'I don't want you digging round anywhere near my psyche,' said Sam. 'Save it for your girlfriend.'

She had said he should come back; and he should, if she wanted him to. He owed her that. And it might prove whether or not her shock cure had worked. He rose, wincing a little. But he had got up without having to think about it; it was a considerable improvement.

He was only slightly out of breath as he knocked on her door; not bad at all. He heard the bolt being drawn back; he must get a bolt for his room, he thought. Especially in view of the thief's activities. It wouldn't surprise him if it was his flatmate who was stealing, just to cause mischief.

Caroline was pale. Her hand shook as she bolted the door again.

'Are you frightened of something?' he asked. Not him, obviously. She'd locked herself in with him.

'I don't want anyone just . . . walking in,' she said, going over to the window.

'Sam's not been here again, has he?'

She shook her head. 'And he's not going to be,' she said. She didn't speak for a long time. Just stood, looking out of the window at the increased police activity.

'Robert killed himself,' she said, at last.

Philip made a grunt of acknowledgement.

'I didn't. I didn't think I could go on living without Andrew, but I didn't try to stop living.'

'Killing yourself isn't a normal reaction,' Philip said, alarmed, going to her. He forgot, briefly, that he couldn't walk the way he used to, and had to hold his breath until the pain passed off. He stood beside her. 'You *can* live without him. Robert could have lived, too. He just . . . panicked, I imagine.'

She looked up at him. 'Maybe I should have killed myself,' she said.

'Caroline,' he said. 'Look – come away from the window. Sit down.' He manoeuvred her to the sofa, and sat her down. 'You've had too much death to cope with,' he said, carefully sitting beside her. 'Do you think that's what Diana would have wanted him to do?' he asked. 'You can't think it's what Andrew would have wanted. He was crazy about you. He told me you'd altered his whole life. He was really upset because I'd missed you—' He broke off, realising what he was saying.

'What's, wrong?'

'I've just remembered that,' he said.

A lot of memories came flooding in on top of that. Too many. Not everything. It was disjointed and confusing, but such a relief that he sighed with satisfaction.

'What have you remembered?' she asked.

'He kept telling me he had a surprise for me. Then eventually he told me about you. He said I'd like you.' He smiled. 'He was right.'

'He said I'd like you,' she said, with an answering smile.

Philip reddened. 'I've made it a bit difficult for you,' he said.

She shook her head.

' "*Everything's gone wrong*," ' Philip said, frowning, as another snatch of that day came back to him. Andrew had said that – just like Caroline had when she met him on the first day of term.

'What?' said Caroline.

'Oh – I was just remembering what Andrew said. I'd had the interview, and you were due back, but you had got held up.'

She nodded.

'And some crisis had happened here,' said Philip. 'I had to get back to London, but I'd missed my train.' He gave a bitter little smile. 'I can't even remember what was so bloody important now,' he said, looking at his stick. 'But he really wanted me to meet you.' He smiled. 'I'm glad I have.'

She smiled back. 'You're so like him,' she said. There were tears in her eyes.

Tentatively, Philip put a hand on her shoulder, patting her.

She drew back. 'You can't give me a cuddle if you're hanging on to that,' she said, taking away his stick.

He held her close as she literally cried on his shoulder. Nothing wrong with his shoulders, like the man said.

The heavy smell of exhaust fumes still lingered in the air around the junior dormitory, and once again the school was alive with uniforms; once again an ambulance stood by helplessly as another dead body was examined; once again Matthew watched the aftermath of sudden, unnatural death.

But this time the scene was sunlit and incongruous. Night seemed the right time for alarms and excursions; the professional, quiet urgency with which these people performed their duties suited a cloak of darkness, and it seemed out of place on a day when the bright winter sunshine flashed its reflection on the windows of the cars that came in a continuous stream up the drive.

Faces appeared at the windows as the news was whispered through the waking school, and boys came and stood in small groups, keeping a discreet distance from the Hamlyns' garage, where all the activity was centred. Matthew hated being one of the crowd, one of those who gathered to watch while other people got on with the job.

He had liked Hamlyn; he was sorry that he was dead. But he *was* dead, and there was nothing he could do about that. That being so, he rather wished he'd found him. Then he would have been in the arena, not in the stands. One day, he would be. One day, he'd be the one called to the scene, like the doctor, who came out of the garage, a girl running behind him, trying to keep up with his long strides. The sergeant and the chief inspector followed, and stopped to speak to Treadwell. What in the world had he been doing, wandering about the grounds at that time in the morning? Matthew wondered if the police had asked him that.

They seemed to be looking over at him, all three of them, talking about him. He thought he was imagining things until they began walking towards him. Being singled out was better than being one of the crowd, but he didn't understand this, and that worried him.

'Could we have a word, Matthew?' asked the sergeant, pleasantly enough.

Matthew had never known dread. He became acquainted with it as he followed them to the headmaster's house, and into the sitting-room, where Sergeant Hill formally introduced him to the chief inspector. Mrs Treadwell eventually realised that she was surplus to requirements, and went off into the kitchen. Nothing ever seemed to touch her, Matthew thought, as he sat down at Treadwell's command. Murder, suicide – she looked exactly the same. No one else did.

Treadwell looked pale and shocked, his hair uncombed, his clothes hastily assembled. Matthew had never seen him without a tie. Mrs Knight had looked like death when he had seen her earlier; even

Waters had been too preoccupied to give anyone the benefit of his opinion. But Mrs Treadwell just fluttered about, as usual.

'The sergeant would like to ask you a few questions,' said Treadwell, sitting stiffly on an upright chair.

Matthew looked politely at Sergeant Hill.

'Friday night,' said Sergeant Hill crisply, and Matthew could only be thankful that he had been allowed to sit.

Helpful. Be helpful, anxious to please, until you know what she knows.

Matthew nodded slowly. 'The night of the ball?' he said.

'You danced with Mrs Treadwell, I believe?' she said.

'Yes,' said Matthew, a genuine puzzlement pulling his brows together. 'All the boys danced with the ladies.'

'Yes,' she said, and opened a notebook. 'You took Mrs Treadwell back to her table when the dance was over?'

'Yes,' he said. 'Of course.'

'What happened then?'

'Nothing,' he replied, to give himself time to think.

She sighed. 'What did you do, Matthew? When you got to the top table?'

This was all wrong. She wasn't going to be a pushover. He should have come forward of his own accord, when he'd meant to. Now he wasn't sure how to play it.

'What did you do when you got to the top table?' she asked again.

She knew. He didn't know how, but she knew already. He was supposed to be telling her of his own free will – shamefacedly confessing, reluctantly imparting the rest of his story. This wasn't right; it wasn't *fair*. But he still had information; he still had something to bargain with. Still, he wouldn't rush in, he told himself. He had to change his game-plan, but he had to be careful; he had to trump the right trick.

'Nothing,' he said again, dropping his head, still hoping that reluctant confession followed by his specific knowledge might swing things in his favour.

'Did you take a pen, Matthew?' asked the sergeant.

He lifted his head and looked straight at her. He didn't think muted heroism would go down very well with her after all; directness might be the answer. And she knew; there was no point in denying it.

'Yes,' he said. 'It was just lying on the table, so I took it.'

Sergeant Hill nodded; Treadwell's mouth fell open as his face grew dark.

Chief Inspector Lloyd turned from his contemplation of the view from Treadwell's sitting-room window, where he had been taking no apparent interest in the interview.

'Did you steal the other things that have gone missing over the last eighteen months?' he asked.

'Yes.' Matthew saw a slight frown appear and disappear on the sergeant's face.

'Why?' said Treadwell, sounding betrayed. 'Why, Matthew?'

'Fun,' said Matthew, looking at the chief inspector.

'What? Speak up, boy.'

Speak up, boy. Somewhere, Treadwell had a headmaster's phrase-book, Matthew would swear. He turned his head this time. 'Fun,' he repeated.

'Fun?' echoed Treadwell. 'You stole for *fun?*'

'Yes,' said Matthew. 'Everyone thought that one of the teachers was stealing,' he said, turning back to the sergeant. 'It was fun.'

'What did you hope to gain by it?' Treadwell asked, his face baffled.

'Nothing. It wasn't really stealing,' Matthew said. 'I was going to give it all back. I was going to leave it somewhere it would all be found after I'd left. That's not really stealing. I kept it all.'

'We haven't found it all,' said the sergeant.

'It was all there,' said Matthew.

'Well,' said Lloyd, 'we'll come back to that. What happened after you took the pen?' He sat beside the sergeant on the sofa.

'I was on my way back to my table when Mrs Hamlyn stopped me. She said she wanted to see me outside, and just carried on walking, as if she hadn't spoken to me at all. So I went out and waited for her.'

'Go on,' said Lloyd.

'She came out and asked me for the pen. I said I hadn't taken it.'

Lloyd looked up. 'Where did this conversation take place?' he asked.

'Outside the Hall, to start with,' said Matthew. 'But it suddenly started raining, and she didn't want to go back into the Hall because there were too many people going in and out of the cloakrooms. So we went into the Barn. She said she'd seen me take the pen. She said she'd have to talk to Mr Treadwell, but then someone else came in, and . . . .' He shrugged. 'I ran away.'

'Who came in?' Lloyd asked.

'I don't know. I couldn't see.'

'How long were you with Mrs Hamlyn?'

'I don't know – just a couple of minutes.'

'What was the point of running away?' asked the sergeant.

'I just ran. I wanted to get rid of the pen, because if I didn't have it she couldn't prove anything. I went back to the house, and waited for about half an hour, to make sure she hadn't followed me, or told anyone. Then I put it with the other stuff. I was going to get rid of it all.'

'I thought you said it wasn't really stealing?' said the sergeant. 'That you intended giving it back?'

'I did,' said Matthew. 'But I didn't intend getting caught. I could say she was mistaken – if I got rid of the stuff, no one would be able to prove anything. But then I couldn't, with the police all over the place. I didn't think you'd find it.'

'You were unlucky, Matthew,' said Sergeant Hill. 'We were looking for a murder weapon. You look everywhere.'

'I didn't think anyone knew about the loft,' said Matthew. 'You can't really see the hatch.'

'A piece of the black bin-liner was sticking out,' she said. 'You panicked a little. You were careless,' she said.

Matthew almost smiled. The pathologist had said that that was how people got caught.

Treadwell frowned. 'Is this amusing you?' he asked.

'No, sir,' said Matthew.

'Did you deliberately cause Mrs—?' He stopped. 'A member of staff to come under suspicion?'

'Yes, sir. Well, I didn't mean it to happen – not at first. But people suspected her, and – well, then I did do it deliberately.' He looked from one disapproving face to another, to another. 'I didn't think!' he said. 'It was just a bit of fun.' He dropped his eyes. 'I'm sorry,' he said. 'I realised that it wasn't right, making people think that she was stealing. That's why I took the pen.'

'Who are we talking about?' asked Lloyd.

'Mrs Knight,' said Matthew. 'But she wasn't *at* the ball, so I thought that if I took the pen people would stop thinking it was her.'

Lloyd sat back. 'So it was really a laudable act, was it?' he asked.

'No, sir.' Matthew was having trouble gauging the chief inspector, and decided that trying to convince him of his concern for Mrs Knight was probably not the most sensible course. 'I thought it would be fun to confuse them, now that they were convinced it was Mrs Knight,' he said. 'I was going to tell you all this.'

'Oh?' The sergeant, disbelieving.

'I was, honestly! But then ... .' He aimed his remarks at the chief inspector. 'I spoke to the doctor who was here,' he said. 'About pathology. Forensic science. That's what I'd really like to do,' he said. 'And I thought if I told you I'd taken the stuff I might not be able to.'

Lloyd nodded. 'Well, that remains to be seen,' he said. 'But why?' he asked. 'Why were you going to tell us?'

'Because it must have been Mr Newby who came into the Barn,' Matthew said. 'His car was parked in there.'

'You could have told us about the car without admitting to the thefts,' said the sergeant, still suspicious.

'I know. But ... .' Matthew paused. 'I know something. I saw something when I was – well, another time. Another time that I took things.'

Chief Inspector Lloyd looked at him, his eyes slightly narrowed, as though he was trying to read print too small for his eyesight.

'Matthew,' he said, 'you have admitted stealing various items over the last eighteen months.'

'It wasn't really stealing,' Matthew said again.

'I am going to ask you to come to the police station to make a statement. As Mr Treadwell is *in loco parentis*, he will accompany you, and will be present during the interview. You can be legally represented if you wish.'

Matthew looked at Treadwell, who seemed as though he might be going to be sick.

'We will contact your parents as soon as possible,' Lloyd went on.

Matthew thought Treadwell was going to faint.

Sam left the art room, feeling hungry. He knew what he wanted; he knew if he gave himself over to it, it would come. But he had to give it time, let it come to him, and he needed something now, something to tide him over. Caroline had said she wasn't ready for that kind of commitment. Thank God for that. He wasn't looking for Caroline's commitment; he couldn't understand how something so trivial as the gratification of sexual appetite could ever assume such dimensions. It would be like having to commit yourself to a plate of chips before you ate it.

Sam would eventually be ready for his commitment; he would work at it, coaxing the colour and light out of his brushes and on to the canvas until it released him, if it ever did. It was wonderful, and dreadful, and no woman could ever produce the feeling of exhilaration he had when he worked, the triumph, the sheer joy that he would experience on its completion. Or the terrible anticlimax of its being over.

In the meantime, Caroline would suffice. Right now, however, food would have to fill the gap being created by the images that danced out of reach; he wandered over to the canteen, but lunch wasn't being served for another hour. He used one of the slot machines, and bought himself a bar of chocolate.

He walked back along the lane, where the images grew suddenly sharper, as he bit into the chocolate. He stopped by the art room, then carried on. He must let the thought germinate, let it come in its own time. He walked slowly, lost in thoughts which were interrupted by the sight of Lloyd and his sergeant getting into a car with Treadwell and young Matthew Cawston.

He watched it drive away, saw Mrs Treadwell look anxiously after it, and quickened his step to reach her before she went back into the house. Matthew, she said, had been stealing.

Stealing may have been their excuse to take him away, but that wasn't why Matthew had been bundled off to the police station. Good old British bobbies. They could always be relied upon to go off at half-cock, firing his bullets for him, and incidentally sharpening the image in his mind; he could see it, he could almost touch it.

It was agony, forcing himself to go back to the flat. Thank God Newby wasn't there. He paced the room, feeling his way cautiously into the image; this was just the start. He had to hold back, had to wait, had to let it take its own time. His only desire was to seize a pencil, sketch his thoughts, but he mustn't. He mustn't force the hard, clear image on to paper, or it would stay like that, like a photograph. When it was committed to paper, it would be pliant, yielding to his pen over and over, until every detail, every line, every curve was perfect. And when it exploded on to the canvas, if he did it right, people who could see past their prejudices would cry for his slot machine, and they wouldn't know why.

He swore when he heard the knock at the door, and didn't open it. But the knocking continued, and he strode over angrily, expecting another visit from the constabulary.

A large, handsome man in a flash suit stood at the door, by no stretch of the imagination a policeman.

'Yes?'

'Where the hell is the headmaster?' the man demanded to know. 'I've tried the school, and his house. The man's nowhere to be found.'

'He's with the police,' said Sam. 'At the police station, I presume.' He smiled. 'We've had some trouble here,' he said.

'Trouble?' The man snorted. 'I'll say you've had trouble! And you're going to have worse trouble, believe you me! Where's his deputy? I want to speak to him.'

Sam grinned. 'I doubt if that will be possible,' he said. 'Unless you've got an Indian guide.'

'What?'

'Suicide,' said Sam, never a man to waste words.

The man opened his mouth, then closed it.

'He was married to Friday night's corpse,' said Sam helpfully. 'He's today's.'

'Now, look!' Sam's visitor was going an interesting shade. 'I want an explanation of what's been going on at this school!'

They'd be coming by the coach load by tomorrow morning, thought Sam. 'You're a parent, are you?' he asked.

'My name is Cawston.'

'Matthew's father?' asked Sam.

'You know Matthew?'

'Matthew is our head boy,' said Sam. 'But, even if he wasn't, I would know him. We don't have that many boys here. And do you wonder?'

'I want to know what the hell's going on!' Cawston roared.

Sam opened the door wider. 'Come in,' he said. 'I'll tell you all about it.'

Treadwell stared at the boy, who sat at the table in the interview room, brazening it out. Opposite him sat Chief Superintendent Allison and Chief Inspector Lloyd; the ranks bothered Treadwell a little. Beside him sat the solicitor, hastily called, wearing a Sunday sweater over his shirt and tie, to indicate just how much he was going to cost. Treadwell hadn't been able to reach Cawston senior yet; he had taken the decision for him, knowing that whatever he did it would be wrong.

'Do you know why you're here, Matthew?' asked the chief superintendent.

'I stole some things,' said Matthew.

'What Matthew means is that he took some things without

permission,' said the solicitor. 'There was no intention permanently to deprive the owners of these articles.'

Matthew Cawston was far and away the brightest boy Treadwell had ever had through his hands; a brilliant career in almost any field he cared to name was virtually a foregone conclusion, and Treadwell had announced that the thief would be expelled. Announcements at assembly weren't legally binding, of course, and he doubted if he really would have carried out his threat in any event, whoever the culprit. The items stolen were so ridiculous, so haphazard, that financial gain could never have been the motive. He had been prepared to have a heart-to-heart with whoever it was, find out what it was all about. Even get them help if it seemed warranted. But Matthew? It simply didn't seem possible.

Matthew was his flagship; when Treadwell would casually suggest that 'one of the boys' show the parents of prospective pupils round the school, it was Matthew whom he detailed to do the showing-round. Clever, but not a swot; strong and athletic, but not a show-off. A tasteful, well-designed, colour-supplement advertisement for the school. A thief.

Perhaps he stole because he was bored, because everything came too easily to him, and he needed the excitement. Perhaps because his overbearing father and his volatile mother had failed him in some way. Or perhaps because underneath all the effortless academic achievement he was just a bad lot.

But, whatever his reasons, if only he had owned up sooner, it might well have been possible to drop the whole thing. To give the boy some sleepless nights, and then tell him that he was being given a second chance. It might even have been possible to keep the alarming Mr Cawston senior out of it, to tell the police that the school did not wish to go any further in the matter of the thefts, and quietly set the whole thing to rest. Why he stole was a question for the psychologists, and didn't really concern Treadwell.

But the sergeant's obsession with the thefts had made any glossing-over impossible. Damn the woman. And the chief inspector, and the chief superintendent. Treadwell would have thought he would have had more sense than to worry about the thefts when two people had died. And it was just the thefts, wasn't it? He cleared his throat.

Matthew looked at him briefly, before his eyes flicked back to the police.

'Don't you want to know what I saw?' he asked.

'All in good time, Matthew,' said the chief inspector.

Sergeant Hill came in then, putting a sheet of paper down in front of Lloyd. Allison read it over Lloyd's shoulder, and left the room. Treadwell was beginning to feel panicky.

'Did you steal a golf-club, Matthew?' asked Lloyd.

'What's your interest in this particular item, Chief Inspector?' asked the solicitor.

The sergeant glanced at Lloyd, and then she answered the solicitor's question. 'Matthew has told us that he took all the items which have gone missing in the last eighteen months,' she said. 'One of them is still unaccounted for. An old golf-club – a niblick, it's called. We would like to know what Matthew did with it.'

Matthew shook his head. 'I didn't steal a golf-club.'

Lloyd took a slow breath. 'The thing is, Matthew,' he said, 'it looks rather as though that club was used to murder Mrs Hamlyn.'

Treadwell thought he was going to die. The statement hadn't taken him by surprise; it had taken no one by surprise. They all knew that they weren't there about some thefts which barely amounted to ten pounds' worth of stuff. But he'd said it now. He'd used the word.

'I didn't take a golf-club,' Matthew repeated, still shaking his head. 'I didn't. But I saw something – why won't you let me tell you what I saw? I saw Mr Newby with—'

'You don't have to say anything at this juncture,' warned his solicitor.

'But I want to! I was going to, anyway! I thought that's why I was here.'

'Tell us now, Matthew,' Lloyd said. 'I'm listening.' But there was no gentle encouragement about his tone this time. This time he meant business, and Matthew obviously knew that.

And he told them, with the odd glance over to where Treadwell sat, about a scene he'd witnessed in the Hamlyns' bedroom between Newby and Mrs Hamlyn. Treadwell listened, his head swimming, hardly daring to breathe.

Lloyd listened, but he didn't comment, didn't ask questions. 'Think about it, Matthew,' he said, and he and the sergeant left. After about five minutes, she came back.

'Right, Matthew,' she said brightly. 'Let's get this statement down on paper.'

The sergeant went through every single item, asking where he'd taken it from, what he'd done with it, checking his answers off on the list she had made of the items she had recovered; Treadwell sat watching, still half-hoping that it was all some sort of nightmare.

He would have sold his soul for a drink.

Caroline pulled a tissue from the box, wiped her eyes and nose, and tried to smile. 'I'm sorry,' she said.

'Don't be silly,' said Philip.

'You must think I do this all the time.'

He looked shamefaced. 'I can't have helped,' he said.

'It only bothered me to start with,' she said, then felt the pain herself as he went crimson. 'Oh, no,' she said, taking his hand. 'I didn't mean to upset you. Please, forget it. It doesn't matter.'

'It does,' he mumbled, like one of the boys being told off. 'Even Sam knew.'

She sighed. 'Yes,' she said. 'He said as much.' He'd said much more than that.

He looked up, appalled. 'He *spoke* to you about it?'

She felt out of her depth. 'Well – yes,' she said. 'You know what he's like! He was trying to put me off – he doesn't think you have any right to fancy me.'

'He's right.' His head dropped again in an agony of embarrassment.

'He *isn't*!' She held his hand tightly. 'It's just another injury, Philip. Like your leg and your back, except it isn't physical.'

He nodded miserably. 'I know,' he said. 'You're right.'

'I'm always right,' she said, smiling. 'You're wrong about one thing,' he said, with a shy duck of his head. 'I don't fancy you.'

'No?'

'Diana Hamlyn told me,' he said. 'The first day I got here. She said I was in love with you. She was right.'

She smiled again.

'But I'd be no good to you,' he said again. 'A physical and emotional wreck is something I don't imagine you need right now.'

'You're not a wreck!' she shouted. 'And I think for a start that you should find somewhere else to live. I know Sam – he'll encourage you to think like that.'

Philip looked up. 'I'm hardly a threat to Sam,' he said.

She shook her head. 'You haven't got Sam figured at all, have you?' she said. 'Has he told you he's not queer yet?'

Philip's eyes widened. 'Yes, as it happens,' he said. 'He told me this morning.' He looked disbelieving. 'You're not saying he is?'

She shook her head. 'No,' she said. 'He makes do with women. But he doesn't like them. And he doesn't want to lose you to the opposition.'

Philip shook his head.

'Oh – you believe macho Sam's stories, do you? Philip – you've got more sex appeal in your left earlobe than he's got in his whole body. I should think Diana Hamlyn's the only woman who ever looked at him twice!'

'You did.'

'No. I didn't – I . . . .' She couldn't explain. And now she was scared again, scared that she would lose Philip.

'You said you didn't discourage him,' he persisted.

'No, because I thought he could . . . .' She looked at him. How could he possibly think he was less attractive than Sam, who would have carried on regardless if she'd dropped dead? She shivered, as she always did when she thought of it, and stood up to try to mask the involuntary movement.

Philip was on his feet, too. 'Well, he *can*,' he said. 'Which is more than I can do, as he pointed out to me only today.'

Caroline closed her eyes. Philip would have shown more

consideration for an inflatable doll than Sam had shown for her. 'Is it that important?' she asked.

He nodded. 'It is if you can't do it,' he said.

'I don't believe you can't do it,' she said. 'But even if you can't, you'd still be a better bargain than Sam.'

'I have to go.'

'No – Philip.' She caught his arm. 'Stay, please. I don't expect anything from you. Just stay with me. I'm scared.'

He looked at her. 'You think Sam raped Diana because of you, don't you?' he asked. 'And you think he was watching you. That's why you're scared. Isn't it?'

She dropped her eyes from his, and nodded.

He moved to the door, and Caroline looked up as he opened it. He turned back to her.

'Sam wasn't watching you,' he said. 'And he didn't rape Diana.'

With that, he left, and Caroline had to sit down, or she would have collapsed.

No, no, not Philip. Please God, not Philip.

'What the hell's going on here?'

The large man who brushed off Jack Woodford's restraining arm stood in the doorway, his face apoplectic.

Jack shrugged, and Lloyd stood up, wishing, not for the first time, that he was taller.

'Mr Cawston,' said Jack quietly. 'Matthew's father.'

'We've been trying to get in touch with you, Mr Cawston,' said Lloyd, coming out from behind his desk, and extending his hand, just as though he imagined Mr Cawston might shake it.

'I was already here!' he roared. 'I wasn't letting my son stay at a place where—' He spluttered. 'And when I get there I'm told that you clowns have arrested him!'

'Matthew hasn't been arrested, Mr Cawston,' said Lloyd, taking Judy's chair, and putting it down in front of his desk. 'He's making a statement.'

'It's the same thing!'

'No,' said Lloyd. 'Do have a seat, Mr Cawston.'

'Er ... Mr Waters is here, too,' said Jack. 'He says he's been asked to make a statement.'

'Oh, yes,' said Lloyd. 'See to it, will you?'

'Yes, sir.'

'Are you in charge of this murder?' Cawston demanded as Jack left, and Judy came in.

'No,' said Lloyd. 'Chief Superintendent Allison is in charge of the murder inquiry.'

'Then get him! I'll speak to the ringmaster.'

Lloyd bit his lip, and nodded, leaving Judy with Mr Cawston while he rang the chief super, who groaned as Lloyd told him what he thought of Cawston so far. 'I'll be right down,' he said. 'Don't say anything, Lloyd. Let me handle it.'

It would probably have been easier for Lloyd to stop breathing, but he went back to his office, and manfully parried Cawston's questions with non-answers until the super arrived.

'Mr Cawston,' he said, after Lloyd had effected a kind of introduction. 'You'll want to talk to Matthew—'

'I want to talk to you! What sort of a circus are you running here?'

Fifteen love. Lloyd had to admire the man's ability to choose a metaphor and stick to it.

'Certainly you can talk to me.' Allison smiled, politely awaiting a question. 'What did you want to know?'

'Why has my son been arrested?' demanded Cawston.

'Your son hasn't been arrested,' said Allison. 'He has been interviewed about the theft from his school of several items over the last eighteen months.'

'What?' Cawston frowned, shaking his head. 'That's not what they're saying at the school. They're saying you think he was involved with this tramp that's got herself murdered!'

No coincidence, then, that Mr Waters had arrived at the same time as Cawston, Lloyd thought.

'I can't be responsible for what "they" are saying, Mr Cawston. We're not saying anything of the sort,' said Allison. 'He has admitted theft. Whether there is a prosecution depends largely on the school.'

Cawston stared at him. 'Matthew?' he said. That took a moment to sink in; then he rallied. 'What the hell did he steal, for God's sake? The crown jewels?'

'The thefts were very minor,' said Allison. 'Only one of the items was worth more than a few pence.'

'And just because of that you cart him off in a police car in front of the whole school?'

'Matthew was brought here in the chief inspector's own car,' Allison said.

'Why was he brought here at all?'

It was weak-wristed; it landed at Allison's feet.

'He was being questioned about his most recent theft by Mrs Hamlyn less than an hour before she was murdered.'

Cawston rushed the net to scoop up the dropshot. 'I knew it! You're accusing him of murder!'

'No, Mr Cawston, we are not. But another of the stolen items is believed to be the murder weapon. If your son stole this item, then we are bound to ask him what he did with it, where he hid it, who might have had access to it – whether he was stealing on his own, or in concert with others. Matthew also wanted to give us information which he felt might be relevant to the inquiry into the death of Mrs Hamlyn. He is here to make a statement. Nothing more.'

For a moment, Cawston blinked a little as the conversational lob went soaring over his head, out of reach. But then he raced it to the base-line, and it came screaming back over the net. '*Believed* to be the murder weapon?' he said. 'You don't even *know*?'

'It hasn't been found yet.'

Lloyd watched Cawston's face with interest as several different reactions chased over them. Anger, disbelief, relief, worry. 'Not been found?' he said, in the end. 'So you don't know that anything he took was used to murder the woman, do you?'

'No,' said Allison. 'But we have to find out. His headmaster was with him, of course. Mr Treadwell thought it advisable to engage the services of a solicitor, who was also present. Your son was interviewed by Detective Sergeant Hill, who is a very experienced officer, and who is dealing with the thefts at the school.' He indicated Judy's presence.

Cawston swung round to look at her. 'And this woman's murder? Is she dealing with that?' he asked.

Allison inclined his head slightly. 'She is involved in the murder inquiry, yes,' he said. 'As one of the last people to see Mrs Hamlyn alive, Matthew is a very important witness. If he were my son, I'd sooner he was here than anywhere else.'

Game, set and match.

Cawston's anger turned to sulky co-operation. 'Can I see him? Can I talk to him, alone?'

Allison smiled, as a constable brought Matthew into the office. 'Matthew is free to leave, Mr Cawston. You can do anything you like with him.'

Lloyd blew out his cheeks as they all trooped out of his office, and sat down again, looking up at Judy. 'Well?' he said. 'What do you make of his story about Newby?'

Judy shrugged. 'He didn't tell us his car was in the Barn,' she said. 'But he couldn't have stolen the golf-club.'

'Why the hell would anyone *want* to steal it?' Lloyd asked.

'To murder Mrs Hamlyn with?' said Judy. She thought about that for a moment. 'With which to murder Mrs Hamlyn?' she suggested, as an alternative.

'In order to murder Mrs Hamlyn,' Lloyd said, with a grin.

'It can't have been that, can it?' she said.

'Why not?' said Lloyd sourly. 'They had a nymphomaniac, a kleptomaniac and a dipsomaniac – maybe they needed a homicidal maniac to complete the set.'

Judy laughed.

'But no one planned this,' he said. 'Even Mrs Hamlyn didn't know she was going to leave the Hall when she did. She took Matthew out to try to get the pen back with the minimum of fuss, and got herself murdered.'

'If Newby's telling the truth,' Judy said, 'then it couldn't have been him that interrupted Matthew and Mrs Hamlyn.'

'He who,' said Lloyd absently. 'No. No, it couldn't.' He tipped his chair back, swinging it gently to and fro on its back legs. 'Sam?' he suggested.

'He admitted being there,' said Judy. 'Would he do that if he had something to hide?'

'He would if he thought that young Matthew had seen him,' said Lloyd. 'Wouldn't he?' He let the chair fall forward.

'But we saw him. That night. He couldn't have cleaned himself up that well.'

'Maybe we just haven't seen the right clothes yet.'

'Lloyd.' She gave him a look.

'It's not so unlikely! He changes out of that music-hall dinner-jacket into something more suitable for taking Mrs Knight out. Realises his pen's gone – goes looking for it. Runs into Diana, and kills her, for whatever reason. Goes back, changes into the jeans and sweater and leaves the premises altogether. We know he didn't go straight to the club, remember. He could have been getting rid of the golf-club, like I said.'

'But he wasn't going out with Mrs Knight by that time.'

'She seemed to think he was. She was all dressed up.'

Judy shook her head. 'She says she was going to go alone. And you can't take any more of his clothes, Lloyd. The man won't have anything left to wear.'

Lloyd smiled. 'Anyway, it might not have been necessary for him to change. He might just have gone somewhere to dry out before he went on to the club – Freddie doesn't think the killer's clothes would necessarily get dirty.'

'He thinks you can rape and murder someone in a downpour and not get dirty?'

'If she *was* in Newby's car, he wouldn't have to get dirty, would he? And the field was frozen – no mud. Freddie says her injuries wouldn't have caused that much blood to splash – especially not if he was at the far end of a golf-club. He might just have got very wet.'

'And you think it was Sam. On no evidence.'

Lloyd knew he had no evidence. But he had Sam. In the interview room. And there was something wrong with Sam's story, if only he could sort out what it was.

'I take it you wrote down what Sam said about his pen?'

'Yes,' she said. She found the page.

Lloyd listened as she read, closing his eyes when she got to the bit that mattered. How could he have just let it pass at the time? Because he let Waters get to him, that's how. He stood up. 'Let's go and have a word with Mr Waters before he leaves,' he said. 'There is something he did that night that could bear a little explanation.' He smiled. 'Or, rather,' he said, 'something he didn't do.'

He deliberately left it at that, enjoying watching Judy's brow furrow as she resolutely refused to ask him what he meant.

They found Waters having his statement read over to him. Lloyd waited until the constable had finished, and Waters had been handed a pen with which to sign it.

'It's an offence,' he said.

Waters looked up. 'What is?' he asked.

'Making a statement knowing it to be false.'

Waters sighed. 'I've had enough of this, Lloyd,' he said. 'Your superior officer is going to hear from me.'

'That'll be nice for him.'

Judy sat down in the seat vacated by the constable, and produced the notebook. The constable stood by the door. Lloyd positioned himself behind Waters.

'Let's look at your statement, Mr Waters. You say you noticed your pen missing, and went to look for it. But that's not what you told us, is it?'

Waters twisted round. 'Of course it is!'

'No. My sergeant wrote down exactly what you said. And you said you thought you had left your pen on the table.'

Waters sighed extravagantly. 'Oh, I do beg your pardon. You are a stickler for detail, aren't you? Bordering on the pedantic, I'd say.'

'So why didn't you go and look on the table?'

Waters swore, screwing up the statement. 'You're going to regret this,' he said.

'I'll tell you why,' Lloyd went on. 'Because you knew where your pen was. Diana Hamlyn told you what had happened – when you were with her.'

'I wasn't with her. I saw her, that's all. With Cawston. Going into the Barn. They left the small door open, and I went to see what was going on. I heard her tell him she'd seen him take a pen, so I knew it had to be my—' He pursed his lips. 'My expletive deleted pen.'

'And you went in.'

The constable had hastily started taking notes. What with him and Judy, this was going to be the best-documented conversation on record.

'No. I left her to it. I went back to the flat. I did exactly what I told you. Exactly what was in that statement.'

'Why?'

'Because I was getting soaked to the skin. It seemed the best place to go.'

'Didn't you want to get your pen back? You seem anxious enough to get it back now.'

Waters tapped his fingers lightly on the table as he spoke. 'I knew Diana. I knew she would go through all the proper channels in dealing with young Cawston. He was denying it – she wasn't going to get anywhere like that. I preferred to deal with him my way.'

'Which was?'

'A clip round the ear. Or two. I'd have got the pen back, don't you worry.' Waters smiled. 'But Diana's demise presented me with an opportunity for much more poetic justice. I let you take him away. And I hope you scared the shit out of him.'

Lloyd sat down on the table. 'Oh,' he said slowly. 'You let us chase after Matthew because he stole your pen?'

'Yes.'

'Or because it stopped us dwelling on the logistics?'

'I don't know words with that many syllables.'

Lloyd bent his head close, and spoke confidentially to Waters. 'Someone interrupted Mrs Hamlyn's interview with Matthew,' he said. 'Someone who seems to have had sex with Mrs Hamlyn, possibly in a car. Newby's car was in there.'

Waters didn't move. Most people pulled away when you got too close. 'Then I suggest you talk to Newby,' he said.

'I'm talking to you.'

'You have no right to keep me here.' Waters sat back in his chair. 'I will be making a complaint to your superiors. This is harassment.'

'How long were you with Mrs Hamlyn?' asked Judy.

'I wasn't with her.'

'Sure?'

'Of course I'm sure. I wasn't with her, I didn't rape her, and I didn't murder her.' He drummed his fingers on the desk. 'When are you going to let me go? I've got work to do.'

'As you said, Mr Waters. We have no power to keep you here. And I don't think you raped her,' said Lloyd. 'I don't think she *was* raped. But, then, you knew that all along, didn't you? So I think that perhaps you went with her, and failed to tell us that.'

Waters grinned. 'Not me. I would have, given half a chance. Any port in a storm, and all that.' He looked back at Judy. 'Even you would have done,' he said. 'I'd have thawed you out, no danger.'

Lloyd contemplated sending her away on some pretext, but he wanted to go on living, and Judy's policy was to ignore Mr Waters. 'So what went wrong?' he asked. 'She was there, the car was there.'

'And Matthew was there,' said Waters. 'Even Diana drew the line at an audience.'

Lloyd sighed. He'd hoped to trick him into admitting that he had been alone with Diana. He had failed.

'And, besides, I didn't want her to know *I* was there. I've told you – I wanted to deal with Matthew my way, and that would have been less than official. And I was getting soaked. I went back to the flat, changed, and went out.'

'At eleven-fifteen, or thereabouts,' said Lloyd. 'But you didn't get to this club until twelve-thirty. What were you doing?'

'I've already told you what I was doing,' Waters said. 'I have co-operated fully with your inquiry, as I will tell your superiors.'

'You have consistently *refused* to tell us what you were doing!' Lloyd shouted.

Waters raised his eyebrows. 'I picked up a prostitute, Chief Inspector. A hooker, a whore, a lady of the evening. That's why I waited until after closing-time – they're thicker on the ground then. Do you want to do me for kerb-crawling?'

'I want to know when you think you told me that before,' said Lloyd.

'I told you at the very start,' said Waters. 'It wasn't an inapposite adjective, Mr Lloyd. Crude, but not inapposite.' He smiled. 'You're going to catch it from your boss,' he said, wagging his finger.

Lloyd got up. 'She had better have a name,' he said.

Waters's smile grew. 'I couldn't give you her name if I wanted to. I wasn't interested in her name. But I don't have to worry about that, because you have found nothing whatever to connect me to Diana Hamlyn's murder, and you know it.'

Lloyd shook his head as the constable made a move to stop Waters leaving, and shrugged. He and Judy walked back along to the office, neither of them speaking. They sat down, and looked at one another.

'He's right,' said Judy.

She had a remarkable talent for stating the obvious. Lloyd wondered if it was worth deploying manpower to try to find whoever Sam was with. The best they could do was find her, that would prove Sam's story. The worst they could do was not find her, and that hardly constituted proof that he was lying.

'Even if it's true,' he said, 'he could still have killed her. She was probably dead before he left the school.'

'How would he have got hold of the golf-club?'

'God knows,' said Lloyd. 'Unless he stole it in the first place.' But that didn't make sense.

'Why did you say that you didn't think that Mrs Hamlyn had been raped?' Judy asked, after a moment.

'Because I don't think she was,' he said tiredly.

Judy stiffened slightly. 'You've joined the chorus, have you? Diana Hamlyn couldn't have been raped; she was the school bicycle?'

'She was in Newby's car with whoever it was.'

'You don't know that!'

'Not yet, but I imagine forensics will prove it.'

'So because she was in a car she can't have been raped?'

Lloyd sighed. 'A car that wasn't going anywhere, Judy. All the evidence suggests co-operation.'

'The evidence suggests a not inconsiderable degree of sexual violence, according to Freddie,' she said. 'You've read his report. He *hurt* her, Lloyd.'

'Maybe she got more than she bargained for,' said Lloyd. 'A professional foul, Freddie called it Perhaps that's why she ran away. Or – maybe it wasn't that unusual, as far as she was concerned.'

'She *wanted* to be treated like that? Is that what you're saying?' asked Judy.

'Possibly. Or at any rate put up with it, in order to get what she needed. Whichever, I think Freddie's right. I think she consented to the sex, and I am inclined to believe that she was killed by someone else. Someone who discovered what was going on, and didn't like it.'

The office door opened. 'A Mr Coleman to see you, Chief Inspector,' Jack said.

His look was one that Lloyd knew well; Jack was the only person he knew who could wink without batting an eyelid. He ushered in a small, plump man with a neat, greying moustache. He carried a large cardboard box, which he held protectively, not without difficulty, under his arm.

'Coleman, Coleman's Outfitters. I thought I really ought to bring this to your attention in person, in view of the circumstances. I do hope I'm not making a fuss about nothing.'

So do I, thought Lloyd. 'Mr Coleman, we welcome any help we can get in a murder case. Well – all cases, really. Do have a seat,' he said as Judy got up.

Coleman sat, transferring the box to his lap. 'I wouldn't want to send you on a wild-goose chase,' he said.

Lloyd was always chasing wild geese. One more wouldn't hurt. 'So,' said Lloyd, smiling. 'I gather the box has some significance?'

'Well – I think so. It was brought back yesterday by a customer – it's one of our hire suits. Now, normally, they're checked over – you know – just to see that we have got the same suit back, but yesterday – well, we're short-handed at the moment, with the stand at the Civic Hall.' He raised his eyebrows. 'You know,' he said. 'The exhibition of non-central traders – to let people know where we are, and so on. A number of my assistants are manning the stand, and so yesterday, when this one was returned, no one checked it.'

Lloyd frowned. It was hardly relevant, but it bothered him. 'But isn't your shop . . .?' He pointed vaguely out of the window in the direction of R. J. Coleman, Gentlemen's Outfitters, smack in the middle of the town centre.

'Yes. But we also have a shop in Queens Estate. Mary Tudor Square. It's quite different. Young, casual – sportswear. You know.'

'Do you?' said Lloyd, startled. What was the world coming to? The Queens Estate shops had had to be boarded up even during working hours in the old days. You knew where you were with it. You could go to the Good Queen Bess at chucking-out time and make your arrest-tally look good. A gentlemen's outfitters? Lloyd shook his head. Queens Estate had fallen to the Yuppies.

'See?' said Mr Coleman. 'That's why we've got the stand. Anyway, we had hired out a number of suits to people at the school where – well, the young woman was – you know. And that meant we had a lot of dry-cleaning to sort out, so I decided to pop in this morning to see what was what before tomorrow. And . . . .' He stood up with difficulty. 'I mean, we expect the odd soup stain, perhaps even a slight tear, but . . . .'

Lloyd sat forward.

'I thought you ought to see it.'

He placed the box on the desk, and grasped the lid, inching it up to reveal folded tissue paper. Lloyd glanced at Judy as she came over to witness the unveiling, and the tissue was drawn away.

The jacket was smeared with mud; dark stains had dried on the lapels, and others, more visible at the time, had been subject to an ineffectual attempt to remove them. One pocket had almost been torn off. Lloyd carefully lifted out the jacket, laying it down, and picked up the trousers. More of the dark stains, under the waistband, and at the tops of the legs, were clearly visible. No attempt had been made to clean them up. The knees were caked with the thin, dried mud.

The shocked silence into which Mr Coleman spoke was almost tangible, and his words wedged themselves into it, seeming not to break it at all.

'It was hired by a Mr P. Newby,' he said.

Lloyd looked at Judy, at troubled brown eyes that held no hint of triumph.

Freddie was wrong.

Chapter Seven

Judy stared out of the window at the darkening sky, as, armed with a search warrant, they drove back to the school. She hadn't formed much of an opinion of Newby, except to register that he was an attractive man. She tried to remember what he had been like the first time she had seen him, when Mrs Knight had brought him into Treadwell's office. What had her impression been then?

Different, she thought. He hadn't been in anything like as much pain, of course. He had been able to walk better; much more quickly, deftly. There had been something almost dashing about him. And that was when she remembered.

'How the hell would he get hold of the golf-club?' Lloyd was muttering.

Judy closed her eyes. 'He didn't have the golf-club,' she said. 'He used his stick.'

'No,' said Lloyd. 'I thought of that, but Freddie said it was something wooden – it splintered. His stick's metal. And it wouldn't be heavy enough – these NHS sticks are—'

'His other stick,' she said, waiting for the explosion.

There was a silence, which was worse.

'What other stick, Judy?' he said, at last.

'Oh, I'm sorry, Lloyd. I *knew* there was something about him, and I couldn't think what it was. I thought it was just . . . . Anyway, he had another stick when I saw him first. A walking-cane. Black. With a heavy silver knob.'

This time the silence seemed to be going to last for the rest of her life. But no such luck.

'Cawston was giving Allison a hard time,' he said conversationally.

The tone didn't fool Judy.

'I wonder what he's going to say when he finds out that the thefts had nothing to do with the murder at all,' he continued. 'I suppose Allison might let me off with my entrails intact. I mean, all he did was go three rounds with Cawston because of some mythical murder weapon that I said junior might have stolen.'

'I'm sorry,' Judy said again, as he drew a breath. 'But I wasn't at the school to see Newby, was I? I was there about the thefts – the man had only arrived that morning. I wasn't taking any notice of him.'

'Some ancient golf-club that we couldn't even find,' Lloyd went on, as if she hadn't spoken. 'Which was stolen last December. Which was kept in a barn. A *barn*, no less, from which anyone could have taken it, and from which young Mr Cawston denied taking it. And, to cap it all, it doesn't matter if he did take it, because Mr Newby used his stick.'

Judy apologised again. If she hadn't been so keen to get her own back on Lloyd, she might have seen the golf-club in perspective. She might never have seen the damn thing at all. Perhaps it was just as well she was transferring.

'Still, all is not lost,' Lloyd said, pulling into the school driveway. 'I'm sure if you need a beat bobby in Malworth you'll put in a good word for me.'

Oh, God. She would be second-in-command at Malworth. Where she would make a habit of getting everyone running round looking for the wrong thing, while overlooking the one thing that only she knew.

The squad car waited outside the staff block, and she and Lloyd met up with its occupants before Lloyd knocked loudly and officially on the flat door.

Sam Waters opened it.

'Christ,' he said. 'You've come mob-handed.'

'Is Mr Newby here?' demanded Lloyd.

'I expect he's in his room,' said Waters, standing aside as they trooped in behind Lloyd.

Judy watched as Lloyd strode across the room to Newby's door.

He knocked, and opened it. She could see Newby as he lay stretched out on top of the bed; he was struggling to get to his feet as she walked across to where Lloyd stood in the doorway.

Lloyd held up the warrant. 'Search warrant, Mr Newby,' he said. 'Right, Sergeant.'

Judy took a step into the room, followed by the uniformed constables.

'No – wait,' said Newby, looking baffled. 'What do you want? What are you looking for?'

Judy took a breath. 'A silver-topped walking-stick,' she said.

She could hear a soft chuckle from Sam Waters, and turned to look at him. He smiled, and left the flat.

'I . . . I lost it. I think it might have been stolen.'

Judy looked back at Newby. Lloyd said that her look made strong men tremble; it certainly saved a lot of time when discovery was inevitable, and Newby was not a strong man.

He blushed. 'Bottom of the wardrobe,' he mumbled.

Judy opened the wardrobe, and moved some bed linen. Underneath was the cane, broken almost in two. 'Chief Inspector,' she said.

Lloyd knelt down, and looked at it, then at her. 'He made a better job of cleaning that than the suit,' he muttered, looking a little puzzled. He stood up. 'Mr Newby, can you tell me how your stick came to be broken?'

'It snapped,' he said. 'The doctor said it might. He told me I shouldn't use it.'

'Why did you lie when the sergeant asked you about it?'

Newby's skin reddened again. 'I had nothing to do with the murder, if that's what you think.'

'Then you have some explaining to do,' Lloyd said. 'Can you tell us how the clothes you were wearing that evening got into the state they are in?' Lloyd waited, but Newby said nothing. 'Where were you between ten-fifteen and eleven-fifteen on Friday night?' he asked.

'I've told you.'

'And you have nothing to add to what you've told us?'

Newby shook his head.

'Do you have your car keys, Mr Newby? We will be taking your car for forensic examination.'

Newby produced the keys.

'And you had better get your coat,' said Lloyd. 'It's cold out.'

'What's happening?' Newby asked.

'I'll tell you what's happening,' said Lloyd. 'You are being arrested on suspicion of murder, Mr Newby. You are not obliged to say anything, but anything you do say will be taken down, and may be given in evidence.'

The constables led Newby to the squad car.

'Here,' Lloyd said, giving his own keys to Judy. 'You take my car back.' He called to one of the constables just preparing to leave the search, and together they went to Newby's car.

The squad car swept away, followed, after a few moments, by Newby's car. Lloyd lifted a hand in salute as they drove off, and Judy walked slowly back to the car. They were never what you expected, even if you had seen it all before. Somehow, you still thought you would know. But no one ever did. Not neighbours, or friends, or colleagues. No one. And especially not the victim.

Waters was standing beside Lloyd's car. He clapped his hands slowly together as she approached. 'I told you so,' he said.

Judy got in, slammed the door, and started the engine, but Waters tapped on the window.

After a moment's hesitation, she wound it down, and he bent down towards her.

'You don't have to rush off, do you?' he said. 'You've got him now – you can take some time off.'

'I have work to do, Mr Waters.'

Waters leaned his arms along the window. 'I just thought that now that I'm no longer a suspect you might come out for a drink with me.'

'Thank you, Mr Waters, but I'm still on duty.'

Waters glanced over to where the other police officers were assembling at the van, ready to go home.

'It doesn't have to be right now,' he said. 'When do you get off?'

'I don't think it would be a good idea, Mr Waters.'

'Oh, come on,' he said. 'No hard feelings.' He winked. 'On second thoughts, I can promise you some,' he said.

'I'm driving off, Mr Waters. If you are still leaning on the car, you might get hurt.'

'But that wouldn't be a nice thing to do,' he said. 'And I can get you and your boss into trouble as – it is, without your adding injury to insult.' He smiled. 'So why don't you just come out for a drink with me, give me my pen back, and I'll forget the whole thing.'

One hand dangled into the car, his fingers brushing her knee. Judy switched off the ignition and removed the keys before he thought of it.

'That's better,' he said, giving her knee a squeeze. 'I'm sure you can be nice when you want to.'

Judy smiled, and looked round at the police van. 'Well,' she said quietly, 'I'll tell you what . . . .' She beckoned him closer to her.

And no one but the predictably and profoundly shocked Waters heard what she said.

Sam watched as she accelerated away. He had never really held out any hope of the sergeant; he had just wanted to rattle her. Instead, she had rattled him. My God, to look at her you would think she wouldn't even know words like that, much less use them. He looked over at the crowd of policemen getting into the van, and went into the staff block, slamming the door. He didn't go into his own flat; he took the stairs two at a time, and knocked lightly on Caroline's door.

He heard the bolt being drawn back, watched her smile fade. She tried to push the door shut again; he wedged his foot in the crack.

'Go away,' she said.

'I've got some news for you.'

'I don't want to talk to you,' she said.

'I was angry,' said Sam. 'I called you names. You're not going to hold that against me, are you? I'd rather you held something else against me.'

'Oh, shut up, Sam. And go away.' She tried to shut the door, but Sam's foot was immovable. A bit painful, with being crushed in the door, but immovable. He smiled. 'Guess who the police have just taken away,' he said.

The pushing stopped, the door opened. Caroline was pale. 'Who?' she asked.

'That's better. Can I come in?'

'No.'

'Then I won't tell you,' he said, sing-song fashion.

She left the door open, and went back into the room. Sam followed, closing it. 'They've taken Newby away,' he said.

'Why? What for?'

'For murdering Diana, that's what for,' he said.

'It's a mistake.' Instantly, without thought.

'It didn't sound like a mistake. Murdered her with his silver-topped cane – doesn't that sound wonderfully decadent to you?'

'You're a liar.'

Sam shook his head. 'They came with uniforms, search warrants, squad cars – the lot.' He smiled. 'See what a narrow squeak you had?' he said. 'Entertaining him up here on your own.' He put his arms round her. 'But never fear – Supersam's here.'

She shook him off. 'Get out.'

'Don't shoot the messenger,' he said. 'I told you so, didn't I? I told you it wasn't healthy. You could have gone the same way as Diana.'

He saw her shiver.

'Just thought I'd let you know you can sleep easy in your bed tonight,' he said, and left.

He heard the door close behind him, heard the bolt being sent home, heard Caroline crying.

He was going to get something to eat.

Philip looked up as they came in. For some moments, Lloyd didn't speak. He looked at Philip rather as though he was considering whether or not to buy him, then walked to the window, and looked out.

The sergeant sat down at the table, her notebook at the ready. She didn't look at him at all. She turned the pages back, making little ticks here and there, then found a fresh sheet, and sat, pen poised.

Lloyd seemed to come to some sort of a decision. He squared his shoulders, and turned from the window. 'Right,' he said. 'You are going to tell us what you did between leaving the Hall at ten-twenty on Friday the fourteenth of February, and talking to us at three a. m. on Saturday the fifteenth. You are going to tell us in detail, missing nothing. And', he said, leaning over the table, his face close to Philip's, 'you are going to tell us now.'

Philip moved back a little. 'I didn't kill Diana Hamlyn,' he said.

'Diana Hamlyn spoke to you, then left the Hall,' said Lloyd. 'You left five minutes later. What did you do after you left?'

'I've told you. I left because I was going to be sick. I went to the toilet – what would you have done?'

'Then what?'

'Then I was sick. When I came out I went to my car, and drove down to the staff block. I've *told* you all this.'

'No, Mr Newby. You omitted to mention that your car was in the Barn. Was there some reason for that?'

'No,' said Philip. Yes. Yes, there was.

'Do you have some sort of explanation of how your clothes got into the state they were in when you took their back to the shop?' he asked.

Philip didn't speak. He should have known he could never be that lucky. But he couldn't tell them. He didn't have to. They had said so.

'Why was your car in the Barn? I thought cars weren't allowed up there?'

'I get a special dispensation,' he said. 'I can't walk very well on the cobbles in bad weather.'

'Whose idea was it?'

'Mine,' said Philip. 'Barry doesn't mind as long as I park in the

Barn and make sure the doors are closed so that other people don't get the same idea.'

But Lloyd was off on another tack altogether by the time Philip had finished explaining.

'How did your clothes get into that mess? How did you break your stick?'

'I fell. The stick broke, and I fell.'

'It must have been some fall,' Lloyd said. 'Where did you fall?'

Philip leaned his head on his hands, his mouth covered, his eyes shut. He didn't want to think about that.

Lloyd got up, and went back over to the window.

'Why did you leave the ball early?' the sergeant asked.

'I was sick. How many more times?'

'You left the toilets, and went to your car. Did you see Diana Hamlyn?'

'I did what I've already told you a dozen times.'

'Which is?'

'I drove down to the staff block, but the light was on in the flat, and I didn't want Sam's company. I'm sure you've seen enough of him to know why.'

The sergeant smiled, suddenly and involuntarily. He hadn't seen her smile before. He would probably have liked her if he'd met her in a more conventional fashion. She reminded him a little of Caroline.

'And then?' she was asking.

And then. Philip felt the heat on his face. 'I needed fresh air,' he said, not looking at either of them. 'I ran down the window and, as I did, I thought I heard someone's feet on the fire-escape. I got out of the car, and walked over, but I couldn't see anyone, so I thought it must have been a shadow or something.'

Lloyd shook his head. 'Not much there to get your clothes covered in mud and blood, is there?' he said. 'When's this fall supposed to have happened?'

Philip's head went down.

'All right,' said Lloyd. 'Let's talk about Mrs Hamlyn. She made advances to you, didn't she? In the bedroom of the Hamlyns' flat on your very first night at the school. Isn't that right?'

'Yes,' he said, baffled.

'And you turned her down.'

'Yes. How do you know that?'

Lloyd smiled. 'There was someone else in the room, Mr Newby,' he said.

Philip shook his head. 'No,' he said.

'Yes.' Lloyd sat back. 'The thief, Mr Newby. The ever present thief.'

Oh, my God. 'Who?' asked Philip.

'Well, since everyone else in the school knows, why shouldn't you? Matthew Cawston.'

'Is that why you took him away?' he said. 'Sam Waters said you thought *he'd* killed Diana.'

'Mr Waters is something of a sensationalist, wouldn't you say?'

'He's something,' agreed Philip.

'But back to Mrs Hamlyn. Did she give up?'

Philip shook his head.

'Did you give in?'

'No.'

'What did she say to you at the ball?'

'She asked how my leg was.'

'That's more or less what she asked you in the Hamlyns' bedroom, isn't it?' Lloyd got up as be spoke, and walked round the table, in slow strides.

'Yes,' said Philip. 'Matthew seems to be a reliable reporter of the facts.'

'So – this time. Was she making another pass?'

'Perhaps,' he said.

'Perhaps.' Lloyd left a space between the two syllables. 'You went out to your car. Did you see Mrs Hamlyn?'

He shook his head. He didn't know what else to do.

'You're sure about that?' Lloyd waited.

Philip wouldn't look at him, wouldn't answer. He didn't have to tell them anything. But they'd got his suit, and the car. His reasons for staying silent didn't exist any more, except that he *had* stayed silent, and they had found out anyway. So his silence looked worse than ever.

'Did you see Mrs Hamlyn?' the sergeant asked.

'No.' His eyes were shut. No one spoke. He could hear Lloyd come closer, and sit down. 'I got to the Barn,' he said. 'And as I went in I could see the rear door of the car standing open.' He looked up. 'I thought someone must have been trying to steal from it,' he said. 'One of the Barn doors had been opened a couple of feet, and I'd left them shut.'

They waited for him to go on, neither of them speaking.

'I looked into the back, and ... .' He looked down. 'And her tights and ... things were on the floor of the car. And her bag.'

'What did you do?' Lloyd's voice was light.

'I stuffed the things into her bag and threw it out,' Philip muttered. 'I was angry.'

'And yet you considerately put her underwear in her bag before throwing it out?'

'I didn't want any of the boys finding it,' he said.

'What about her shoes? What did you do with them?'

Philip shook his head. 'I didn't see her shoes,' he said.

'You drove over one of them.'

'I didn't *see* them! I drove off, and did what I've already told you umpteen times.'

'But you haven't told us this umpteen times, have you? You didn't tell us this at all. Why?'

Newby shook his head. 'I – when Sam said you thought she had been raped, I thought she was just making trouble for him for some reason. Then you said she was dead. And you'd been looking at Sam's clothes. I thought ... .' He dropped his head in his hands. 'I didn't want to get involved,' he said. 'I knew what it would look like, if you saw my clothes.'

Lloyd sat back, hands behind his head, smiling at him. 'That is what it looks like, Mr Newby,' he said. 'Your story explains away any evidence of Mrs Hamlyn's presence in your car, and any of your prints that we might find on her bag. Very good. But it doesn't explain one thing.'

'I've told you. I fell.'

'No, not that. We'll come to that later. No – what bothers me is *why* she was in your car.'

What was wrong with the man? He'd just told him why she was in his car. 'I would have thought it was obvious,' he said. 'I was a decoy. That's why she came and spoke to me. She had arranged to meet Sam. It's obvious!'

'Don't you lock your car, Mr Newby?'

'The back door doesn't lock.'

'Who knows that?' asked the sergeant.

'I don't know! It's not a secret.'

'So you think that she was in your car with Sam Waters,' said Lloyd.

'Yes.'

'But she thought that you would be in the Hall until the small hours. Sam would have had the flat to himself. Why the back of a car? Why the back of *your* car, Mr Newby?'

Philip shook his head. 'I don't know,' he said. 'I didn't think – I just . . . .'

'I think I know why,' said Lloyd. 'I think it was you she was meeting. You expected to find her in your car, and you did. But Sam had left early, so your flat wasn't available, and Mrs Knight was in the Hamlyns' flat – the car had to do.'

'No,' said Philip.

'Doesn't that make more sense?'

'It isn't true!'

'Look,' said Lloyd, crouching down beside him. 'I don't think you set out to rape her. But after giving you every reason to believe that she was ready and willing, I think she changed her mind. I think perhaps she was more interested in a stolen pen than she was in you, and you didn't like that.'

The frown deepened. 'What?' said Philip.

'Matthew had run away. She wanted to go after him, maybe. I can imagine she might have felt torn between you and carrying out what seems to have been regarded as her job. Pastoral care, Mr Treadwell called it. So, she let it go too far before she changed her mind.'

'What?' said Philip.

'Well, of course, that's just my scenario. For whatever reason, she changed her mind.'

'What?'

Lloyd rose. 'You do see what I'm getting at? I mean – whichever – she was obviously co-operating at that stage. But then – to go back to my scenario – she says, "It's no good, I'll have to try to find Matthew," or "I'd better speak to the headmaster," or her husband, or whatever. It was something like that, wasn't it?'

Philip's head was just shaking, all the time. He had no idea what the man was talking about.

'Well, maybe she was just fickle,' said Lloyd. 'But she changed her mind, and you didn't like that. She ran away from you, but you caught her, and you raped her. She got away again, you chased her on to the field, and this time you killed her. Otherwise how did your suit get covered in mud and blood? How did your stick get broken? You went back to your car, and that's when you threw out her bag.'

'Me?' said Philip. 'I chased after her? Like this?'

'Ah, but that's another point,' said Lloyd. 'You weren't like that, were you? You could move pretty fast before, according to everyone I've spoken to.'

'Not that fast.'

'How fast was that? How fast was she running?'

Philip sighed.

'Well,' said Lloyd. 'I'm afraid you are going to have to accept our hospitality for the night, Mr Newby. The forensic and pathology tests which we are doing will produce all the evidence we need to charge you. I suggest you think again about legal help.'

Philip shook his head. He didn't need legal help. Roll on tomorrow.

'What in the name of God Almighty is going *on* here, Treadwell?'

Thus had the chairman of governors greeted Treadwell, who had been home from the pub for about half an hour; long enough to consume one more large Scotch, and pour a second. The man must have been lying in wait for him, watching for him coming back.

Marcia had been home, but it transpired that she had stayed in the back room, not answering the phone, not going to the door. Because of the newspapers, she had said, when Treadwell had taxed her with it.

'Theft, rape, murder – suicide?' He came in, uninvited, past Treadwell; a small, round ball of self-importance with a ginger moustache and a bald head over which he persuaded lacquered strands of hair from a parting above his left ear. 'A pupil arrested – a teacher arrested? Do you imagine for one moment that the school is going to survive this?'

Treadwell shook his head. 'Drink?' he asked, waving his own glass by way of encouragement.

'Why not?' he said, sinking into an armchair, where the light from the table-lamp glinted on his frameless spectacles.

'I'll resign, of course,' said Treadwell, handing him an equally large whisky.

'Too bloody true you'll resign!' He took a gulp of his drink. 'But what good's that going to do? How many of them have already taken their boys away?'

Treadwell shrugged. 'I've been out all day,' he said.

'Who was minding the shop?'

Treadwell smiled weakly. 'Well,' he said, 'in view of the depletion of our ranks, I think probably Caroline Knight would take over.'

'Then we'd better find out.'

'Marcia!' Treadwell sat down on the sofa as his wife came in from the kitchen. 'Go and ask Caroline if she'll be good enough to join us,' he said, and watched her scuttle off.

'It was touch and go as it was, Treadwell. This place has been trading on a reputation it hasn't had for years.'

'Well,' said Treadwell into his glass, 'it's got one now.'

'I seem to remember you went on the wagon after you got banned.'

'Yes.' Treadwell topped up both their drinks. 'Struck me as silly. If I couldn't drive, why the hell shouldn't I get drunk?'

'Because you're supposed to be in charge of this place!'

'Now wait a minute,' said Treadwell. 'I didn't employ these people – I didn't employ Hamlyn or his wife. I didn't employ that so-called artist—'

'What's Sam Waters got to do with anything? You employed the murderer!' He leaned forward. 'And the so-called artist has been telling me some very interesting stories,' he said.

'I'll bet he has.' The chairman seemed to be regarding Sam in a rather more favourable light now that he was comparing him to rapists and thieves.

'Like how you found Mrs Hamlyn in the Barn with some odd-job man or other.'

Treadwell had another swallow of the water of life.

'How come the governors didn't hear about that? How come you sacked this man and kept Hamlyn on?'

'I didn't find Hamlyn in the Barn with the odd-job man.'

'You knew what that woman was like, and you did nothing about it. You railroaded Hamlyn's promotion through. You employed Newby – you insisted that we keep his job open. If you had acted responsibly, neither of these people would have been here, and none of this would have happened.' He finished his drink. 'Have you any idea how difficult it is to keep this place going at all?' He shook his head. 'We won't survive this,' he said again.

Marcia ushered in Caroline Knight. Treadwell looked up. 'Ah, Caroline,' he said. 'Have a drink. We're celebrating the demise of St Rasputin's School for the Sons of Gentlefolk.'

'No, thank you, Mr Treadwell.'

'Am I right in assuming that you took charge of the exodus?'

'Mr Dearden did, really. I manned reception when we realised the scope of the enquiries, and Mr Dearden actually spoke to them.'

'People wanting to know if their sons were still alive and kicking?'

Caroline's eyebrows rose slightly. 'Basically, yes,' she said. 'Most of the young ones have actually gone. Their parents haven't withdrawn them,' she said to the chairman. 'Most of them just said they would rather they had them at home until this was all sorted out.'

The chairman looked at her bleakly. 'Do you think they'll be back?' he asked.

'I don't know.'

She looked tired, thought Treadwell.

'This chap Newby,' said the chairman. 'He was pestering you a bit, wasn't he?'

'No,' said Caroline.

'Oh,' he said. 'Waters said something. Perhaps I misunderstood.'

'Or perhaps Mr Waters misunderstood,' said Caroline.

Treadwell made the mistake of draining his glass; now he'd have to offer his guest another. On the other hand, perhaps he just wouldn't. He picked up the bottle. 'Well,' he said. 'They've got him now. So it is sorted out, isn't it?'

Both the others looked coldly at him.

'Why don't we just ring these people up and tell them it's all right?' he said. 'The police have got him, and their children will be safe and snug in the corridors of St Bluebeard's for another term.'

The chairman rose. 'Well – thank you, Mrs Knight,' he said, and turned to Treadwell. 'You'd do well to leave that alone,' he said. 'The papers have got on to this – they'll want interviews, I expect. It seems that Mrs Hamlyn's activities are already public knowledge.'

Treadwell raised his glass to him. 'You shall have my resignation in the morning,' he said, and smiled at Caroline. 'You could do worse than make Mrs Knight the head teacher, you know.'

'Head teacher of what?'

The door banged, and Treadwell looked up at Caroline. 'I've never actually closed a school before,' he said. 'I've had to resign before, but up until now I haven't had to count the dead and injured.'

She didn't speak.

'Oh – don't worry. You won't find me in a haze of carbon monoxide. You see, I don't think it was my fault.'

'Don't you?'

He was a little surprised. 'Ah – you agree with the revered chairman. I insisted on employing Newby – yes, I did. I thought he'd had a raw deal. Still do. It was probably because of the accident that he . . . .' The booze was making him less inhibited than usual. 'Don't think he was quite . . . you know.' He searched his pockets for a cigarette. 'Do you smoke, Caroline?'

'No.'

'Ah, no vices.' He tapped his glass. 'I have a vice. A couple of vices. But – you shouldn't be here, you know. We only take flawed human beings at St Judas Iscariot's. Seconds. Factory rejects.'

'I think I'll go now, if you don't mind, Mr Treadwell.'

'I blame . . . well, I blame the school – evil spirits. Who do you blame, Caroline?'

She looked at him. 'Not Philip,' she said.

'No. We agree on that. Not Philip. Philip was a victim of circumstance.' He nodded. 'Good night, Caroline.'

He finished his drink, and got to his feet. A little unsteadily, he walked round the room, switching off the umpteen table-lamps that Marcia favoured, lighting-wise. She had gone to bed, of course. She always did when he was drinking. Silly place to go, since that was where the one thing she was hoping to avoid always took place. No barns for Marcia. No back seats.

No, Barry. He could hear her already.

Monday morning, and Matthew's parents were rowing, as usual. Only this time they were rowing in public, in Chief Inspector Lloyd's office, with Lloyd and the sergeant as their audience.

His father had made him apologise. They had been rehearsing all morning in the hotel room, until someone came to see his father, and released Matthew for half an hour.

So he had apologised. Then they had all started chatting about him as if he wasn't there.

'We'll have to find another school,' his mother had said. 'But I'm sure he can manage without for a week or two – he's had a terrible shock, poor lamb.'

That had started it. The poor lamb sat back and closed his eyes while they argued. He'd have liked to smoke, but neither of his parents knew that he did, and there would be hell to pay if they found out, even from his mother.

'He's got exams,' said his father. 'In three months.'

'He'll pass anyway,' said his mother. 'If he could get all these O levels at that place, he can pass a couple of A levels standing on his head.'

'He can't pass them if he doesn't sit them!' roared his father.

'Well,' said Lloyd, obviously trying to bring the interview to an end, 'I'm sure you have—'

'He is *not* going back to that place!'

Matthew knew his mother was more than a match for any chief inspector.

'This isn't really any of our—' tried Lloyd, and gave up.

'Why not?' demanded his father. 'They've got him now – it's all over.' He turned to Lloyd. 'Isn't that right? You've got him?'

'A man has been arrested and is being questioned about the incident,' said Lloyd carefully.

'All over?' said his mother. 'They arrested Matthew! What does that prove?'

'They didn't arrest Matthew,' his father said, his voice quieter. 'He confessed to stealing. And the school is *asking* us to keep him there when they could have been expelling him.' He turned to Matthew. '*Stealing*!' he shouted, aiming a cuff at him.

Matthew didn't even try to move out of its way, because it was never intended to land.

'Well,' said Lloyd again, 'if you don't—'

'The school say they'll forget about the thefts,' said his father. 'The police have got the right man now – Matthew's got very important exams to sit. Disrupting his schooling now is—'

'Disrupting his schooling? What do you think all this has done to him?'

'Very little, from what I can see!'

'You'd send him back to a school that allowed that sort of woman amongst growing boys?' She looked at Sergeant Hill. 'What sort of man would do that?' she asked her.

His father turned to him again. 'Did she try anything on?' he demanded to know.

Matthew shook his head.

'See? She left the boys alone – and the school didn't know what she was like.'

'Of course they did! And Treadwell couldn't care less!'

'He has resigned,' said his father, as though he was talking to a small child. 'That's why he doesn't care. They're appointing someone else. They've got the guy that did it. It's all over now.'

'You've just taken him out of that place,' said his mother. 'You can't change your mind now.'

'I'll tell you what I've just done!' his father yelled. 'I've just paid for a whole year's schooling! I've just forked out for a whole new bloody uniform! I've just heard how much that solicitor's charging, and I've just lost the chance of a bloody good contract because I had to be here, that's what I've just done! And he's going back, understand?'

Matthew saw his mother's head tilt slightly as the truth dawned, and she really did understand.

'That man at the hotel this morning,' she said. 'The one with the moustache. He offered you some sort of deal, didn't he?'

His father didn't reply.

'He did! You're going to send your son back to that place sooner than have to pay another school! That's why he was there in the first place, because it was cheap – and now what? A rebate? Is that what it is? A free term? Money's all you can think about when your son's *life* is in danger?'

'His life isn't in danger, you stupid woman! It was an isolated accident. Matthew only got involved because he was breaking the law himself. He's damn lucky not to be charged with it!' He turned again to Matthew. 'What the hell were you playing at?'

'It was fun,' said Matthew.

'Was it?' said his father. 'And this pen – that was fun, was it, taking it from right under this woman's nose?'

'It was getting too easy the other way. And I wanted to confuse them.'

'What?' His father frowned. 'What do you mean, confuse them? You're confusing me, I can tell you that.'

'They all thought it was Mrs Knight,' Matthew explained patiently. 'She wasn't at the ball, so if I could take something from the top table it would make them all suspect one another. It would have been better that way. It was a joke,' he said, with a shrug.

'Who's Mrs Knight?' asked his father.

'The history teacher.'

'What made them think it must have been her in the first place?'

'Her husband was killed in a car accident – she went a bit strange for a while.'

'In that place?' said his mother. 'How could you tell?'

Matthew laughed.

'You think that's funny?' asked his father. 'You thought it was funny to let everyone think she was stealing? Because she'd lost her husband?'

Matthew shrugged again; this time the blow did land. Tears of surprise and pain sprang to Matthew's eyes as his father turned to Chief Inspector Lloyd, and shouted over his wife's shocked protests. 'We're going, don't worry.'

Matthew found himself being pulled to his feet and propelled from the office. The final humiliation was when his father, still holding his collar, turned back.

'It's the school that wants protecting from *him*!' he roared.

Almost four o'clock, and Caroline was trying to conduct a class. It wasn't easy. She placed the card on the easel. 'This, for instance, might be how the tabloids would have reported the sinking of the Spanish Armada,' she said.

The facsimile paper, which she had drawn with painstaking care, should have produced a laugh. The banner headline read 'MY NIGHTS OF LOVE WITH WILL – EXCLUSIVE: ANNE HATHAWAY TALKS TO THE SUN', and down in the left-hand corner, with a couple of column inches, was 'ADIOS, AMIGOS!'

A couple of the boys smiled politely.

'Well,' she said. 'That's the idea, anyway.' She left it there; some of them might stop and read some of the other news items that she had culled from the history books to amuse them.

'The idea is to write up brief newspaper accounts of anything that takes your fancy during Elizabeth's reign. Any style you like. But factual, please. If you want to do mock-up newspapers like I've done, I can let you—' She stopped speaking as she saw Sam through the small glass pane in the door.

'I've got card and felt pens, and so on. Just tell me what you need. And these old history books – you might find the style a bit odd, but they're full of little anecdotes and things that you might like. Historians today don't believe in telling you that Drake finished his game of bowls before he sailed.' She had expected there to be some interest by this point. 'Kitty says that you can use the typewriter in the office when it's available.'

'When do you want them by, Mrs Knight?' asked a voice at the back.

She smiled. 'End of term,' she said. 'You don't have to do it at all, if you don't want to. But, if you do, I suggest you do it in groups of three or four.'

'We'll be lucky if there are three or four of us left by the end of the term,' said another.

'Then, whoever is still here, if they want to do it, can do it!' Caroline shouted.

They looked startled; she would have thought that they would be beyond that by now.

'Look,' she said. 'This is difficult for everyone. I think the best thing we can do is put it to the back of our minds, and carry on as normal.'

Someone laughed. Sam was still hanging about. She looked back at the class.

'Will you be taking us for English, Mrs Knight?'

Oh, God. Philip. 'I don't know,' she said.

'Did he really kill Mrs Hamlyn?'

'I don't want this topic discussed,' she said. 'As far as I am concerned, this is a history period, and that is what we should be doing.'

The bell rang, and the last few words were drowned in the chair-scraping exodus. When the doorway had cleared of grey blazers, Sam was still there.

Caroline started putting things away in her briefcase.

'Did you do this?' Sam asked, after a moment.

'Yes.' She closed her briefcase.

'It's good. I didn't know you were artistic.'

'I'm not.' She got up.

'You'd have made a good draughtsman.'

He turned, catching her arm as she passed.

'Let go,' she said.

'Now, Caroline,' he said. 'I'm not a murderer. That's your other friend.'

'What are you doing here? What do you want?'

'I've started a painting.'

'Have you?'

'Yep.' He turned back, and smiled at the mock-up. 'But I don't actually paint – not for a while. I mustn't. I mustn't paint, or it goes wrong.' He let go of her arm.

She was listening, interested despite her desire to run away, and she put down the briefcase.

'This is a kind of gestation period,' he said. 'It makes me hungry.'

He was moving all the time. His hands would be in his pockets, then out; he rocked slightly on the balls of his feet. He was fidgety, nervous. She had never seen him like that.

'Then maybe you should go and have something to eat,' she said.

'I will,' he said, his head turned away, looking at the mock-up. 'But it's more than that. It sharpens my senses. My reactions. My appetites.' He turned to her. 'And you and I have some unfinished business,' he said.

'It's going to stay unfinished.'

'No,' he said. 'No, it's not. I'll come to your flat, and we'll finish it. OK?'

'I don't want you in my flat.'

'Fine. You come to mine. I'll be alone. My flatmate's moved out.'

'Find someone else, Sam.'

'That's like telling me to read the end of another book,' he said.

'What does that matter?' she asked, picking up her briefcase again. 'If you don't know which book you were reading in the first place?'

'Look – maybe . . . well, maybe I was a little quick off the mark. I'll behave better this time if you will.'

'There isn't a this time. I thought perhaps I needed you. I was wrong. I did behave badly, and I'm sorry.'

She walked out, leaving him standing by the easel.

Boys flowed like a grey river through the building, on the staircases, in the corridors, swollen by tributaries from the open classroom doors. She stood on the landing, and watched the building empty, pouring its contents out on to the cobbles. The grey streams ran down the slope, seeping along the lane, dribbling into the houses.

She became aware, gradually, that Sam was standing beside her.

'Happiest days of your life?' he said.

She shook her head.

'They were of mine,' he said.

All things considered, Lloyd thought, as evening fell, it hadn't been a bad day. Cawston senior had made junior apologise to Allison before they left, and he in his turn had been almost pleasant to Lloyd.

Freddie had promised to give top priority to an examination of all the things they had discovered; soon, it would all be over.

They had found the missing buttons in Newby's car, and they would find something on the stick, however carefully he'd cleaned it. The silver top was engraved with an intricate pattern, and anyone who had ever stripped paint from carved wood knew just how difficult it was to remove all traces. Microscopes were wonderful inventions.

And the clothes spoke for themselves. They had found his shirt under the bed, and you didn't have to be a pathologist to recognise bloodstains when you saw them on a white shirt. The mud on the suit gave all the classic indications.

But he wanted to know *why*. Why he had done it, why he had made such a half-hearted job of covering his tracks, come to that. Why had he just taken the suit back to the shop, for instance? Judy had asked that last night, and it still bothered Lloyd.

He had told himself that if law-breakers had brains the crime detection rate would be even lower than it was. He had told himself that the man must be severely disturbed, and didn't even think about the consequences. He had told himself that it was deliberate; he was, after all, already receiving psychiatric help, and he had subconsciously wanted to get caught, knowing that he'd gone over the edge.

But Philip Newby came across as a sane, level-headed, intelligent man who was suffering permanent injury from the car crash, and who was being treated for the depression which had resulted. So why, having done it, did he not either give himself up, or work a little harder to conceal the evidence?

Maybe he would be going for diminished responsibility, and try to cite his lack of a cover-up as proof that he was a brick short of the load. Maybe he had prepared some sort of story that would have satisfied the shop, had they asked, and thought that the police would never know. But he knew it wouldn't satisfy Lloyd, so he simply wasn't even trying it on him.

Lloyd stopped at the machine, got one plastic cup full of lethally steaming liquid for Judy, and punched the buttons again. He got his own, and looked round for a plastic thing with holes in it, but there wasn't one, and he had to grit his teeth, a red-hot cup in each hand, all the way down the corridor. Once, people had made him coffee. Brought it in. Instant, but better than this stuff which seemed to have been designed purely as a weapon. He had had to give instructions that it must never be served to a prisoner until it had cooled.

He got into the office, gave Judy her coffee, and sat down still feeling disconsolate. He was about to be given all the evidence he needed for a conviction, and he had expected to feel something.

Maybe triumphant, if he had felt he was putting away someone who deliberately preyed on women. Maybe even sad, if he felt that the murderer was just as much a prey to his own impulses. But all he felt, when he thought about Newby, was puzzled. Why would he suddenly do a thing like that?

Some of them were called by God. Seek out wicked women, use them, destroy them. Newby seemed to have about as much truck with God as Lloyd himself, and it did seem, now he came to think of it, a little bit as though he himself had suddenly raped and murdered someone. He smiled. Maybe he could be a character witness. It must have been totally out of character, a complete bolt from the blue, because Newby didn't split infinitives.

The phone rang; Judy answered it. 'Freddie,' she said. 'For you.'

'Freddie,' he said, picking up his extension. 'You've surpassed yourself this time.'

'I've had everyone working on it,' said Freddie. 'Since the crack of dawn. But it's not as simple as it seems. Before I start, I agree that Newby's clothes show all the signs. I know that you found what appeared to be the murder weapon in his wardrobe.'

Lloyd closed his eyes. 'Appeared to be?' he repeated dully.

'Lloyd – if Newby raped and murdered someone, it certainly wasn't Mrs Hamlyn.'

Chapter Eight

Lloyd looked at Newby for a long time without speaking. Judy settled herself at the table with her notebook.

'Well, Mr Newby,' he said, when he had got Newby practically squirming in his chair. 'It seems your stick didn't kill Diana Hamlyn – it's made from a different kind of wood from the murder weapon, and bears no traces of having been used to assault anyone. It seems that the blood on your suit is probably your own, and it seems that you are not the man who had sexual relations with her.'

'I told you that,' said Newby. 'Does this mean I can go?'

'I don't think you really believe that,' said Lloyd. 'You are a witness. A reluctant one, at that.'

'I had nothing to do with Mrs Hamlyn.'

'No,' said Lloyd. 'It seems that whatever you were doing to get into that state, you weren't doing it with Mrs Hamlyn. Her clothes are not muddy at all. None the less, it is your duty, Mr Newby, to help the police in any way you can.'

'I don't *have* to, though, do I? I mean – duty is a very nebulous concept. I am under no obligation to speak to you.'

Lloyd gave a concessionary nod. 'But then again,' he said, 'you have no right of silence. You did have – when we were accusing you of something. But we're not any more. And, clearly, you wouldn't be indulging in philosophical musings about duty unless there was something you're not telling us.' He sat down.

'Oh – so because I *haven't* committed a crime . . . .' Newby's righteous indignation petered out, and he covered his face.

'However,' Lloyd said.

Newby took his hands away, slowly.

'Your blood *is* a match for the stains found at the foot of the fire-escape,' said Lloyd.

Newby's face coloured painfully, and Lloyd glanced at Judy.

'Don't you think you had better just tell us?' she asked gently. 'We want to know what happened to you. *Did* you see someone? Was it a fight, or something?'

'No.' The word was muffled as his hands went over his face again.

Newby waited for her to speak, but Judy could play that game better even than Lloyd, though he would never admit that to her. Very few people could stand silence in the middle of an interview. They almost always felt obliged to expand upon the last thing said.

Judy just sat, and waited for him. Newby had spoken, and she would wait for ever for him to continue, if she had to. At least, that was the impression she gave, even to Lloyd. He took a stroll round the room, stopping to read the notices. He had read over half of the advice to people in police custody before Newby spoke again.

'I drove down to the flat, and I waited in the car park for the light to go out,' Newby said. 'I didn't want to see Sam, not after what I'd found in the car. I felt . . . .'

Lloyd groaned silently. Not the same story again, please. He strained to hear what Newby was saying.

'I felt as though I'd been used. I *had* been. My car had been. Other than that, I wasn't much use to anyone. I didn't want to see Sam.'

Lloyd sat down opposite Newby as he spoke.

'My head still felt a bit woozy, so I ran the window down for some air. And . . . and I heard feet on the steps. And I thought I *saw* someone.'

There was another long, long silence.

'I went up after whoever it was. I'd had too much to drink – it was crazy. It's metal, it was wet and slippery – anyway, I went up.'

Newby's head was on his hands, his fingers digging into his scalp. 'There was no one there,' he said, his voice clearer now. 'But – but there was a gap in the curtains, and I saw Caroline. She –

she was changing, and ... and I ... .' His face was crimson. 'I watched her,' he whispered.

'You watched her undressing,' said Lloyd, getting up. So that's what it was all about, he thought tiredly.

'Yes.' He took his hands away, but his head was still bowed, his face still painfully red. 'And then she saw me, and I turned to get away. I put all my weight on the stick, and it snapped.' He looked up. 'It had a crack in it,' he said helplessly. 'I shouldn't have been using it.'

Lloyd sighed. Deeply, audibly, dramatically.

'I fell, but the jacket pocket got caught on the railing. Then it ripped, and I went headlong down the steps. I tried to get up, and I couldn't. Eventually, I managed to kneel, and I realised my nose was bleeding.'

Lloyd started walking round the room while Newby spoke. He listened to him with half an ear, because the evidence from the fire-escape already bore him out, more or less, and they had discovered a thumbprint on the handle of the rear door of the car which wasn't Newby's.

'When you went into the Barn,' he said, interrupting whatever Newby was saying, 'did you touch the rear door of your car?'

'I closed it,' said Newby.

'How?'

Newby frowned. 'I closed it,' he said. 'The usual way – what do you mean, how?'

'What's the usual way?'

Newby thought. 'I – I just pushed it, and it slammed.'

'Has anyone had occasion to open it since?'

'Not to my knowledge,' said Newby pointedly.

'Thank you.'

Lloyd had a theory to work on. One that he had abandoned on seeing Newby's suit; one that had come right back into the reckoning.

'I was frightened that Caroline might have called someone,' Newby went on, having left a suitable interval to be sure that Lloyd had finished his detour. 'I was frightened people would come looking. I crawled away until I could stand up. And when I did I saw Sam go to his car, so I went to the flat, and lay on the bed. I was trying to get my clothes off when you came in with Sam.'

Lloyd turned to look at him. 'So you were Caroline Knight's Peeping Tom all along,' he said.

Newby closed his eyes, and nodded.

'Well, that solves that little mystery, doesn't it?' Lloyd shook his head. 'Mrs Knight may wish to take the matter further, of course, but I have more important things to do than waste time on you. You can go.'

Lloyd wondered what Mrs Knight would do. She could, he supposed, lose him his job. Sam Waters had said that Newby had been making a nuisance of himself with Mrs Knight; perhaps they should have put two and two together. He felt sorry for the man, but then he wasn't the one on whom he had been spying. And Mrs Knight would have to be told. 'Mr Newby,' he said. 'You're free to go.'

Newby didn't move.

'Mr Newby,' said Judy. 'I'll see if I can arrange a lift back to the school for you.'

'I don't want to go back there.'

'You can't stay here.'

Newby looked up at Judy. 'I'm not like that,' he said. 'Truly, I'm not like that.'

Judy looked a little nonplussed. Clearly, something was required of her. She smiled a little. 'Try not to make a habit of it, then,' she said.

Newby stood up, stiffly and painfully. 'I would like a lift back,' he said. 'If it's possible.'

Judy went to find out; Lloyd looked at Newby, who stared down at his feet.

'I couldn't . . . .' Newby shook his head. 'I couldn't tell you.'

'You had to tell me in the end,' said Lloyd.

He nodded. 'I'm sorry I wasted your time,' he said.

'Do you think your arrival in the Barn scared them off?'

Newby shrugged.

Something had, thought Lloyd. So who was with her? He still

thought that Waters, fresh from his rejection by Caroline, might well have taken advantage of finding himself alone with Diana Hamlyn. The kerb-crawling had only been mentioned in case they found some evidence of a sexual encounter on his clothing. Another word with Waters was indicated.

'If you could come with me,' Judy said, coming back, 'I'll show you where you can wait. It might be a little while, but there aren't any buses, and it's cheaper than a taxi.'

Lloyd went back to the office, and gave some more thought to his theory. Sam had been with her, and something, someone had scared them off. Not Newby – he would have seen them. Someone before Newby. Someone who became enraged at what he discovered. There was the usual objection. How could he have got hold of the golf-club? But as he doodled he realised something.

He looked up when Judy came back in. 'So,' he said, smiling. 'The hunt is back on for your golf-club, isn't it?'

Judy nodded. 'We've done the immediate area,' she said. 'And all the usual places – the bins, and so on. We can move on to the school building proper, if you think that's likely.'

Lloyd agreed that they should, as the phone rang and he was summoned to Chief Superintendent Allison's office. It didn't sound as though it was going to be too friendly an encounter.

Lloyd knocked, and went in. He was not invited to sit down, as Allison carried on writing something for some moments.

'I,' he said, still writing, not looking up, 'have just been on the receiving end of what was called "a word to the wise".'

Lloyd arranged a look of polite interest on his face, just in case Allison bothered to look at him.

'I don't know about you,' Allison went on, putting down his pen, 'but I feel apprehensive when conversations start with those words.' He clasped his hands, making a steeple with his forefingers, and looked at Lloyd for the first time.

Lloyd kept his face expressionless, and just had to hope that it didn't come out as mutinous. He was clearly not being invited to speak until he was asked a question. Which, if he had got Allison's measure, would be coming up any minute.

'Samuel Cody Waters,' he said. 'How many times has he been seen during this inquiry?'

Lloyd pursed his lips. 'Oh – twice, three times . . . I'm not entirely certain, sir. But Sergeant Hill will—'

'Don't bother the sergeant,' said Allison. 'If you've lost count, I don't wonder that he's beginning to feel like a marked man.'

'He was very unco-operative,' said Lloyd.

'That's not against the law, Chief Inspector.'

Lloyd gave a brittle smile. 'You're the second person who's told me that today, sir,' he said. 'I am aware of that. But a lack of co-operation does tend to draw out our enquiries.'

'Lack of co-operation,' repeated Allison. 'That's not quite what I've been told. Is it true that Mr Waters offered us both the sets of clothes that he wore that night for forensic examination?'

'Yes,' said Lloyd wearily.

'Did he come to the station voluntarily to make a statement concerning his movements that night?'

'Yes, sir.'

'Then I fail to see where this lack of co-operation comes into it. What did you want him to do? Write a thank-you letter?' He tapped the tips of his forefingers together as he spoke.

'The statement that he made was—' Lloyd began.

'Was what? False?'

'Not exactly,' said Lloyd.

'Did it contain any false*hoods*?'

'No, but—'

'But what?'

Christ. If he'd let him finish a sentence, he might find out but what. 'But he was using us!' he said firmly. 'Sir.'

'Using us? Oh – you mean because Cawston had stolen his pen? Well, yes – that would never do. Involving the police in bringing a thief to book? Whatever next?'

'Sir, I'm sure you know what—'

'Have you at any time during this inquiry found any evidence – circumstantial or tangible – to link Mr Waters with this murder?'

'No, sir.'

'Have you found any evidence that he has committed any offence of any sort?'

'No,' said Lloyd.

'Then it's hardly surprising that he resents being treated like a criminal.'

'He has been treated with—'

'With discourtesy and disrespect. Those were his words, Chief Inspector. Are they accurate?'

'He has been treated with as much courtesy and respect as he has shown towards us,' said Lloyd.

'Look, Lloyd. The papers have got on to this. Apart from the obvious circulation value of Mrs Hamlyn's activities, it appears that Waters himself is something of a celebrity in the art world.'

'He used to be,' agreed Lloyd. 'I'd have thought he would have welcomed the publicity.'

'Well, he doesn't! And neither do I. I've got telephone calls stacked up from papers wanting to know if we suspect Waters. Do we?'

'No, sir.'

Allison's eyebrows shot up.

'But I do think that he was involved,' said Lloyd.

'Think?' repeated Allison. 'This isn't a cops-and-robbers television show, Chief Inspector. Leave your hunches at home. And unless and until you have some justifiable reason to *believe* that Mr Waters can cast any light on the incident at the school on Friday night neither you nor any other officer is to question him on the matter again. Is that understood?'

'Sir.'

'Now – Sergeant Hill. I want a word with her. And I want you present.'

Allison sent for Judy, and Lloyd waited for her knock, feeling more apprehensive for her than he had for himself.

'Come!' said Allison.

Judy came in, and stood, hands behind her back, while Allison busied himself once again with something on his desk. But at least he looked at her when he spoke to her.

'Sergeant Hill,' he said. 'You are in charge of the inquiry into the thefts at this school, I believe?'

'Yes, sir.'

'Are we still holding property belonging to Mr Waters?'

'Yes, sir,' Judy said. 'It was one of the stolen items recovered by PC—'

Allison raised a hand, stopping her going into the detail that she was clearly about to give him. 'Is it the case that all the other items have been returned to their owners?'

'Yes, sir.'

'Why hasn't Mr Waters's pen been returned?'

Lloyd stepped forward a little. 'I thought it might have some connection with the murder investigation, sir.' He didn't dare look at Judy. 'I asked the sergeant to hold on to it,' he lied.

Allison nodded, and turned back to Judy.

'But, acting on information given to you by Mr Waters, you apprehended the thief. At which point you knew that the pen could be of no further use in the investigation. Mr Waters, along with others, agreed not to prosecute. Why hasn't Mr Waters's pen been returned to him?'

So much for his gallantry. He had got himself into trouble for being a male chauvinist pig, and all for nothing.

'I'm afraid I haven't got round to it, sir.'

'You will get round to it now. Today.'

'Yes, sir.'

Rain was suddenly thrown against the window, as the evening grew dark and blustery.

'And a point for both of you,' he said. 'Mr Waters also alleges that an investigating officer used obscene language to him. I understand that he declined to name the officer concerned, but I have been asked to draw the matter to your attention. As far as I am concerned, I strongly disapprove of unofficial complaints, and I do not want to know who it was, even if you find out.'

He stood up. 'What I do want', he said, 'is for the future conduct of this inquiry to be free of any such petty nonsense as this business with the pen, or the least hint of personal scores being settled. And I want that damn golf-club found!'

They were excused; back in the office, Judy took out her notebook, and began writing in it.

Lloyd sat down, disgruntled. 'Who the hell does Waters know?' he asked.

'It's all in the handshake, or so I'm told,' said Judy, still writing.

'Waters is a Freemason?' said Lloyd incredulously.

'According to Bob Sandwell, who knows everything,' said Judy. 'And so – according to Bob – is the deputy chief constable.'

'Wouldn't you just know?' muttered Lloyd.

'I've got some better news,' she said. 'At least, I think it is.'

'Oh?'

'I asked Mary Alexander if I could share with her until the transfer.'

Mary lived in the block of flats behind Lloyd's block. He smiled. 'Well, you would be nice and handy,' he said. 'But if you're not going to Barton you can't be sure it'll be in June. She might not want a lodger indefinitely.'

Judy smiled. 'You are in an optimistic mood today,' she said. 'I haven't finished. She said yes of course I could, but how would anyone know which flat I actually lived in? I can use her address and, if anyone asks, she'll say I live there.' She smiled. 'I'm sure she won't mind a phantom lodger for as long as it takes.'

Lloyd sat back, his hands behind his head, and looked at her. 'So this is it?' he said. 'You've moved in? For keeps?'

'You try getting rid of me.'

Lloyd smiled.

'Well,' she said. 'You heard what the man said. I'd better get the sensitive flower's pen back to him.' She opened the door, and looked back at him. 'How polite do I have to be?' she asked.

'A bit more polite than you were the last time, by the sound of it,' Lloyd said, picking up his coat. 'I'm coming with you.'

Lloyd tried out his theory on the way to the school. 'Changing your clothes isn't all that easy when everyone's in formal dress,' he said. 'People would notice.'

He could feel the pull of the wind on the exposed country road, and slowed down, despite his instinctive desire to drive faster to get away from it.

'If it was someone who returned to the dance, he must have,' said Judy.

Here we go, thought Lloyd, as he launched his theory. 'Or been noticeably wet,' he said.

'Like Treadwell?' she suggested. 'He never did tell me why he didn't phone Mrs Knight back,' she said, raising her voice slightly as the rain battered the car.

Lloyd was relieved; his theory might not get the bad reception he had expected. 'I've been wondering about him,' he said.

'He went looking for her,' Judy said. 'And got soaked to the skin. And he was gone from the table for quarter of an hour.'

Lloyd nodded. He had been thinking about it for some time; it made sense of Hamlyn's statement, and his suicide note.

'But where did he come by the golf-club?' Judy asked, right on cue.

'Ah.' He let his foot press slightly on the accelerator. 'He's one of the few people who *could* have come by it,' he said. 'He found it in the first place.'

'Last December,' objected Judy, like his straight man. 'It doesn't make sense.'

'Who says it was last December?' asked Lloyd.

'That's when it was stolen,' she said.

'Who says?' he repeated.

There was a little silence. 'Treadwell,' she said.

The journey back had been worse even than being arrested in the first place. Back to face Caroline finding out what a pathetic mess he was. Back to face dismissal and *everyone* knowing what a pathetic mess he was. Including Sam.

He had been relieved that Sam wasn't there, and had gone into his room, shutting the door, wishing he had a lock. He had closed the curtains on the dark evening, on the school, on everything, and now he lay on the bed, wishing he could just die. Hamlyn had had the right idea.

He closed his eyes, trying to block out his thoughts, but he couldn't. He had been accused of murder because he couldn't bring himself to tell them that he had watched Caroline through a gap in the curtains. His stick had snapped because it had a crack, and it had a crack because he had smashed it down on the table the day he arrived. He had smashed it on the table because of what he had become; because all he could do was look up women's skirts and down their blouses. Because of what he had become, he had watched Caroline through a gap in the curtains. A wicked, vicious circle from which he could never, never escape.

He didn't open his eyes when he heard his door-handle turn. Sam, he presumed. Caroline must have told him; he would be here to give him the benefit of his opinion. But he couldn't say anything worse than Philip was already thinking.

'They told me.' Caroline's voice.

Oh, God. Caroline. He kept his eyes closed. Make her go away. Please, make her go away. But she didn't.

'Well?' she said. 'Aren't you going to say anything?'

'They thought I'd raped Diana,' he said. He opened his eyes. 'I suppose I should take it as a kind of compliment.'

'Oh, for God's sake, Philip! Stop feeling so *sorry* for yourself!' She closed the door, and came towards the bed. 'There's nothing wrong with you.'

'What?' he said.

'I was ill, too – but I did something about it, for God's sake!'

'You pulled yourself together? Well, bully for you, Caroline.'

'Yes! And so could you, if you weren't just lying there thinking what a terrible thing happened to *you*, as though nothing terrible ever happened to anyone else!'

'It doesn't hurt when I lie on my back,' he said, offended.

'And if you're going to watch me undress . . . .'

Philip's eyes widened as, arms crossed, she seized her sweatshirt.

'. . . then watch me. Don't peep through windows to do it.' She angrily pulled the sweatshirt over her head.

It landed on the bed; Philip picked it up, absently folding it neatly.

'All right, you were badly hurt,' she said, kicking off her shoes, unzipping her jeans. 'Maybe you'll always be in pain – so what? You're alive, Philip – Andrew isn't.'

He laid the shirt down on the table beside the bed.

'You can walk – some people can't even move!' She stepped out of the jeans, kicking them away. 'Can't feed themselves – can't even talk. There's nothing wrong with you except what's going on in your head.' She peeled off her tights. 'If you want to spend the rest of your life the way you are, then don't do it round me – go and have fantasies about someone else.'

The Marks & Spencer bra and pants were discarded impatiently, and she looked at him. 'It hurts you to undress?' she said. 'Right. I'll do it.'

And she did; quickly, efficiently, irritably, like a nurse who was already late going off duty, except that she got on to the bed with him which, as far as he could recall, the nurses had refrained from doing.

She lay beside him, her head resting on her hand, not touching him, not speaking. Just looking at him. For the first time, he looked into her eyes; they were beautiful, and he had never seen them before. Then she bent her head, and her mouth was on his. She pressed close to him as they kissed, moving against him, awakening sensations that he had almost forgotten. She drew away, and he reached out to her, touching her face, her neck, her shoulders.

'And if you're not in pain when you lie like that,' she said, smiling down at him, 'then lie like that.'

She was real. His tongue had found an unsuspected gap where a tooth should have been; she had a vaccination scar on her arm. He caressed full, slightly heavy breasts, and his fingertips found the occasional blemish as they moved down the small of her back to a bottom no firmer than it should be. He could see a little broken vein at the top of her thigh.

She was real. Hands that worked, that washed dishes and Marks & Spencer underwear were arousing him, exciting an eager, almost instant response from the hunger that had fed too long on insubstantial fantasy.

She was real. Her legs had tiny bristles on them that rubbed against his skin when their imperfect bodies joined together. She didn't cry out in ecstasy; it was over too soon for that.

Matthew would never forgive his father for what he did at the police station. Making him look a child, a fool, in front of the chief inspector. Making him come back. But that hadn't been as bad as he had thought. He was no longer head boy but, far from being shunned, he had been inundated with questions; his status as murder suspect – never actual, but not denied – had eclipsed the fact of his having been the thief, and what might have been a sticky return to the school had turned into a positive triumph. Newby's arrest had been attributed to him; he had liked that. Newby had been perfect; nervous, obviously having physically overstretched himself somehow. Being led on by Mrs Hamlyn every chance she got. And his car had been parked in the Barn; it had all made sense.

But he and Mrs Hamlyn hadn't been interrupted by Newby; Newby had obviously convinced the police of that, or they wouldn't have released him.

So he had been trying to piece together what he knew, and what he had gathered. He wished that he could be shown round the forensic laboratory while the investigation was going on; then he would know what they knew. As it was, he had to rely on what he'd seen, and heard. And overheard.

He frowned when it occurred to him. No, he thought. That would be impossible.

Or was it? The more he thought about it, the more he thought about the little things, like the doctor had said – the little insignificant incidents, snatches of conversation, moments – the less impossible it became.

Matthew smiled to himself. The police might know things that he didn't, but the traffic wasn't all one way. He knew who else could have stolen the golf-club.

He nervously licked his lips as he knocked on the door, which was answered by Treadwell himself.

'What do you want, Cawston?' he said wearily. 'I've seen more than enough of you lately.'

'I'd like to ask your advice,' he said.

Treadwell seemed to think this funny; he let Matthew into the sitting-room.

'At your service,' he said, pouring himself a drink.

'Mr Treadwell?' Matthew said. 'Should I say I'm sorry to Mrs Knight?'

'No,' Treadwell replied. 'It's possible that she didn't realise that she was the subject of gossip. And if she did, it certainly wouldn't help to know that it was a deliberate act.'

'It's just that she was so nervy,' Matthew said. 'On Saturday. And I realised that she'd been that way since the accident really.' He dropped his eyes from Treadwell's.

'What's the accident got to do with it?' Treadwell asked.

'I must have made things worse for her. I'd really like to tell her I'm sorry.'

'That's too bad,' said Treadwell. 'I'm not giving you that luxury. And if I hear that you have said one word to Mrs Knight about the thefts I will kick you back out again, Cawston. I'm still the head for the moment, and don't think I wouldn't do it. Now, go away, and stay out of my sight.'

Matthew left, just as Sam Waters crossed the road to the lane; he followed a little way behind as he went to the canteen, waiting outside in the wet, windy darkness while Waters ate three courses, still watching as he strode away from the canteen.

He stepped back into the shadow of the doorway as Waters passed him, deep in thought, then followed him back into the lane, and saw him go into the art room.

He walked quickly along the lane, and knocked on the door. On getting no reply, he walked in.

'What the hell do you want?' Waters roared.

'Sorry, sir,' said Matthew. 'It was just that I saw the light going on, and I thought perhaps someone was messing about in here.'

'Well, they're not, so you can just piss off.'

'Sir,' said Matthew, determined to say what he had really come to say.

'Oh, for Christ's sake – what?'

'Sir – you know that I stole those things?'

'Yes, Cawston, I know that you stole those things. And I know that you stole my pen. And I knew that was why you were with Mrs Hamlyn, but I didn't tell the police that because I thought you deserved to be scared out of your wits. I trust you were.' Waters sat down at the table as he spoke, but he wasn't relaxed. His foot tapped quickly, as though he was listening to fast music.

Matthew realised what he had said. '*You* were there,' he said slowly. 'You were there when Mrs Hamlyn spoke to me.'

Waters's foot stopped tapping. 'You mean you didn't know?' he said.

Matthew shook his head. But he knew now. And the police had seen Waters over and over again, but they hadn't arrested him; it fitted. It all fitted.

Waters's foot began to tap again, slowly this time. 'What do you *want!*' he demanded.

'I'd like to ask a favour, sir,' said Matthew.

'From me?'

'Yes, sir,' he said. 'You see, everyone thought it was Mrs Knight who was stealing.'

'You made bloody sure everyone thought it was Mrs Knight.' He jumped up again, and paced the room.

Matthew nodded. 'I want to apologise to her,' he said. 'But Mr Treadwell won't let me talk to her about it.'

'Why not?'

'He thinks she'd rather not know that I was doing it on purpose,' Matthew said, then took a deep breath. 'But I'm sure she already knows,' he said. 'I mean – she'll have worked it out, won't she? It could hardly have been coincidence. Not all those times.'

Waters snapped his fingers, still hearing his music. 'What's that got to do with me?' he asked, sitting down again, hooking one leg over the other, his foot moving, moving.

'Will you tell her I'm sorry?' he asked.

Waters grunted.

'And – sir? Could you tell her that I didn't take the golf-club? I want her to know that.'

Waters frowned. 'What golf-club?' he asked.

'The one that went from the Barn just before Christmas,' said Matthew, watching him carefully.

Waters frowned. 'What about it?' he asked.

Matthew's eyes widened. 'Didn't you know?' he said. 'The police think that it's the murder weapon.'

Waters again stopped his constant movement just for a second. 'Do they now?' he said.

'Will you tell her, sir?'

'Why pick on me, for God's sake?'

'Well,' said Matthew. 'She's a friend of yours, isn't she, sir? I mean – I've seen you go out with her.'

'You know she's a friend of mine,' repeated Waters, in a low voice. 'You've seen me go out with her. You know too bloody much, Cawston. You know everything that goes on round here, because you never stop watching people, do you?'

Matthew had always watched people. People were usually very interesting.

'Will you speak to her for me, sir?'

'Yes! Stop calling me sodding sir and piss off!'

Matthew turned to go.

'And Cawston,' Waters called.

He turned. 'Yes, s—' He bit off the rest of the word.

'Don't play with fire,' he said.

Perhaps it *was* still all a nightmare. Treadwell poured himself a considerable pre-dinner whisky, and checked the drinks cabinet. He'd have to go to the off-licence for more soon. At least he could drink it in the open. He could get as drunk as he liked, because he was all washed up anyway.

Unless it was a dream, of course. In which case he could still get as drunk as he liked. And when he woke up Diana would still be alive, and he wouldn't even have a hangover. He watched Marcia lay the table for one. She wasn't speaking to him because he was drinking. It was no great loss; she was not one of the world's great conversationalists.

He wished Matthew Cawston hadn't mentioned the accident. How much did he know about what went on that day? Sometimes, he thought that Matthew knew everything about everyone. It was an uncomfortable thought.

Why, when God knew how many people were swooping on the school to take their sons away, did the Cawstons, of all people, have to bring theirs back? He had come in that morning with his father, who had said that after some discussion it had been agreed that Matthew should after all finish his education at the school. Matthew had looked a touch chastened; it was to be presumed that Mr Cawston had had enough of his smart-alec son. He had even been made to apologise.

'I'm very sorry for all the trouble I've caused you,' he had said. 'And thank you for being prepared to overlook what I did.'

It had been a bit like watching a hostage read a prepared statement. But the slightly mutinous look had gone with this latest visit, to be replaced by a Uriah Heep humility; it didn't suit him. And it hadn't given Treadwell the satisfaction he had hoped it might when he had dismissed Cawston from his presence. Why did he have to go and mention the accident?

The doorbell rang, interrupting his thoughts on Matthew. Marcia announced the arrival of Chief Inspector Lloyd and Sergeant Hill, and retired to the kitchen, presumably to eat her solitary meal. Treadwell didn't mind his being interrupted; he didn't really feel like eating.

They came in, bringing with them the cold, blustery night which he had managed to shut out with the help of his liquid refreshment.

'Mr Treadwell,' said Lloyd. 'We wondered if you could tell us a little about the golf-club.'

Treadwell frowned. What did they want to know about that for?

'Well,' he said, 'it's not bad. Not bad at all – not sure if you need to be a member. But' – he looked at his watch – 'you'd have to hurry. They stop serving quite early.'

From the looks on their faces, he didn't think that that could have been the information they were seeking.

'No, Mr Treadwell,' said the sergeant. 'The golf-club – the one that went missing.'

'Oh!' Treadwell frowned again. 'Someone said Newby used his stick,' he said. 'Are you still interested in the golf-club?'

'Mr Newby has been eliminated from our enquiries,' said Lloyd.

Suddenly, Treadwell felt very sober indeed. 'Not Newby?' he said.

'No.'

Treadwell sat down heavily.

'Does that bother you?' asked Lloyd.

'No,' he said. 'No. I'm glad. I like Newby.'

'May we sit down?'

'Oh, yes, yes.' Treadwell waved an expansive arm at the chairs. Not Newby. He'd have to tell Lloyd. But not with that damn woman here.

'About the golf-club,' said Lloyd. 'You know exactly when it went missing?'

'Yes. Saw it before lunch – rang the chap who might be interested, and arranged to have lunch with him. At the golf club, as it happens,' he said, with a weak attempt at a smile. 'Went back to pick it up, and it was gone.'

'When was this?'

'December the . . . whatever it was. It's on the list.'

'You're sure about that?'

'Yes. When I asked Mrs Knight to organise a do for the sesquicentennial, I said I'd like to include the older boys in some way. I thought that perhaps we could clear the Barn, and have a disco or something, but it wasn't possible, so we just let them come to the proper do. Anyway, it was when I was seeing if clearing it out was feasible that I found the niblick.'

'When my sergeant came about the thefts, you didn't mention the golf-club.'

'No, I'd made a note of them all, but I hadn't made a proper list. And it slipped my mind – I mean, it didn't even belong to anyone.'

'You said you'd let her have a list, but the first time she saw it was on Saturday.'

'I forgot all about it,' said Treadwell. 'There weren't any more thefts reported.'

Then the man seemed to change tack completely. 'When we spoke to Mr Hamlyn,' he said slowly, 'he said that he had suggested that his wife might be with Sam Waters as some sort of revenge.' He looked politely at Treadwell. 'What do you suppose he meant by that, Mr Treadwell?'

Treadwell shrugged slightly. 'Revenge for Sam having had an affair with his wife, I suppose,' he said.

'But that was an amicable arrangement, according to Hamlyn himself. He and his wife had arrived at an understanding.'

Treadwell frowned. 'I don't quite know what . . .' he said.

'We think he may have been trying to upset someone else. Someone at the table. Someone who had an interest in his wife. Someone who wouldn't be too happy to think that Sam was with her.'

Treadwell thought. The chairman? No, he decided. Too interested in himself, if he was any judge.

'He felt as though he had been given some sort of gift,' Lloyd went on. 'To ease someone's conscience. Could that have been his promotion, Mr Treadwell?'

'But I'm the one who put him up for promotion,' Treadwell said. 'The chairman just went along with it – very reluctantly, I might add. He thought Hamlyn was too old.'

'The chairman didn't leave the table,' said Lloyd. 'And Hamlyn believed that his remarks actually caused his wife's death. I don't think he suspected the chairman.'

'Then who?' said Treadwell.

'You went looking for Mrs Hamlyn, Mr Treadwell.'

Treadwell was totally bewildered. 'Because Mrs Knight wanted to speak to her,' he said.

'Why didn't you ring Mrs Knight back?' asked the sergeant.

Oh, God. He'd have to tell them. He opened his mouth a couple of times, but he couldn't. 'Chief Inspector,' he said, 'would it be possible – I mean, could I speak to you alone, do you think?'

'Sergeant?' Lloyd said.

'Certainly,' she said, getting up. 'I have something else to do.'

Lloyd twisted round as she got to the door. 'Judy!' he called, and got up, speaking to her too quietly for Treadwell to hear what he was saying. He came back into the room as the outside door closed. 'Right, Mr Treadwell,' he said, sitting down again.

'I couldn't . . . well, not with a young woman . . . .' Treadwell wasn't at all sure that he could anyway.

'You were about to tell me why you didn't ring back to say that you had been unable to find Mrs Hamlyn,' Lloyd said. 'Why, Mr Treadwell?'

'Because I did find her.'

Lloyd just nodded, as though he'd known that all along. 'Well – I saw her.'

'Where?'

'In the Barn.'

Lloyd looked stem as he spoke. 'Why didn't you tell us this before?' he demanded. 'Why didn't you tell the chief superintendent that night? Why didn't you tell anyone at all, Mr Treadwell?'

'Because . . . I had got it all wrong, you see. I hadn't got the picture – it took a while to get it all sorted out.'

'Three days?'

'No, well—'

'Then let's sort it out now, shall we?'

'I went into the Barn, and—'

'Wait. Did you expect to find her there?'

The wind howled round the house; Treadwell poured himself another drink.

'No. When I was on the phone, the small door to the Barn was open, and I could see Newby's car. I thought he'd left some time before that, and I went to see if he was all right. With it being so wet and slippery underfoot.'

Lloyd nodded encouragingly.

'But then ... .' Treadwell ran a finger round his shirt-collar, which was damp with perspiration. 'As I got to the door, I heard ... sounds,' he said, producing the final word as quickly as he could.

'Sounds?' Lloyd frowned. 'What sort of sounds?'

'Oh, you know the sort of sounds!'

'No,' he said, sitting back. 'Suppose you tell me?'

For a moment or two Treadwell's lips moved, but nothing much came out. His hands moved, too, as though their waving about would suffice. 'Sounds,' he said again. 'You know. Sort of ... well ... moaning, heavy breathing – you *know*!' He hated Lloyd for making him tell him, but at least he wasn't that woman.

'Did she call whoever she was with by name?'

Treadwell gulped his drink, and shook his head. 'Not unless his name was God,' he said, in a heroic attempt at a joke.

Lloyd didn't laugh. 'If they were in the car, how were you able to hear so clearly?' he asked.

Outside, the wind and the rain danced wildly together. Diana had danced wildly, Treadwell thought, beginning to feel pleasantly hazy. But you would never have thought it to look at her. She had been pretty, and vivacious, but she had always dressed sensibly, and she had *been* sensible. Bordering on wise, even. But she had danced wildly. He smiled a little.

'Mr Treadwell? How could you hear what was going on in the car?'

He sighed. 'The rear door was open,' he said. 'I could see that when I went in.'

'Why did you go in?' Lloyd's face was unfathomable. He just asked questions, and listened to the answers.

'Because I had to put a stop to it. Suppose one of the VIPs ...' Even now, in the new-found freedom of his resignation, Treadwell couldn't bear to think of it. 'I called out. Asked what was going on,' he continued. 'There was silence, then a sort of scuffle, and then someone got out of the car and opened one of the big doors. That's when I could see that it was Diana Hamlyn, as if I hadn't already guessed. I followed her, and she was going in the direction of the playing-field when I got out. Then I heard the doors being pushed open properly, and Newby's car came out.' He shrugged a little. 'He was driving very fast. Too fast. I don't think he saw me.'

'What did you do then?'

Treadwell reached for the whisky, and poured two this time, handing Lloyd a glass whether he wanted one or not. He took it; no nonsense about not drinking on duty. 'I walked around,' he said.

'In a downpour?'

Treadwell nodded. 'I walked around, thinking what a god-awful night it had been, and how I didn't want to go back in to the chairman and his wife and Hamlyn being so . . . .' He took a deep swallow. 'But I did.'

Lloyd sipped his drink, and didn't speak. The wind huffed and puffed, but it couldn't blow Treadwell's house down, because it was in ruins anyway.

'I didn't ring Caroline back because it still wasn't eleven, and Diana was on her way home,' he said.

'Or perhaps,' said Lloyd slowly, 'perhaps when you followed her to the door, you picked up the first thing that came to hand. The golf-club.'

Treadwell felt once again as though he had turned over two pages at once. 'The golf-club? But it wasn't there any more and, even if it *had* been, why—?'

'You say it wasn't there,' Lloyd said, interrupting him. 'But I don't know that. It might not have gone missing in December. We only have your word for that. As far as we know, it could have gone missing on Friday night, and been put on the list on Saturday. Perhaps you picked up the golf-club, caught up with her as she crossed the playing-field, and killed her.'

Treadwell almost choked on his drink. 'Why in the world would I do that?' he asked.

'Because you were having an affair with her.'

'An affair? Me?'

'That's what Mr Hamlyn seems to have thought,' said Lloyd.

Treadwell almost laughed. 'I feel flattered, in a way,' he said. 'If Hamlyn thought that I could ever have coped with Diana.'

Dancing wildly with Diana. It was a nice thought, but he couldn't even talk about Diana's wild dancing, never mind take part in it. He put down his drink. He really shouldn't drink this fast.

'He thought that was why he was promoted. He said he felt like a wife whose husband suddenly buys her flowers. He thought you had a guilty conscience, Mr Treadwell.'

'If he thought that, he was quite wrong. I pushed for his promotion because he had already been passed over twice, and it wasn't fair. And, as I've already told you, I thought that Diana would have been an asset in that particular situation.'

'He thought that that was why you sacked Lacey. And you went looking for her, Mr Treadwell. Where you'd found her last time.'

'I went into the Barn for the reason I have given you,' said Treadwell. 'Yes, I did find her again.' He finished his whisky, his two-minute-old promise forgotten. 'Only last time it was a summer's day,' he said. 'And I could see all too clearly what they were up to.'

He looked at Lloyd, the whisky deadening the embarrassment he still felt when he thought of it.

'She couldn't have cared less,' he said. 'She laughed. She actually laughed. Said something about having been caught in the act, and laughed, Mr Lloyd. And there was I, shocked, embarrassed, looking as if *I* had been caught in the act.' Chance, he thought, would have been a fine thing. 'And that's why I sacked Lacey. It was something I could do. To prove that I was in charge of the situation.' He smiled. 'But I wasn't,' he said. 'Diana was.'

Lloyd nodded slightly. 'Have you any idea who she was with this time?' he asked.

'I presumed it was Newby.'

Lloyd shook his head. 'We know it wasn't Mr Newby,' he said. 'Diana was in his car with someone *else*?'

'She must have been,' said Lloyd. 'Do you have any idea who it was, Mr Treadwell?'

'I suppose it must have been Sam,' said Treadwell. 'Hamlyn was right.'

'Did you touch the car when you were in the Barn?' he asked. Treadwell shook his head.

'You won't mind letting us have your fingerprints? Just so that we can make sure?'

'If you think it's really necessary.'

Lloyd put down his glass. 'If I think it's *really* necessary,' he said, 'I will fingerprint everyone who was here on Friday night. At the moment, I think it would merely be helpful, Mr Treadwell. And I'm sure you want to be helpful.'

'I don't mind,' said Treadwell, resigned. 'I think, to be perfectly truthful, that I am past caring.'

'You didn't go back in,' said Lloyd. 'Didn't you feel the urge to sack anyone this time?'

Treadwell shook his head. 'Do you know the play *An Inspector Calls*?' he asked.

'Yes,' said Lloyd, a little puzzled.

'We don't know what the consequences of our actions will be,' Treadwell said. 'I sacked Lacey. Lacey was a driver. I needed a driver, because I had been banned.' He raised his glass in a salute to the constabulary, and realised it was empty. 'And he came in handy, running errands to the town, picking people up, that sort of thing. He picked Newby up from the station when he came for his interview.'

Lloyd picked up his drink again, and sipped it. 'And he should have taken him back?'

Treadwell sighed. 'But he didn't, because I dismissed him. Told him to get off the premises. Newby missed his train as a result, and Andrew drove him back to London.' He shook his head. 'If I hadn't sacked Lacey, the accident couldn't have happened.' He poured himself another. 'I've felt responsible ever since. For Knight's death, for Caroline's illness – because she *was* ill, Mr Lloyd, even if stealing wasn't, as it turns out, one of the symptoms. I feel responsible for Newby's disability – for everything.'

Lloyd covered his glass with his hand, as Treadwell advanced with the bottle.

'So I didn't want to go back into the Barn, and face anyone. Finding her in almost exactly the same circumstances had brought it all back, and I didn't want to do anything about it at all. And I thought, then, that everything with Caroline was going according to plan, despite that. So I didn't ring her back.'

'And when you found it hadn't?' Lloyd hadn't forgotten his original question. 'Why did you tell no one about this?'

Treadwell gave a deep sigh. 'Robert said he'd had enough at about ten to one or so,' he said. 'And then, the next thing I knew, he was back. He came up to me at the table, and he said, "Diana's dead", just like that. "Diana's dead. Someone's killed her." ' He stopped speaking, as he remembered the moment.

'Go on,' said Lloyd.

'But I thought he'd been *home*. I thought he had found her with Newby, and ... well, flipped. After the way he had been behaving at dinner . . . . Anyway, when I found out what had actually happened to her, it was such a shock that I wasn't thinking at all. It wasn't until Marcia asked me who was minding the juniors that I realised that Diana had never *got* home. I said I'd have to go and tell Caroline what had happened, but Simon Allison suggested I send someone else. Quite right. I'd had – I'd been ... I was drunk,' he finished defiantly. 'And because I was drunk I wasn't capable of sorting it all out.'

'When were you capable?'

'When I woke up next morning, with a thick head. Simon had said that someone was coming to see me, so I was going to tell him. But it wasn't a him! I didn't expect a woman, for God's sake! I couldn't tell a woman what I'd heard, what had happened!'

'That was two days ago. Why didn't you tell me? Or Mr Allison?'

'I was going to. But then there was Hamlyn, and Matthew, and I didn't know whether I was coming or going. Then you arrested Newby, and I thought it was all over. I thought that was who she had been with, and now you had got him.'

Lloyd sat back, nursing his drink, deep in thought. Then he spoke. 'Why should I believe any of that, Mr Treadwell?' he asked.

Treadwell shrugged a little.

'How do I know you didn't follow her on to the playing-field and kill her?' he asked.

Treadwell looked at him. 'If Mrs Hamlyn was killed with the golf-club,' he said, his voice quiet, 'then . . . .' He paused. 'Then you should ask Caroline Knight. She was with me when we found it. She'll confirm that it was stolen that day.'

Lloyd listened; but Treadwell still couldn't tell what he was thinking.

Caroline watched as Philip's eyelids began to flicker, and smiled at him as he opened his eyes.

'Have you stopped being cross with me yet?' he asked.

Caroline buried her head in his shoulder. 'I was cross with us,' she said. 'For letting the accident hurt us more than it had to. I haven't pulled myself together any more than you have.'

He kissed her, and she smiled. 'I told you you could do it,' she said.

'Not very well,' he said.

She laughed. 'Oh, Philip! It'll get better. Yesterday you were practically suicidal because you thought you couldn't do it at all. Are you never satisfied?'

'I was,' he said. 'But I don't suppose you were.' His arm tightened round her.

'I just wanted to be with you,' she said. 'I wanted to prove to you that you weren't a wreck, and . . . I wanted to prove to myself that I wasn't Andrew's widow any more.'

'But you are Andrew's widow,' he pointed out, showing the same literal turn of mind as Andrew himself.

'I was ill,' she said. 'After Andrew died. Really ill.' She smiled. 'I was seeing a psychiatrist, too,' she said. 'You're not the only one.'

He nodded. 'I know,' he said.

'But it wasn't helping. And one day I realised that I had to stop being Andrew's widow,' she said. 'I had to live my own life again, and I had to do it without the help of medicine men.'

'Perhaps you should have moved away from here,' Philip said.

She nodded. 'I wasn't thinking logically. I just wanted to prove to myself that I was still me. I needed to put some sort of full stop to widowhood.'

She stiffened as she heard the front door to the building open, relaxing when someone knocked at the flat door.

'I thought it was Sam,' she said. She wasn't looking forward to seeing Sam. 'Shouldn't you see who it is?'

Philip smiled. 'I don't feel like entertaining visitors,' he said. 'I don't know about you.'

Another knock; louder, going on for a little longer.

'It could be important.'

'Then they'll come back.'

A third knock. She and Philip stopped speaking, and listened as the footsteps went, and the front door banged shut. A woman's footsteps. Whoever it was, she had gone.

'What were you going to do?' Philip asked.

'What?'

'About stopping being Andrew's widow.'

She lay on her back, no longer looking at Philip, but still close, still touching him. 'I was going to sleep with Sam,' she said.

'Wasn't that a bit drastic?'

She laughed. Drastic hardly covered it.

'Why Sam?' he asked. 'Of all people?'

'Because he was a sitting duck,' she said. 'Always so keen to prove how macho he is. I knew it wouldn't be difficult to interest him in the project.'

'I got the impression that was his project,' said Philip. 'He put the idea into your head in the first place.'

No, she thought. It was the other way round. Sam had embraced the idea that a night with him would cure everything, but it had been her idea. But sex wasn't important. It had seemed to be before, but it wasn't. It *had* been important to Philip; that was why she had come to him. Because she could do something for him that his psychiatrist couldn't; it was as simple as that.

She turned, and kissed him again. 'It was my idea,' she said. 'Sam just tried to convince me that I was right, and he almost succeeded. I went out with him a couple of times, but I couldn't make myself get involved with him. So, I planned it all. For weeks. Friday night,' she said. 'That's when I was officially going to stop being a widow. We were going to a film, we'd be back late, he'd ask if he could stay, and I would say yes.'

'Simple as that?'

'I thought so.' She sighed. 'But when it came to it I couldn't.' She sat up and looked at Philip. 'I really did treat him very badly,' she said.

'You still think you caused it all, don't you?' said Philip.

She didn't answer.

'You didn't, Caroline. Sam might have gone with her, but he didn't rape her. They were in my car, for God's sake! I don't know why the police thought it was rape.'

Caroline shivered slightly. 'I do,' she said. 'Sam isn't what you'd call gentle.'

'Is that why you didn't go through with it?'

She shook her head. 'I couldn't go through with it because I had already stopped being Andrew's widow,' she said. 'I'd met you.'

'Are you waiting for someone, miss?'

The loud voice startled Judy, who was having a cigarette in Lloyd's car, and had opened the window in the vain hope that he wouldn't know.

'Oh, it's you,' said Des. 'You're the policewoman, aren't you?'

'That's right.' She pitched her own voice at his level.

'It's cold out here,' he said. 'I'm just going to do the boiler – would you like a cup of tea and a warm?'

Waters wasn't in his flat, so she had been unable to put into practice Lloyd's last minute instruction to be polite at all costs. She couldn't go back to Treadwell's, and Judy, crossly waiting in the car for Lloyd like a child outside a pub, couldn't think of anything much nicer than a cup of tea and a warm. She walked with Des back to the school, and the wonderfully cosy boiler room. She sat at a little table while Des filled the kettle, then watched, transported, as he opened up the bottom of the boiler, and removed the hot ashes.

The smell made her six again. Six, in her grandmother's cottage which her father had tried, without success, to make his mother modernise. He would tell her of the joys of electricity, how clean the cooker would be, how easy it would be to heat the house, how she wouldn't have to rake out ashes and heave coal about. He would offer to pay for all the work to be done. And she would say that she had always done it, and always would. And she always did.

Des's boiler was much bigger, even more trouble, even hotter, and more awkward. But, like her grandmother, Des expertly shovelled up the ash and deposited it in a metal container. 'Bloody nuisance, these days,' he bellowed, as he carried it to the door, and put it outside.

'Plastic bins,' he explained, as he came back and spooned tea into the pot. 'You can't put the ashes straight in any more. Got to let them cool down first.'

Perhaps, she thought, Des was a reincarnation of her grandmother, as he sat beside her, leaving the tea to brew. No tea-bags for Des or Gran.

'How long have you worked here?' she asked.

'Thirty years near enough. Since it was a real school.'

She smiled. 'Isn't it a real school?'

'That lot? You ought to know by now – you've been asking enough questions.'

Judy decided that being non-committal was the wisest course when everything you said had to be shouted at the top of your voice.

Des handed her a mug of tea, and indicated the milk-bottle and the bag of sugar, which had a soup-spoon in it.

'Des,' she said. 'Was Mrs Hamlyn involved with anyone at the school?'

Des laughed.

'I mean recently,' said Judy.

'I don't know about that bloke with the stick,' said Des. 'She might have been, but I don't think so. She went about with that artist for a while. She wasn't too fussy.' He drank some tea. 'Mainly, it was people outside,' he said. 'I'd see her driving off in the evenings. I think since the business with Jim she didn't want to cause any more trouble here.'

Judy didn't think she had the strength to go checking up on Diana's outside contacts. She could feel the increased heat on her face before Des began to shovel coal in on top of the fiercely glowing embers, banking it up for the night.

'Hard work,' she observed.

'No,' he said scornfully. 'I'm used to it. Antiquated, though – you'd think they'd spend some money and get a new one, at least.'

'How often do you have to do it?' Judy knew that on a cold Monday morning she would hate it, but right now it seemed like a lovely job, full of warmth, and the sights and sounds and smells of her childhood.

'Night and morning,' he said. 'Every day but Saturday. Let it out Saturday, and clear it out proper on Sunday morning.'

Judy smiled. 'So why were you raking it out on Saturday at lunchtime?' she asked. 'Don't forget, you're talking to a detective here, Des.'

Des's face was blank.

She laughed. 'Just a joke,' she said.

'But I wasn't,' he said. 'I wasn't here on Saturday. It's my day off. Always has been. I'm at home with my feet up on a Saturday.'

'You don't live in?'

'Not me. Never take a tied house. If you lose your job, you lose your home.' He frowned. 'Your lot used to have to have police houses, didn't you?'

'Mm.' Judy wasn't really listening. 'Someone was in here on Saturday,' she said. 'Raking out the boiler. I heard them. Myself.'

'Well, I'd like to know who was messing about with my boiler,' said Des.

Judy nodded. 'So would I,' she said, putting down her mug. They had searched all the bins; it was the first thing they did after the playing-field. 'Des – that container that you put out the back door – how often do you empty it?'

'When it's full,' he said.

'Do you have something I could use to poke around in it?' she asked.

Des walked slowly over to the boiler. 'A poker works best,' he said.

Judy smiled, and held out her hand, but Des pulled the poker back. 'No,' he said. 'These ashes are red hot. I'll look for whatever it is.'

And he looked, and they found it. The metal head, which wasn't going to burn up, and the murderer knew it. The metal head which someone had had to come back for, to rake out of the ashes before Des found it. Which couldn't be put into a dustbin, because the police were emptying them all.

Sam couldn't concentrate; he walked back over to the staff block, frowning as he saw the light. He hadn't left the light on. He never left lights on.

Caroline and Newby sat on the sofa, with the fire going full blast.

'I thought they'd banged you up,' he said to Newby.

'I've been released,' he said.

'Well, well, well.' Sam turned the fire down, and picked up a beer. 'So we've still got a murderer at large,' he said.

'Could we drop that subject?' Caroline asked.

'A bit difficult,' said Sam. 'It isn't every day even this place has a dead body in the middle of the playing-field.'

The knock on the door was all too familiar. 'Fat chance of the subject being changed,' he said, opening the door to find the sergeant. 'Good evening, Sergeant Hill,' he said. 'Do come in.'

'No, thank you.' She handed him his pen, and he signed a receipt with it.

'Is that all?' he asked.

'You've got your pen back,' she said.

Sam smiled broadly. 'Had your knuckles rapped, have you?'

'I was told you had complained, and I was asked to give you your pen back.' She took a breath. 'But I suppose I—' She stopped speaking as Chief Inspector Lloyd arrived.

'Now what?' said Sam.

'Not you, Mr Waters,' Lloyd said, his foot on the stair. Sam wanted to let him go upstairs, but he felt he had done enough already. 'She's in here,' he said.

Lloyd and the sergeant came in. Asking about the golf-club.

'Perhaps you could confirm when it went missing from the Barn?' Lloyd was asking Caroline. 'Mr Treadwell wasn't certain.'

'December the fourteenth,' she said.

Lloyd smiled. 'Very precise.'

'It's in my diary,' she said. 'Barry wanted to see if we could clear the Barn.'

'What's a golf-club got to do with it?' asked Newby.

'They think it murdered Diana,' said Sam.

Lloyd looked at him. 'No,' he said. 'We think someone murdered Mrs Hamlyn with it.'

'Sorry,' said Sam. 'It's a pity you can't arrest me for murdering the language, isn't it?'

The sergeant took Lloyd to one side, and spoke quietly to him.

'It seems', Lloyd said, looking up, 'that the golf-club was indeed the weapon used.' He was watching their faces as he spoke; everyone's, not just Sam's. 'And perhaps,' he said, 'since I have you all together, one of you might know who Mrs Hamlyn was likely to have been seeing recently?'

Sam laughed.

Lloyd raised an eyebrow. 'All I know is that you have all told me – in your various ways – that she couldn't keep her hands off men. Odd that, because every man I speak to was apparently as pure as the driven snow as far as she was concerned.'

'You give me a guest-list,' said Sam, 'and I'll show you half a dozen blokes that I know about, and another half-dozen that I suspect.'

'Right,' said Lloyd. 'I'll do that, Mr Waters. Any information would be most helpful.'

Sam frowned. 'I don't see how,' he said. 'Everyone would be coming and going – getting drinks, going off and talking to other people, going to the gents' – how can you sort out who nipped out for a quickie with Diana? It would be like looking for a needle in the proverbial.'

'When it comes to a murder inquiry', Lloyd said, 'we look for needles in haystacks and anything else they might be in, however unpleasant. And we very often find them.' He opened the door. 'Good night,' he said to the assembled company. 'Thank you for your time.'

Newby and Caroline, said good night; Sam let Lloyd almost close the door.

'A word of advice, Chief Inspector,' he said, catching the door-handle.

'Yes, Mr Waters?' Lloyd reluctantly turned to look at him.

'Whoever murdered Mrs Hamlyn would have had a hell of a job doing it when she hadn't just been screwing someone.'

Lloyd paused for a tiny moment. 'Thank you,' he said.

Sam stood for a moment at the door, as Lloyd and the sergeant left.

She had been going to say something when Lloyd arrived, he thought. He wished he hadn't tried to needle her so much. She had more go about her than most women. He might almost have found her good company, if things had been different. Oh, damn it all. She shouldn't have tried hanging on to Walter's pen.

Walter Smith, a year ahead of him in school, one of the half-dozen or so black pupils whose parents had somehow managed to get rich enough to send their sons there. Smith had looked after him; he'd kept him out of trouble. He'd interested him in art. And when they had finished university, and Sam had gone to art college, he'd had the pen engraved, with the 'WS' linked along the side, for Walter's birthday. It was his first design. Walter Smith was the only other human being for whom Sam had ever had any time, and time was the one thing that had been denied to him. His wife had given Sam the pen back when Walter died from a heart-attack at the ludicrous age of thirty. It could just as well read 'SW', she had said. Sam already knew that.

Sam closed the door, and swore.

Newby sighed. 'Is that aimed at someone in particular, or just the world in general?' Sam swore at Newby.

'Well, so long as we know where we are,' said Newby amiably. 'Did I hear Sergeant Hill saying you had *complained* about her?'

'Storm in a teacup,' said Sam. He paused. 'What do you think of the good lady sergeant, Philip?'

'I don't know. I haven't seen any reason to complain about her.'

'No, I want to know. I'll bet you wouldn't kick her out of bed, would you? She's your type – like Caroline.'

Newby blushed, not looking at Caroline.

'I mean, you could mistake her for Caroline, at a distance, couldn't you? You must have noticed. Does she get you going, too?' Sam watched Newby's discomfort with totally unconcealed pleasure.

'All right,' said Newby, looking up. 'Yes, I've noticed a resemblance, and no, she doesn't get me going. So whatever it is you're trying to do, give up.'

'Just as well she doesn't,' said Sam. 'If you ask me, her boss is knocking her off.'

'You would think that, wouldn't you?' said Newby.

'I'll bet I'm right,' said Sam. 'And I'll bet that you and the lovely Mrs Knight here have become more than just good friends since I saw you last. Which surprises me, Newby. I didn't think you had it in you.'

'Come on, Philip,' said Caroline, standing up.

'Don't leave on my account,' said Sam. 'I've got work to do.'

Rather you than me, he thought, as he left Newby to Caroline's devices, and went back to the art room, ready at last to start work. He knew he was right about them, and about Lloyd and his lady. And he hadn't given Caroline the message from Cawston, because now he understood it, and understood that he had never been meant to pass it on.

And he knew he was right about that, too. His work was surrealist, if it had to be given a name, but Sam painted people; not everyone realised that. He knew what made people tick.

He just didn't like them very much.

Chapter Nine

They were alone in Philip's flat, having passed up the school breakfast in favour of toast and tea.

'When all this is sorted out,' Philip suddenly said, his voice firm, 'we're getting out of this place.'

Caroline looked up quickly, making the tea she was pouring spill on to the table.

'Oh,' said Philip, flustered. 'Unless – oh, hell, I'm taking too much for granted. Sorry.'

'No,' she said, mopping up the spilled tea with a tissue. 'You're not. I just didn't know that you felt the same.'

He smiled. 'I told you I did.'

She finished pouring the tea, and handed him his. 'So you did,' she said.

'And we'll leave here? As soon as we can?'

'It might be difficult,' she said.

'No,' said Philip. 'We just get into our cars and go. To hell with this place – it won't last the week anyway.'

'I mean finding somewhere that we can work together,' she said.

Philip looked a touch uncomfortable. 'Ah,' he said. 'I wasn't really thinking about our working together.' He cleared his throat unnecessarily. 'In fact,' he said, 'I'm not so sure that it's a good idea, on the whole.'

'Of course it is.' She drank some tea.

'But . . . .' Philip thought for a moment before carrying on. 'But I think that that's one reason why it was so difficult for you when Andrew died,' he said.

'I loved him,' she said.

'I know, I know.' Philip put down his mug. 'But if you had worked somewhere different – well, that part of your life would have carried on . . . . I mean, it wouldn't have altered. Whereas you were so close, so . . . involved with him that . . . .' He dropped his eyes from hers. 'Well, you lost your bearings.'

'I've found them again.'

'Yes, but you should have a life of your own. You said so yourself.'

'I've got you,' she said, then wondered if all this was his way of backtracking on what he had said. 'Or am I taking things for granted now?'

'You've got me,' he said. 'I'm not sure why you want me. But I still think that you should have your own job, and your own friends. I'm not so sure that living in one another's pocket is a good idea,' he said again.

'That's what Andrew said.' She smiled at him, at the kind, concerned eyes looking so earnestly into hers. 'His exact words. I don't think it is living in one another's pockets. I think it's perfectly possible to live and work together, and be a team. That's not living in one another's pockets.' She drank some tea as she watched Philip prepare his argument. 'Sam's probably right about the chief inspector and Sergeant Hill,' she said. 'They manage.'

Philip shook his head. 'You don't know that he's right,' he said. 'And even if he is, you don't know that they manage.' He smiled. 'And even if they do, they don't *live* at the police station,' he added.

'We don't have to live wherever it is,' she said.

'Is that what you told Andrew?'

She laughed. 'We didn't have much choice,' she said. 'I talked him round.'

Philip smiled, a little uncertainly. 'Well,' he said, getting up from the table. 'Time enough to discuss that. We'd better get to work – if we have any pupils left.'

'I've got a free period,' she said.

'It's all right for some.'

She went to the door with him, and discovered the thaw. The weather had finally made its mind up; water poured from the roof as the snow melted.

Philip smiled. 'Spring,' he said. 'Just right for new starts.'

Caroline frowned as she saw the crowd of boys in the lane. She glanced apprehensively at Philip. 'What's happened now?' she said, her heart sinking.

They walked quickly towards the lane; Caroline wanted to run, but she kept to Philip's pace.

'Mrs Knight!' someone called as they got closer. 'Mr Waters won't let us in!'

She left Philip behind, pushing through the crowd of boys to the building. Through the window, she could see Sam, working on his painting, oblivious to everything but what he was doing. She let out a sigh of relief.

'It's all right,' she called to Philip, as he came through the crowd to her. 'It's just Sam being even worse than usual.'

Philip banged on the window, on the door; if Sam could hear him, and he could hardly not hear him, he didn't indicate it by so much as a twitch.

'Bang goes my free period,' Caroline said. 'Right, boys. Single file. You'd better go to my form room.'

The boys pushed and jostled into a wavy grey crocodile, and set off.

Philip shook his head. 'Trust Sam,' he said.

'What are we going to do about him?' asked Caroline. 'He can't get away with this.'

Philip glanced in. 'Leave him,' he said. 'He's being bloody-minded as usual. He'll probably unlock the door as soon as we've gone.'

'You'd better go to your class,' she said. 'I'll find something for that lot to do.'

'Right. See you at lunchtime.'

'Mrs Knight!'

Caroline sighed. It was obviously going to be one of those days, and she might as well accept it. She turned. 'Yes?' she said.

'Mrs Knight, Mr Treadwell said to ask you to go to his house, because the chairman of the governors would like to speak to you.'

Caroline looked at Philip, at Sam, at the small crocodile on its way to the main building, and back at the youth who had given her the message. 'Right,' she said. 'Please tell Mr Treadwell that I'll be along in a moment.'

The boy ran off, and Caroline thought. 'Philip,' she said, 'which group have you got?'

'5C,' he said.

'So you'll have a prefect, won't you? Can you ask him to supervise the class while you go and keep an eye on the kids in my form room? I'll be there as soon as I can get away.'

'All this so as no one finds out what he's up to?' Philip asked, with a nod through the window at Sam.

Caroline nodded. 'I think it's the least I can do,' she said.

Philip didn't seem convinced of the necessity, but he sighed, and shrugged his shoulders. 'All right,' he said.

She watched him go, walking quite quickly even on the cobbles, some confidence back in his step. He waved as he went round the bend in the lane, and she waved back, her heart light for the first time in months.

He was so like Andrew.

Sam worked quickly, with a thin brush and bright oil paints. Harsh colours, harsh subject. But every stroke was applied with infinite patience, total concentration. He had been with it all night; it had started as a mark on the canvas. Just one line, the dominant line, the angle from which everything else would follow. Building it up, piece by piece. And he wouldn't stop until it was finished; he never did. By the time he first loaded the brush, the painting was there, in his head.

It never quite looked like it did in his head. But sometimes it got close, and one day – maybe today – it would come exactly right. Red. Red, and white.

He had heard the commotion outside the door, he had heard the banging on the window. But he had heard the birds start to sing before the sun rose; he had heard the school waking up. Heard cars arrive, and people walking along the lane outside. You could hear these things, but you didn't have to listen.

It had been so long since he had painted, so long since he had felt the release that it gave him. Sometimes, he wished he didn't use it all up at once like he did; he wished he could cover it up and come back to it again and again. But he couldn't let go, not once he'd got it. If he left it, it might not forgive him.

So he worked on, and he heard more people pass, another group of boys congregate and disperse, another knocking at the door. People calling his name. Then it went quiet again.

Sam could see that there was very little left to do; he didn't want to let it go, and yet he longed to. He wanted to stand back and look at the image in his head. The image that had come to him, stealing up on him, covering his eyes so that he couldn't see it. That was the worst time, when he couldn't sit still, and he was hungry all the time. And this was the best time; the moments before he looked at it.

He laid down his brush, not looking at the canvas. With his back to it, he cleaned up, put everything away. Washed his hands. Tidied up the room. Once he looked, it would be over.

He looked, and it was there. The image in his head. It was there, on the canvas.

He sat down, elated, exhausted, his head in his hands. Too soon, the moment was over. Already, he could see that the image hadn't translated exactly. He hadn't got enough power, enough energy into it. He had taken too much care. He should have slashed some of the colour on. He should have . . . .

But no matter. Another image would come. Because he was painting again. In a year, if he could survive it, he would have enough for another exhibition. Sam painted fast and furious when he was really working. Meticulous, but fast. Like a machine. Like a computer, programmed with the brushstrokes, with the image inside its brain in coded messages. Sometimes he felt that he could start in one corner and build the picture up from there, so little did he seem to have to do with its execution.

And now he could look at it dispassionately. It was neither perfect nor disastrous. It was – what was it one of the papers had called him? – technically sound. He smiled. A put-down. But he was used to put-downs. Nobody *liked* what he did, but people like

Newby appreciated it. Art critics didn't. He recalled some of his reviews, knowing he would read them again if this one ever saw the light of a gallery. '... depicting the sort of obvious, crude, colourful violence that is exploited on the cinema screens every night', according to one. 'The substitution of machinery for women as a focus for the brutality is as subtle as it gets.' He was right. Violence *was* obvious and crude. It wasn't subtle; why should he be?

Another knock. Not banging, like before. Just a knock. Slowly, like an old man, he got up, and unlocked the door.

'Hello,' she said.

'Sergeant Hill.' His voice was hoarse. 'Come to evict me?' She gave him a little smile. 'No. I've come to thank you,' she said.

'What for?'

'Not shopping me,' she said.

'Oh, that.' He sat down again, wearily. 'I deserved it,' he said.

'Yes,' she said. 'But you could have got me into trouble, all the same.' She looked at him. 'Have you been here all night?' she asked. 'Mr Newby said you were painting.'

He sighed, running a hand over his stubbled chin. 'I've finished,' he said, a little wistfully. He waved a hand at the canvas which stood facing the wall. 'You can be the first to see it, if you want.'

She looked a little dubious at the honour. 'I don't know anything about art,' she said. 'You want Lloyd for that.'

'No,' he said. 'I want you.' He nodded to it. 'Go on,' he said. 'See what you think.'

With a slight shrug, she crossed the room. He watched as she walked round the easel; he saw her look of polite expectation vanish, saw her eyes unwillingly move over it before she turned her head away.

'Does it disturb you?' he asked.

'Yes,' she said.

'I hope you're typical,' he said.

Her eyes moved back to it. 'Who buys a painting like that?' she asked.

Sam smiled. 'You wouldn't fancy it hanging in your sitting-room?' he asked.

'Would anyone?'

He shook his head. 'Probably not,' he said. 'A collector might buy it, or a gallery. If my reputation survives the critics.'

'Turner's did,' she said.

'I thought you knew nothing about art?'

'I'm being taught.' Another look at the painting. A slight frown. 'Poor Mrs Hamlyn,' she said, and left.

Sam looked at it. Just coloured marks on canvas. An optical illusion. He smiled. He had told himself people would cry for his slot machine; the sergeant hadn't cried, but it had touched her, all right. And one was all you needed.

Philip ate alone. Caroline had never returned to relieve him of Sam's art class, and her attempts to save Sam from himself fell apart when the next class was refused entry to the art room, and she hadn't been around to organise cover. It had been sorted out, eventually, with classes doubling up. Sam had emerged after Sergeant Hill had seen him, only to shut himself in his room. When Philip had left the flat for the canteen, Sam's snores had followed him to the front door.

Treadwell had abdicated responsibility for the whole affair, and Philip had no intention of involving himself, so the rest of the day would presumably be as chaotic as the morning. Though not as chaotic as it might have been; the normally packed canteen was quiet, with so many of the pupils taking an unscheduled break, and the doubled-up classes were not much larger than the normal ones.

Philip looked up as someone came in at the other end of the long room. He half-rose, trying to catch her attention, then realised that it was the sergeant. He had thought, for a moment, that it was Caroline. He sat down again, his heart pounding.

Sam had planted the idea last night. Deliberately, maliciously. He had been able to ignore it then, but now . . . .

He watched as Chief Inspector Lloyd joined the sergeant at the counter, his eyes never leaving them as they chose their meals, and sat down in a corner. The chief inspector was doing all the talking; she just sat, and toyed with her food like Philip himself.

Then Caroline really did come in, not stopping to pick up food, but coming straight to where he was, sitting down, her eyes shining with excitement. 'You'll never guess,' she said.

'I won't try, then,' he said. Seeing her made him feel better, and he actually began to eat.

'I've been offered a joint headship,' she said. 'With Mr Dearden. They think they should have a woman head teacher because of the girls coming next year.' She smiled. 'No interviews – nothing. A straight appointment.'

Philip stopped chewing.

'Isn't it great?'

Philip didn't know which aspect of it he found least entrancing. He looked round the huge canteen, with its odd groups of people eating. 'Are you sure anyone will be coming next year?' he asked.

'Oh, I'll get it going again,' she said confidently. 'The way it ought to be.'

Philip smiled. 'Well,' he said, 'if anyone can do it, you can.'

She put her hand on his. 'I know I can,' she said.

'I just don't think that this place is for me.'

'It won't *be* this place! They've all gone, Philip. Or they're going. The Hamlyns, Sam – Treadwell.'

'It's still the same school,' said Philip.

'But it's not *their* school any more,' she said. She sat back a little. 'But if you feel you have to leave, then I'm coming with you,' she said.

Andrew's voice. '*If you've got to leave now, I'll have to drive you.*' Andrew's voice, his face. Even his car. He could see it all now. A warm sunny summer day. An open-top car. '*Everything's gone wrong. Caroline can't get back, and it seems that Treadwell's sacked the bloody driver.*' Getting into the car, Andrew irritated because Philip wasn't going to meet Caroline after all. '*Found him in the potting-shed with the maths teacher's wife, would you believe?*' he had said, as they drove off. The potting-shed. He'd called it the potting-shed, in fun. That was what had made him think that there was a garden. *'I've told Caroline she's got Diana Hamlyn to thank if I get led astray by the bright lights.'*

And if he got killed? Philip's eyes rose slowly to Caroline's.

'Philip? We don't have to stay. I just thought it would be good, because we wouldn't have to find somewhere that we could both work. We could do it right – teach them to stop and smell the roses.' She squeezed his hand. 'But it really doesn't matter, Philip. We'll go. We'll find something else.'

He looked at her, then let his eyes move towards the sergeant. Dark, slim. *It could have been you,* he'd said to her, when she had asked.

The figure that he had glimpsed on the fire-escape; the figure that hadn't been there any more when he got to the top. Caroline had been there.

The police had suspected Sam because he had changed his clothes. Caroline had been changing her clothes.

But he looked at her, and he knew he didn't care. He couldn't leave without her, and he couldn't take her away when she was so enthusiastic about the job. He smiled, and shook his head.

'We'll stay,' he said. And he would be with her, whatever happened. They were a team.

'Are you deep in thought or in a huff?' Lloyd asked.

Judy put down her knife and fork and stopped pretending to eat. 'Neither,' she said.

He smiled. 'Oh – I almost forgot. It seems that single-handedly you managed to flush Sam out of his bolt-hole. He came out just after you left, apparently, and you are fast becoming a folk-hero.'

Judy managed a smile, but she couldn't get that picture out of her mind.

'Did he say something?' Lloyd asked, his voice angry. 'Because if he did—'

'No,' she said. 'No, he was fine.' She looked at Lloyd. 'I think maybe he was even nice,' she said.

'*Waters?*' was Lloyd's only comment.

She hadn't told Lloyd about the painting. He would only make fun of her.

'If you're not going to eat that, could we take a walk round?'

Judy looked out at the weather. Long spits of rain streaked the windows down one side of the hall, as the afternoon grew greyer and wetter. 'A walk round,' she said.

'A walk round to the car, then, if you're frightened of a bit of weather.' He pushed his chair back. 'Come on,' he said.

Matthew Cawston, alone, as usual, came in as they were leaving, his blazer spotted with the quickening rain, running a hand over wind-tousled hair. Polite. Pleasant. Debonair, even in his school uniform, as he had been the first time she met him. Not the vulnerable boy she had seen on Friday night, that she had been conned into thinking she saw in Michael. She felt foolish every time she thought of that. Sometimes, she knew just how lucky she was to have Lloyd. She ought to tell him that some time. They walked through the lane to the car park, and they sat in the car as the wind grew wild.

'Both Newby and Treadwell think it has to have been that nice Mr Waters who was with Diana,' Lloyd said.

Judy groaned. 'Oh, Lloyd. Aren't we in enough trouble? Don't keep going after Sam. Why would he want to kill Diana Hamlyn?'

'I don't think he did,' said Lloyd.

The wind murmured round the car, ready to let rip again.

'You think Treadwell caught them together,' Judy said, a little wearily. 'But that doesn't make sense.'

They had been through his theory on Treadwell; why, Lloyd had wanted to know, had Diana run away from him this time? She hadn't before. She had laughed, made a joke of it. So why run this time, unless he was chasing her with murderous intent? Which would have been fine, except that Freddie had just half an hour ago quite unequivocally confirmed that the golf-club was indeed a niblick, and the murder weapon. End of theory. It hadn't so far produced any more clues as to who had wielded it. All Freddie could tell them was that it had been wrapped in some sort of plastic, probably a bag.

Lloyd tapped the steering-wheel thoughtfully. 'Logic,' he said. 'You're fond of that.'

'All right,' said Judy. 'Let's look at it logically.'

'Let's.'

'We now know that the golf-club is the murder weapon.'

'Check.'

The wind suddenly blustered, rattling the window. Judy shivered, and Lloyd switched on the engine, putting the heater on full.

'And it was stolen last December,' she said, caught in a blast of cold air from the heater. Why were car heaters cold to start with? Other heaters weren't. That never seemed entirely logical to her.

'Check,' said Lloyd again.

Judy was aware that she was being manipulated in some way; he was making her go through his theory for him, whatever it was, so that she couldn't dismiss it out of hand. It had to be a Lloyd special.

'So,' she said carefully, hanging on to the logic. 'Either it was somewhere that the murderer just happened to find it when he needed it, or . . . .'

'Or it was stolen for the purpose?' Lloyd supplied the alternative, unable to wait for her.

'And that's simply not possible,' Judy said firmly. 'You said yourself it wasn't. No one knew that Mrs Hamlyn was going to see Matthew stealing that pen. No one knew that she was going to leave the Hall when she did.'

Rain started to fall steadily, blown almost horizontal by the wind, drenching the car, streaming down the windscreen, blotting everything out.

Judy took out her notebook, flicking through the pages. *Eighteen months*, she kept reading. Eighteen months, she thought. She had written it down so many times. She frowned. 'Eighteen months,' she said.

'What?'

'I keep hearing it.' She pointed to the places in the notebook as she spoke. 'The stealing started eighteen months ago,' she said. 'The odd-job man was sacked eighteen months ago. Newby's accident was eighteen months ago.'

'That isn't coincidence,' said Lloyd. 'His accident happened *because* the odd-job man was sacked. And Andrew Knight was killed in the accident,' he said.

Judy looked up from her notes.

'Everyone thought Mrs Knight was the thief,' said Lloyd. 'Because the thefts began at about the same time. And she was having some sort of breakdown.'

'Yes.'

'So everyone thought she had stolen the golf-club, presumably,' he said.

Judy confirmed that with a nod.

'But because she didn't take the *other* things, everyone's discounted her. Yet she was the only other person who knew it was there. If Treadwell didn't take it on the off-chance of finding Diana with another man . . . .' He sat back. 'Sometimes things are just the way they seem. Mrs Knight did take the golf-club.'

'Why?'

'To murder Mrs Hamlyn,' said Lloyd. 'Your friend Sam Waters gave me some advice last night. Remember?'

'*Whoever murdered Mrs Hamlyn would have had a hell of a job doing it when she hadn't just been screwing someone.*'

Judy remembered. She hadn't written it down.

'The sex had nothing to do with it,' said Lloyd. 'It doesn't matter who she was with in Newby's car. It doesn't matter who discovered her. She was going to be murdered. She was *always* going to be murdered.'

'By Caroline Knight?'

Lloyd nodded.

'But if the golf-club was stolen in order to murder her, then it *has* to have been planned,' said Judy doggedly. 'And it couldn't have been.'

'Oh, yes, it could. It was. The murder was planned. The whole evening was planned.'

Judy's eyes met his. 'By Caroline Knight,' she said slowly.

'She planned everything. She arranged the date of the ball, and then she arranged to babysit rather than attend. She arranged to go to this midnight movie thing with Sam, so that Diana would have to leave early, and walk across the playing-field just when she did.' He looked at Judy. 'She happened to be running away from Treadwell, but that doesn't alter the fact that she was crossing the playing-field exactly when she would have been anyway.'

Judy was looking through her notebook again.

'But Sam almost spoiled it,' Lloyd said. 'He wasn't supposed to come until eleven o'clock, and there she would have been, all ready to be escorted to her midnight movie. As it was, he came early, and she had to get rid of him so that she could wait for Diana crossing the field. She kills her, and then goes back up the fire-escape. Newby saw someone who just disappeared, remember. That's because she went in the door on the balcony. And he said it could have been you. Caroline Knight looks like you, Judy.'

So she had been told. Judy turned the pages.

He looked up in the general direction of the Hamlyns' bedroom window, though nothing could be seen through the windscreen but the blurred shape of the building.

'And Newby went up after her, and watched her changing. We said whoever it was had to have changed, and we *know* she did. We've known all along. And why was she changing? Sam wasn't taking her anywhere.'

'But why?' Judy asked. 'Why would she kill her?'

'*An Inspector Calls*,' said Lloyd.

Judy frowned.

'It's a play. By a man called J. B. Priestley. It shows you that everything you do has consequences, some you might regret. Treadwell mentioned it – now I know why. He said he felt responsible for Andrew Knight's death, Caroline's illness – and everything.'

It was hot and stuffy now; Lloyd switched off the heater, and sighed.

'Because Diana Hamlyn chose to seduce Treadwell's driver, Andrew Knight died. Because Andrew Knight died, Caroline had a nervous breakdown. And now Diana Hamlyn's dead. That's what 'and everything' meant. It all goes back to the accident. Eighteen months ago.'

'But why would she steal the golf-club?'

'Why not? Someone was stealing anyway. Chances are if she used something of her own it would get traced back to her. But if she stole something in the middle of a spate of thefts – something she had no intention of using for two months . . . .' He spread his hands. 'Any real investigation would prove she hadn't stolen the other things, and no one would connect her with the golf-club. And that's exactly what happened.'

That wasn't what Judy had meant; she let it pass, as she read her notes.

'And remember what she was like when we saw her that night?' asked Lloyd. 'She was surprised when we said we thought Diana Hamlyn had been raped. Surprised – and worried.'

Judy found what she was looking for.

'She disposed of the club in the boiler room,' Lloyd went on. 'And retrieved the head on Saturday.'

There were more efficient murder weapons than an old golf-club, thought Judy. And Caroline Knight had got rid of Sam because she didn't want his company any more. She had changed because she wanted to see the film, simple as that. And she had been surprised at the rape, just like everyone else, because Diana Hamlyn was anybody's. And she was worried about the rape, just like all the women living in the school were worried. But Judy didn't voice her opinion, because that was all it was.

'Well?' he said. 'Say something.'

He moved slightly, inadvertently touching the horn. The sudden noise made Judy start, and she remembered something. Something relevant, but not something she had written down. She had facts – one that she had just remembered, with the sudden noise of the horn.

'Caroline Knight didn't go in by that door,' she said, almost absently.

Her logic took her through the notebook, ticking things off. Facts. Things she had seen. Heard. Incidents, like Jim Lacey turning up. Little things that she had puzzled about. Because a lot of things had seemed odd, to her. Not any more. As usual, it took Lloyd on one of his flights of imagination to make her see it. Because Lloyd always picked up the things that mattered; he would throw them down in a corner for her to sort out, and now that's what she was doing. Why entertain her lover in the back of a car? Who would *want* to steal a golf-club? Difficult, to change your clothes when everyone's in formal dress: people would notice. Sometimes, things are just the way they seem. What about her shoes?

'There's the window,' Lloyd said impatiently. 'She would use it to open the door.'

Judy looked up. 'I am the crime prevention officer,' she said. 'I know about sophisticated tricks like that.'

'Then why couldn't she have done it?'

'She could have,' said Judy, delighted as she always was when she could pick Lloyd up on his use of the language. 'I simply said she didn't. Or Philip Newby wouldn't just have heard footsteps, would he? He would have heard the door opening. It, if you'll pardon the expression, would waken the dead.' Not quite; Hamlyn had slept on in his fume-filled garage, when Mary Alexander had opened the door on to the balcony to tell them she had found the suicide note.

Lloyd stared at her. 'Yes,' he said, with the puzzled frown that he always had when his theories bit the dust. 'Yes.' The frown went, to be replaced with a slight defiance. 'Newby's covering for her. Maybe he was in on it. He was hurt in the accident, wasn't he?'

Now, she gave him her look.

'Oh, all right,' he said.

She smiled. 'Now,' she said. 'I'll ask you a question. It's your own question.'

'Go ahead,' he said, with a sigh. 'You look like a gun-dog. Who am I to argue when you look like a gun-dog? You are invariably pointing in the right direction.'

'Why *did* Mrs Hamlyn run away from Treadwell?' she asked.

The chairman had left, thank God, and Treadwell closed the front door with a deeply grateful sigh. The man seemed to think that he should have done something about Sam Waters barricading himself into the art room. There really wasn't much he could have done, even if he had wanted to, but Sergeant Hill had winkled him out, somehow. He didn't know where Sam was now, and he didn't care. He was having nothing to do with it. He didn't hire him, and he wasn't going to fire him. He would gladly hand that pleasure over to Mr Dearden and Mrs Knight.

He went through to the kitchen where Marcia was putting away the crockery. 'Lovely lunch,' he said. 'You almost put the old sod in a good mood.'

'Don't swear,' she said.

'You should have joined us.'

'It was none of my business,' she said.

'Marcia, Marcia. My sudden retirement from academic life *is* your business.' He stretched. 'Early retirement,' he said. 'I can see us now, pottering about the garden, joining the Darby and Joan Club—'

'Where?' she said. 'Where will this garden be? Where will we go? What will we do?'

'Don't panic.' He sat down at the kitchen table. 'He says he can get Stansfield District Council to house us. A flat, probably.' He smiled. 'We'll have to potter about the window-box, I suppose.'

'You've been drinking,' she said, and turned away.

He watched as she put away plates and cups, and stood up. 'Yes,' he said. 'I've been drinking.' He slipped his arms round her waist. 'Dance with me,' he said.

She stiffened.

'I'm not drunk.' He smiled at her. 'Not yet. We used to go dancing,' he said. 'You wouldn't dance with me on Friday night. You danced with young Cawston, but you wouldn't dance with me.'

'He wasn't drunk.'

He held her tight. 'Dance with me now,' he said.

'Don't be ridiculous! Let me go!'

Dance, Marcia. Dance wildly. Once. Just once. But you couldn't force someone to dance, he discovered, as he tried vainly to push her round the room. You couldn't overpower a woman just to dance with her.

The doorbell brought the undignified grappling to an end. 'I'll get it,' he said.

Detective Chief Inspector Lloyd and Detective Sergeant Hill. Wonderful. Come to arrest him for attempted dancing.

'I'm afraid we're going to have to take up some more of your time, Mr Treadwell,' said Lloyd.

'Well, I've got plenty of that,' said Treadwell, showing them into the sitting-room. 'Can I interest either of you in a drink? I'm going to have several.'

They shook their heads in unison.

'What embarrassing questions do you have for me today?' he asked, pouring himself a Scotch of magnificent proportions.

'We would like to ask you some questions,' Lloyd confirmed. 'And I would like you to get Matthew Cawston here, if you would.'

Treadwell frowned. 'What do you want with him?' he asked.

'We think he may have information which is relevant to this inquiry,' said the sergeant.

Treadwell picked up the phone, and caused Matthew to be found.

'On Friday night,' Lloyd said, as they were waiting, 'you went into the Barn. Were the big doors open or closed?'

'Closed,' said Treadwell. 'I couldn't see Diana until she opened one of them.'

Lloyd nodded, and asked no more questions until Matthew arrived, and was invited to sit down.

Lloyd asked Matthew the same question about the doors, and Matthew gave the same answer.

'And, when you were interrupted, which way did whoever it was come in?'

A frown crossed Matthew's brow. 'From the Hall,' he said. 'He came in the small door.'

'He?'

'Well . . . whoever.'

'And which way did you run?' asked Lloyd.

'The other way.'

'You had to open one of the big doors?'

'Yes.'

Lloyd looked at Treadwell, then back at Matthew. 'You were running away,' he said. 'I presume you didn't close it again.'

'No,' said Matthew guardedly.

'So who did?' Lloyd asked Treadwell.

'It's surely quite obvious,' said Treadwell, forced into talking about this again, with not only a woman but also a boy present. 'They wanted privacy,' he said, in a stage whisper.

'They?'

'Diana and . . . whoever she was with,' said Treadwell. Lloyd considered that. 'Privacy,' he said. 'Yes. Yes, they would. So *they* closed the big door again.'

Treadwell grunted.

'So why did they leave both the car door and the small door open?' asked Lloyd. 'Not much privacy there. You could hear everything that was going on.'

Oh God. Not in front of Matthew, of all people.

Lloyd smiled. 'I don't expect an answer, Mr Treadwell,' he said. 'I just wanted to be certain that we understood about the doors.'

Matthew half-rose from his chair.

'Oh – the sergeant has a few more questions for you, Matthew,' Lloyd said. He turned to Treadwell. 'I'm afraid you will have to be present,' he added.

Treadwell shrugged. He was still the boy's headmaster, just.

'The thefts, Matthew,' said the sergeant.

My God, the woman never gave up, thought Treadwell. 'Oh, really,' he said crossly. 'The school has agreed not to prosecute. And you are certainly not going to take up any of my time, plentiful though it is, going over all that again.'

'Before I ask you anything, Matthew,' said Sergeant Hill, as though Treadwell hadn't spoken, 'I have to tell you that you are not obliged to say anything, but anything that you do say will be taken down, and may be given in evidence.'

It would be taken down all right, thought Treadwell, as the sergeant's thick notebook made its usual appearance.

'And you can have a solicitor present, if you wish.'

Matthew shook his head, puzzled, smiling.

'You were stealing for eighteen months,' she said.

Matthew nodded briefly.

'Eighteen months,' she repeated. 'That's a long time.'

Matthew said nothing. There wasn't much he could say, Treadwell supposed. Time was relative, after all. It was a long time compared to a day. It was a very short time compared to a millennium. Treadwell didn't even try to sip his drink.

'No one ever saw you,' she said. 'No one caught you. No one suspected you. They even suspected someone else altogether, because you wanted them to. That was clever, Matthew.'

Poor Matthew, thought Treadwell. How do you react to that? A self-deprecatory smile hardly fitted the bill. Modest denial was just as bad. He almost felt sorry for him.

'So why did you get caught on Friday night?' she asked.

'Bad luck,' Matthew said.

'No. You were good, Matthew. You never took anything that mattered to anyone. You would wait for weeks and weeks between thefts, so that you could pick just the right moment, and just the right item.' She leaned forward. 'But this time you took something expensive. Something that meant a great deal to someone. Because it didn't matter what you took, did it? This time, you wanted to get caught.'

Treadwell's glass stopped at his lips, as he looked at Matthew.

Matthew frowned. 'Why would I want to get caught?' he asked.

'So you could get Mrs Hamlyn alone,' she said.

Treadwell put down his glass.

'If she actually saw you steal, she would have to do something about it,' the sergeant went on. 'And she wouldn't take you to task in front of all those people. She would take you aside.'

Matthew shifted a little in his seat. 'I don't see why I would want her to do that,' he said.

'You knew what she was like,' said the sergeant. 'You'd seen her in action. Trying to seduce Mr Newby the very day he arrived at the school. It got you going, didn't it? You wanted her. That would be even better than stealing – that would really be cocking a snook at everyone. Having a teacher's wife. And easy. All you had to do was get her alone, and indicate your interest. She was anyone's, wasn't she?'

Treadwell picked up his glass again. He wasn't sure how much of this he could take. If Marcia had ever spoken like that, he would . . . but, then, perhaps the sergeant danced.

'And she did take you aside. It started raining, and you went into the Barn. Even better.'

Matthew was shaking his head, smiling a little.

'When we began this investigation, it looked like a straightforward rape and murder,' she said. 'Then all sorts of things came to light. We found out what Mrs Hamlyn had been like, and we found out that the sexual intercourse probably hadn't happened on the field at all. So it was possible that she hadn't been raped. We found out that it had actually happened in Mr Newby's car – Mr Newby found her underwear there, so he knew she hadn't been raped. Mr Treadwell actually heard her with someone. He knew she hadn't been raped.'

Treadwell looked at Lloyd, who seemed to be having nothing to do with any of this. It was nonsense, anyway. Whatever Diana Hamlyn may have been, she certainly didn't get involved with pupils, and this woman was suggesting that it was *Cawston* she was with when he heard . . . . He didn't finish the sentence, not even in his head.

'But sometimes, Matthew,' said the sergeant, 'things are just the way they seem.'

Matthew had lost the supercilious look.

'Right at the start, we were asked who the hell would need to rape Diana Hamlyn. And the answer is – a pupil would need to rape her, if he wanted her. Mrs Hamlyn would have nothing to do with you, would she, Matthew?'

Matthew's face had the closed expression that Treadwell had seen when he had apologised to him, as Sergeant Hill went on.

'It did happen in Mr Newby's car. But Mrs Hamlyn didn't get in voluntarily, did she? You opened the door, and you pushed her in. She tried to struggle – kick. Her shoes came off. Outside the car. She was pinned down in the back of a small car – she couldn't fight you off. And when you had had enough you ran. Your first thought was to get rid of the pen, deny everything. So you ran to where you kept the things you had taken. And you left by the small door.' She glanced at Treadwell. 'That's why you found it open,' she said, and turned back to Matthew.

'You had stolen everything that had gone missing here for the last eighteen months,' she said. 'And when you put the pen away you saw the golf-club. Because you had stolen it, of course. Who else would want to? Sometimes things are just the way they seem.'

Treadwell took a gulp of whisky.

'You realised what you had done. You had hurt her – you knew you were in deep trouble. She would tell. She would report it. You couldn't rely on lying your way out of violent rape. There she was, making all that fuss, and there it was, a ready-made weapon.'

Not a flicker of emotion showed on Matthew's composed, blank face as he spoke. 'You said that Mr Treadwell heard her with someone,' he said. 'According to you, I was at the other end of the school by then.' He looked at Lloyd. 'She can't have it both ways,' he said.

'Mr Treadwell went into the Barn,' said the sergeant. 'Diana Hamlyn got out of the car, and pushed open one of the big doors. Just moments later, Mr Newby drove his car out, having spent some time removing the articles he had found in the back. So if she had been in the car with someone, then Mr Newby would have found whoever it was still in his car, wouldn't he? But all he found were the tights and pants that she pulled away from her ankles in order to run away before anyone saw her. And what Mr Treadwell heard was someone shocked, hurt, in pain ... .' She paused. 'And alone,' she said, looking at Treadwell. 'Moaning. Trying to catch her breath. And asking God to help her.'

'*Not waving*, Mr Treadwell,' Lloyd said quietly, '*but drowning*.'

Treadwell looked away. He didn't need poetry quoted at him to know that he had jumped to the wrong conclusion. The sergeant was doing well enough in her own more prosaic way. But he had gone in. He would have helped her. 'She ran away!' he said, in his own defence.

'Yes,' said Sergeant Hill. 'She ran away. She ran towards the playing-field. Towards home.' She turned back to Matthew.' You knew she wouldn't go back into the Hall, not in the state you had left her in. She would go home. You ran to the junior dormitory, and you went up the fire-escape. But you saw Mrs Knight and you realised not only that Mrs Hamlyn hadn't reached home, but also that when she did Mrs Knight would see her. Now you really panicked. You had to get to Mrs Hamlyn *before* she got home. So you ran back down. And that's when Mr Newby saw you. He saw you on your way down, not up. That's why there was no one around when he got there. But he had caught a glimpse of you; he said he thought it was a boy, and sometimes, Matthew, things are just the way they seem.'

Treadwell knew that he ought to be on the phone to the solicitor. But, if Matthew hadn't thought of it, why should he? Everyone knew he was a drunken incompetent.

'You ran across the field; you met Mrs Hamlyn, trying to get home. And you made certain that she never did.'

She sat back. 'You thought you'd got away with it. But we got on to the pen, and you had to think fast. You tried to make us think it was Mr Newby. You had your story about him, which was true. You had raped Mrs Hamlyn in his car; that had to help. But it didn't work, did it? You had to think of someone else. Someone plausible. Since no one believed it was rape any more, it didn't have to be a man. But it did have to be someone who could have stolen the golf-club. And who was the only other person ever suspected of stealing? She even had a motive – you discovered that when Jim Lacey came here. You were there, Matthew. You heard him – everyone heard him. He was talking to Des, and Des is deaf.'

Treadwell put down his glass. '*That's* why you came here talking about the accident!' he said. 'Making sure I remembered she had a motive. Knowing that she was with me when we found that club, because you were there, too, weren't you? Following her about, waiting for your chance to steal something.'

There was a silence after Treadwell had spoken; everyone looked at Matthew, who never took his eyes off the sergeant.

'You've got no evidence,' he said at last. 'You've twisted things to fit. But you've got no evidence to back it up, because it isn't true.'

'I think I have evidence,' she said. 'Or, rather, a witness.'

Treadwell looked at Matthew, who seemed distinctly uncomfortable. He looked back at the sergeant, waiting to see what she did next, his drink forgotten. He would have paid good money for a ticket to this show.

'You see, Matthew, you must have got terribly wet. We know you didn't get any blood on your clothes, but the golf-club just wasn't heavy enough. You had to get down into the snow and the slush to finish the job. You must have been wet through.'

Matthew sat up a little in his chair.

'And you went back to the school, once you'd killed her. You disposed of the club in the boiler room, and went into the Hall from the inside door. You were there only minutes after you had murdered Diana Hamlyn, and your clothes must still have been wet.'

Matthew's eyebrows lifted a little. 'Has anyone told you that they were?' he asked.

'They might not have looked wet,' she said. 'But you wanted to establish that you were in the Hall. So you asked the headmaster's wife to dance with you.' She moved forward again. 'Shall I ask her?'

Matthew didn't react.

'Marcia!' Treadwell shouted, making everyone jump.

She appeared, looking even more flushed and flustered than ever beside the cool, collected Sergeant Hill.

'Mrs Treadwell,' said the sergeant, 'you told me that Matthew danced with you on Friday night. Once when all the boys danced with the ladies, and once later on. Do you know what time that was?'

Marcia looked at Treadwell.

'Tell the woman!'

'About twenty past eleven, or so,' she said. 'I know, because I—'

'I want you to think carefully, Mrs Treadwell,' said Sergeant Hill, gently interrupting her. 'Were Matthew's clothes wet?'

She frowned. 'I'm sorry. I don't know what you mean.'

'It's hardly an oblique question, Marcia,' groaned Treadwell. 'Were his clothes wet or weren't they?'

'Wet?' she repeated. There was a long silence while she puzzled over the question.

The sergeant gave her an encouraging smile. 'Perhaps not wet,' she said. 'But were they damp?'

'No,' said Marcia.

'Are you sure?' the sergeant persisted, but it was a lost cause, and she knew it.

'I'm quite sure,' said Marcia. 'His clothes were dry.'

Trust Marcia. Trust her to be decided for the first time in her life when everyone else wanted her to be undecided. Treadwell watched her as she walked back into the kitchen, then turned to look at the sergeant.

She looked at Matthew, and gave a little shrug. 'I was wrong,' she said. 'Your clothes were dry.'

Matthew inclined his head a little.

There wasn't a lot more she could say, Treadwell thought. Cawston senior would have a field day with this. Sergeant Hill would be lucky to be directing traffic come nightfall. No wonder her boss had stayed out of it.

But she did have more to say, her voice crisp and clear in the silence.

'Why were they dry, Matthew?' she asked.

Matthew felt the dread again. He didn't speak; he didn't look at her, as her voice went on.

'According to you, you went out to speak to Mrs Hamlyn, and it started to rain. You went into the Barn. You were interrupted by someone, and ran away. Through the rain. The rain that was so hard that Mr Waters's jacket was still damp hours later. But you didn't get wet.'

'I waited in the House. For a long time. I told you that. I got dry while I was waiting.'

'And then you went back to the Hall. It was still pouring – Mr Treadwell got soaked to the skin just walking round the Barn. But you went all the way from Palmerston House, which is at this end of the school, to the Hall, which is at the other end, without getting wet at all. Not even damp. You were dry, Matthew. Your clothes were dry. How did you manage that?'

'I had my coat on.'

She shook her head. 'You didn't have a coat,' she said. 'I saw you in the crowd. You weren't wearing a coat, and you weren't carrying one. And only Mrs Hamlyn's coat was in the cloakroom. Try again.'

Matthew hated her. She had been cleverer than him. He didn't like that. But that wasn't enough. It couldn't be.

She smiled. A cold, hard smile. 'I'll tell you how you did it,' she said. 'We knew whoever did it had to have changed his clothes. And who could change out of formal dress without people noticing? Someone in a school uniform, that's who. You murdered Mrs Hamlyn, you ran back to the House, and picked up your old uniform. The one you had outgrown. The one your father had to replace this term. I imagine you stuffed it into one plastic bag, and the broken golf-club into another. You ran through the rain to the school.'

Matthew was beginning to panic again. The panic that had engulfed him when Mrs Hamlyn wouldn't stop sobbing like that, and he had run away, the blood pounding in his ears, still sure he could hear her when he got to the House. The panic that had made him careless with the loft door. He mustn't be careless. He mustn't panic.

'You burned the club, and you changed your clothes. You hung the uniform you're wearing now up to dry. No one was going to go into the boiler room until Sunday.'

How did she know what he had done? He wasn't left in doubt for long.

'I told you that I saw you later that night, Matthew. In the crowd. I saw someone whose trousers and sleeves were about an inch too short; a boy, still growing. But that's not how you looked last month. And it isn't how you look today. I don't think you get taller and shorter, Matthew.'

It should have worked. He had spoken to everyone he could think of about the accident, and the golf-club incident. It *had* worked; the rumours had hit the classrooms by lunchtime. Mrs Knight might have killed her, they were saying. The police are here again. Not enough for them to charge her, but enough to suspect her. Enough to keep him out of it.

It had *worked*. So why was he here? How did she know, how did she work it out?

'I know someone like you, Matthew,' she said.

Perhaps she read minds, too.

'He had me fooled,' she said. 'But I don't get caught the same way twice.' She paused. 'The next day, you went to help Mrs Knight set up a project in the school building. You raked the metal head of the golf-club out of the ashes, and put it in the ashcan. You picked up your uniform, and put it in your briefcase.'

It was all circumstantial. His father would get lawyers who could make mincemeat of her case.

'You can't prove any of this,' he said.

'Oh, yes, we can. You're interested in forensics – you should know that. We have a thumbprint. We have threads from your blazer. We have samples from the victim, and now we even have a thing called DNA testing. Genetic fingerprinting. Do you know what that is, Matthew? It means that all sorts of things can be proved that could once only be suggested. Paternity, for instance. Right of inheritance. Rape. Murder.'

Panic took hold; Matthew leaped up, and ran from the room, from the house, smack into the arms of two police officers in the doorway.

The sergeant came out, followed by Lloyd; Treadwell brought up the rear.

'You should have let her live, Matthew,' she said.

Matthew stopped trying to struggle free. It wouldn't get him anywhere even if he could. He hated Sergeant Hill.

'She wasn't about to tell anyone. Her husband had just been made deputy head. Think about it – think about her history. Think about the headlines. She wasn't going to report it – she ran away from Mr Treadwell sooner than have to explain.'

Matthew's eyes widened. She was right. She was right. And his body sagged a little, his weight taken by the policemen who held him, one on either side.

'But maybe Mrs Knight would have made her tell the police,' she went on. 'And we would have charged you. But what would have happened? A sixteen-year-old schoolboy and a woman like her? A nice middle-class sixteen-year-old schoolboy and a woman with a reputation like Mrs Hamlyn's? She had to have led you on. She had to have been asking for it. And the violence was . . . well, within reason, shall we say? A professional foul – that's how I understand it was described. And that's how they would have seen it in court. A guilty plea, a show of remorse and, my God, Matthew, you would have got so many Brownie points they would have probably sent her to jail instead.'

Matthew swallowed.

'But you murdered her,' she said. 'And perhaps she didn't die in vain. Perhaps she saved a lot of other women going through what she went through in that car.' She stepped back a little, and looked at him for what seemed like for ever.

'Now you can take him away,' she said.

He hated her.

They had put on his film. After all the other programmes, where no one would notice it. But Judy had; she had gone to bed without the attendant nagging of his fantasy. He got up when it had finished, and took his mug into his suddenly tidy kitchen; he wasn't sure he could get used to that. He couldn't just leave it, like he would have done before. He washed it up, put out the light, and went back through to the living-room. Television off, video off, lamp – his eye caught Judy's ashtray. He would have to add that to the list, he thought, examining it carefully before putting its contents in the waste-basket, as though the cigarette that she had stubbed out two hours ago might suddenly leap into life-threatening flame.

He went round doing his usual check of windows and gas-taps. Putting the cat out, he called it in his head. Not that he had a cat. Not that he would put it out if he did. He liked cats. He wondered if Judy would like one, and realised that she might loathe them for all he knew. It had never been discussed, because all he and Judy had ever talked about was work and the triangular relationship in which they had always found themselves. Now at last they had the time to talk about other things.

He tiptoed into the bedroom, and undressed in the dark, easing himself into bed beside her. He liked going to a bed that had Judy already in it.

'Was the film good?' she asked.

'Sorry,' he said. 'I tried not to disturb you.'

'Some things disturb me,' she said. 'You're not one of them.' She switched on the light, and smiled.

He put his arm round her, not sure whether to broach the subject that had been bothering him.

'Judy,' he said slowly. 'Was there anything personal in what you said to Cawston? About what Diana Hamlyn had gone through?'

She shrugged a little.

'You haven't been . . .?' He was getting like Treadwell, he thought.

'Raped?' she supplied, shaking her head. 'No.'

'But something,' Lloyd said. 'Something of the sort.'

She looked faintly surprised, then gave an unamused laugh. 'Yes,' she said. 'Something of the sort has happened to me.'

'When?' he asked, alarmed.

'Years ago.' She sat back a little. 'Lloyd,' she said, shaking her head. 'Go out tomorrow, and ask ten women in the street. I guarantee you that something of the sort will have happened to seven of them.'

He frowned.

'Oh – they don't report it,' she said. 'They aren't raped. They manage to run away, or someone happens to come along at the right time. Or they talk their way out of it. But they know what could have happened if they'd failed.' She smiled a little sadly. 'Something of the sort will have happened to Mrs Knight, and Mrs Treadwell,' she said. 'Something of the sort has happened to almost every woman you have ever met.' There was a little silence before she spoke again. 'If Alsatian dogs were as unpredictably violent as men,' she said, 'the breed would long ago have died out.'

Lloyd thought about that. 'So what's to be done?' he asked.

'I don't know. All I know is that when I saw Diana Hamlyn I knew it could have been me. But I lost sight of that, until I saw Sam's painting.'

Lloyd had seen it, too, now. He didn't care for it.

An elegantly shod foot, thrusting in from the edge of the canvas, kicking to death a slot machine that had failed to produce one of the red-wrapped goodies which were spilling out in its death throes, staining the snow-covered ground, trampled, crushed, no longer wanted. Only destruction would satisfy.

'I saw it,' Judy said, 'and I knew I was letting her down. Because that was what it looked like when we saw her, and that was what it *was*, whatever Freddie said, whatever anyone said.'

Lloyd nodded.

'Sorry,' she said. 'I don't actually hold you personally responsible.' She kissed him on the cheek. 'Good night.'

She left the light on; he liked to read. He picked up his book. Perhaps one day she would complain about the light, about his late hours; the honeymoon wouldn't last for ever. But he was almost looking forward to that. He looked at her, at the dark head on the pillow beside him, and swallowed a little as he remembered her arrival on Saturday night. Angry, hurt, clutching a huge blue laundry-bag.

But give her someone like Sam Waters, and she could hold her own all right, he thought with a smile.

'Did Sam Waters make a pass at you?' he asked. 'Is that why

you said whatever you did say?' He hadn't asked what she had said; he was sure he would rather not know.

'Yes. I told him exactly what I would do to him if he didn't take his hand off my knee. And I meant it.'

He smiled. 'Was I once in danger of whatever dire punishment you threatened?'

'You didn't make a pass,' she said. 'You said: "I'm a married man with two children, and I'm falling in love with you. Is this going to be a problem?" ' She smiled.

He remembered. 'And you said yes,' he replied. 'How right you were.'

But it wasn't a problem any more.

'I can take you out to dinner!' he said, suddenly aware of the new world opening up. 'We can go to the pictures – we can go for walks.' He abandoned his book. 'We can go on holiday,' he said, beaming.

'I'll hold you to all of this,' she said.

He put out the light, holding her close in the darkness.

'Lloyd?' she said, after a few minutes.

'Present.' He stroked her hair.

'Is your first name biblical?'